BARNEGAT DARK

A Novel

BARNEGAT DARK

A Novel

Daniel J. Waters

Cover Design by James Zach / *ZGraphix* / *Mason City, Iowa*
Author Photo © Jean Poland Photography

I'D LOVE TO CHANGE THE WORLD
Words and Music by Alvin Lee
© 1971 Chrys-a-lee Music Ltd. Copyright Renewed All Rights
Administered by BMG Rights Management (US) LLC
All Rights Reserved Used by Permission
Reprinted by Permission of Hal Leonard LLC

JERSEY SHORE AND LONG BEACH ISLAND MAPS
Courtesy of Ryan Martz & Doug McCarthy / Fire & Pine
Bluffton, South Carolina
www.fireandpine.com
Used by Permission

For Pam, Jessica, Michael & John
Always the best chapters of my life

I'd love to change the world
But I don't know what to do
So I'll leave it up to you

"I'd Love to Change the World"
Alvin Lee/Ten Years After (1971)

High Bar Harbor

Barnegat
Light

Loveladies

Harvey Cedars

North Beach

Surf City

Ship Bottom

Brant Beach

Beach Haven
Crest

Brighton Beach

Beach Haven   Peahala Park
Park

Haven Beach

The Dunes

Beach Haven Terrace

Beach Haven Gardens

Spray Beach

Little Egg
Harbor Yacht

Holgate

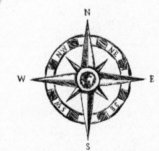

Forsythe
Wildlife
Refuge

Atlantic Ocean

Long
Beach
Island

Beach Haven

Atlantic City

Ocean City

Cape May

OCTOBER, 1970

-1-

Jingletown Neighborhood
Oakland, California

THE SHABBY THIRD-FLOOR walk-up was less than ten straight-line miles from campus but it might as well have been a million, the young man thought. He looked at the small group of people all of whom were sitting or squatting around a moth-eaten Oriental rug. Empty cartons of takeout and greasy food wrappers littered the place. Scattered on the rug were a few items he recognized but there were some things he had never seen before and had no idea what they did.

"What did you think a revolution looked like?"

The question came from a pretty woman with dark, short, center-parted hair. She wore no make-up but still had the aura of a high school cheerleader.

"I guess I didn't really have any idea," he said.

"Well," the woman continued, intently molding something that looked like gray Play-Doh, "Revolution is dirty and smelly and dangerous so if you want to be involved you better get used to it."

"What's that in your hands?" the young man asked.

The young woman sitting next to him answered his question.

"That is what we like to call Chanel Number Four," she said, "and there's enough right there to level this whole block."

"Oh shit," the dark-haired girl said. "Everybody run!"

The young man tried to stand but then instinctively dropped back down and covered his head. A loud bang followed. It was followed by raucous laughter. He opened his eyes.

"I love newbies," the dark-haired woman said with a grin. She sniffed the air with an actress's practiced theatricality. "And you didn't even shit your pants so you've successfully passed the first test."

The man sitting next to her held up an exploded party-popper.

"This ain't Greenwich Village," he said and tossed it over his shoulder.

The girl next to him spoke again and in her voice he detected the flat accent of the Plains he'd grown up with. "You should probably head back now," she said. "You don't want to be hoofing it in this neighborhood when it's dark. The Brown Berets own the streets at night."

"Hoofing it" caught his attention. It was a farm girl expression, he thought.

The dark-haired woman nodded in agreement. He thought he heard one of the others call her Gina or maybe it was Angelina. They weren't exactly high on using anyone's real name he had quickly surmised. "We'll find a way to get in touch with you," she said, still kneading the wad of Play-Doh. "Don't come back here unless we tell you to. Check the personal ads in *The Daily Cal*. We like to support it now that the fascist pigs don't have editorial control anymore." She leaned toward him. "Whisper your name in my ear."

The young man did as he was told.

"OK, so…let me think. Got it. Look for a message to the Blessed Virgin, which is also your handle in this group from now on."

The young man looked perplexed.

"What? You should be happy. My first thought was to call you BVD but there are so few revolutionaries named after underwear."

Laughter rippled through the group.

"I guess I better be happy with Blessed Virgin, then," the young man replied. He raised himself from the floor and the girl sitting next to him offered her arm in support. He looked into her face. Farm girl, he thought again. Definitely. One of the Dakotas or maybe even Nebraska.

He silently exited the apartment and navigated the three flights of narrow stairs, stepping out from an entryway that reeked of urine into the warm California sun. An old song by the Rivieras popped into his head. None of the people in the apartment looked like revolutionaries, he thought. No beards, no berets. They were just out there a havin' fun, he mused. And they certainly didn't look like the "radical leftists" his high school teacher had railed against in Civics class.

A group of Latino youths perched on a stoop across the street eyed him suspiciously as he began the twenty minute trek back to Fruitvale Station. If The Revolution had a historical district, he thought, this was it. The Black Panthers had been founded by Huey and Bobby at Merritt College over on Grove Street and the Chicano Revolutionary Party had its roots here. But they at least *looked* like revolutionaries he decided. The people he'd just left were all white, educated and quite possibly privileged and so they looked like – he paused to see if any of the Latino boys were following him – they looked like everybody else.

As he quickened his pace it dawned on him. That was exactly what made them dangerous.

Twenty five minutes later, as the train approached, he heard a loud sound almost like an explosion in the distance somewhere behind him. The Oakland International Airport was just a few miles away he knew and so reasoned it was probably just a jet's sonic boom.

He boarded the instant the doors opened, deciding it was better not to turn around and make sure.

MAY, 1971

-2-

Barnegat Light State Park
Long Beach Island, New Jersey

ALMOST TWO HUNDRED FEET above the ground the wind was working hard to whip Chief Mickey Cleary's Ray-Ban Wayfarer sunglasses from her face and fling them out into the churning Atlantic Ocean. She decided it was safer to take them off and tuck them in the pocket of her uniform blouse.

"Which one is his?" Mickey asked, shouting to be heard above the offshore breeze.

"I'll know it when I see it," replied Loretta LaMarro, shouting back. "It has an open cockpit and it's the only one with two seats."

Mickey was sure it was just her imagination but she thought she could feel the lighthouse swaying slightly with each salty gust. She put both hands on the railing and scanned the cloudless sky.

"I hope you don't mind me saying this," Mickey said, "but Mayor Billy doesn't really seem like the daredevil type."

"Oh, he's not," Loretta answered. The wind had lulled for a moment. "But he is cheap. Mr. Tomalino, the man who owns Paramount Air Service, promised him a discount if he took a ride on the tow plane. I think he'd do a wing walk if it meant he could get it for free."

Mickey laughed. "Well I know I'd pay to see tha-"

"Wave! Wave!" Loretta exclaimed. "I think that's him."

Mickey looked southward down the long, narrow expanse of the island on whose northernmost tip they now stood. She heard the sonorous drone of a propeller engine and after forming a makeshift visor with her hand she peered out over the waves.

"See it? Billy said it had double-decker wings. I think he called it a biplane."

"I got it," Mickey said as the wind gusted again. For a moment she was jolted back in time to two summers earlier, watching Dickie Robichaux launch himself into oblivion from almost the exact spot she now occupied. She could see his face, silhouetted by the searchlights and hear the loud *whump* of the helicopter's rotor. She was the last person on this earth he'd spoken to and it was this notion and not the words he said that haunted her still. He had looked her right in the eye – a firm, calm, utterly fearless gaze – and she didn't realize he was going to jump until he did.

"See them? See them?" Loretta asked. "Right there." She pointed skyward.

Mickey saw them. It was indeed an old biplane, mustard yellow with blue markings and horizontal red and white American flag stripes on its tail fin and rudder. It was trailing one of the ubiquitous advertising banners that would soon appear almost continuously every day, buzzing over the shoreline from Cape May all the way to Island Beach.

ADVERTISE WITH PARAMOUNT AIR!

The banner rippled, its five-foot tall letters snapping in the breeze. Hundreds of them would fly on the same route all the way through Labor Day shilling everything from Steel Pier concerts and Coppertone to bars and bowling alleys. Mickey recalled clearly the first one she'd ever seen, just after she'd moved onto to Long Beach Island. She'd been working on her first police cruiser, a '66 Chevelle SS that she'd just passed on, with some reluctance, to one of her departing deputies. She could still see what to her at the time was the cryptic phrase trailing the plane:

DUNES 'TIL DAWN

It had taken three years until she actually visited the infamous local establishment on Longport Boulevard. The Dunes bar sat on the corner where the main roads leading from Ocean City and Somers Point intersected. Ocean City was a totally "dry town" due to a series of Blue Laws still on the books from the days of its Quaker founders. Somers Point, on the other hand, had no such aversion to alcohol but its bars and clubs had to, by law, stop serving it at two a.m. and had to close up shop an hour later. A late night with Ronnie the previous summer had revealed The Dunes to be the shore's one and only true after hours joint. Its Egg Harbor Township address allowed it to stay open and pouring drinks for virtually all twenty-four hours although it did close for a while after the liquid breakfast rush was through. They'd had fun that night, listening to a band that had finished its gig at The Bay Shores up the road and still wanted to play. But ultimately Mickey felt like she saw enough miscreants, drunk, disorderly and otherwise, just doing her day job. She also doubted it was a great idea for her, as Surf City's Chief of Police, to be seen mingling with the fairly rugged clientele the place seemed to attract. She never went back.

As the plane drew closer Mickey could see her borough's Mayor, the Honorable William Patrick Tunell, in the open forward seat ahead of the pilot's. He was wearing a comical-looking barnstormer's cap and goggles. Loretta had told her he'd found them after rummaging for more than an hour through the Clearance bins at Ricky's Army/Navy Store.

"He looks like Snoopy from the comics," Loretta said with a wrinkled grin. "Please don't tell him I said that, of course."

"He'll never hear it from me," Mickey replied.

The single propeller engine noise grew louder and the plane grew closer. Mickey used a little trick Ronnie had taught her from his military sniper training. She curled the fingers on her right hand into a crude telescope. Keeping her left eye closed she held it to her face and squinted through it with her right eye. The plane and its occupants came into sharper focus.

"I take it back," Mickey said to Loretta. "He actually looks pretty daredevilish after all. All he needs is a long white scarf."

Loretta put her hand to her mouth. "He has one," she laughed. "But he thought he would be sitting behind the pilot. I bet a nickel they wouldn't let him wear it."

Mickey envisioned the scarf flapping in the pilot's face as he tried to navigate and had to laugh at the image it conjured in her mind.

"Oooh – I think he sees us." Loretta began gesticulating as the prop noise escalated in volume.

Mickey watched as Mayor Billy began waving in return. She could see him turn his head around and shout something at the pilot. Seconds later the yellow plane dipped its wings three times in quick succession.

"That was for us," Loretta yelled. She sounded like one of the schoolgirls she used to teach, Mickey thought.

The biplane passed them and the engine drone began to fade as the breeze carried it and the intrepid aviators downwind and away from them.

"Billy told me that Andre, he's the owner of the planes, said they can't fly too close to the lighthouse. Something about the way the wind swirls around it can make the airplane or the banners do funny things."

"Like crash into it?" Mickey asked, dropping her hand from her face and reaching for her sunglasses.

"Well he didn't say that exactly but I suppose that's what he meant." Loretta pulled a pair of Foster Grants from her own pocket and slipped them on.

"I like the new shades," Mickey said.

"They're the same ones Jackie Kennedy always wears."

"I think it's Jackie Onassis now," Mickey replied.

The two women moved cautiously toward the little walkway that would take them from the circular observation deck back inside and out of the freshening breeze. Mickey let Loretta go first, offering her arm to steady the older woman on the first step down.

Once they were inside Loretta said, "I'll never call her that. Never. She'll always be Jackie Kennedy to me."

Loretta had told Mickey the story enough times. The one and only time she'd ever cried for in front of her third grade students was when the news of the young President's assassination had crackled over the tinny loudspeaker in her classroom.

"She was my model of grace and dignity when Jim died," Loretta continued. "So that's how I always want her to be. At least in my mind."

Two hundred and seventeen pie-shaped metal steps lay ahead of them on the circular stairway inside Barnegat Light. Mickey put her Ray-Bans back on. The upper reaches of the spiral stairs were drenched in the sunlight that filtered through the windows of the lamp room and two round porthole windows in the tower itself. Tiny prismatic rainbows appeared on the brick wall and then vanished. Loretta pointed at one.

"What does that remind you of?" Loretta asked.

"Tinkerbelle," Mickey answered immediately.

"They still show 'Peter Pan' on TV. The one with Mary Martin. I watch it every time," Loretta added.

"Say, did you think you could feel the lighthouse move a little when we were up there?" Mickey asked as they descended. Loretta's hard soled shoes clanged with each step.

"Old Barney here is as solid as the Rock of Gibraltar," Loretta replied. She patted the bricks for emphasis. "Not bad for guy who's a hundred and twelve years old. Too bad more people don't come to visit him. He's like a member of the family to the year-rounders. But, I guess, when you've stood in one spot for that long people kind of stop noticing you. Maybe wouldn't even notice if one day you weren't there."

"Uh, huh," Mickey said as the metal squeaked. "But what I want to know at the moment is - how old are these steps?"

"You worry too much," Loretta said, keeping one hand on the wall as she descended. "This lighthouse will be here long after you and I are both gone."

Mickey scanned the tuck-pointed red bricks. "It looks different on the inside," she said, "but that can't be right. It must be an optical illusion."

"Nope, you're right," Loretta said turning her head slightly. "It's really two towers, one built inside the other. The inside one is a straight cylinder like the cardboard tube in a roll of Scott Towels. The outer one tapers like a cone all the way to the top."

"How do you know all this?"

"I love going to the library and they have a whole section on the Island's history. I know that you think Billy and I spend all our free time drinking martinis and making whoopee but just because I stopped teaching doesn't mean I've stopped learning."

"You're wrong about what I think," Mickey said. "I don't think you two spend much time drinking martinis at all."

Loretta stopped and tuned toward her.

"You are a very perceptive young woman, Michaela Cleary," she said with a wry smile. "I can see why our little town and its handsome mayor think so highly of you. Plus, just look at all the excitement you've brought our little glorified sandbar in the past four years. Who needs this casino gambling nonsense they keep talking about when we've got you?"

Loretta continued carefully down the gratework stairs which now oscillated noisily as the two women circled the central support pole which rose toward the lamp room like the spinal column of some gigantic museum dinosaur.

"I'm not sure excitement is really the right word," Mickey replied. She steadied herself with a palm against the cool interior brick.

"Perhaps," Loretta replied, "Perhaps drama might be a better description. Isn't that what your reporter friend from the *Daily News* said? Gannon was his name, wasn't it? Or maybe it was Gannett. Anyway, he said your arrival on Long Beach Island precipitated more drama in two years than the entire shore had seen in two decades."

"That's not exactly praise, Loretta. You know that, right? And it almost was two years ago that he wrote that piece. Not much drama since then."

"Yes, but he did refer to you as a 'lovely lass of the law' if I'm not mistaken. He seemed quite fond of alliteration in his prose. And also of you, I'm guessing."

"Yes, he is - was. Fond of alliteration," Mickey said.

"It must work," Loretta continued. "I mean, he got nominated for a Pulitzer Prize for those articles about that awful motorcycle gang in the Pine Barrens and then he got a job with the *Evening Bulletin*. I was quite surprised the *Inquirer* didn't snap him up after the Pulitzer nomination." They were halfway to the base of the lighthouse.

"But, unfortunately, he didn't *win* the Pulitzer Prize" Mickey answered. "He told me they gave it to newspaper reporter from a Chicago paper for an expose` he did about student radicals and the Students for a Democratic Society, the SDS. Mike said violent protests by rich, white college kids in a Midwestern metropolis was a much sexier subject than plain old murder-for-hire and drug dealing in the middle of God-forsaken pine forest. And the *Inquirer* is probably a little too stodgy for Mike Gannon. He's not a guy that does well on a short leash and he doesn't much like the idea of sharing what he's working on or any scoops he gets with his editors."

Loretta stopped. "I've read about those SDS people. They

like to blow things up. Along with themselves, occasionally. And speaking of scoops – have you told him yet?"

Mickey put both hands on the railing. "Who? Mike Gannon or Mayor Billy?"

"Ronnie," Loretta said patiently. "Your might-as-well-be husband after all this time. Have you told him?"

She had caught Mickey slightly off guard and she seemed to know it.

"Ronnie is," Mickey said, fumbling for the words, "Ronnie is going through some stuff right now. I don't know what it is, Loretta, and I don't know how to help him. So I just listen to him, give him his space and let him do his own thing."

"You don't think he's sick do you, dear?"

"Physically?" Mickey replied. "No, I mean I don't think so. He's lost a little weight but he was always pretty lean and mean to begin with." She looked down and noticed that her foot was tapping rapidly on the metal step. She willed it to stop and then continued. "But ever since Nixon ordered that soldier released from prison last month he's been, I don't know, different. Consumed you could almost say. He went to that May Day Rally of Vietnam veterans in Washington and now it's like all he talks about. How they have to end the war by any means necessary."

"You mean to tell me the lieutenant who killed all those people in poor little Bunny's village is out of prison?" Loretta asked. "I guess I missed that. Maybe I should spend more of my library time on Current Events."

Mickey sighed heavily. "Ronnie says that the guy certainly didn't kill five hundred unarmed civilians by himself. And he didn't do it without orders or at least approval from above. But they let everyone else off the hook above and below him in the chain of command. He says we can't win now even if we are the good guys."

"But he's always been against the war, at least from what you've told me. He fought in it. And quite bravely, everyone says."

The column of light they were bathed in disappeared as the sun inched slowly westward.

"Yeah, but he's never been like this before," Mickey answered. Both women removed their sunglasses. "This is different. It probably sounds silly but right now he's just not the Ronnie Dunn I know. He's getting connected with people who are really, and I mean *really* not just against the war but against the government and probably baseball, apple pie and Chevrolets, too. It's a pretty radical crowd from what I can gather. And it worries me. Really worries me to be honest."

"So you haven't told him."

"No," Mickey said as they resumed their descent. "I just keep waiting for a right time that never seems to come. Plus I'm not that late. Just a week tomorrow. But I'm usually like clockwork."

"You could have the rabbit test, you know."

"Dr. Harman says it would be too early still. She says if I go another two weeks without a visitor then we can do the test."

"If you had a piano you could play a little Brahms."

Mickey smiled. "Sorry. No piano. But I do have a Carole King album I've been saving. I assume now you have to go pick up Mayor Billy at the airstrip?"

"Yes, and in the convertible of course. I'll drive by your police station on the way back – just so you and the fellows can see the scarf in all its glory."

Mickey nodded and they took the rest of the steps in silence. When they reached the bottom and stepped outside into the light Loretta took Mickey's hands in hers.

"Men are like boats and women are like moorings," Loretta said. "It's OK to let the boat drift away a little. Just don't lose sight of it. And don't ever let go of the rope."

"Thanks. I'll try to remember that," Mickey said and pulled Loretta in for a quick hug. "And tell His Honor he looked, um, dashing up there. Not like Snoopy at all."

"We watched 'The Blue Max' on NBC's Saturday Night at the Movies last week. I think that's where he got the idea for the scarf. My Billy's a looker but he's no George Peppard. But I'll be sure to tell him. Dashing – yes, he'll really like that."

Loretta walked over the crunching gravel towards her red Mustang. Mickey thought about what she'd said as she headed toward her new cruiser.

"Right," she whispered to herself. "Don't let go of the rope."

The Palace
24 Scott Street
Riverside, New Jersey

THE PALACE DINER HAD never been a joint known for keeping up with the times but at least it was trying, Candy thought. When she was little it had been labeled a teen hangout, frequented only by "big kids" and the occasional brave parent who came looking for them. It gave the place a mix of mystery, wonder and the faint suggestion of illicit, unspoken danger. When she became a big kid herself it was a safe place to be with her friends, run by a nice family who handmade wondrous chocolate and candy eggs at Easter. Now it was a little piece of who she had once been.

She looked around and saw beaded curtains hung at what appeared to be possibly random locations. Faded posters of Elvis Presley and Frank Sinatra hung next to newer ones featuring The Who and Jimi Hendrix. Just above their booth was a framed, full-page ad for a Tom Jones concert at Cherry Hill's Latin Casino in 1969, the year Candy had graduated from Holy Cross High School. Candy's mother had wanted to attend the show with several of her old high-school girlfriends but her father had forbidden it, perhaps fearing a panties and hotel-room-key throwing frenzy like that described in the story he'd read aloud at the supper table from behind his copy of the *Philadelphia Daily News*. It was his last real act of spousal subjugation, Candy considered, before a lifetime of Lucky Strikes and lung cancer took him six months later. Her mother still had her unused ticket, held fast by a Sealtest milk bottle-shaped magnet, hanging on the refrigerator door.

Candy had brought her new college boyfriend home with her but she was starting to have second thoughts about the decision already. She could see that her hometown was dying. Which meant that he could certainly see it, too. It was a slow and a subtle demise, but she sensed it all around her. Every local kid she knew was, like herself, working hard to make sure they were going to be able to get out. Only family ties pulled them back for visits that were usually painless as long as they didn't last more than a few days.

Brad was still talking. The other two young people in the booth, girlfriends of hers from high school, were listening with polite and perhaps occasionally genuine attention. She was glad for once that he was so completely self-absorbed, thinking perhaps he wouldn't really see what she now felt acutely was the obvious shabbiness from whence she had sprung.

Candy flipped through the offerings on the Crosley *Select-O-Matic* miniature jukebox which was parked at the juncture where their table met the peeling wallpaper. Interspersed with The Mamas and The Papas, Deep Purple and the Strawberry Alarm Clock were still plenty of songs by Bobby Darin, Ricky Nelson and the Four Seasons. She was impressed that there were a few obviously recent additions, identifiable by the whiteness of their vertically arranged title cards. James Taylor, Rod Stewart and even Isaac Hayes she noticed. Maybe there was a little hope for the place and the town after all. She came across "She's a Lady", one of the songs she planned to use in her upcoming semester project. Her mother had asked her at breakfast exactly how a baccalaureate degree in Women's Studies was going to translate into a job offer after graduation. Candy didn't really have an answer.

"...but what really opened my eyes," Brad was saying with intense inflection, "was this guy I met - purely by accident, mind you - during my campus exchange semester at UC Berkeley."

It was a story Candy had heard numerous times before but she tried to act as if she too were actively listening.

"Berkeley's up in northern California," he added for good measure. "Just outside San Francisco. You can see the Bay from it."

Candy made silent note of his assumption that total academic, cultural and geographical ignorance by his boothmates was somehow presumed. Her gaze wandered to their waitress, a woman who had to be in her fifties, Candy figured. She was sitting at the diner's counter on one of the silver-with-red-upholstery circular stools and working something in front of her with an eraser. Candy thought it was probably their check until the woman picked it up and blew off a tiny cloud of rubber and graphite. It was a crossword puzzle. She looked over her shoulder and caught Candy's gaze. This triggered her waitressing instincts. She hustled to their booth.

"Another round of Vanilla Cokes?" she asked.

"This one's on me," Bradley Vreeland, Jr. declared magnanimously. The waitress's white plastic name tag identified her as Josephine. She stared at Candy.

"I know you. You're a Catanzariti. You're Julie's little girl, aren't you, honey?" Josephine asked.

Candy smile and nodded. "Yeah. But she goes by Catan now. Since my dad died."

Josephine planted a hand on one hip.

"Well, your mom and I went to RHS together. We were good friends way back then. Thick as thieves the teachers used to say about us. And I think my son Henry – he likes to be called Hank now – he was in your class in grade school at St. Peter's. Up through the third grade, anyway. After that we switched him to public school. We just didn't have the money and CCD classes were free. In fact I'm almost certain you were in the same class. Did you have Mrs. LaMarro?"

The name instantly brought a grin that lit up Candace Catanzariti's face.

"I loved Mrs. LaMarro," Candy replied. "Is she still teaching?"

Josephine scribbled something on her pad and shook her head. "Oh, no, honey. No, she's gone. It's been a few years now."

"You mean she *died*?" Candy asked, worry and shock infusing the question.

Josephine laughed. "No, no. At least not that I know of, anyway. She retired from teaching and moved down the shore. She's probably still there."

Candy breathed a sigh of relief.

"Yeah, Hank loved her too," Josephine continued. "She was a real keeper. Your mom had an older sister – became a nun if I remember right. That was a waste of womanhood, I'll tell you that, she -"

"My Aunt Agnes," interjected. "She's still a nun. Works with orphan girls in North Philadelphia. We don't see her much. She's been Sister Innocentia for a long time now."

Josephine laughed. "Innocentia?" she said. "That's rich. No offense honey but if she's an Innocent then I'm the Queen of Sheba. I'll go and get your Cokes."

The warm air was still moving from Josephine's departure when Brad resumed his story. She knew it by heart. Sitting in the shadow of the Campanile, the strange guy with the side-part and glasses who was wearing a coat and tie at a school where everyone, including the professors, wore jeans, tie-dye, beads and dashikis. The briefcase that spilled open. How Brad helped him retrieve and reorder all of the typed pages that had threatened to blow away.

Brad was saying, "So I asked him, 'This your thesis?' He looked like he could be a PhD candidate in Physics or Mathematics or something. 'No,' he says,'" Brad continued. "'More like my manifesto.' So then I said, 'You're a Communist?'" He just gave me a weird look and said, 'No, I am not a Communist. I am an agent of change. A prophet crying out in the wilderness of modern society. Someone who understands that you can't eat your cake and have it, too.' And then he just took off, like he was on a mission. Never ran across him again but I was really struck by that phrase he used – agent of change."

Candy was already mouthing what she knew came next.

"*Agent provocateur*," Brad said with what Candy always thought was way more French accent than necessary. A Maurice Chevalier imitation performed by Pepe` Le Pew. She had already agreed to spend the whole summer break bumming around with him but what she really wanted was to take him down the shore. She knew he'd grown up somewhere in Minnesota and had never even seen the Atlantic Ocean. Candy was so sick of hearing about California and Berkeley and "the Bay." It sounded like a place that was a carbon copy of Grinnell College but with much better weather.

Brad rattled on until Josephine approached with a tray of sweating Coca-Cola glasses. He finished with his usual capper, "And so the first thing I did when I got back to Grinnell, Iowa was join the campus SDS chapter. Or what was left of it anyway."

Candy gathered up their empty glasses and pushed them toward the end of the booth while Josephine set down the fresh ones. "Thanks, doll," Josephine said.

"Does Henry – I mean Hank – does he still live around here?"

Candy asked. Nicknames were never used or even allowed in the little Catholic school and so well into adulthood classmates automatically and unconsciously called each other by their full first names.

"Yes and no," Josephine answered. "His mail still comes to the house but he joined the Marine Corps right out of high school. He writes pretty regularly but he says they read their mail before it's sent over and he'll get in trouble if says where he is."

"I remember Henry," Candy said. "He was a very nice boy."

Josephine smiled. "I'll tell him I saw you when I write him back."

"Oh, he's not going to remember me," Candy replied.

"I'm pretty sure he will," Josephine said. "He cried for a whole month when we had to pull him out of St. Pete's. He would sit at his old desk during CCD classes until he got too big for it. Anyway, he was allowed to say he got to Saigon OK but that was all. I just hope he's someplace safe."

Before Candy could stop him Brad interjected. "Well if he's there as a member of the armed imperial invasion forces then there probably isn't any place that's actually going to be safe." Candy kicked him hard under the scarred Formica table. Her friends, the identical Carswell twins, grimaced.

"I really hope he is, too," Candy said, ignoring Brad's rejoinder.

"You kids can pay your bill at the register," Josephine said. She turned without another word.

"My, you are most certainly provocative," Denise Carswell said. She stirred her Vanilla Coke with a paper straw. "Inappropriate certainly but nonetheless provocative."

"Somebody has to stop this immoral war," Brad replied, his cheeks red. Candy wasn't sure if it was from anger or embarrassment.

"Um, I think you may be misinterpreting or maybe just mistranslating that term," Denise's sister Deborah said. Her tone was mildly condescending but somehow she managed to retain a hint of kindness.

"No, I don't think so," Brad answered. "It means someone who provokes a change."

If Brad had bothered to ask, Candy mused, he would have known that the twins were both attending Princeton on full rides. Denise was pursuing a double-major in French and Economics while Deborah was studying International Relations and had already spent a semester abroad. Denise was heading to Paris in the fall. Candy thought for a moment about rescuing him but then decided he could sizzle on the social skillet just a little bit longer.

"My sister here is the French major," Deborah continued, turning up the burner a bit. "But my understanding of the term, politically anyway is that it means someone who does or suggests something that draws someone *else* into committing an act for which that person will be blamed or punished. Very often, an *agent provocateur* is actually an *agent de police*." Her diction was exquisite, Candy thought. "I'm really not sensing your plan is to become an informant, now is it?" Deborah asked.

Denise could barely conceal her amusement and Candy almost felt sorry for Brad, but she decided a little ego deflation might do him good. The Carswell girls had always possessed the odd ESP that twins exhibit and she knew Brad was now facing the tip of a very sharp and double-edged sword.

"Then maybe what I mean is that I want to be an *agent du change*," Brad shot back. She could tell by Denise's wrinkled nose that he had mangled the term, the pronunciation or perhaps both.

"It's actually *agent* de *change*," Denise corrected. "And that would make you a broker at The New York Stock Exchange. Don't take offense, but you don't strike me as a three-piece suit kind of guy."

Brad was clearly becoming flustered by their superior intelligence. "OK, OK. Look, I just want to stop the war," he said, the normal shade of paleness slowly returning to his cheeks. "And by whatever means necessary. I honestly don't care what you call me as long as I can help accomplish that. So kids like, like Henry stop coming home in flag-covered boxes."

Candy closed her eyes.

"Ah, but now you're talking about power," Deborah said. "You think you might have some power to stop the war. But power comes in several flavors just like Coke." The twins' voices were so similar Candy had to peek to see who was speaking. She knew Brad was in intellectual quicksand at the moment but hadn't yet gone completely under.

"Legitimate power," Deborah pressed on, "Like the government or the law, that's Vanilla Coke. What you're talking about now is Coercive Power – doing something that *makes* the war stop or at least forces the people who are waging it to stop. Like Aristophanes' *Lysistrata*. That's what every protest, every act of civil disobedience, every Molotov cocktail and every pipe bomb at a Post Office is based on. What you want is, I don't know, you want a, a Tabasco Coke."

Candy laughed at the thought and the tension eased. "My scholarship didn't come with a stipend," she said, desperate to change the subject. "And neither did Agent Brad's here. I'm trying to convince him that we should try to hook summer jobs down the shore, rent some shack and live like beach bums. You can't visit New Jersey and not go down the shore, right? Can you believe he's never played SkeeBall or had saltwater taffy or Copper Kettle Fudge in his whole entire life?"

"Down the shore," Brad said. "Why does everyone say that? Just say going to the beach like they do in California."

The three girls chuckled.

"'Cause this isn't California," Denise chided. "This is Jersey, man. Nobody here says they're going to the beach. You want to see the ocean or bake on the sand you go down the shore. That's just how it is. *Lingua franca*. The language of the people. Say anything else and you'll immediately arouse – no, you'll *provoke* suspicion. Not exactly something an *agent* of any stripe wants to do."

Candy wasn't sure but she thought that confronted by the cumulative intelligence sitting across from him, Brad actually appeared humbled.

"Hey," Deborah chimed in, "Come on now, paleface. Don't get us wrong. We're with you all the way on stopping the war. Even soldiers who were in Viet Nam are organizing against it. Last month in Chicago."

"Yeah, but protests and sit-ins aren't going to do it," Brad said quietly. "It's going to take something big. Something people will notice. Something they'll remember."

"I'm sorry, Brad," Denise teased, "But did you say your last name was Baader or Meinhof?"

"Meinhof is a woman," Brad deadpanned.

Denise smiled. "I know. I was just checking your violent radical I.Q."

Candy fished a dime out of her jean shorts and plopped it into the coin slot on the top of the *Select-O-Matic*.

"So, do you have an idea?" Deborah asked. "I mean, outside of the obvious ones like the Pentagon or the Empire State Building. Have you considered the Moorestown Mall?"

"People are always more concerned about what's in their own backyard," Brad replied. "But it has to be something they have an emotional attachment to." He was absent-mindedly stacking several of the slightly tapered and fluted plastic salt and pepper shakers on top of each other.

Candy flipped through the carousel of vertically arranged song titles. She punched the square buttons, depressing "C" in the top row and then "4" in the bottom. After a few hisses and pops an acoustic guitar riff slowly made its way across the booth.

"Oh, so maybe you do have something in mind then?" Denise said.

The table went quiet as the new song by the British group Ten Years After suddenly went up-tempo with a flurry of strummed chords and drumbeats.

"No, not really," Brad replied. He half-smiled at the Carswell twins. "But I'm pretty sure I'll know it when I see it."

"Well please remember to tell us so we can be conveniently out of whatever town you decide upon," Deborah said with a laugh. The twins eased themselves out of the booth. Brad did the same. Candy waited for him to go for his wallet. When he didn't she pulled five one dollar bills from her front pocket and laid them on the table. She drilled Brad with a look. The Carswell twins exchanged pleasantries with them and then departed. Candy tried to wave to Josephine but the older woman kept her back toward them. She turned to Brad.

"That was a really shitty thing to say to our waitress," Candy told him. "I *live* here, you know?"

Brad looked down at the treadworn black and white squares of ancient linoleum. He waited for Candy to slip out of the booth. As she moved toward the door he laid a five dollar bill on their table. As he turned to leave his hip grazed the top of the banquette seat. The tower of stacked shakers wobbled for an instant and then tumbled down with a clatter.

THURSDAY
JULY 1st 1971

-4-

Surf City, NJ

MICKEY COULD FEEL THE pool of perspiration between her shoulder blades wicking its way up her uniform blouse in just the time it took her to walk from her cruiser in the SCPD station's small parking lot to its back door. The stick-on dashboard thermometer she'd picked up at Pep Boys had read one-hundred degrees. She figured the humidity to be only slightly less than that. When she stepped inside, the abrupt Freon-generated cool of the air-conditioning gave her a shiver.

"It's hotter than blue blazes out there," Mickey said, invoking the expression her father often used. She looked around and noticed Charlie Higgins' desk was empty and Denny Dippolito was on the phone. He held up an index finger.

"Hang on a second," he said into the receiver. "She just walked in." He looked at Mickey. "It's Rich. Want to say hi?" Dip's voice was still raspy and probably always would be from the near-fatal choke hold Dickie Robichaux had put on him when he'd snatched Bunny from the station back in 1969.

Rich Rodriguez had been one of her deputies then as well and had stayed with her until he was offered the Chief's position in Rehoboth Beach, another resort town across the Delaware Bay. He'd left just after Memorial Day and his presence was truly missed. But she knew that Delaware was where he'd grown up and where he'd been a star athlete so she'd let him go with her blessing and also her beloved Chevelle SS cruiser. She fanned herself with her campaign hat and reached for the receiver

"*Hola, amigo,*" she said. "I only want to know two things. First, how are Colombia and the rugrats and second, how's my car?"

She nodded and smiled at the answers.

"OK," she said. "I don't know about how you do things at your shop but this Police Chief has work to do. Here's Dip." She handed the phone back to Dippolito then tossed her hat so it caught on the wall hook, a trick it had taken her three years to perfect. Dippolito gave her a thumbs up and continued talking.

Mickey sat down at her desk. On it were several folders. The top one bore the printed seal of the new Jersey State Police. Taped to it was a pink "While You Were Out" note. She recognized Charlie's meticulous style of cursive handwriting:

E Driscoll called X 2
Please call him PHL Field Off ASAP
(215) 555-5309

Evan Driscoll, she thought. He'd been an up-and-comer with the Bureau in '67 when she'd been a brand new Chief and all hell had broken loose. In the years and, as Loretta put it, the dramas that followed he'd been a hovering presence, contacting her several times each year. Most were on fairly thin procedural pretenses, but they always included an open invitation to discuss, as he put it, "career advancement opportunities" over lunch or dinner. He'd taken her brush-offs with good humor but he didn't stop offering. In the meantime he'd ascended to a Deputy Director position with the Bureau, the job that had been J.J. Durkin's in 1967. Mickey had trusted Durkin implicitly and although she felt Evan Driscoll was always honest and appeared to be a classic straight-arrow, her instincts told her he had an interest in her that extended beyond the strictly professional. He always managed, she noted, to slip in a question about her marital status or an offhand remark about his continued bachelorhood and his difficulties meeting "the right one." She knew the FBI had a file on her which meant that Evan

Driscoll knew much more about her than she would have ever told him herself. It was not a comforting thought.

Mickey had only a general idea of what he was calling about. But whatever it was she hoped it was important enough that she could keep any personal talk to a bare minimum. The idea seemed outlandish – there was nothing on Long Beach Island of any major strategic significance except maybe the land-locked schooner *Lucy Evelyn* over in Beach Haven and it certainly wasn't going anywhere. It was probably a bigger danger to itself, she thought, She never could understand why a hundred-year-old wooden ship would stock so many candles in a below decks Gift Shop.

She tapped her fingers on the note, took a deep breath and picked up the phone to make the call.

Steel Pier   1000 Boardwalk
Atlantic City, NJ

They were packed as tight as sardines in a tin, Candy thought, except this time the brine was on the outside. The child next to her had brought along her beehive swirl of cotton candy which was now rapidly liquefying in the fetid air and sticking to Candy's white t-shirt.

"All I see are wood pilings, algae and lots of barnacles," Brad said. His face was pressed against one of the eye-level portholes on what the sign called the Submarine Diving Bell and promised it would be *The Thrill of a Lifetime*! "There's so much sand swirling around. Is this all it does?"

Candy smirked. "Geez. What did you expect for a dollar? *Twenty Thousand Leagues Under the Sea? Moby Dick? The Kraken?*"

"Well, I mean, a fish would be nice – or maybe a dolphin. I guess I expected a little more than an underwater sandstorm and slimy telephone poles," Brad replied with a shrug. "I can see those really well, though."

"It's Flipper's day off," Candy deadpanned. Just over their heads was a microphone that looked like something that had been lifted from a Drive-In Theatre pole. The experience only lasted five minutes but she was already feeling claustrophobic. Then all of the children and many of the adults began shouting after receiving instructions from their ride-along guide to send "messages from the deep" to the landlubbers on the pier above.

"Should I start the FISH cheer?"

"Don't you dare," Candy commanded.

Instead Brad began singing softly. "And it's one, two, three, what are-"

Candy pinched his arm.

"Commie," she heard a woman say.

"Fascist," Brad replied.

"Just let it go, would you?" Candy said. "Jesus, it's almost the Fourth of July."

"All the more reason-"

"OK, folks," the attendant shouted. "Everyone hold on tight – we're going to begin our ascent from the briny depths of Davy Jones' Locker in five, four, three two-"

The chamber shot upward courtesy of its own natural buoyancy. The smaller children screamed and several of the adults gasped loudly. The Submarine Diving Bell bounced a few times and then came to rest. Green ocean water rushed past the portholes as the steel tank began its slow pneumatic rise up the gantry tower and back into the rickety embrace of the pier. When the door opened another group of undersea adventurers was already queued up and chattering excitedly.

Candy and Brad were among the last to exit. As they did, an older man in the line with a gray brush cut yelled "Which one's the Pinko faggot?" The breeze wafted a pungent bouquet of roasted peanuts mingled with body odor.

A woman wearing a pair of white cats-eye sunglasses and a black sleeveless top pointed at Brad.

"Him," she said, almost spitting the words out.

"Love it or leave it, asshole," an unseen voice shouted.

"Oh fuck me," Candy said under her breath. "Let's go."

The Submarine Diving Bell's attendant stepped over and ushered them quickly along a fraying yellow rope and away from the murmuring line. Candy heard someone say something about freedom of speech in a raised voice but she did not turn around to see who it was. She grabbed Brad around the waist and hustled him toward a sweating crowd of people waiting for the giant Ferris Wheel.

"Tough crowd," Brad said.

Candy was picking clots of spun sugar off her shirt.

"It's a tough state," she said. "But we like it that way. Remember you're a guest here so try to play nice with the other adults, OK? This is our only day off. There's a time and there's a place. This is neither."

"A time and a place," Brad repeated.

Candy did not at all like the way he said it.

"So what's next?" Brad asked her.

Candy looked at her wristwatch and then up at a large placard. "The Diving Horse," she said. "But we only have ten minutes and we want a good seat. It's pretty cool. You'll really like it."

"I'll really like it only if I get to ride the horse," Brad replied.

Candy ignored the remark and kept walking.

Pic-a-Lilli Tavern
Shamong Township, NJ
The Pine Barrens

Ronnie Dunn couldn't help himself. He kept looking up from their table at the two pictures displayed prominently above the beer taps behind the bar. They were hung side-by-side and festooned with black crepe paper and little American flags. A pine-board sign that looked like it had been made with a child's Burn-Rite woodburning set rested crookedly below the frames on angled two roofing nails It read "Brothers ~ Together Forever."

"What's the problem, Dunn?" Stellwag asked. "Shit, you look nervouser than fresh meat walking point. Relax, brother. No Charlie in here, man. Only thing can kill you is this horse-piss beer."

Ronnie exhaled hard. "Yeah," he said. "You're right, LT. It's nothing."

Stellwag leaned in and lowered his voice. "Listen. Both those crazy motherfuckers are dead. KIA. So completely KIA that they didn't even need Glad Bags. And don't kid yourself, brother. Nobody gives a shit how or who and nobody's one bit sad about it. It's just an old Piney place keeping up appearances is all."

Ronnie Dunn looked up again. The Bowker twins stared back. They way they'd both gone out, Ronnie considered, meant even the pit of Hell would not present a new experience.

"I heard it took the coroner three months to positively identify BoDean," Stellwag said between sips. "He didn't have any of his own teeth and there wasn't any kin. They say when they brought in the bones he thought at first they were from an animal, like maybe a wild pig. Until he saw the skull. And that's all there was

- just bones. Not a scrap of flesh. And I heard they ended up with some extra wrist bones which they still can't explain."

Ronnie drank from his bottle of Carling Black Label. He was only responsible for one of them, he knew. The one of whom nothing remained, unless those were the extra wrist bones they found in the skeleton frame of the burned out Chevrolet . Stellwag was right. Both brothers had been blots on the very notion of civilized humanity. He'd taken a chance dragging Mickey to The Dunes one night. He knew he wouldn't ever be bringing her here.

Stellwag told him the Pic-A-Lilli had always been a "Locals Only" bar with a sign that said as much until the old gravel road it fronted became the paved Highway 206. Once ignorant tourists on their way to the shore started mistaking it for a quaint roadside stop, the locals soon found other places to imbibe and a new owner decided tourist cash was just as spendable and much more readily dispensed.

Stellwag drank deeply from his bottle and tapped Ronnie's. "That chapter is over, soldier, and that book is closed. Now drink up or we'll have to leave here sober."

Ronnie drained his Black Label. "Hey, Mabel," he said and motioned to the barkeep for two more. As they waited for a new round a diminutive man in cowboy boots and a snap-button Western shirt got up from his table and approached them.

"You boys look like you might'a served overseas," he said. "Viet Nam I'm assuming." Ronnie noticed that although he dressed like a cowboy he didn't sound or act like one.

"Two tours each," Stellwag replied. "Different units, different sectors, but at the end of the day when you're in the shit it's all pretty much all the same."

"You for or against finishing it?" the little man asked.

Ronnie laughed. "Finishing it? Buddy, there's no finishing it. There's just getting out of it."

"Peace with honor the President says," the sawed-off stranger replied.

Stellwag leaned in. "Listen. It's another country's Civil War. North and South, same as ours was. There won't be any peace and there sure as shit won't be any honor."

"I'm sorry to hear that," the little man said. "Name's Barstow. Most people just call me Cowboy. I seen you lookin' at them pictures of the Bowker boys. Sad ends but good riddance to the pair of them, I say. They were like dangerous animals."

"So I've heard," Ronnie added. Kurt the bartender brought over two more Black Labels.

"Let me get those," Cowboy Barstow said. "Least a grateful citizen can do."

"Appreciated," Stellwag said. "Considering that not everyone shares your sentiments these days, you know."

"What they ought to have up there is a picture of old Harry Leusner. He used to be a regular here too. Somebody burnt him up one night when he was just sittin' in his little lean-to. Old Loose Nuts, he never hurt anyone."

Ronnie noticed Stellwag shifting in his chair.

"If I didn't know better I'd say somebody put a flamethrower to him – maybe like an M2A1."

Ronnie and Stellwag looked at each other. It was the model used by ground troops in-country until flame-throwing tanks appeared.

"That's a pretty good technical guess," Stellwag said.

Cowboy shuffled his feet. "I'm sort of a student of weaponry," he said. "Especially incendiaries. A hobby of sorts. Just booksmarts, though. I try to never touch anything more dangerous than a kitchen match myself. I lost a good truck to fire – I just thank the good Lord I wasn't in it at the time."

Ronnie wasn't sure why the little man felt compelled to share all this information with two strangers but he nodded anyway.

"You boys enjoy the beers," he said next, turning away. "Maybe I'll see you again." He returned to his seat at the bar.

Ronnie noticed that Stellwag had gone quiet.

"Y'OK there, LT?" he asked.

Stellwag drank the fresh bottle of Carling in one gulp. He looked at Ronnie. "Let's get out of here," was all he said.

▲▲▲

Outside the humidity was oppressive. Stellwag doffed his leather vest and stood bare-chested in the bright sun which glinted off his dog tags. "Don't tell anybody I took it off." He slung it over his shoulder so the Sons of Satan MC patch was displayed. "Did you think that was a little weird?" Stellwag asked

"The little cowboy?"

"Yeah. He didn't look tall enough to have ever been inducted into any branch of the armed services."

"He didn't look tall enough to ride the slide at Morey's Pier in Wildwood," Ronnie replied. "And like you said – pretty savvy on the weaponry for a civilian. Yeah. Weird. So, what are your archrivals The Druids up to these days?" Ronnie asked.

"Pretty quiet," Stellwag said. "Those newspaper articles really brought the whole law enforcement house right down on top of them. It was the investigative reporting equivalent of Operation Arc Light which, I guess, also makes the pen mightier than the B-52. There are still FBI surveillance teams snooping around the Pines. We've had to scale our operations way back and it's been nearly two years. They have gone deep underground with whatever they're running now."

"You're way too smart to be a dirtball biker even if you are the leader of the pack," Ronnie said. "You know that right? Anyway, did you realize that Arc Light is still going on? Man, that is a shitload of ordnance dropping every damn day. Not that it does any good."

"Well, it didn't stop Tet from happening," Stellwag replied. "Before I transferred to Dust Off I flew over half of my combat missions with the Razorbacks in just four days when that shit came down. I'd rather have a Thumper or even some Willie Pete, personally. You know a little bit about that, I think." Ronnie didn't answer. "How much ordnance do you still have stashed?" Stellwag asked.

"Enough to defend a perimeter," Ronnie replied. "You?"

"Enough to take on a regiment of NVA regulars, maybe a little more. Mostly explosives, small arms and ammo – not much need for - what'd that little guy say - incendiaries? So if you need anything that goes 'Boom' just say the word."

"No Agent Orange?"

"Oh, man," Stellwag answered, "I still worry when I think about how much of that shit we were exposed to. They still swear it's safe."

"Yeah, well they still swear we're winning," Ronnie answered. "And thanks, but I have plenty of noisemakers."

Stellwag looked around the parking lot. "Your little ballgame still on for Saturday?"

"Fourth of July on the third of July," Ronnie said. "Maximum exposure and response. You sure you and the Sons don't want to saddle up for it? There's power in numbers."

"I think we'll sit this one out in the Piney DMZ," Stellwag answered. "My guys want their 201 Files to stay closed. Let me know what the BDA ends up being, though."

"I'm sure you'll read about it," Ronnie said. "It'll be in all the papers."

"You sure you know what you're doin'?"

Ronnie smiled. "Never been more sure," he said.

Stellwag slipped his vest back on and plucked a pair of Army aviator's round-cornered rectangular sunglasses from its slit pocket. The gas tank on his blue Harley-Davidson Electra Glide sparkled in the sunlight. He pointed to Ronnie's black Royal Enfield. "Still riding the Schwinn, I see. Or does that say Sears and Roebuck? And is that a bell I see on the handlebars?"

Ronnie laughed. "Hey, watch it. This here is a real soldier's motorcycle," he said. "That thing," he pointed to the big Harley, "is a goddamn two-wheeled suburbanite station wagon. All it needs are wood panels on the forks."

A plane buzzed overhead and the two men looked up.

"A biplane," Stellwag said, shading his eyes. "Man, would I love to grab the stick on that bird."

"You could fly that?" Ronnie asked.

"Fuckin' A, bubba" Stellwag said. "Brother, I flew, and with some distinction I might add, the Huey Iroquois helicopter. Which means I can fly damn near anything. I could probably fly that new Boeing 747 if you gave me an hour to read the flight manual. Stick, rudder and thrust plus angle of attack. Powered flight is actually pretty simple. Scary, but simple." The aerial advertising banner being towed by the little plane came in to view.

TAN DON T BURN ! USE COPPERTONE

"Don't burn," Stellwag said. "Now that is always good advice, isn't it? How's my favorite Police Chief?"

"She's doing OK," Ronnie said. "Down one deputy since Rich Rodriguez left so no time off over the Fourth. And the crowds of shoobies just get bigger, crankier and more demanding every year."

"Well tell her I said hello – and tell her to make sure that reporter friend of hers watches his back along with his ass. The Druids are not exactly a forgive-and-forget type of organization."

"Roger that," Ronnie replied, hopping on his bike. Stellwag mounted the Harley and fired up the big V-twin four-stroke engine. It came to life with a guttural roar. Then he twisted the throttle to crank up the rpm's and the noise level. Ronnie grinned and saluted him then kick-started the Enfield which thrummed at a full hundred decibels lower. Stellwag snapped a return salute then peeled out with a double belch of black smoke from the twin pipes, sending sand and gravel flying.

Ronnie balanced on his bike and looked up again at the receding message. The next time he met Stellwag for a beer, he decided, he'd pick a different spot.

Surf City, NJ

Charlie Higgins walked in just as Mickey put down the phone.

"Hail, hail, the gang's all here," he said in his deep Carolina drawl.

"Got room for one more," Mickey responded tilting her head toward the empty desk where Rich Rodriguez had sat for almost four years.

"I see that. Any news on a replacement for El Kabong yet?" Charlie asked.

Mickey and Dippolito both laughed. "Mayor Billy swears they're looking," Mickey answered, "but my bet is at this point in the summer we won't see anyone sitting in that chair until next May."

"So then it's just us until next Tuesday?" Dippolito asked. With the Fourth falling on a Sunday the king tide of tourists was already starting and wouldn't ebb, they all knew, until at least Monday - five days hence.

"Afraid so," Mickey replied. "This heat wave might help us, though. Wears people out pretty early. Davey Johnson says the Ship Bottom boys would be willing to help out if we need them."

"Two things I know," said Charlie, settling back in his chair. "Crime doesn't pay and stupidity never sleeps. We should all just bunk here and get our shuteye in shifts like they do on ships. Go home to shower or show passionate affection to a loved one, maybe, but that's it."

"That was my thinking, too," Mickey added.

"So you agree that passionate affection qualifies as duty time under the dire straits we currently find ourselves in?" Charlie asked.

"As in 'marital duty'?" Mickey asked with a grin.

"I hope not," Charlie replied, "as none of us sitting here are currently married."

Mickey was going to tease him about his long lunch hours which had begun soon after he met his girlfriend when the LBI Central Dispatch radio crackled. Arlene Shields' familiar voice poured out from the single round speaker.

"Surf City this is Dispatch. Be advised the LG's are reporting a disturbance near their stand at 14th Street and are requesting assistance. Repeat, LG's at 14th Street request assistance. Copy?"

The lifeguards were asking for help, they all understood, most likely with unruly or inebriated beachgoers but there were sometimes other reasons.

Mickey nodded at Dippolito and he hit the Talk button on his microphone. "Copy, Dispatch. Is this by any chance a medical situation?" Mickey knew the lifeguards also called the PD if there was a water rescue or a heart attack to help manage onlookers and to clear a path for the ambulance crew.

"My Reply is No," Arlene said. She often tried to add a little humor to the dry, newly-scripted patter required by her handbook by quoting answers from the popular *Magic 8-Ball*. Mickey had one of the black plastic toys on her desk. The box it came in said it was made by a company in New York City called Alabe Crafts. It had been a Christmas gift from Arlene herself. Mickey later found out she'd bought one for all eight Police Chiefs on Long Beach Island. Ever since the local Radio Shack had started selling cheap police-band scanners to the general public their previously private and sometimes irreverent transmitted banter had to be curtailed.

"Copy that." Dippolito said simultaneously reaching for his hat and patting his gun. "I'm on my way."

To their surprise the radio crackled again. "Be advised, Surf City, the LG's specifically requested you send the Cavalry. Copy?"

Mickey and Charlie immediately rose from their chairs.

"Copy that, Dispatch," Dippolito replied, "SCPD 1, 2 and 3 all rolling." There were squeaks and scrapes from scuffing chairs as the three law officers headed for the door.

"Hey, Dip," Mickey said when they hit the parking lot.

"I know, I know, Chief," Dippolito replied. "You don't need to remind me every time. Leave the shotgun in the car."

1011 Boardwalk
Atlantic City, NJ

Candy was tired and Brad was obviously bored. They had just stepped off one of the few remaining three-wheeled wicker rolling chairs on which they'd ridden the length of the boardwalk. Brad had embarrassed her first by asking the young black man whose job it was to push the chair if he wanted to switch places with him and then by suggesting that the owner of the chair service was surely named James Crow. Both Candy and the young black man looked at first confused and then mortified. Now Candy was handing him a generous tip and apologizing for Brad's boorish behavior. She also thanked him for narrating their little tour. Candy saw that his name, Andrew, was embroidered on his sweat-soaked but otherwise neatly creased white short-sleeve shirt

"Tell your boyfriend to be cool. This is just my summer job and I actually like it a lot. People are friendly and I make better tips than if I was waiting tables or whipping weeds. I've done both before and this is a breeze compared to those gigs. The little old ladies from Philly and the suburbs are the best. I pushed Frankie Valli all around last week but he wore a hat and sunglasses so nobody would recognize him."

"Where are you going to school?" Candy asked.

"Glassboro State right now," Andrew answered. "Majoring in Business Administration but I'd like to get into Penn and then maybe even Wharton after that. Maybe get a job in one of those gambling casinos they say will be coming here soon. Big dreams I know."

"Well, good luck," Candy said.

"You?" he asked. Brad had taken a seat on one of the brightly painted wood and cement benches near the railing that faced the ocean. He was furtively glancing over his shoulder at her. Candy knew Andrew was chatting her up. She decided to let him continue since Brad was watching.

"I go to Grinnell," she said.

A quizzical looked passed over Andrew's face. "No offense, but is that a high school? I'm from just outside of Camden, but there's still a lot of little towns around here I've never even heard of."

"Actually, it's a college. It's in Iowa. But I grew up in Riverside. Went to Holy Cross."

Andrew smiled. "I graduated from Camden Catholic," he said. "We played you in the Parochial A playoffs. Beat your behinds pretty bad as I recall. You had too many white boys and that's a fact. We ended up losing to Don Bosco even though they had too many white boys as well."

"I think you did and I'm sure we did," Candy replied. "I'm majoring in Women's' Studies now."

"Darlin', every college guy I know is majoring in the study of women," Andrew replied.

"You got that right," Candy said. Now he was flirting with her, she decided. She was waiting to see how long it would take Brad to walk back over – or whether he would even bother.

"Just here for the day?" Andrew asked.

Candy nodded yes. "I have a summer job with The *SandPaper* in Surf City."

"So you a reporter – kind of like Lois Lane? Or maybe a photographer."

"Not exactly. Mostly I make coffee, pick up doughnuts or takeout at Bill's Luncheonette and run errands all day. I do get to write some articles, though. And depending on the article I might take a few pictures. " Candy paused. "Like tomorrow, I'm spending the whole day with the Police Chief in Surf City, Mickey Cleary. She's the only woman Chief on the Island. I think she might be the only one in New Jersey. Kind of a 'day in the life' type of piece. It's not much but it's something to put on my resume` anyway."

"No, that sounds cool," Andrew said. "You should do a story about these chairs – they're about as old as the damn Boardwalk itself I think. Lots of famous folks sat right where you did over the years. They're a regular tradition," he paused a beat and then continued, "or at least tha's what Massa Crow tell me." Then Andrew flashed a wicked grin, openly mocking Brad's patronizing offer and doing it, Candy realized, quite possibly within earshot.

"Touche`," Candy replied. "Maybe I will."

An elderly couple approached. "Maybe I see you around," Andrew said. He nodded to the older couple. "Looks like I have customers. Nice meeting you…" He paused, obviously waiting for her to fill in the blank.

"Candy," she said. "Candace actually but no one calls me that."

"I got it. Candy. Candy Girl, like in that song by The Archies a couple of summers ago. What was it? 'Sugar, Sugar'?" He motioned for the older couple to take a seat in the chair. "You be cool now, Candy Girl. Remember, it's Andrew. Andrew Sarjeant." He handed each of his new riders a straw fan. "Like I said, maybe I see you around sometime. Surf City. Newspaper. I'll remember." Andrew stepped behind the chair, gave a heaving grunt and started off with his new fares. The ancient yellow pine boards underneath creaked and groaned with the weight. "So where you lovely folks visiting from today?" she heard him ask as the big spoked wheels began turning.

Candy walked over to the bench and sat next to Brad. The light green ocean was as flat and as calm as a swimming pool. Tiny excuses for waves lapped weakly at the beach. Candy thought the tide was probably going out judging by where a stripe of wet beach remained but it was hard for her to really tell. Iridescent heat waves shimmered above the sand and a cacophony of music and chatter from hundreds of transistor radios hung in the motionless air. The Rolling Stones' "Brown Sugar" was playing on one nearby.

"Exchanging pleasantries, political polemics or maybe just phone numbers?" he asked without looking at her.

"Don't be a dipshit, Brad, OK? I mean seriously, Jim Crow?" Candy opened her purse, pulled out a Virginia Slim, lit it then turned her head to blow the smoke away from his direction. "I apologized on your behalf and, for your edification, his name was Andrew, he goes to college around here and he probably takes home more money than you do hooking and unhooking letters on airplanes all day. He really didn't sound at all like he was being oppressed or persecuted by Whitey or The Man."

"Hey, Paramount Air pays pretty well," he replied. "Mr. T is a great person to work for and there will be a lot of overtime starting tomorrow. One of the pilots even said maybe I could ride along for a loop in one of the trainers." Candy remained quiet "That reminds me," Brad continued, "Can we pick up a copy of your little newspaper around here?"

Candy looked at him funny.

"It only comes out on Wednesdays, remember?" she said and took a quick puff on the long cigarette. "It's not The *New York Times*. And anyway, no. We don't distribute it way down here. Just on the Island and a few of the little mainland towns across Little

Egg Harbor and Barnegat Bays. Why? It's mostly ads anyway." He seemed to hesitate, she thought, but then he answered her.

"Right. That's why. I saw an ad last week. Guy had a motorbike for sale. Two seater. I thought it might be fun. If he's still advertising it then it would be in yesterday's issue. Maybe we could check it out. I think it might be on our way back."

Candy stubbed out her cigarette on the bench then dropped it between the slats.

"There might be an old copy in the car," she said. Candy was still feeling angry and frustrated but realizing they still had two months of cohabitating ahead of them, she decided to sue for peace with or without honor. "Come on," she said and reached for his arm. "The big Planter's Peanuts store is right there. Let's go grab a sack for the road. Maybe get enough so we can sit on the beach and eat them with some beers while we wait for the sun to go down."

Brad put his arm around her. "OK," he said. "I suppose, when in Jersey…"

"That's the spirit, farm boy," Candy replied. "We'll put some sand in your shoes yet."

-5-

14th Street & Ocean Avenue Beach
Surf City, NJ

ALL THREE CRUISERS ARRIVED within thirty seconds of one another, light bars flashing and sirens wailing. Once parked, they left their lights on, killed the sirens and got out. Mickey led the way down narrow the beach path at the end of the crumbling asphalt road. Charlie was right behind her. As she had instructed, Dippolito began flanking north along the weathered wood-and-wire snow fence that guarded the dunes, scanning for any runners.

"Isn't this the same place that-" Charlie said as they trudged through the hot, sugary sand.

"Yes it is," Mickey replied, not letting him finish. "Let's just hope it's alcohol and not PCP this time." A second later Mickey got her first glimpse of what could only be described as a melee. She figured at least twenty people were going at it "full-tilt" as her father liked to say. The lifeguards, all just college kids, were shouting and blowing their whistles but they had obviously given up trying physically to intervene. Mickey did her best to rapidly assess the combatants. They were all white, she noticed right away, so at least it wasn't racial. There were more and more of those blow-ups every summer it seemed and she thought they got uglier each time. It took her another few seconds but then she caught a glimpse of the beach blanket, saw the differences in age and hair length she knew.

"Not PCP, right?" Charlie asked. "Just tell me it's not PCP

this time."

"Worse," Mickey replied, bringing up the electronic bullhorn she held in her left hand.

"What could be worse than PCP?" Charlie asked. He tugged on the cord that held his own whistle and it flipped up.

Mickey looked at him, tilting her lips away from the bullhorn's mouthpiece.

"Politics," she said.

Charlie blew his whistle. Mickey did the same with hers but only when she amplified it with the bullhorn did the participants momentarily pause, turning toward the ear-splitting sound. Then they went back to fighting.

"Well, shit," Mickey muttered. She unsnapped her holster and withdrew her sidearm. She pointed it toward the ocean and raised it to a forty-five degree angle. She quickly scanned for anyone or anything out further than the shoreline. She had been taught never to fire straight up. A falling bullet, the weapons instructor at the academy had told her, returned with such speed that it could still seriously wound or kill someone despite its small mass.

Seeing nothing she pulled the trigger.

This brought the burgeoning riot to an immediate standstill. Mickey holstered her gun and closed the snap. She tried the bullhorn again.

"Everybody put their hands in the air," she said, the bullhorn's loudness setting cranked to Maximum. In the stagnant air and with a dead calm sea the sound was even further magnified. "I said...hands in the air. And move away from anyone near you. I want to see daylight otherwise everyone ends up with an arrest on their record. Now move!"

To her mild surprise the crowd did as they were instructed. Charlie slid to Mickey's right and Dippolito closed in from behind and to her left, triangulating the group. Dippolito reached for his nightstick but Mickey waved him off and stepped toward the group.

"OK," she said, now foregoing the bullhorn. "You can all put your arms down." She moved methodically between the sweating, sand covered bodies. For a moment she thought they were all men but then she spied several young women who looked considerably worse for the wear. A ring of beachgoers had gathered. She nodded to Charlie and he began methodically moving them back and away. Dippolito did the same on his side.

"OK," Mickey said. "Now, Simon Says everybody sit their asses in the sand."

The still-panting group complied. Mickey weaved between them until she spied it again. She reached down and picked up the beach blanket. Its design was a huge American flag with the usual red stripes but on the blue background were fifty white Peace Signs in place of the usual stars. The people palpitating and perspiring on the beach looked evenly divided between what the Mayor referred to as hippie freaks and what the newspapers called Middle Americans. Except for the women – she couldn't tell what side they'd been on and figured they just went all in with whatever their husbands or boyfriends did. She made eye contact with one girl who looked familiar, a freckled redhead who had filled out considerably since the last time Mickey had seen her. Mickey pointed at her.

"Susy, right?" The girl's eyes darted in alarm. "Don't worry," Mickey said to the group. "She's a repeat offender not a Narc." Relief tinged with gratitude washed over the girl's face. "I may need to deal with you later, young lady, so don't go anywhere."

Mickey grabbed the ersatz flag blanket by its corners and shook out the sand, intentionally spraying the former brawlers who rubbed at their faces and made spitting sounds trying to get the grains out of their mouths and off their tongues.

"We're gonna have a quick Civics lesson here and then maybe, maybe I might let you go. But if I hear any crap from even one of you then you can all plan on getting your fingerprints registered with the New Jersey State Police." She handed the flag blanket to Charlie who'd taken up a position next to her, his thick forearms crossed over his chest. Some more easily bored rubberneckers had already wandered back to their coolers and their sand chairs but many sat or stood quietly within earshot.

"This," she pointed toward Charlie, "is a blanket that looks like our flag. But it isn't our flag. If it was we'd be having a different conversation. One of the things that the actual flag guarantees is that you are free to express yourself in public." She noticed that some of the more muscular men had tattoos she recognized as military. "Some of you risked your lives for that flag and you take offense because you feel that it's being disrespected. Some of you don't think what's being done in the name of that flag is necessarily right."

Mickey paused and tossed the bullhorn to Dippolito who bobbled it but managed to hang on.

"But my job and my deputies' job is to serve and protect all of you regardless of which side you choose. Which means I will not, I repeat – I will not let you beat the crap out of each other in my town on my beach in broad daylight. Are we clear?"

There were head shakes and mutters from seated group in front of her.

"Who owns the blanket?" Mickey asked.

The freckled redhead raised her hand.

"Yeah," Mickey said with a laugh. "We are definitely going to talk later. Now come get it." The young girl stood and walked toward Charlie. Several of the men in the group glared at her. "OK," Mickey continued. "Everybody on their feet." They all complied, many brushing sand from their legs or trying to dislodge it from the more intimate areas of their bathing suits.

"Now, if you don't particularly care for this artistic rendering of Old Glory then you will gather up your chairs and your umbrellas and whatever else and you will follow Deputy Higgins here no less than one hundred yards north." She pointed to her left. "If free expression is more your bag then you will follow Miss Susy and Deputy Dippolito no less than one hundred yards to the south." She pointed to her right. "Furthermore, this ends right now. I'm not going anywhere and Surf City occupies only one single square mile of this island so if you decide to rekindle hostilities and violate the holiday truce I am declaring then I can promise you this - I will be much less reasonable the next time. It will soon be the Fourth of July and that is supposed to be a celebration of freedom – and freedom means, unless your plan is to disrespect or hurt someone, freedom means you have a right to express your opinions and ideas without getting hassled or beaten up. It's been that way for almost two hundred years and we are not changing it today. Now, let's start moving."

Charlie leaned close to her. "Isn't that the 'Death to Pigs' girl? From the last time we were here?"

Mickey chuckled. "Yup, that's her - in the pale flesh. Her parents must still rent or maybe by now they own a house up the street." She reached down and retrieved the spent nine millimeter shell casing from the sand.

"Man," Charlie said. "She certainly grew, um, up. How did

you ever remember her name?"

"She wrote us a letter of apology, remember?" Mickey said. "I still have it in my desk. Dotted all the i's with little hearts. I'm pretty sure she's still not street-legal, so let's keep a watchful eye on her, OK? My guess is she's going through a wild-child phase just to annoy her parents. I'm betting she has a lowlife boyfriend they absolutely hate."

"You ever know anybody was like that?" Charlie asked with a smirk.

"Not for a long, long time," Mickey replied.

Charlie nodded and left to herd his assigned political faction up the beach. Dippolito did the same with his slightly younger and scragglier crew. Mickey started her trudge back toward the dunes. There were some murmured thanks from the remaining sunbathers to which Mickey gave only a quick wave in response.

"Hey, Chief," a man called from behind her as she got to the rickety fencing. "Chief," he yelled again. Mickey turned around. He looked about forty and was deeply, almost too deeply she thought, tanned. His skin looked like the oiled leather on one of her old baseball gloves. A thick gold chain with a circular medallion and a bull's horn charm nested in an overgrown garden of salt-and-pepper chest hair. A pair of mirrored sunglasses dominated his face. Otherwise, she noted, all he wore was a size-too-small Speedo racing suit, which she quickly decided provided considerably more information than she either needed or wanted. He did not have a beach tag and she wondered where he would pin it even if he did.

"Hey, Chief. You didn't arrest anybody?" he said. "Seriously? After all that? You didn't arrest even one of those longhair hippie instigators?" Mickey intentionally kept her gaze at eye level and away from the contents of the skimpy suit.

"If I arrested everyone in Surf City who got into a fight in a week I'd have to turn the Ebb Tide Motel into a jail just to hold them all."

"I pay taxes here," he persisted. "Pretty high taxes in fact. I shouldn't have to deal with Viet Cong sympathizers in my face and on my vacation. This is the United States of America not Red China. I was in the Reserves. I shouldn't have to put up with this."

Mickey took off her Ray-Bans. "Sir, first let me thank you for being a loyal Reservist. Second, let me remind you that you pay those taxes you mentioned for me and my deputies to keep the peace and to provide a level of safety for you and all these other fine people who live and visit us here. Which is exactly what we just did. I try to be a fair person but this heat wave is making people a little crazy. Tempers tend to rise right along with that red mercury in the Pepsi thermometer downtown. And the ocean is like bathwater which doesn't help the situation."

The man would not relent. "This is still just a pricey resort town. You know what having a house down the shore is costing me? And I only use it for three months out of the year. So during those three months I don't expect to see anti-war protests or desecration of the flag. You should have arrested them. That's your job."

"If I arrest one then I have to arrest them all." Mickey said and took a breath. "It wasn't a real protest and it wasn't a real flag - just a beach blanket that sort of looked like a flag and a difference of opinion that got out of hand. So I suggest you let it go and get back to working on your sunburn. I sure hope your wife brought along the Noxzema."

"Yeah, yeah, yeah. You're one of them, aren't you?" he persisted.

Mickey was losing patience. "One of them? If you mean an American then, yep, I'm one of them. Now if you'll excuse me I do have other duties so-"

"No, I mean one of *them*. I bet you have a framed picture of good old Hanoi Jane right on your desk. Maybe with her autograph, even."

Mickey realized her foot was tapping rapidly and waited for it to stop.

"Sir, do you have a shirt and a towel with you today," she asked.

"Yeah, of course I do, why?"

Mickey tried not to smile. "Because I'm going to need you to put on the shirt, wrap the towel around your waist and accompany me back to the station."

"You're crazy," he said and began to turn away. "I'm not going anywhere with you. Broads got no business being police officers anyway if you ask me."

Mickey straightened her shoulders and hooked her thumbs into her gun belt. "Sir, please don't make me add Resisting Arrest to the other pending charges I'll be filing."

"What the fu- . What the hell are you talking about? What

other charges?"

"Violation of the Borough's Beach Tag Ordinance, Disorderly Conduct and -" she lifted her right hand. Without even glancing down she pointed theatrically to his groin. "Indecent Exposure."

The man was too shocked to reply.

"Be aware that although I'm not required to do so I will grant you the courtesy of exactly one minute to explain to your family why you're going to be late for dinner this evening. Now go gather up your things and come right back. I don't want to cuff you in front of everyone but make no mistake, I will not hesitate to do so."

The man seemed to struggle processing what had just transpired but he turned without a word and headed for his little encampment, his shoulders slumping noticeably. The rear view, Mickey decided, was not quite as offensive but it was certainly no less unattractive. It reminded her of a comment Dippolito made when he'd returned to work one Monday after taking advantage of a fourteen-dollar weekend special at Sunshine Park, the nudist colony in Mays Landing. He'd gone there hoping to spy some Atlantic City showgirls getting what the big sign out on Route 50 promised was a "Total Tan." What he'd found instead were paunchy middle-aged suburbanites and wrinkly retirees.

"Believe me," she remembered him saying. "That isn't anything anybody wants to see."

Hyde Park Neighborhood
Chicago, Illinois

The plastic radio rested precariously on the window sill, its extensible silver antenna poking through one of several holes in the screen. Lake flies crawled on the outside until they found ingress. It was the only place reception wasn't completely blurred out by static.

"There should be something on the news by now," one of them said.

"Try another station," a young man suggested.

"Leave it where it is."

The command came from a dark-haired woman in upscale hippie chic. None of the other three people in the shabby apartment dared to question her and she did not bother to look up from her copy of the *Chicago Daily News*. Stock prices, Cubs and White Sox scores and the local weather forecast droned on from the studios and announcers of WBBM but nothing about the event they were listening for.

"Maybe it didn't go off," said a young woman with lighter hair and fair skin.

The dark-haired woman ignored the comment. From a back bedroom came the sound of a muffled shout and the scraping of shoes on a bare wooden floor. A younger man with long, unkempt hair stood and disappeared down a hallway.

"We have to take out the trash, first," the dark-haired woman said.

"Why?" the younger woman asked. "Why can't we just leave him in there and blow town."

"Because he puts the entire network at risk, that's why." This came from a man with thinning hair and glasses who appeared older than his compatriots. "When you're fighting a revolutionary war spies are always dealt with in the same way."

"But what if he's with the FBI or the CIA?" the young woman's voice pleaded. "Just leave him. We still have the safe house in Oakland. We could be back by Sunday."

"Oh, look," the dark haired woman said. She had discarded the *Daily News* and was now perusing the previous day's issue of the *Sun-Times* newspaper. "The Student Drama Society is doing Ibsen's 'Hedda Gabbler' this weekend.' How deliciously ironic. Should we go? We should definitely go. It says all SDS members and supporters are admitted free. Everybody have their membership cards?"

A forced riffle of laughter followed.

The dark haired woman stared out the window at the sprawling urban campus of the University of Chicago. "What we really need - what we really, really need is for the National Guard to shoot some more students," she said. "We had our moment last year. Our one big chance. Right after Kent State. And we missed it."

The older man lit a joint, took a few tokes and then handed it off. "Yep. Bases loaded, nobody out and somehow, somehow we didn't score," he said with a cough. "Nobody's listening to us now. Nobody cares. College kids are back to worrying about getting high and getting laid. We had our chance when joining a march or a protest demonstration made both of those things more likely. And we had free advertising every time they played that goddamn song-"

"Four dead in O-hi- o," the younger woman sang.

The dark-haired woman nodded in agreement. "And so, comrades in arms, it falls to us to take the fight right to them even if no one else wants to. Kent State was like Pearl Harbor, we had their hearts and we had their minds – and we let it slip away." She puffed on the glowing blunt and passed it on. "Any message from our friend the Blessed Virgin? His Holy Day of Obligation is fast approaching."

"He's supposed to call this afternoon. We told him to find a pay phone, preferably in the middle of nowhere," the younger woman replied. "We placed the number of the phone booth up the street in a newspaper ad. Was there anything special you wanted me to tell him?"

The dark-haired woman cracked a thin smile. "Just make sure he trusts his local munitions dealer," she said. "It's the only link in the chain that's out of our control. And you know how much I hate it when things are out of our control. Say, does New Jersey have a National Guard?"

"Every state has a National Guard," the older man answered. "Why?"

"Just thinking one or two moves ahead. Maybe... maybe we need to worry less about protesting something and focus more on, you know, provoking something. I don't know how Nixon did it but even if he's not calling us bums anymore we've definitely become the bad guys in the public's consciousness. So... we need to rewrite the script. The pigs and the politicos have to go back to being the villains in this drama. I am not going to let a bunch of hardhats in New York City call the tune here."

"I'm not sure I understand where you're going with all this," the younger woman said. "What would we do?"

The dark-haired woman continued. "Who's the Governor of New Jersey? Is he the kind of guy who would send in the troops?"

"Cahill," the older man answered. "William T. Cahill." The joint had made its way back to him and he produced a paper clip from his pocket and expertly slipped the moist end of the burning stub into its grip. "And that's hard to say," he rasped after two quick tokes and a loud exhale. "He once worked for the FBI. And he was a prosecutor in Camden which is one tough town. But he is a Catholic. He went to a small Jesuit college up on the Main

Line in Philly. Liberal Arts, but only modestly liberal. He's not a lifelong politico like Rhodes over there in Ohio so it's hard to say just how reactionary he'd be. Jesuits pride themselves on being thinkers first. Very big on questioning literally everything. They'll argue with you even if they agree with you."

The two women looked at him with quizzical expressions.

The older man coughed. "Excuse me," he said with a huff. "Remember I do have a PhD International Relations and I do teach Political Science as well as Government at the university level. Tenure track I might add. Governors are the wild cards in any political deck. That's why I keep files on all fifty of them."

The dark-haired woman declined the proffered joint. "What I'm thinking," she said, "is that while destruction of federal property is still good – something like this is better. A cultural landmark instead of a faceless government building for once. When we blow up a Post Office it just pisses people off because then they don't get their welfare checks. So this is definitely new territory for the movement. But if we could somehow connect it with, let's say, the unfortunate death, no, wait, the state-sponsored *execution* of an ordinary kid from middle America, that might be enough to re-light the fire. Kent State, Act Two. Is there a train from here to New Jersey? Or a bus?"

"I think the Blessed Virgin was planning on being a hero, not a martyr," the younger woman said. She was once again ignored.

"The Pennsylvania Railroad – sorry – what do the fascists and robber barons call it now, Amtrak? I think it has a direct run from Chicago to New York but not Philadelphia," the older man answered. "But I'm pretty sure there's a train that runs from New York to Atlantic City. Or at least to Philadelphia. So you could get close. But passenger trains and major train stations are easy to watch and you'd have to negotiate at least three of them. Buses, although they are a truly shitty way to travel, buses do go literally everywhere and it's much easier to blend in with the rabble on a Greyhound than on the Broadway Limited."

The dark-haired woman banged her fist on the floor. "OK, then," she said. "Pack up your troubles, Sister Fargo," the dark-haired woman said. "You need to be in the Garden State by Saturday so get busy checking timetables. You decide train or bus just so you get there. But don't tell the Blessed Virgin you'll be miraculously appearing to him just yet. Check in with me along the way and we'll work out the rest of the details on the fly. And for this assignment I'm changing your name. The time has come."

"To what?"

"Sister Christian. I don't know, I just like the way it sounds."

The younger woman stood. She did not look at all happy but said nothing.

"There is one more thing before you go," the dark-haired woman said. She reached behind her and stuck her right hand, which was missing the fourth and fifth fingers, underneath one of the torn couch cushions. After some digging she pulled out a nickel-plated revolver, dangling it by the trigger guard between her thumb and index finger.

"Are you fucking serious?" the girl cried.

"Yes, I am completely fucking serious," the dark-haired woman replied without emotion. "What did you think a revolution looked like?"

-6-

U.S. Highway 9
Oceanville, NJ

THE CAMARO HAD BEEN the love of Candy's life when she got it in 1967 just after she turned seventeen. But it was not aging all that well and she knew it. They had decided to use it for the drive from Iowa, Brad's light blue VW Bug being mechanically suspect and only marginally roadworthy even on a good day. She suspected his continued ownership of it had become something of an affectation since he made a point of educating anyone within earshot that Volkswagen translated from German as "the people's car." Candy had no idea what Camaro meant, if anything, but it sounded very cool and, in the long run, that was really all she cared about.

At the moment, however, the pride of the General Motors plant in Norwood, Ohio was anything but cool. The air conditioner had quit providing even mildly cool air in mid-June after a series of intermittent work stoppages that lasted anywhere from a few minutes to several days. The car's paint color was listed as Ermine White which she was currently thankful for since she was seated on the hood of the coupe, just behind the transverse black stripe that circled the front cowling. She loved the fact that the wide stripe, which was easily ten degrees hotter to the touch than the surrounding metal, was the only contrasting color on the car's exterior. Although she never told anyone she always thought of the car as her own white stallion, like the Lone Ranger's horse

Silver. Candy looked over the top of the roofline and back down the pitted asphalt road they had pulled off from fifteen minutes earlier. Brad was on a New Jersey Bell pay phone. The air wasn't moving at all but she noticed he had still tried to pull shut the folding glass door on the battered silver and red booth. Its tall oblong outline was tilted slightly against the flat horizon at the same angle of declination, she decided, as the Leaning Tower in Pisa.

Brad had been unusually vague on the details of the motorbike and its seller and he had taken with him the copy of *The SandPaper* she had found wedged between the white bucket seat and the black center console. The windows of the phone booth were smeared and mud-spattered. On the side facing her there was a large spider web crack which appeared to be the result of a thrown rock. She mused it could also have been a caused by bullet but decided that was much less likely. She couldn't see Brad clearly but even through the murky panes his movements appeared animated. Candy had read enough cheap novels that the phrase "gesticulating wildly" immediately sprang to mind. She was a good writer, everyone told her, and her high school teachers were sorely disappointed when she didn't major in either English or Journalism. Only Peggy Collier, the school's full-time Librarian, had been upbeat about her planned course of study. Candy had idolized Collier her from the day she insisted on being addressed as "Ms." and loved it that she always dressed smart and chic and anything but frumpy. She had made Candy promise that when she got her degree she would come back with the answer to just one question.

"I want you to tell me why," Ms. Collier had said one winter afternoon as Candy dutifully scribbled it in her Composition Book, "Why the average man is more terrified of being laughed at by a woman than he is of being shot by one." Candy hadn't really understood the question at the time but she promised to try. Now, after two years of parsing history, literature and popular culture, a thin beam of academic light had begun to cut through fog, guiding her closer to what she hoped might be an answer.

The door of the booth had jammed in the half-open position and Candy could hear Brad cursing. She hopped off the Camaro's hood and walked back toward him. By the time she got there he had extricated himself through the narrow but somehow still passable opening.

"Sold it this morning," Brad said flatly and started toward the car.

"All that –," she half smiled as the next word formed on her tongue, "Wild gesticulating over something that's already sold?" She trailed after him, a peloton of sweat droplets forming rapidly on her forehead. "Jesus, I figured you had to be haggling over the price or something."

Brad answered her but did not slow his pace or turn around. "Somehow we got to arguing about politics."

"So even a motorbike is a political statement now?" she asked. "How? Did it have 'Love It or Leave It' on the license plate or maybe an American flag gas tank like the one in 'Easy Rider'? Was it a Honda made by oppressed Japanese factory workers?"

"Let it go, Candy," he said. "I really don't want to talk about it."

"OK, OK . Fine. You want to drive for a while?"

"Not really," Brad replied. He yanked open the passenger side door and got in.

At Brad's suggestion they had avoided the speedier Atlantic City Expressway and Garden State Parkway routes back to Surf City on the notion that the back roads would be free of not only toll booths but also the "Mongolian hordes," as he phrased it, of tourists that were sure to be clogging the major arteries in their collective rush to start the extra-long holiday weekend. Candy didn't really mind. The old thoroughfares conjured up happy girlhood memories of family car trips to Wildwood, Ocean City and what to her back then had seemed the pure and magical fairy tale allure of Atlantic City. Often, she recalled, they would go just for the day, changing and showering in the rickety, barely private white wooden stalls of commercial bath houses then stopping for pizza and a whole pitcher of Pepsi on the way home. Invariably, she would pass out in the big back seat of the turquoise Chevy Brookwood, sated, sunburned and exhausted. She could almost feel her father's arms cradling her as he carried her up the stairs to her tiny cupola of a room, lit by the soft glow of a Tinkerbelle nightlight, and laid her in the small canopied bed.

By the time she got to the Camaro's driver's side door Candy thought she was going to cry.

Brad was fumbling with an old Esso road map which was threatening to come apart completely at every one of its folds. "So where are we?" he said.

"Asks the man with the map," Candy shot back.

"Seriously," Brad replied. "Where the fuck are we?"

Candy laughed.

"We're miles from nowhere," she began to sing. "So I guess I'll take my time."

He refolded and handed her the map. "Sorry," he said. "But we're all out of tea for the Tillerman, I'm afraid."

Candy took the flimsy stack of paper from him. On its rectangular cover page was a faded drawing of a happy family in a red convertible parked next to a pair of Esso gas pumps. A helpful and crisply uniformed attendant was giving directions to the panoramic vistas in the distance. "*Happy Motoring!*" was printed at the bottom. Gingerly, she unfolded the map but only so the southern sections of the Garden State and its network of roads great and small appeared. Out of Atlantic City she knew they had taken U.S. Route 30, nicknamed the White Horse Pike. *Well, how perfect that is*, she thought. The last sign she remembered had been for a poorly maintained County road that they had turned onto just outside Absecon. It had serendipitously led them straight to old Highway 9, the newer version of which was technically now the high speed but heavily patrolled Parkway. She was sure pretty Old Nine would eventually get them back close to Long Beach Island.

"I'll know better when we get to an intersection," Candy said, dropping the map on her lap. She slipped the key into the ignition, pumped the gas pedal twice and the Camaro's six-cylinder one-hundred-and-forty horsepower engine kicked into life. Her father had purposely purchased the lower power package, assuring her he didn't want her driving what he called a "suicide machine." The dash vents gamely poured out hot, stale air. Candy shifted the 3-speed automatic into Drive and pulled back onto the baking tarmac.

"Could you at least navigate?" she asked. "Taking the back streets was your idea, remember?"

"You're the Jersey girl," he said in reply. "Nothing around here makes any sense. Where I grew up if a road sign says north then you know you're heading north. Here you could be going straight south towards the equator."

Candy took out the square, oversized Ray-Bans she'd bought from a pretty blonde sales clerk at Bamberger's and slipped them on. The light blue lenses gave the view through the windshield a slightly surreal quality. She had her hair twisted into a pony tail and the back of her neck felt, just like the song by the Lovin' Spoonful said, dirty and gritty.

"Can we turn the radio on at least?" she asked.

Brad reached over and twisted the silver knob. Joe Niagra, the self-named Rockin' Bird was DJ'ing on WDAS. "Can you get WMMR on this?" Brad asked.

"Bradley, this is a '67 Chevy, remember?" Candy answered, scanning the road for any kind of waypoint sign. "No FM and the 8-Track hasn't worked in a year. So, sorry. Anyway, why is everybody so hot on FM radio now? The DJ's talk so low you can hardly hear them and all the songs are twelve minutes long and are either by Traffic, the Doors or Pink Floyd." She reached across and turned up the volume. "She's a Lady," by Tom Jones blared out. Candy began to sing loudly along with the "*Whoa, whoa, whoa*" part of the chorus.

"Really? You *like* this song?"

Candy laughed so hard she snorted. "No," she said turning it up even louder. "I absolutely *hate* this song. Fucking hate it. Like meeces to pieces. But I'm using it as part of my junior year capstone project." Brad barely nodded. The song faded out in a hail of brass and undulating sine-wave *whoa-whoa's*. Then, without any intro, the marimba-laced opening riff of the Rolling Stones' "Under My Thumb" came on. "OK, now," she said, "That asshole. He did that on purpose."

"Did what on purpose?"

Candy slowed as an unmarked intersection appeared on their left. She braked to a complete stop in the road and looked down at the map. "I think I know where we are now. We just need to keep going straight." She let up on the brake and they resumed traveling. Brad turned down the radio volume.

"Who did what on purpose?" he asked again.

"The Rockin' Bird," Candy said. "He definitely played those two particular songs back to back on purpose," she said. "They're both completely demeaning and derogatory toward women. Like, sure," Candy continued, "She's a lady. But let's get one thing straight - she's *mine*, like my property. And oh, yeah, she always knows her place - which is right under my thumb. Well fuck him and fuck that."

A sign appeared on their right.

SMITHVILLE 2 mi
TUCKERTON 20 mi

Candy remembered a restaurant. Was it in Tuckerton? No, she realized, it wasn't Tuckerton. It was Tuckahoe. A name not a town. The Tuckahoe Inn. And it was well south of them by now she thought.

"Really? There's an immoral and unjust war going on and you're worried about what's on AM radio?" Brad asked. "Besides, it's Tom Jones for Christ's sake."

"Careful," Candy replied. "You definitely do not want to end up a casualty in the War of the Sexes which, by the by, also happens to be both immoral and unjust and has been going on for a hell of a lot longer. And for your information Tom Jones didn't write 'She's a Lady'. Paul Anka did. What a schmuck."

Brad turned his head and looked out the rolled down passenger window.

"I meant Paul Anka was a schmuck, not you," Candy clarified as they approached another intersection. Two single lane roads left the highway at acute angles and heading in opposite directions. Candy took neither of them and continued on what she assumed was still U.S. 9 North. Mick Jagger's preening vocals faded and once again, without any of the usual DJ patter, a new tune began, this one heavy with electric bass and organ. Candy recognized it immediately. So did Brad who immediately turned the sound back up.

Ray Manzarek's Fender electric piano percolated lazily out from the dashboard speakers. Brad closed his eyes. Candy could see his head bobbing slightly as the song's rain and thunder sound effects kicked in. She pressed the accelerator. The Camaro responded. She'd come to a decision. When they got back to Grinnell she was going to wait a week after classes started.

Then she was going to dump him.

Surf City

The big Admiral window air-conditioner was working overtime but it was still warm inside the station. Mickey hadn't realized Admiral even made air-conditioners until the mayor had gotten a deal on them when an appliance store in Sea Isle City went belly up over the winter. He'd bought seventeen of them, the place's entire remaining inventory and its single floor model. The PD had gotten the floor model which arrived complete with tiny red ribbons tied in Gordian knots to the louvered vents. The beast seemed to have only two "comfort settings" as it said next to the big control knob. The current one was what Dippolito named "Neil Diamond" because, he said, it was "just never going to get cool enough." Mickey referred to the only other interior climate alternative as "Morgue Mode" because it made everyone feel like they were stiffs on ice.

Mickey grabbed a folded copy of the local newspaper to fan herself. She licked a salty drop of perspiration from her lip and watched as several more fell to the desk blotter. The office was empty. She looked at Rodriguez's bare desktop and reflected on just how much of the load he had silently shouldered for her over the years. He'd be a good Chief, she knew. She also knew that Charlie had turned down an offer to head up Campus Security at a small but wealthy college in North Carolina. Eli or maybe Elon University, she thought it was called. It wasn't far from where he'd grown up and where he still had family so his passing on the opportunity had surprised her. After what they'd been through together it sounded like a good job with better money. She would have traded mobsters and psychopaths for rowdy college kids any day.

Mickey looked at the wall clock. She had agreed to meet Evan Driscoll for what she insisted needed to be a quick and strictly business dinner. Given the traffic jam she'd just witnessed on Long Beach Boulevard she doubted he'd make it on time. Ronnie had a week off but she knew that as a Forest Fire Service incident commander he could get called at any time. But the humidity was high and it had been more than a year since the last conflagration. He told her he thought they might skate by with just the No Campfires policy to get them through the holiday. It had taken a few years but Ronnie said he felt like they were starting to come around to his view that the Pine Barrens needed the fires, that they were part of a natural cycle to clear the forest floor of its burden of suffocating deadfall. They weren't ready for his "controlled burns" idea just yet but he felt was making slow progress on that front as well. They were letting the wildfires rage as long as they didn't threaten life or permanent structures. The Pinelands Jetport was still a drawing board project but local politicos and a shady cabal of out-of-state investors were insistently keeping it alive and dreaming of Atlantic City as the next Las Vegas.

Mickey still worried about Dippolito. It was more than the permanent rasp in his voice, which was like coarse grit sandpaper rubbing on her psyche with every word he spoke. Two years ago she had made the decision to leave him alone with Bunny knowing he was no match by himself for Dickie Robichaux, who had been a tunnel rat in Vietnam. What had later come to light was that Dickie had also had a hand in the "fragging" of Charlie's brother Darnell, an Army lieutenant. Darnell had survived, losing a leg, only to be intentionally and murderously overdosed with morphine in a stateside VA hospital months later. The original incident had been laden with racial overtones, Darnell having been one of the few black officers serving "in the shit" as Charlie put it. The truth, Charlie would find out, was that Darnell had stumbled on Robichaux's heroin smuggling operation which, Charlie said, reached an embarrassingly long way up the chain of command. The Army investigated but the CID man assigned to the case, a Warrant Officer named Cole Prejean, was told to stand down when he started to get too close for the Pentagon's comfort. Ronnie tried to help for a while, having served two tours himself, but once Nixon had intervened in the *My Son* massacre case he'd suddenly lost all interest.

"If they don't care about justice for five hundred defenseless women and children on the cover of LIFE Magazine," Ronnie told her, "Then they sure as shit are not going care about justice for one Negro lieutenant discovered dead in his VA bed." Mickey found this new hard-edged cynicism troubling, especially when every discussion she had with him now seemed to end with his insistence that "someone needs to do something."

Mickey sniffed the air and quickly realized that the acrid odor she noticed was hers. She decided that as soon as one of the deputies returned she'd run home and grab a fresh uniform blouse and, if there was time, a quick shower. She didn't need to impress Evan Driscoll but on the other hand neither did she need to gross him out. Mickey didn't think the months-old and possibly impotent dispenser of Secret Roll-On in her desk drawer was up to the job. She was also worried that Driscoll would pitch an FBI job again, which she would decline – again. What she did want to hear was what intel he had and how a tiny little beach town could possibly fit into it.

She fanned herself several more times with the paper then

set it down and unfolded it. *The SandPaper* had merged with *The Beachcomber* and Mickey usually flipped through its ad-jammed pages just to see what was going on in the other Island communities. Her term as head of the Chief's Council would be ending in December and she was hoping Davey Johnson would step up and take over the job. Between Arlene in Dispatch and Loretta on the social scene, Mickey's ear was always close to the ground and so scuttlebutt rarely escaped her. But every once in a while some item in the thick little paper would surprise her.

Then she remembered something.

Her big desk blotter calendar was still on June so she quickly peeled off the 17 x 22 inch ink-defiled sheet to expose July's thirty-one boxes. In the square marked 2nd she'd written:

N' paper reporter w/ me all day - - - - Candy???
? OK'd 6/17 – meet here @ 9

The word Candy threw her for a moment. She couldn't think of any reason she'd need or want candy. Maybe the reporter wanted to bring candy? Did she tell the reporter to bring candy for some reason? That didn't sound right. Had to be a name. She flipped open the paper and looked for the masthead. In small but easily readable print there was a bold heading that said "TSP Summer Staff – Welcome to Surf City!" Mickey scanned the short list of names until she found it.

Candace M. Catanzariti, Riverside, NJ (Grinnell College, IA)

Candace.

Candy.

Obviously. But what was "IA"? Indiana? Or maybe it was Iowa? Mickey wasn't sure. She still had trouble remembering ZIP codes and they been around for eight years, arriving at the same time the new two-letter State abbreviations had been introduced. She didn't use many of either outside of the local NJ, PA and DE ones.

But Mickey now recalled the conversation – she'd been busy that day but it had seemed like an OK idea. The girl was nice on the phone - pleasant and intelligent but, Mickey sensed, very direct. It did surprise her a little to now learn that this Candy was a South Jersey girl – she remembered thinking she had to be from somewhere else by her accent. Especially the way she said the word "water." Mickey knew from her one and only trip to a National Police Chief's Association conference in Chicago that the native Delaware Valley pronunciation always came out sounding like *wooder*. This became a source of some amusement to the local Midwesterners attending the meeting who had also politely informed her that there was no such thing as a "lozenger." The girl on the phone hadn't said *wooder* so either she wasn't originally from New Jersey or maybe this Grinnell College, wherever it was, had modified her way of speaking. Mickey's dad Patsy was fond of the saying "When in Rome" and she wondered if it also applied to Iowa or maybe Indiana.

She looked at the name again and found herself smiling. *Candace Catanzariti*. Jesus, she thought, wouldn't Mike Gannon, with his profound love of alliteration, be proud of that one? Someone had once told Mickey that the repeated consonants in first and last names were "a real Ginzo thing." She looked over at Deputy Dennis Dippolito's desk and almost laughed out loud. She could immediately think of a half-dozen more people she knew whose names fit the pattern. All of them were Italian.

Candy Catanzariti. "Doesn't it just roll off the tongue?" is what Gannon liked to say. Now Mickey was curious to see what kind of girl came attached to the name. For an instant another memory arrived – skinny little Bonne Nuit "Bunny" Tran wearing a Batman t-shirt singing and bouncing madly on the cot in one of the empty jail cells. She had spent a completely sleepless sleepover with Rodriguez's three "rugrat" daughters at which she'd been introduced first to the world of Barbie Dolls and then to the completely fictional rock group The Archies. The latter came courtesy of a scratchy 45 rpm record and a Kenner Close'n Play phonograph. "Sugar, sugar" and "Candy girl" were the only words in the song Bunny knew since the recording was in Spanish, but she had nonetheless belted them out with unbridled enthusiasm and at the top of her lungs.

Mickey reflected that she hadn't heard from Bunny or her mother Yvette in over a month which was unusual for them. She took a tooth-marked Flair pen and wrote on the calendar in the square marked 7 th. Call Bunny + Yvt with news.

The seventh was almost a week from now. That's good,

she thought.

It would give her plenty of time to break the news to Ronnie.

Hammonton, NJ

Cowboy Barstow looked around. Seeing no one, he inserted the silver key into the extra-heavy-duty Yale padlock. The shed door made a cracking sound as he opened it. Cowboy reached inside and felt until he found the old round switch. It required a half-turn clockwise and clicked loudly when it alternately completed or interrupted the current flowing through the loosely strung insulated electrical conduit. A trio of bare two-hundred-fifty watt overhead bulbs blazed on.

The shed's interior belied its real purpose. Various hand tools and small gardening implements either hung from rusting ten-penny nails or rested against the salvaged barnwood walls. The floor was three-quarter-inch A-D plywood and an oval-shaped braided rug covered a large area of it in the center of the rectangular building. Cowboy carefully rolled the rug back into a dusty tube. The underside had retained most of its color, autumnal shades of red, brown and ochre woven tightly together in concentric bands. The door he'd cut into the floor was roughly six feet by three feet and sported an even larger padlock, this one by Masterlock, secured by a thick metal hasp that slipped over a U-bolt that had been placed full-thickness though the horizontal door.

Cowboy jingled his key ring until he found the correct one. He'd been careful to have a new key made and had discarded the original, which had borne a stamp-pressed Masterlock logo, so the new key couldn't be readily matched up should he ever lose possession of the ring. The duplicate hadn't been perfect, having been cut by a disinterested part-time salesman at Repece's Hardware & Lumber, but on this day it slipped in with less difficulty than usual. Cowboy set the lock aside and flipped back the hasp. From the near wall he grabbed a short length of rusting rebar and slid it through the U-bolt. Grasping it on either end he lifted the door and rotated it back on its hinges until it leaned against a 4 x 8 framing stud.

The pit that now yawned below him was dark as sin. Cowboy flicked on his Eveready "Big Jim" flashlight lantern and set it at the edge of the aperture. He crab-scuttled until his legs dropped in. With the toe of first one boot and then the other he found the iron ladder he'd welded together himself. Shifting his weight from his arms to the wide step, he reached with one hand and grabbed the lantern. He pointed it down into the subterranean chamber which was larger in all dimensions than the shed above it. Critters and spiders so far had not been a problem. The floor was cement and the walls were red brick that he'd tuck-pointed himself and then sealed against the reach of leaching groundwater. Outside the brick walls he'd tiled six feet deeper than the floor on all sides. He couldn't do much about dust and flying insects, however, so he pulled the blue bandana he'd tied around his neck up and over his mouth and nose and then carefully descended the remaining steps.

Once both boots were on the rough but level floor he shone the heavy flashlight around methodically. It had an incandescent lamp the size and shape of a car headlight on one end and a bulbous red combination light/flasher on the other. They were connected to each other by a thick silver handle. The whole shebang screwed on to the terminals on top of a 6Volt battery with a thin metal mounting plate, the large dry-cell accounting for most of the three-pounds of deadweight. Cowboy set the lantern on a small work table and pressed the bubble plunger switch twice. This turned off the bright incandescent and turned on the red taillight. It took Cowboy's eyes a few seconds to adjust to the soft ruby glow but once they did his night vision made seeing the room's contents much easier.

Cowboy moved carefully to a far corner and pulled out a heavy wooden box. He carried it back, setting it down on the sturdy pine table. He'd carpentered the table himself out of leftover plywood and 4 x 8's and had braced the legs and top with angle-irons. The box's one-piece top was snug but he was able to lift it free without having to pry it. He moved the Big Jim closer and studied the contents. They were fearsome looking even in repose.

Cowboy was not certain how his prospective client planned on utilizing the weapons or exactly how many he was interested in. The box before held plenty. He moved to the opposite wall and removed a narrower but similar wooden box and returned with it to the table. This one had never been opened so he extracted a flathead screwdriver from his work belt. Its top was secured with only flimsy finishing nails and so the lid popped free with just a few squeaky twists of the blade. He brushed away some of the loose packing straw, withdrew the cylinder and checked it for rust or corrosion. Finding neither, he replaced the heavy object and tapped the lid back down with the handle of the screwdriver. He reset the lid on the other box as well. A mother bird with lots and lots of baby birds, he thought to himself. Cowboy looked at his watch. The prospective buyer had seemed to be in a hurry to make the purchase but yet wouldn't commit to a firm meeting time. Unlike most of his clientele, this one had not haggled even a single penny on the price. This surprised Cowboy but he made it a point never to ask about a customer's intentions, source of capital or political leanings. The buyer only said he needed to take possession before Sunday. Cowboy never brought a buyer down into the underground cache itself but decided he didn't want to have to climb into the pit again. He switched the red light off, pushed again on the plastic bubble and lit the big lamp, squinting and shielding his eyes from the instant brightness.

He lifted the canvas tarp from its hook on the wall and laid it out on the floor. He set the larger box on it and then the smaller crate on top of the larger one. Next he threaded the rope he had carried down with him through the four brass corner grommets and pulled on it to create a sling. He hitched the rope to his belt, grabbed Big Jim and started his clamber back up the ladder. Above him in the shed he had a block-and-tackle assembly that would span the width of the opening in the floor. He would slip his end of the rope through the double-pulley and then hoist the merchandise up, leaving it in the shed until the buyer arrived.

It was an unusual choice, Cowboy thought as his head cleared the floorboards. The thick rug had kept the plywood underneath in pristine condition and Cowboy could clearly read the familiar green Weyerhaeuser trademark stamp on the sheet that was now at eye-level. So unusual, Cowboy decided, that just maybe he would break his own rule and ask a few questions this time.

But just maybe.

7

Surf City

THE FRONT ENTRANCE TO to the eponymous Wally Mitchell's Restaurant faced Long Beach Boulevard, just off the corner of North 8th Street, one oblong block and eight overpriced houses from the ocean. Wally's, as everyone who hadn't been parachuted onto the Island called it, was an unprepossessing structure which made it seem all the more inviting. The strake-sided second floor had a flat tar-paper roof and permanent aluminum awnings. There was a phone booth near the corner and across the side street sat the three-story Surf City Hotel. The Hotel had a slightly nicer dining room and a bar with its own Wurlitzer organ, Mickey knew, but she wanted to make sure her agreed-to meeting with Evan Driscoll didn't last any longer than necessary. Wally's ambience did not encourage lingering and neither did its wait staff which in the summer was a mix of grizzled middle-age veterans who took the food orders and teenage girls who poured water and coffee, served fountain drinks, bussed the shaky tables and, most importantly, kept a steady stream of college boy lifeguards patronizing the premises. It locked its doors at night only to clean up and restock. The free-standing trapezoidal sign out front rose proudly from a large wooden flower box and told the passing public everything they needed to know.

Wally Mitchell's

BREAKFAST
LUNCH
DINNER

OPEN

A matching CLOSED sign had once been hung hook-and-eye over the bottom letters at night but it had blown away in the fall of 1967 when Hurricane Doria passed through with winds strong enough to sink a boat off Ocean City.

Mickey had wrangled a square, wobbly table near the plate-glass front window. It gave her a view of the Boulevard and the comings and goings of Wally's patrons. Noting the line of cars crawling the main drag in both directions, Mickey hoped Driscoll's arrival wouldn't be interminably delayed.

A cute young girl in cutoff jeans gave her ice water in a ruby red-plastic tumbler and black coffee in a chipped china cup. Mickey spooned an ice cube from the water glass into her steaming coffee. As she watched it dissolve she felt a hand on her shoulder and reflexively brought her hand to rest on her holster.

"Mind if I sit for a minute?"

Mickey craned her neck around and smiled. Doc "Juice" Guidice smiled back.

She took her hand away from the gun and pointed to the seat on her right. The older man wriggled himself in. Mickey patted his hand.

"How's my favorite Police Chief," he asked.

"Just watchin' the world go by," Mickey replied. "How are you feeling?"

Guidice gave her a grin. "As Mark Twain once said, reports of my demise have been greatly exaggerated."

"Did you get new air filters for the old jalopy or did you just drink a quart of water from Lourdes?"

"I'd never drink the water at Lourdes," Guidice said. "Comes straight out of the Cooper River, you know."

"I meant the shrine not the hospital," Mickey said, referring to Our Lady of Lourdes in Camden.

"Actually," Guidice continued, "I found myself a new doc up in Stratford. Nice fella. A little older but I like that. You'll get a kick out of this - he was a beach cop in Wildwood in his younger days. So we have a lot to talk about."

The cute waitress returned with a pitcher of water in one hand, a Bunn glass coffee pot in the other and a drinking glass pinned between her elbow and torso.

"Is this the party you were waiting for?" the young girl asked.

"I'm just an aging interloper," Guidice said before Mickey could answer. "I won't be staying." The girl turned and headed toward the bustling kitchen. She had a Peace sign patch stitched on each back pocket of her cutoffs which, Mickey noticed, were short enough to reveal just a hint of each cheek.

"I see you're not hooked up to your scuba tank anymore," Mickey said. "That has to be a good sign."

"I use a little oxygen at night but otherwise I'm fit as a fiddle. I'd be ready for love, too, but I'm afraid it would take a derrick to raise that I-beam again."

Mickey shook her head. "OK, Doc, I really didn't need to know that. But I'm glad you're feeling better, anyway. So, is your new sawbones a Dago or a Jew?"

Guidice laughed. "I much prefer to use the terms Neapolitan and Hebrew these days, but the answer is neither one. He's a full green-blooded Mick just like you. Take off the white coat and you'd swear he was a Leprechaun. Always after me Lucky Charms, I tell him. Damn good lung doctor, though."

"And what medical professional doesn't appreciate cereal box humor, right?" Mickey deadpanned.

"How's my old pal Patsy these days?" Guidice asked. "Don't think I've seen him around lately, although I don't have much call to go to Ship Bottom unless it's to cross the bridge."

Mickey sipped her coffee and winced. "Oooh, this is terrible," she said. "Anyway, Dad amazes me. They took that slug out from around his spine, you know." Guidice didn't take the bait so Mickey continued, "And since he found that little dog, or I should say since that little dog found him two years ago, he started walking her everywhere and now he's ten maybe fifteen pounds lighter."

"I should stop by, I suppose."

"He's gone until next week. South of the Border," Mickey explained.

"Patrick Aloysius Cleary? In Mexico? Ha! I'd pay a wooden nickel to see that."

Mickey laughed. "No, not quite that far south," she said. "South as in Carolina – right below the border with North Carolina. Right off I-95."

"That tourist trap?" Guidice said, "Jesus, kid, you'll probably have to wire him money to get back home. I think they charge for fresh air at that place. So who's watchin' that little doggy in the window?"

"Took her with him," Mickey replied. "Said since she's a Mexican Chihuahua she'd probably feel right at home."

"I'm sure he thinks it barks in Spanish," Guidice quipped. "Did he take the Bel Air? Geez, how old is that clunker now?"

"It's a '57 but I did some major work on it over the winter," Mickey said switching to the water glass and trying to get the taste of the coffee out of her mouth. "He'll never sell it. He loves that car."

"Ah, who'd want a '57 Chevy anyway?" Guidice said with a dismissive shake of his head.

"Probably nobody," Mickey replied. "You still have the Grand Prix?"

"Yeah. But I like to pronounce it Grand Pricks. Seems more fitting, somehow. You're waiting for your soldier boy, I s'pose?" Guidice asked. "Hot date?"

"I am waiting," Mickey answered, "But for none other than Deputy Director Evan Driscoll of the FBI."

Guidice's eyes widened. "A DD now. Huh. Must'a finally caught Al Capone. Whatever happened to his boss? Can't think of his name off the top of my head. Another bloody bog hopper I think."

"J.J. Durkin," Mickey said. "I'm going to ask Evan that myself. He's not with the Bureau anymore, that's all I know."

"Hoover has to be pushing eighty," Guidice said. "You think he would'a quit by now."

"Durkin told me years ago that the only way Hoover ever leaves the FBI is when they carry him out of his office covered by a white sheet. Maybe that's why he moved on. No room at the top."

Guidice shifted in his chair. "Missed you at the big funeral," he said.

"I sent private condolences to the Ragone family," Mickey replied. "I thought my being there might be a distraction, you know?"

"It was a nice service," Guidice said. "The Archbishop gave the homily. Surprised it wasn't the Pope. You'd never've known that Dante Donatello Ragone personally whacked or at his behest had somebody else whack at least a hundred people in his illustrious career. He was the walkin' font of all holiness to hear it told. I'll lay even money that Danny Rags gets canonized before Blessed John Neumann does."

Mickey laughed at that one and took another drink of water. Guidice pressed on.

"There were a lot of wiseguys there that I'd never laid eyes on, though. This next generation of hoods – they're really different and I don't mean that in a good way. Little Rags was, as you well know, Danny's only kid." Guidice paused. This time it was Mickey who did not take the bait and so he continued. "So with the *paterfamilias* finally gone I think they're gonna haf'ta shoot it out to see who takes over."

"What about the Rocca's?" Mickey asked, referring to the rival Philadelphia Mafia family.

"Carmine had a bad stroke, you know, and his brother Bobby, well he doesn't want anything to do with anything 'cept ink and paper, so their piece of the big tomato pie is up for grabs now, too."

The young waitress returned with a sheepish look. "Excuse me, Chief Cleary," she said to Mickey. "Did your coffee taste, um, kind of, uh, funny?" She reached to remove the cup and saucer.

"Yeah. It was awful. Why?"

"Um, I think it might have had some, um, some urn cleaner in it. I'm really sorry."

Mickey looked at the cup. "I only took a sip," Mickey said. "Let me ask the medical expert here. Am I a goner, doc? Give it to me straight – I can take it."

Guidice adjusted his bifocals. "Unfortunately, in my experience even one drop is usually quite slowly but quite painfully fatal," he said gravely. The waitress went white and Mickey thought the girl might swoon. "Hey, hey, I'm just kidding," Guidice said. "Young lady, does the stuff you dump in the coffee urns come from a package or do you make it yourself?"

"Uh, I think Wally, I mean Mr. Mitchell, I think he mixes it up from a clear bottle with a white cap. Is she gonna be OK?" She turned to Mickey. "I mean are *you* gonna be OK? You're gonna be OK, right?"

"It's probably just vinegar and water," Guidice said. "I think she'll be just fine."

"Mr. Mitchell said to tell you, he says your tab is on us today.

I am so, so sorry."

"Sweetheart," Guidice said, "With all the crap the good Chief here has to swallow in her line of work it might actually turn out to be good for her."

"You probably don't want more coffee," the girl said.

Mickey shook her head. "Maybe a Fresca if you have it? With plenty of ice."

"Um, no Fresca. Is Tab OK?"

"Sure, a Tab would be fine," Mickey said.

"It'll be free," the girl told her. "Refills, too. As many as you want. I am just so sorry." She turned and beelined for the fountain. Guidice leaned in.

"Did it *taste* like Seven Seas Italian Dressing?" he asked.

Mickey nodded in the affirmative.

"Good, because that commercial stuff really will kill ya." He winked. "And now your dinner's free. Beats dropping a live cockroach in the fried clams, doesn't it?"

The girl quickly returned with the Tab and Mickey took a long drink. "So spill your guts," she said and suppressed a tiny burp. "Who's gonna be the new Don Corleone?"

Guidice rubbed his chin. "Mother of God," he said. "That book. Worst thing that ever happened to organized crime if you ask me. These young Turks think it's some kind of friggin' manual. And worse, they all think they're Sonny which, as you can imagine, creates a bit of an organizational challenge."

"Yeah, but who's the smart money on?" Mickey inquired.

Guidice dropped his voice. "You're not gonna believe this. Turns out old Danny Rags had a half-sister down in Florida. Nobody knew about her all these years but him. Even Graziella, Danny's wife, well, his widow now I guess, even she didn't know. This half-sister she, of course, has a kid – boy named Domenico. Only this Domenico, he likes to call himself Little Nico. You know, like Little Caesar, I'm guessing."

"Edward G. Robinson, right? Black and white movie from about from a million years ago?"

"Half a million years ago, kid. I ain't that old. Anyway, this cocky punk, this Little Nico, he figures he's blood so he should be next in line for the throne, no questions asked. 'Course, obviously not everybody sees it the same way. But since he's been in Florida all these years he doesn't have any local beefs and the cops and the

Feds up here never seen him or heard of him. The new *consigliore* is pretty hot for him to take over since nobody has paper on him. But he's getting' pushback from Bobby Nads, an old *capo* who wants to see his nephew Bruno move up."

"Bobby Nads?" Mickey asked. "That's a name I don't think I know."

"Real name's Robert D'Agoni. Mid-level muscle. His own kid is a dentist up on the Main Line. Lower Merion or maybe it's Merion, I think. They're all the same. Pretty ritzy molars up that way. And totally legit if you believe that."

"I have to ask. Bobby I get. But why Nads?"

Guidice laughed. "It's easy, kid. Robert D'Agoni becomes Bob D'Agoni. Bob D'Agoni becomes Bobby D'Agoni. Bobby D'Agoni becomes, what else, Bobby D'Agonads. And Bobby D'Agonads-"

"Becomes just plain Bobby Nads. I got it." Mickey drank more of the Tab. "But now back to this lawyer. I met him, didn't I? Santucci's his name, I think? He was the guy with you in the Mayor's Office two years back."

Guidice looked around. "Yeah. Tommy Santucci. But I don't remember if he was there with me and Tony Mart that night or not. Anyway, sharp kid – he's got all the graft and all the payoffs hidden in so many fake companies and Swiss bank accounts you'd think the Philly Mob was Atlantic Richfield or maybe Campbell's Soup."

"He just bought a house here in Surf City," Mickey replied. "Santucci did. Sherry, the nice real estate lady, she told me he paid cash. It's not that far from our place. Now how come he doesn't have a nickname?"

"Because lawyers usually don't shoot anybody. No bones, no name. That's the rule. It's also why you don't see Artie Petroni around no more."

"Well that's a relief," Mickey said. "On both counts."

"Hey, between havin' a police chief, an Army sharpshooter and now a wiseguy shyster all watering their lawns or maybe it's shampooing their shells together on Saturday mornings, yours is gonna be the safest neighborhood on the Island. I bet if you ask her, that realtor lady will tell you that the money he forked over was all twenties and fifties. Non-sequential bills, too."

"You mean you think it could be counterfeit?" Mickey asked. Now she wondered if this was what Evan Driscoll wanted to talk to her about.

Guidice shook his head. "No, I'm sure it was real green cabbage, freshly cleaned and pressed. Just don't ask your new neighbor where it came from is what I'm saying. It could make for an awkward conversation."

"Would the FBI be looking at that? I mean if there was even a chance it *was* hot off the presses?" Mickey asked.

Guidice reached over and took a long drink from Mickey's water glass. "No. The Secret Service is who goes after paperhangers. The FBI, they would be more interested in house painters." Mickey gave him a quizzical look.

"And don't be surprised," he said. "If more of your neighbors start selling their places at a tidy profit to families whose names end with a vowel."

"And why would that be?"

Guidice made a fist, blew twice into the curl formed by his thumb and forefinger then mimed shaking and throwing a pair of dice.

"Snake Eyes," he said. "Chiefy, the casinos will be down here before you know it. That's why this power struggle across the river is so important. It's not going to be about street book or addicts in North Philly anymore. Now it'll be all about high rollers, grand-a-night call girls and lucrative union contracts for laundry and maintenance. The rats will come because they want to be near not just the cheese this time but the cheese factory itself. They'll rape and they'll rob Atlantic City and eventually leave it bleeding in the ditch but they would never even think of living there. Mark my words, kid. This time next year we'll have a dozen new Neapolitan taxpayers on the rolls and that's just in our little drinking town. *Capisce?*"

Two Ocean City lifeguards, instantly identifiable by their bright red O.C.B.P. sweatshirts, squeezed into the table next to them. They both acknowledged Mickey with respectful nods.

"Aren't you boys a little far from your home sandbox?" Mickey asked them.

They were blonde and bronzed and both had residual specks of zinc oxide on their noses. One was slightly taller and had a patchy mustache. "Scenery's better up here," he said with a big smile. The cute waitress materialized at their table as if she'd just been conjured out of thin air.

"Can I get you two handsome gentlemen anything to drink?"

she cooed.

"Couple of Vanilla Cokes to start," the boy without the mustache said. The girl turned and, very slowly this time Mickey saw, sauntered away from them. Tilted heads and approving glances followed her.

"So what was that about house painters?" Mickey asked returning to Guidice. He glanced around again. "I'll tell you another time. I think your date just arrived. You can spot a Fed a mile away. They must all get issued the same mail-order catalog."

Through Wally's squeegee-streaked window Mickey spied Evan Driscoll standing outside the Surf City Hotel looking around. He wore a blue blazer with a pink button-down pinstripe shirt which was open at the collar. Cuffed khakis and, to Mickey's surprise, brown Sperry Top-Siders and not the usual Florsheim wingtips completed the uniform.

"I should get going," Guidice said. "I'm supposed to be meetin' Sam the Holy Ghost across the street for a Scotch or three. Sometimes Larry Ferrari drops in to play their big Wurlitzer organ. Give Patsy my best, kid. You can even pet his yappy little pooch for me."

"Sam the Holy Ghost has a nickname," Mickey commented.

"What I said. Lawyers don't shoot anybody. Santaspirito just happens to mean Holy Ghost in Italian. But probably good for Sam if somebody even thinks he probably didn't but he maybe possibly might have shot somebody. Maybe they decide to settle instead of goin' to court."

"OK. Now I feel better," Mickey said.

Guidice put his hand on Mickey's forearm and spoke to her quietly. "You don't smoke, I know, so that's good. Don't start. Lay off booze completely. And tell the druggist at Galdo's you want a big bottle of vitamins. I don't mean Flintstones or the One-A-Day's. You want ones that have extra iron. Read the label – you gotta make sure it doesn't say DES anywhere on it. Call me if you're not sure. That stuff is a lot worse than coffee pot cleaner for both of you. And remember to drink lots of water or the extra iron will bind you up and you won't cra-, you won't defecate for a month. Got it?"

Guidice got up.

"How did-"

He patted her on the head. "Kid, I was a G.P for forty years.

I might be retired but I'm not stupid." He slid past the returning young waitress and was gone.

Mickey's thoughts were still swimming when Evan Driscoll sat down. He had a thin leather valise from which he immediately withdrew a manila folder.

"Smart choice of location," he said, looking around. "At Quantico they teach that the first rule of espionage is to hide in plain sight whenever possible. So what's good here?"

"They're known for their S.O.S.," she said. Driscoll peeked at the laminated menu card on the table.

"Is that a seafood dish?" he asked. "Stop On Sight? Or maybe a nod to the Sons of Satan?

Mickey started to laugh. "Noooo, it's creamed chipped beef on toast. Get it?"

Driscoll looked perplexed.

"The toast is the shingle," Mickey clarified. "Which makes the stuff they put on top of it the-"

"I got it," Driscoll said. "And the – stuff - is what they're famous for?"

"I'm not sure famous is exactly the right word. But it's what a lot of people order so it must be pretty good. Otherwise I'd probably go with the chowder and a grilled cheese."

"No, I'll try it," he said and set the valise next to his chair. He kept the folder in his hand. The waitress turned away from the lifeguards and spoke to him. "Something to drink?" she asked.

"Coffee," Driscoll replied. "Black, no sugar. Thank you, honey." The girl looked at Mickey.

"Make it two coffees," Mickey said. The girl's shoulders sagged in relief.

When she left Driscoll scooted his chair as close to hers as it would go. She didn't recognize his after-shave but she liked it.

He surveyed the surrounding tables.

"Chief Cleary," he said and then paused. "Would you be offended if I called you Mickey? We do have a bit of history."

History was putting it mildly, Mickey thought, since four years earlier Driscoll had been ready to arrest her for the murders not only the young Ragone boy but also of two FBI agents and a Mafia lawyer.

"No, that's fine," she replied.

"And please," he said, "Call me Evan. There's no reason we

can't be relaxed and informal while still remaining professional. And there's a high likelihood that we'll be conversing a number of times over the next several days."

"Hmm. OK. Can I assume what we will be conversing about is what's in that folder?" She nodded toward it.

"Yes, you can," he answered. "Let me start, though, by asking you one simple but important question."

Mickey waited.

"Are you familiar with the term 'domestic terrorism'?"

8

Surf City

SLY AND THE FAMILY Stone were on the radio singing "Family Affair." Ronnie was vaguely aware of it but he wasn't really paying attention.

The modest one-level beach house they had bought from the Ianuzzi's was starting to feel less like the previous owners' and more like he and Mickey's, Ronnie thought. They had finally cured the mysterious and persistent rank odor in the spare bedroom first by pulling out the carpet and finally by tearing up all of the floorboards and steaming off the wallpaper. Ronnie had half-expected to find body parts beneath the boards but ended up seeing only splotches of organic matter of indeterminate origin. They didn't appear to be animal or rodent droppings and after he'd mopped the sub-flooring with a concentrated bleach and water mixture the room had ceased smelling like, as Mickey put it, death and Windex warmed over.

Once the sale was completed the Ianuzzi's had decamped from Long Beach Island so quickly they might have conceivably left visible skid marks, a fact Ronnie found odd since they had enjoyed an active social life with their neighbors and friends. They sold their red Mustang convertible to Loretta LaMarro and bought a smaller home in Ocean City which they sold a year later. When last heard of they'd sent their son to an out of state college and spent their summers quietly in Stone Harbor. Ronnie knew their son had been friends with the Ragone boy. He'd had some tangential connection to the boy's demise on the dark and dusty beach road, an initially routine vehicle-pedestrian accident that had gotten FUBAR and spawned a literal and political firestorm in its wake. Mickey always ducked the question but Ronnie suspected that the generous deal they'd gotten on the house was in unspoken exchange for expunging the Ianuzzi boy's name from any and all of the official inquiries and documents. He assumed the lowball sale price of the Mustang to Loretta was also part of the family's wish for clean break from not just the events of 1967 but also from the shadier participants in the Summer of Love's fatal dramas.

Ronnie had laid the new hardwood flooring himself. For the several weeks the job took he had slept more soundly and felt better than he had in some time. He'd even started taking long, solitary runs which seemed to lift his spirits in direct proportion to how much they exhausted him. But April's Presidential decision had pushed him back toward some kind of edge. And over that edge, he knew, was a deep and black hole with no bottom. He had been acquaintances with Lieutenant Claude Stellwag, then friends of a sort and now, apparently, drinking buddies.

But theirs, he knew, was a bond forged only by misery – the same misery shared by anyone who'd ever gone to war thinking they could go back to being the same when they returned as when they left. Stellwag was far from stupid or lazy or even criminal – Ronnie knew he could just as easily be working in Center City, wearing a suit and tie from Boyd's or John Wanamaker's and taking the Lindenwold High Speed Line home to a wife and kids in Westmont. Instead, Ronnie realized, he was still fighting the same war, taking the same hill over and over - and still looking after his men. But it was only the enemy, Ronnie had come to realize, not the battle that had changed. It wasn't Charlie or the NVA inside the wire anymore. Now it was the society that did not reserve a place, forget a pedestal, for its returning warriors. The Sons of Satan, he figured, were men without a country even in their own country. Stellwag, Ronnie believed, was refusing to turn his back on them. And nobody was giving out medals for that.

The phone rang.

Ronnie managed to extricate himself from the couch but by the time he got to the wall in the kitchen where it hung it had stopped. The note from Mickey said she was having a quick meeting with "our FBI friend" at Wally's and would stop home as soon as she could.

She was trying to help him, Ronnie knew. But she couldn't. This he also knew. He wondered about his planned action, his "ballgame" as grunts always referred to it, and what effects beyond the immediate shock and dismay it would have on her and them and everyone around them. Maybe it was better, he considered, that her department was shorthanded and that she'd hardly be home over the holiday. It would give her what the Army brass called "plausible deniability." And it wasn't like they had kids together or even a dog to look after or to keep them somehow connected.

Ronnie glanced over at the counter. In an oversized bowl a solitary goldfish swam happily between a sun-bleached replica of a medieval castle and a bubbling deep sea diver who was missing one arm. Mickey had named the fish Yossarian, after Joseph Heller's "*Catch-22*" antihero. She had read the book after Ronnie'd left it lying around. She had decided that the fish's dilemma was the same – it had no way out of its situation that arguably was or was not crazy. Ronnie walked over and tapped a few flakes from a round plastic container into the bowl.

"Down the hatch, Private Y," Ronnie said, replacing the red cap. He hoped he hadn't done this earlier in the day. Overfeeding, Mickey warned him, was the Mortal Sin of piscine ownership. When Ronnie had told Stellwag about the name they had both laughed. They both understood. Then Stellwag had shared his own philosophy – the one he called Catch-23.

"Catch-22 only applies in-theatre," Ronnie recalled the LT saying somewhere between beers. "Catch-23, now that kicks in when you get home." Ronnie remembered the explanation. "If you come back the same," Stellwag had said slowly, "meaning you come back and you are *not* totally fucked up by what you've seen, then you must have been totally fucked up before you left."

Ronnie thought about all the pictures the mission photographers had taken in *Son My*, clicking away while an almost unthinkable massacre unfolded through their viewfinders. With maybe one exception, Ronnie figured, they weren't fucked up when they arrived. But he knew it didn't take long for them to get to the point they got to. He thought about "Haystacks" Calhoun, the Sons of Satan's' gigantic sergeant-at-arms and his dozens of belly scars – the ones from his multiple shrapnel wounds and the multiple surgeries endured to repair them. The people who were at that moment pouring on to the Island, Ronnie knew, they didn't want to see them, they didn't want hear about them – they didn't want to even *know* they happened. They were coming to escape. And they were more than happy to consign Calhoun and everyone like him to a lonely patch in the pines or its equivalent. They wanted beer and bunting. They wanted food and fireworks. They wanted to pretend everything that really was going on in the world really wasn't.

Ronnie crossed to the refrigerator and grabbed another of the clear bottles of Miller High Life. It would be his last one, he decided. Or maybe his next-to-last one. He still had work to do before Saturday's ballgame.

Historic Town of Smithville
Galloway Township, NJ

Candy had reconsidered. She now decided she'd wait a week after they got back to Grinnell and then *think* about whether or not to dump him.

"How did they ever get it here?" Brad asked.

He was looking out at the small body of water where the *Thomas M. Freeman* rode calmly at anchor. The sleek white oyster boat, colloquially known as a bugeye, had a low-slung profile and swept-back lines. Some even called them "racing" lines and their visual conflation with the craft's two bare, aft-canted masts made it look like it was still crisply making headway out on the broad Chesapeake Bay even as it bobbed safely on "Lake" Meone, a lovely if somewhat overstated pond.

Candy looked at the little plaque. "They sailed it from Chesapeake Bay up the Inland Waterway, then out to the Atlantic, back across Delaware Bay and then up the Mullica River. Next it was, let's see here, Bass River Marina, Nacote Creek, Port Republic Lake then…it just says overland to Lake Meone which is where we are." Brad, she noticed, hadn't taken his eyes off the boat. "Never seen a lake before?" she teased. "Isn't Minnesota supposed to have like a thousand of them?"

Brad turned around. "Ten thousand," he said. "As in 'Land of 10,000 Lakes'. That's like the state motto or saying, or maybe it's just the official state nickname. Like you guys call this 'The Garden State'."

"Really? And for the last two years I thought Minnesota was the 'Land of Sky Blue Water'," Candy replied in earnest.

"That's probably what it should be but that, that is actually the advertising slogan for Hamm's Beer. And technically it's, 'From the Land of Sky Blue Waters.' Waters, plural, with an 's'."

"So why not just call it The Lake State? Or The Sky Blue Water State - you know, like the Sunshine State, the Keystone State or, what's Iowa again, the Hawkeye State? You don't hear us calling New Jersey the Land of Ten Thousand Gardens. And another thing, do they go around every so often and count all ten thousand lakes just to make sure it shouldn't be The Land of 10,001 Lakes or 9,999 Lakes?"

"You're mocking me," Brad said. "Aren't you. You are. Admit it."

"You take everything so personally." Candy said this with a smile. "It must be a Midwestern thing. Thin-skinned my dad would have said. Drives me nuts at Grinnell to be honest. I really don't need or want to see a freaking smile in every freaking aisle when I go to buy tampons. It's creepy, if you ask me." She looked at her watch. "We still have almost an hour until they said we'd have a table."

"Which restaurant was it again?"

"The Lantern Light," Candy replied. "Which is fine. We're not dressed for the Smithville Inn or Quail Hill which works out well because we couldn't afford either of those anyway. The Posset Shop had snacks and sodas but it closed at five. What name did you give them?"

"Yours," Brad said. 'And it's pop, not soda."

"We're in Jersey, remember? So it is most definitely soda. Please don't embarrass me at dinner by asking what kind of pop they have. And you gave them my name? You gave them Candy?"

"No. I gave them Catanzariti. Since, like you said, we're in New Jersey. One thing I've learned is that you get treated better if you have an Italian last name." He pronounced it like *eye*-talian and Candy rolled her Italian eyes.

"I'm pretty sure that only holds true at *Ih*-talian restaurants or businesses," she said, stressing the short initial vowel sound. She hooked her arm through his and gazed around, marveling at all the rustic and historical buildings, some still being erected while others were getting repaired or spruced up. "The last time I was here," Candy said, "I was with my parents and my grandmother when I was real little. But I still remember. It was a big deal and we were all dressed up like we were going to church.

My grandmother, she had come over from Italy when she was like twelve. She married my grandfather when she was probably fourteen or fifteen. Nan's name, we called her Nan or Nanna, was Caterine – it means 'pure.' That's what my mother wanted to name me. My father said he wanted a more American sounding name and, by God, he always won, so Candace it was. Edgar Bergen, the famous TV ventriloquist, he had named his daughter Candice a few years before I was born and my dad liked the sound of it. But her name had an 'i' so that's why Dad decided he would spell mine with an 'a'."

They started walking. Candy didn't know why Brad had become noticeably and thankfully more companionable but she decided to just enjoy it rather than analyze it. She had lied about the Camaro's dashboard temperature gauge reading HOT because she knew from the map they weren't far from Smithville and she didn't really care if they got back to the Island before dark or not. Brad had to be up early but she wasn't due at the Surf City Police Station until nine.

"Minnesota names are kind of all the same," Brad mentioned as they strolled. "They're all just variations on a theme. Somebody's son – Lars or Sven or Ole or Knut or maybe the name of the frozen Scandinavian village your family came from just so they could live in another frozen village. And, usually, nobody's first name really means anything. That's why they're so plain. I was one of four Brad's in my high school class. There were three Lutes, five Heidi's and, you'll love this, two Luverns –they were both guys. It's a really huge state but the demographics are pretty bland when you get right down to it. I would bet you could name every male baby Sven Larsen or Lars Svensson, or Swenson – it's the same - and no one would even notice it or think twice about it."

"What about girls?" Candy asked. She couldn't think of any two girls in her grammar school class who shared the same first name.

"Sarah Olson or Heidi Knutson. It would be the same. Nobody'd blink an eye."

It was a real, honest-to-God conversation for a change, Candy mused to herself. No politics, no self-righteous moral outrage, no "Power to the People, Right On" bullshit. Something had happened to him in California, she often thought. Something not so good, either, she suspected. Something more than a chance run-in with one random straight-arrow in a place where there was a good chance the entire population was not comprised of gentle people with flowers in their hair. A subtle sort of contamination, she considered, of that cloying, annoying Midwestern niceness that she so enjoyed poking fun at.

Maybe it would pass, she hoped. Maybe it would veer offshore, pushed by its own circular energy like one of those coastal hurricanes that male chauvinist meteorologists designated using only female names. As if to say women were the gender who were capricious, unpredictable and destructive. Candy seriously doubted she would live long enough to ever see a Hurricane Brad. Then a disturbing image popped into her mind - the eerie, beautiful but short-lived window of absolute calm that existed when the "eye" of one of those storms passed directly overhead.

Brad was still talking and Candy realized she'd missed at least the last few sentences if not more. "Did you just ask me something?" she said.

"Your project," he said. "Do you have a name for it yet?"

Candy tried to focus. "Um, yeah, I have a couple of working titles but nothing final. The title to me is everything. I never start a paper or a project until I have a title"

"I want to hear them," he replied. "Your titles are always so clever. Sometimes I think most people don't really appreciate them or understand that they're slyly but highly subversive. They are, right? Intentionally quite subversive, I mean."

They were now at the far end of Lake Meone. The sun was getting lower and the air was thankfully starting to cool down a bit. Brad pointed to the gently swaying bugeye.

"I get that more people are able to enjoy it this way," Brad said. Candy detected a hint of wistfulness. "But it was built to sail the ocean. Here, it's kind of like a fish in a bowl. Safe from storms and rocks but now and forever with nowhere to go."

Candy admitted she had not thought about it that way. "At least it's on the water," she replied. "Not like the poor *Lucy Evelyn*, encased in rocks and cement for all eternity."

"I suppose," Brad answered. "So, anyway, come on. Tell me your subversive working titles."

Candy thought hard. "OK, but don't say anything. I haven't decided on one yet and I don't want you to unconsciously bias me for or against any of them."

Brad drew his index finger across his lips as they continued their stroll. Candy continued.

"Number one. 'Under Your Thumb, question mark, You Don't Own Me.'" She paused to let it sink in. "Number two. N-O R-E-S-P-E-C-T, all caps with en dashes, colon, The Objectification of Women in Popular Music." Candy looked over. Brad barely nodded and she couldn't read his poker face so she kept going. "Number three. Different Drums, colon, Women and Power in Popular Music. And number four, Now It's OUR Party, O, U and R in caps, em dash , You Can Cry If You Want To." She watched Brad trying desperately to stifle a smile.

"What?" she asked. "What? Not subversive enough?"

"OK," he said. "Seriously. You need to write four papers. Or maybe four books. Or one paper and three books just so you can use all of them. But you have to use *all* of them."

Candy clapped. "Mister Brad Vreeland, come on down!" she said, mimicking The Price is Right's announcer Johnny Olson. "That, sir, that was exactly, no, wait, that was *precisely* the right answer. There may be hope for us yet." She had meant to say 'hope for you' but realized instantly that was not what had come out of her mouth.

Brad appeared relieved at having avoided what Candy knew surely must have felt like standing under the Sword of Damocles. "OK, she said, "So what are you going to call yours?"

He got a faraway look. "Truthfully, I didn't have the foggiest idea until we were driving here and listening to the radio. Turns out I'm pretty happy the tape deck was broken even if I did have to listen to Donny Osmond eight times. But seeing that boat is really what kind of did it. "

Candy shrugged. "Okay, so what is it, then? It's 'Imagine,' right? It has to be 'Imagine.' Just don't say 'Paint it Black' or 'Sympathy for the Devil.' And please don't let it be 'Peace Train,' OK?"

Bradley Larsen Vreeland III laughed out loud. "You're close," he said."I did think about 'Imagine' but I'm just not a big John and Yoko fan."

"Soooo? Come on. Pretend it's the Academy Awards. And the winner is...?"

"The winner is...'Me and You and a Dog Named Boo.'"

They had reached the far side of the sparkling pond. Candy stopped. "OK. Now who's mocking whom?" she asked.

"Just wanted to make sure you were paying attention," he

said. They resumed their slow meander. "I was pretty set on 'Time Has Come Today.'"

"Chambers Brothers," Candy said and tugged on his arm. "Have to say, a bold choice for a boy who is, to put it mildly, just a wee bit *white* for that genre, don't you think?"

"Yes. I considered that. I thought it might look like - what did the guy I had at Berkeley for Intro to Poli Sci call it? Cultural appropriation?"

Candy smiled at him. "So, right words but wrong vibe?"

"My mom always uses the expression 'right church wrong pew'," Brad

replied, "but I think this would be a case of possibly the right pew, but definitely the wrong church." Candy nodded in agreement.

"OK," she said. "Enough suspense. What is it?"

Brad stopped and looked at her. His expression, she thought, was not worrisome but neither was it in any way comforting. She waited.

"I'm going to call it 'Rider on a Storm'," he finally said. "Rider, singular, without an 's' and I changed the article from 'the' to 'a'."

"Yeah, I caught that," Candy said in a subdued tone.

In her mind the calm eye of the hurricane appeared overhead. And in that stillness her heart sank just a little.

Surf City

Evan Driscoll had been true to his word, Mickey thought. He'd been all business, except for remarking he had expected to see a wedding band on her finger by now. Mickey had said something about the Fifth Dimension's "Wedding Bell Blues" and they moved on without further mention of the subject.

She had left her new cruiser idling at the curb. Ronnie was passed out on the couch, empty Miller bottles standing next to it like bowling pins. He could sleep it off right there, she decided.

She made sure the appliances were turned off and then started writing him a note.

Let a sleeping dog lie — call PD
in AM when you are up

She tacked it to the side of the Frigidaire near the phone with a wooden magnet that had been painted to look like a watermelon slice. She moved toward the door but then stopped. Her fingers drummed on her holster. She turned back, took down the note and wrote some more.

Not sure what to do for you. SB —
Am sure 1 thing — R deep M high
Mick

Back up went the note and the slice. Mickey took a deep breath, tapped Yossarian's bowl and walked outside into the waiting embrace of the salty, sultry summer night.

FRIDAY
JULY 2nd, 1971

-9-

Surf City

BILLY TUNELL WAS ON his third can of Sugar Free Dr. Pepper. The first two sat neatly on a corner of his mayoral desk. Mickey wondered if the lack of sugar was compensated for with more caffeine given his current state of agitation.

"Why don't we just have the lifeguards yell 'Shark!' every half hour starting at High Noon today? Wouldn't that be spiffy?"

Mickey was sitting in her customary seat, a worn wood and vinyl-upholstered armchair on the opposite side of the polished teak desk. Except for the doll-house sized washer and dryer the bric-a-brac on top of it shared a seafaring theme. Mickey's favorite was a gimbaled ship's compass on the edge nearest to her. A large to-go coffee from Bill's Luncheonette steamed in her left hand, most of it already gone. She noticed that the nameplate on his desk, which at her last visit was the size of a Scrabble tile holder, had been upgraded to one at least twice as large. Beneath the Gothic block letters which identified William Patrick Tunell was a smaller subscript, engraved in cursive, which further proclaimed *Mayor for Life*. She waited while His Honor chugged the last few drops in his can. When he reached to open the small Kenmore refrigerator which held the rest of his cache she answered him.

"There hasn't been a shark attack or even a credible shark sighting since 1916," she said calmly."But that doesn't mean fins in the water are necessarily dolphins."

The mayor-for-life plopped back in his large leather swivel chair, popped open the fresh can and took a sip. "Do you know the details of the 1916 attacks?"

"You got me there, Your Honor," Mickey replied. "I thought I was doing pretty good to come up with 1916."

"Well I do," Tunell said. "So allow me to enlighten you because there are eerie similarities to our present day."

Mickey sipped her coffee and peeked at her watch. It was pushing eight-thirty and she knew the college girl reporter would be arriving at the station soon.

"The attacks took place over twelve days," Tunell continued, "beginning on the First of July. The weather then was exactly what it is now – a veritable tropical heat wave. The victim was a young man from Philadelphia who had his leg bitten off and then most inconsiderately bled to death on the Manager's desk at the old Engleside Hotel in Beach Haven."

"With all due respect, sharks are not in my jurisdiction or purview," Mickey said hoping to move the proceedings along.

"And neither are – what did you call them?"

"Domestic terrorists."

"Right, domestic terrorists, whatever that actually means."

Mickey shifted in her seat.

"In 1916," Tunell continued, "There was a resultant panic which was very costly to the Island in terms of both prestige and revenue.

"But that's because there was an attack. A fatal one."

"My point, exactly," Tunell said. "To my knowledge, there have been no threats, no fires, no exploded or unexploded bombs, no graffiti, no flag or bra-burnings, no protest marches and no Buddhist monastic self-immolations. And seldom is heard a discouraging word. Am I correct so far?"

Mickey nodded. "But," she responded, "I saw up close just how little it took to set off a beach brawl of not-quite-biblical proportions but on its way there. If we had shown up ten minutes later than we did a hundred people would have been duking it out. And all over a teenager's questionable taste in beach blankets."

"Your point is well taken, my dear," Tunell answered. He

leaned back in his chair which squeaked in complaint. "But hear me out. If you were telling me that you knew that the Chicago Seven or Jane Fonda were coming here to spend a long weekend I'd agree. But they're not." He sipped at the Dr. Pepper. "Remember, we're just a little drinking town with a big fishing problem. We don't have any, any – what was that term you said your FBI friend used – any targets of opportunity. No boardwalk, no Diving Horse or Diving Bell, no Steel Pier. We have mom and pop businesses, paved roads, sand and ocean. And that's true for basically every town on this Island. Even if a band of commie pirates does succeed in hijacking the *Lucy Evelyn* I don't think they'll get very far. The old girl is in more imminent danger from all the wax candles in her cargo hold than she is from any radical miscreants. And the market for cowrie shells is, I believe, at an all-time low. The only ruinous thing that can happen this weekend is that Little Willie Wanamaker's liquor store runs dangerously low on or, God forbid, runs out of fermented hops and distilled spirits."

Mickey checked her watch again. The girl would just have to wait for her. Mayor Billy was on one of his rolls.

"I mean," he continued after a quick breath, "I suppose someone could poison our supply of saltwater taffy or threaten to hold hostage the entire retail supply of suntan oil or Frisbees but short of that, my dear, short of that-"

"I understand, "Mickey said. "But the FBI came to see me, not you. I saw what they have. And there's a message on my phone to call Major Joo at the State Police. I'm sure it's not to wish me a Happy Fourth. Look, Mayor Billy, there's a lot of anger and division in the whole country right now. Even Ronnie's not speaking to his father again over this massacre thing. And he idolizes his father."

"As he should," Tunell added. "He was a hero at Guadalcanal."

"Right. But people are walking around just feeling generally, excuse the term, pissed off. It's hot, it's humid and in two hours it'll be blanket to blanket and boobs to bellies out there. We get a lot of families here but I'm betting the percentage of *happy* families is at an all time low. Ronnie said when they were in the jungle or out on the river on patrol they'd just get a sense that things were going to go south. They called it 'feeling the vibe.' Mayor Billy, I am 'feeling the vibe.' I just want a little leeway to stamp out the small fires before they get out of control."

Tunell drained the can and set it with the others. "I do

understand your concern. I do. But let me reiterate a conversation we had when you arrived here in 1967 – another year fraught with rampant social unrest as I recall. People come to this town, to this Island to escape the turmoil. They don't want to bring it with them. They don't want to hear about it, read about it or be reminded of it. They want to be transported back to a simpler time – peanuts and Cracker Jack, if you will. For only one quarter of the calendar year, three short months, that's what we are here to provide. I only ask that you and your deputies do your best to safeguard those people, to serve and protect them while they indulge that, and there's no other word for it, that fantasy."

"You're right about that. It is just a fantasy," Mickey said. She stood and reached for her hat, grabbing it by the wide brim. "Oh, and I spent a little of the taxpayers' money, just so you know. I had Dippolito buy a whole case of cheap walkie-talkies and I distributed them to the girls who are checking beach tags. A visionary idea, by the way – the tags, not the radios." Tunell rolled his eyes at the sarcasm. "Anyway, it's partly for their own protection and partly because they're the closest thing we have to advance scouts or spotters. I told them to call if anything, and I emphasized that I did mean *anything* just doesn't look right to them."

"Good idea," Tunell replied. "I'll approve the purchase post-haste. Speaking of unhappy families as we were, did you by chance arrest someone on the beach yesterday? Because *his* family is most unhappy. I sent Sam the Holy Ghost over to calm them down. A visit from the borough's kindly but ruthless solicitor will usually do the trick of avoiding messy litigation."

"Technically, I didn't arrest or even charge him. I gave him a complimentary ride in the front seat of an air-conditioned police cruiser from the beach at fourteenth all the way to the bay at Division and Barnegat Avenues."

"Which just happens to be the furthest geographical point within borough limits from where you picked him up," Tunell noted.

"Hmm," Mickey said, smiling. "I guess I hadn't realized that."

Tunell tilted his head and looked at her over his bifocals.

"Anyway," Mickey went on, "I said the walk back would give him, as our spiritual advisor Innocentia always says, a prolonged opportunity to contemplate his actions and consider appropriate penitence. Make sure Sam Santaspirito knows that little detail.

The guy should be thankful I didn't charge him." Mickey laughed. "And tell the Holy Ghost we really need to pass a law tomorrow against Speedos on any male over twenty-five. Ever see something you just wish you hadn't?"

Tunell smiled. "It's why I got rid of all my full-length mirrors, dear child. Did you happen to assign the poor man any Hail Mary's or Our Father's?"

"Penance is mine, sayeth the priests," Mickey replied. "Look, I've been here almost five summers now. And I do remember that conversation, mostly because you were sitting in your old Lincoln with that horrible Kelly Green paint job."

"Careful," Tunell interrupted, "Earl Scheib may be listening. Oh and did you hear? Larry Ferrari was in town last night. He played the Notre Dame Fight Song at the Surf City Hotel in my honor even though it was, sadly, also in my absence."

"Anyway," Mickey persisted, "I'm not exactly learning the ropes anymore. We both know this is a just a little barrier island. Probably be underwater in a hundred years, who knows? I think of it as a barrier to the whims of, as Doc Guidice likes to say, the goddamn Atlantic Ocean out there. It exists to protect the mainland. It's not a magical kingdom. It's not America's Riviera, no offense." Tunell indicated he took none at the mention of his failed advertising campaign slogan from two summers before. "And I see enough day in and day out to stand here and tell you, it is not a barrier to problems. This Island does not protect us from what's sitting and stewing inside every person in every car that's rolling over the causeway bridge right now. It's the same set of problems and disagreements, they're just packed closer and tighter and now the heat is turned up to High. We might as well be a Presto pressure cooker. At least let me try to keep the lid on it. That's my job."

"Indeed it is," Tunell said in a conciliatory tone. "And I can think of no one more suited to that task. But, I still think your concerns have been, perhaps, unhelpfully exaggerated by outside law enforcement agencies wanting something showy to do. If I were you I would worry more about sharks than I would about terrorists."

"Well that would be a lot easier," Mickey said with a small grimace. She started moving toward the office door. "For one thing, I know what a shark looks like."

Paramount Air Service
Rio Grande
Cape May County, NJ

It wasn't even eleven o'clock in the morning and Brad Vreeland was already shot. He walked into the Paramount Air Service shed where the bins of letters and the boxes of fasteners were kept. He headed straight for the Igloo ten-gallon galvanized metal water tank. It looked like a trash can with a plastic spout, Brad thought. He remembered the ones they made themselves on the farm being a lot bigger and sturdier. Brad knew he smelled like a truly noxious mix of Avgas and body odor but hadn't thought to bring another shirt with him. Mr. Tomalino did not allow them to work bare-chested.

"Tired already, there, Old MacDonald?"

The question came from Thomas "Gumby" Gambacorta, one of the aerial advertising company's airplane mechanics who were tasked with keeping the twelve Piper Cubs as well as the two old biplanes safely and almost continuously aloft.

"This is insane," Brad replied searching for a cup or any reasonable facsimile of a drinking vessel. "Man, I walked beans and de-tasseled corn every summer all the way through high school. That was hard, dirty work. This is, like I said, nuts." Brad was on a ten minute break and realized almost a fifth of it was over already. He spied a large plastic funnel and picked it up. He sniffed it, shrugged then wiped it out with the crusty sweat rag from his back pocket.

Gumby watched in amusement. "Long as it didn't get used for 80/87 it probably won't kill you." 80/87, Brad knew all too well was the type of aviation fuel the most of the fleet's reciprocal Lycoming piston engines burned by the thousands of gallons...

"Death would be a relief right now," Brad replied. He put his thumb beneath the funnel's narrow outlet, held it under the spout and depressed the button. Nothing came out. "You have got to be shitting me," he half-cried.

"Hang on there, Farm Boy," Gumby said. He tilted the gray cylinder forward. Clear water poured out in a thin stream and pooled in the funnel. "There. Look at that. Just like an old cow pissin' on a flat rock."

A propeller droned loud, low and close. They were supposed to use rubber ear plugs but Brad had already lost the pair he'd been given when he clocked in at eight o'clock.

"Who you callin' a farmer, bog boy?" Brad shot back. The Gambacorta family, Brad had learned, were big-time cranberry growers. He could hear the pilot throttling down, almost gliding he knew. Then came the clink of the grapple. An instant later he heard the rpm's increase to a whine as the plane – it sounded like a Piper Super Cub – started its climb with a new banner trailing behind.

"Drink up," Gumby instructed. "It's gonna be a banner day in the banner business. Mr. T says in addition to overtime all you letter monkeys will get a bonus based on how many we can get up there."

Brad gulped down the water, wiped his face with the rag and turned toward the hangar's open doors. "Better check that Super Cub when it gets back," he said to Gambacorta. "It's missing – worse now than it was this morning." He sat the funnel on top of the cooler.

Gumby gave him an odd look. "How is it you know so much about light planes?"

"I don't know much, really," Brad replied. "Our spread back home was big so we would do our own crop dusting and later some aerial topdressing. I've just been around single engine props like these since I was a kid."

"What'd your family's operation dust with?" Gumby asked.

"We had one of the first Ag-Cats," Brad replied. "Yellow. That thing was amazing. Like it just knew what to do."

"Biplane," Gumby said, "Wings were offset. Grumman, right?"

"Grumman said they made it and they stamped their name on it but their factory was overloaded making planes for the military so they gave the actual manufacturing job to a company in upstate New York, Schweizer Aircraft Corporation, SAC. My dad used to tell me it stood for Strategic Air Command. For a long time I believed him."

"Hey Minnie Mouse!" a voice shouted from outside the hangar. "Break's over. Let's go."

"Farm Boy's helpin' me with something," Gumby called out – "I need him for at least another ten." He nodded at Brad. "Shee-it, son, just how many nicknames do you have around here?"

Brad grabbed the funnel off the water cooler. "Let's see. Farm Boy, farmer, Old MacDonald, Paleface, Minnie Mouse – I guess 'cause I'm from Minnesota – Mr. Green Jeans or just Green Jeans, Mr. Douglas, Mr. Haney, Eb, Arnold Ziffell, Alf, Ralph oh, and of course shithead and dumbass."

"I gave you those last two," Gumby said proudly and tilted the cooler on its bottom edge.

Brad filled the funnel again and drank its contents down. He offered it to Gumby who declined.

"The fellas do enjoy their 'Green Acres,'" Gumby said. "Shame they canceled it."

"Yeah," Brad replied, "I'm fuckin' heartbroken about it."

"You ever get to fly that old Ag-Cat?"

Brad hesitated. He looked down at the shed's dirt floor. "Nah. I don't know how to fly. My Uncle Sven, he was spraying DDT one spring and got tangled with some power lines. He was dead before they could get the canopy off. Mom wouldn't let me even sit in a duster after that."

"Vreeland!" Another shout. "Come on, asshole."

Brad looked at Gumby. "Oh, yeah. Asshole – guess I forgot that one," he said and walked out into the unforgiving heat.

Once on the narrow tarmac he pulled on his heavy canvas gloves and waited for the little plane that was on approach. Inside the cockpit, he knew, the pilot was getting ready to pull up on a large lever which would let the banner and its two-hundred and fifty feet of tow rope drop to the ground. Brad's job was to retrieve the banner and tow bar along with the rope and haul them to the hangar where the letters would be disassembled and the tow cable rolled up and readied for another flight. The plane would then circle and return to pick up a waiting banner with a new rope and grapnel let out by the pilot and attached through the tail wheel. The pilots usually took four or five of the tow cables along with them. The plane's wheels would never touch the ground until it was either low on fuel or had used all its tow ropes.

Brad watched the banner drop and hustled out toward it, laughing to himself. The story and the name Uncle Sven had just popped into his head. Gumby had bought every single word of it.

Had he ever flown a plane?

The correct answer in Minnesota would have been, "Yah sure you betcha," he knew. But no one needed to know that, he had decided. They would find out soon enough. And, as he was often reminded, he wasn't in Minnesota anymore.

-10-

Surf City

MICKEY CHECKED THE STATION'S baking asphalt lot for signs of a "foreign car" with Indiana or Iowa plates or even a strange bicycle. She did not see either. Traffic was already getting thick and so the girl might have had to park some distance away, she reasoned. Mickey rolled the new cruiser into the space marked "CHIEF" and headed for the back door of the SCPD's now four-year-old station house. She punched the buttons for the code on the Unican 1800 lock. 1, 9, 6, 7 for the year the old one had been leveled. She turned the bolt and pulled it open. The big Admiral AC was on Morgue Mode and Mickey shivered a little when the arctic air came in contact with sweating skin. She scanned the room and caught site of her - Candy Catanzariti.

"I got hung up at the Mayor's Office," Mickey said over the din of the behemoth shimmying in the window. It cut out half way through the phrase making it sound like she had shouted it.

Dip and Charlie looked up. The girl, who was wearing Dippolito's patrol jacket to fend of the artificial chill turned around.

"I got hung up at the Mayor's Office," Mickey repeated in a softer tone. She moved to toss her hat on the peg and then decided just to hang it there this time.

"Miss Catanzariti," Mickey said extending her hand. The girl had been busy making a fresh pot of coffee at the one gallon Bunn urn.

"Chief Cleary," the girl answered reaching hers out to shake.

She surprised Mickey by immediately adding, "I usually prefer Ms. Catanzariti if we're going to be formal but I was hoping you'd be OK just calling me Candy."

Mickey was taken aback slightly but recalled her initial impression of the girl on the phone – pleasant but direct. She had a dazzling smile with very light olive skin and dark eyes. She wore her black hair in a short but highly becoming style that Mickey would call pixie-cut. The term made her think for just an instant about her father's little dog with the same name. She hadn't heard from him and hoped that meant he was enjoying, as the brochure she'd seen at his house said, "*Siesta All Day, Fiesta All Night.*" Mickey realized she still held the girl's hand and quickly released it.

"In here or in the cruiser I'll just call you Candy," Mickey said. "If we're out in public or interacting with the citizens I'll refer to you as Miss, I'm sorry, Ms. Catanzariti. Probably work best if you call me Chief Cleary or just Chief. Agreed?"

"You betcha, Chief," Candy replied. "And thanks for doing this. It's pretty exciting. The last story I got assigned was about a woman in Surf City whose dog runs away like clockwork every summer but always comes back." Mickey shot Dippolito a look and noticed his gaze was fixed solidly on the girl.

"Hopefully we'll have a good day today," Mickey said. "Gunfights, hostage situations, civil unrest, bomb threats, the occasional bank robbery – Surf City is a real hotbed of criminal activity on most weekends. Isn't it, deputies?"

They both nodded.

"Just last week we had a saltwater taffy shoplifting spree," Charlie intoned. "Thieves took everything but the Wintergreen and Cinnamon. Nobody likes those. Not even taffy thieves."

The girl appeared confused and unsure how to react. Mickey took her by the arm. "What Charlie means, in his own humorous way," she said, "Is that what we do, ninety-nine and forty-four one-hundredths percent of the time anyway, is protect the citizens of Surf City from themselves and, on occasion, from each other. And search for lost dogs." She glanced at Dippolito who was, she noted, still looking, no, still staring at the young and quite lovely Ms. Catanzariti. Mesmerized was the word Mike Gannon would probably use, Mickey thought. "You've had a chance to meet Deputies Higgins and Dippolito, I assume, due to my unavoidable tardiness," Mickey said.

"Just so you know, Chief. We didn't ask her to make the coffee," Charlie clarified. "The child just went right to it."

Mickey sat down at her desk and motioned for Candy to take the straight-backed wooden chair at its side. Dippolito brought over two cups of coffee and set them down in front of the two women.

"Thank you, Deputy," Candy said.

"It's my, my, my…distinct pleasure," Dip answered. He was almost stammering.

"Can you get me the Overnight Log please, Dennis?" Mickey asked him. She had never, ever called him Dennis before while they were working. It seemed to break the spell.

"Right away, Chief," he said.

Mickey took a sip of the coffee and nodded approvingly. "I might hire you just so you can make coffee," she said. The girl looked at her funny. "Ohhh, right," Mickey said. "I didn't mean it like that. Probably didn't sound too liberated, did it? What I meant was that the coffee is just really good." She looked at Charlie. "For a change."

Candy smiled. "Well I'm glad you like it," she replied. "I get a lot of practice over at the newspaper. Now where did I put my bag?" She scanned the office. Dippolito almost tripped on his own feet fetching it for her. Mickey again looked over at Charlie. He held up a notepad with a jagged line drawn on it in black Magic Marker. Seeing Mickey's expression he put the pad down and mouthed "later" to her. Candy meanwhile reached into the yellow canvas beach bag with red plastic handles and pulled out a stenographer's notebook.

"If it's alright with you I'd like to start with some background questions." Candy said in a matter-of-fact tone. She produced a pink-barreled Parker Pen with a silver top from the depths of the bag.

Wow, Mickey thought. Quite direct.

"I read what Mike Gannon wrote about you in *The Philadelphia Daily News*," Candy said. "But that was really sort of a puff piece with a little yellow journalism mixed in. I don't imagine you think of yourself as, what did he call you? Right, this lovely lass of the law. I mean, you don't have that on your business card or your resume` I assume."

Mickey was nonplussed. "Uh, no. I guess I don't. We just have plain SCPD business cards we hand out, not any personal ones.

And so far I haven't needed a resume`."

"You should each have your own card," Candy said. "People are more likely to contact you with information if they have a name to go with the number. It both implies and establishes a personal connection. Reporters do it all the time that way. Somebody has nothing to say when you interview them so you leave them your personal card. You make a big deal about hand writing a second number on the back. Usually it's just a different office phone but you tell them it's an inside number. Bang - an hour later they're spilling absolutely all the beans to you on the phone. I bet the printing company we use at The SandPaper would do them for almost nothing. I can ask if-"

Mickey interrupted her, making a conscious decision to take back the reins of a conversation that felt like it was galloping headlong away from her.

"Do you have a card?" Mickey asked.

Without hesitation the girl reached down. For a second Mickey was reminded of the cartoon character Felix the Cat and his Magic Bag of Tricks. The girl handed Mickey the card.

"Candace with an 'a'," Mickey said, studying it. "I like that. It's unique."

"My dad said he didn't want people confusing me with Candice Bergen."

"I can see how that could happen," Mickey replied. "Can I keep this?" The girl nodded. "Now, you obviously know a lot about me," Mickey said, "which is good. I'm impressed. You did your research before you walked in here. But I don't know a single thing about you. I did make the bold assumption that you were not a career criminal with a rap sheet as long as my arm and that you are not currently wanted by the FBI."

The Admiral AC kicked back on with a clank.

"Dip," Mickey said, looking over. "Could we switch to Diamond Mode?"

"What's Diamond Mode?" Candy asked.

"Technically it's Neil Diamond Mode," Mickey answered. "As in it never gets quite cool enough." The girl laughed out loud and clicked her pen.

"OK if I use that?" she asked.

"Why don't we check and see if Neil Diamond is playing the Steel Pier this summer before you print that. I don't want any angry PR people calling me up or picketing outside the station. And I personally like the guy. 'Girl, You'll Be a Woman Soon.' I love that one." She saw Candy wrinkle her nose. "Not a good choice, I take it?"

Candy put down her pen. "I'm the wrong one to ask. But I really like his music and that's a really good song, you're right."

"But?"

"But the message it carries isn't 'you'll be a woman soon.' The real message is 'you'll need a man.' Says who? And for what?"

"It's just a song," Mickey said, laughing, "It's not like Neil Diamond is the Manchurian Candidate."

Candy squared her shoulders. "It is just a song," she said. "But it's song after song after song. And the message is always the same. 'Bobby's Girl,' 'She's a Lady,' 'Under My Thumb' – a squirming dog? Really? A squirming dog. What would you do if someone called you a squirming dog?"

"She'd shoot them 'tween the eyes with that big-ass gun on her hip," Charlie called from his desk. "That's what our Chief Cleary would do. And it'd be justifiable homicide. I'd swear it on a stack of King James Good Books."

Mickey was simultaneously surprised and entertained by the girl's intensity. *Spunk* her mom would have called it. She decided to let her continue.

"So if you're a girl, this is what's playing on the radio all day. Which means that this is what's playing in your head all day. Which means after a while you start to believe it. Yeah, OK, I guess I must be just a faithful, thankful, squirming dog who always knows her place and someday I'll need a man." Candy Catanzariti exhaled sharply. The room was warming up and she slipped off the patrol jacket. To Mickey's amusement, Dip was trying desperately to pretend he wasn't watching her do it. The girl, Mickey observed, had on a crisp white blouse with a Peter Pan collar, a blue jean skirt that covered her knees and cute tan espadrilles with white anklets. It was the perfect outfit for a girl reporter and, to Mickey's great relief, she also appeared to be wearing a bra. It occurred to Mickey that if she weren't then she and Charlie would probably have ended up having to resuscitate Dippolito right there on the station house floor.

"Okay," Mickey said after a moment. "But what about that Lesley Gore song?"

"'You Don't Own Me,'" Candy said. "It's great. I love it. It should be the national anthem of the entire Woman's Movement. And it was written by two guys from Philly if you can believe that. But it's one song. One song. Still, God bless Lesley Goldstein and her gift to girls everywhere."

"Lesley Goldstein?" Mickey asked.

"Lesley *Sue* Goldstein," Candy replied. "That's Lesley Gore's real name. Born and raised in the heart of Brooklyn, New York."

"Well that is definitely something I didn't know," Mickey said. She decided the rpm's had gotten high enough that it was a good time to clutch and shift gears. "It says in *The SandPaper's* staff listing that you're from Riverside?"

"Yep, that's my little town," Candy answered. "I was born there – Zurbrugg Memorial Hospital. It's still going which is amazing considering how ancient it is. My dad used to say Jesus had his appendix taken out there by Saint Luke. When I was little I thought it was Zoo Bug Hospital. He, my dad not Jesus, he called me Zoo Bug until I was about ten."

"What does your father do?" Mickey asked.

"He's dead," Candy answered without hesitation or pause. "Lung cancer a few years ago. Smoked like a chimney."

"I'm sorry," Mickey replied. "I know how hard that is. My mother, her name was Eileen, she died when I was a teenager. I miss her every day. She called me Little Black Irish until her – until the last time I heard her voice."

"What did she die from?" Candy asked.

"A sudden illness," Mickey answered. She could never quite bring herself to say the word suicide and "a fifth of Four Roses and sixty Seconals" was a bit more information than she thought most people really wanted.

"My dad was kind of a tyrant," Candy said. "I mean, he loved my mom and she loved him but I think she's OK with the fact that he's gone. It's like she can have a life of her own now while there's still time."

Direct and honest, Mickey mused. There were worse combinations. "Isn't Riverside where they have that great bakery?" she asked. "The one that makes the cream doughnuts?"

"Yeah, L & M Bakery. It's actually in Delran but only by a block. How did-"

Arlene's voice materialized from the Dispatch radio. Mickey

held up a finger.

"SCPD, this is Dispatch. Please respond to Wanamaker Wine and Spirits. Proprietor requests immediate assistance. Code 4. Copy?"

Charlie depressed the button on the microphone base.

'Dispatch, SCPD. We copy and are rolling Code 4. Wanamaker Liquor Store."

"This is a first," Mickey said as they stood. She looked at Candy. "You ride with me. Leave your bag here but you can bring your notepad and pen."

"I also brought a camera along," the girl replied.

"Yeah, um, OK," Mickey said. She reflexively patted her holster and grabbed her hat.

"What do you think it is?" Candy asked, gathering her things.

"Probably any one of ninety-nine just plain stupid things but it's always possible that it's one dangerously stupid thing. Most crime is born out of stupidity or desperation or, a lot of times, the combination of both. Hope for the best but rig for the worst is what the local boat captains always say. Everybody ready?"

The deputies nodded and they all filed out the back door. Mickey kept Candy right in front of her. Charlie and Dip brought up the rear. They exited into blinding sunlight and undulating humidity. Mickey listened for the door to shut and latch behind them. She pointed Candy to her Chief's cruiser.

"Holy shit," the girl cried. "You're kidding me. This is your friggin' police car?"

The Plymouth Barracuda's custom dark blue-on-white paint job sparkled in the sun, the morning glare reflecting almost painfully off the chrome.

"Oh, you mean this old thing?" Mickey replied as they approached it.

"I mean, seriously, holy shit. Gannon's article said it was a Chevelle SS which I thought was truly boss. But this is a 'Cuda cop car. This is well beyond bad."

"It gets me where I need to go," Mickey said. She opened the driver's door, slid behind the wheel and popped the automatic door locks. Candy climbed in on the passenger side and buckled up the lap belt. Mickey ignored her own seat belt and cranked the big-block 425 horsepower V8 engine into rumbling, growling life. She checked her mirrors and waited to let Dip and Charlie pull out first. They all hit their sirens and roof bars and began the weave in and out of the congealing traffic on Long Beach Boulevard heading toward Little Willie Wanamaker's place. He'd upgraded the little shop's name and window lettering to include the classier-sounding "Wine and Spirits" but that, as far as Mickey knew, was the only thing he'd upgraded. The place still smelled like a frat house on a Sunday morning every time she stopped in to check on him.

Mickey thought about her earlier conversation with His Honor the Mayor. She really and most sincerely hoped that Little Willie had only run out of beer.

▲▲▲

Ronnie shook out four Anacin tablets and washed them down with one of Mickey's cold green bottles of Fresca in one continuous gulp. The headache wasn't bad but it was insistent, like a horsefly trapped between a closed window and a screen.

He dialed the SCPD station number and got only a recorded message. He thought he could hear sirens somewhere outside but, with the hangover still humming and buzzing between his ears, he couldn't tell whether they were fire, ambulance or law enforcement. Plus, their house was close enough to the borough line that there was at least an equal chance they were from Ship Bottom and not from Surf City.

He hated falling asleep on the couch. His spine always felt like a rusted gooseneck lamp when he woke up. He decided he'd go stand in the shower and then try Mickey after he was cleaned up. Ronnie looked at the note lying on the counter. Michaela Cleary was a woman of few words much of the time. An occupational hazard he assumed. He tacked it back up with the watermelon slice magnet and meandered down the hallway.

River deep. Mountain high.

It was their catchphrase for how they felt about each other. They both had trouble saying 'I love you' and this snippet from the song seemed to fill that space nicely. They weren't Ike and Tina Turner but they both understood what it meant.

River Deep. Mountain high.

Ronnie turned on the faucets and engaged the occluder on the tub spout, directing the entire flow of water up to the shower head. He couldn't shake the feeling and that's why she couldn't help him. The river was still deep and the mountain was still high – but now they were surrounded by an impenetrable canopy of green jungle.

-11-

Cavanaugh's MainLiner
City Line Avenue
Philadelphia, PA

THE ESTABLISHMENT'S ONLY WINDOW faced out onto side of the busy artery that led away from the City of Brotherly Love and out toward its fabled Main Line. The three men in the booth along the wall to the right of the long bar were the only patrons, the front door having been locked. Foot traffic outside was light. Neighboring St. Joseph's College had been on summer break since early May. Cars traveled mostly in one direction as the suburbs emptied out and headed for the Delaware River bridges and the siren song of the Jersey shore.

Thomas F. Santucci, Jr., Esq. waved a hand to get the bartender's attention.

"Hey, Terry," he said. "What time does the french fry man come in?"

Terry was gray-haired but still fit, only the barest hint of paunch visible at his waist. He wore a short sleeved white shirt and a narrow black bow tie. He had come to the United States with his parents from County Kildare in Leinster Province and still retained a bit of brogue, something which seemed to amuse and intrigue his college customers. He steadfastly refused to utter any words related to either the Lucky Charms cereal or Irish Spring soap advertisements and once brandished a Louisville Slugger at an unlucky, uncharming and less than springtime fresh undergraduate who drunkenly persisted in the request.

"I think I just heard him come in," Terry replied.

"Can he cut up some cheese and crackers for us real quick?" Santucci asked. "And then maybe some fries as soon as the grease is hot."

Terry Spollen lifted the hinged section of the bar and headed for the tiny kitchen to relay the request.

Santucci checked his watch. "Diane's packing the car so I don't want to get home too soon." He envisioned his wife in the driveway of their sprawling home in Merion, one of the wealthiest Zip Codes in the country, and sipped his still frosted glass. "Nothing is better for me than thee," he said, lifting the mug by its thick glass handle.

One of the other nattily but casually dressed men in the booth leaned in.

"Tommy, I know it's a freakin' holiday and all we need to make some kind of decision here," Bobby Nads said.

"I agree," Santucci replied. "Nature abhors a vacuum. Especially a power vacuum." He wasn't sure either compatriot understood the proverb but at the moment he was not particularly interested in explaining it to them.

"I know he's like my own flesh and blood but I gotta say I still think Bruno is a good choice." Tommy Santucci acknowledged Bobby's support of his loyal but somewhat slow-witted nephew. "Domenico seems like a nice kid and all," Bobby Nads continued, "but he's kind'a young. And, if I may say so, a little brash for my tastes."

"He's a strutting, preening peacock," Santucci replied. He spied Terry exiting the kitchen and gave him an inquiring look.

"He's slicing the cheese right this second and just waiting on the oil to bubble," Terry said and slipped back behind the bar. "You guys good?"

"Maybe another round when the fries are ready," Santucci replied. "And tell your guy – what's his name?"

"Ralph."

"Tell Ralph we'll be sure to show our appreciation to you both. Where's Rose?" Rose was a kind, older but often befuddled waitress who had worked at the bar since it opened. Tommy always left her a twenty no matter how what the check came to.

"I gave her the weekend off," Terry said and rested his back against the big NCR cash register next to the taps. He glanced up occasionally at the television mounted on brackets above to see how the Phillies were doing. They were playing the Expos in Montreal and Rick Wise was behind in the count and on the scoreboard early in the first game of a doubleheader.

"But he's Danny's blood," the third man in the booth said. "Blood is blood. It's like trump is in Pinochle."

Santucci held up a finger. "That reminds me. Once we get the management situation figured out I want you guys to meet someone I've gotten to know in New York. Someone who could be very valuable in establishing our presence in Atlantic City a few years from now. He's only twenty-five but he likes real estate and his daddy's bankrolling him. Anyway, I agree. The blood thing is something we have to weigh strongly in making a selection."

"For fuck's sake, Tommy, this ain't the English throne," Bobby Nads said. "We're talking about neighborhood mooks, not dukes and freakin' duchesses."

"Exactly," Santucci replied. "Think of it like this. We really don't need a Don anymore. If people, including the Feds, want to believe it's still like in that book, I say fine, let 'em. But that's not the world we live in today. What we need today is a front man. Like a rock and roll band has a front man. Bruno, he's like Fabian or Frankie Valli. Little Nico, he's more like Mick Jagger. Question is - who is going to sell more records? That is all we care about. How many records?"

Jerry Castagnoli laughed. "Tommy, I love you like a brother, but sometimes I think you went to school for too long. You're way too smart. Thinkin' too much, maybe. Crime is pretty simple. Steal as much as you can for as long as you can and do whatever it takes not to get caught. Bing, boom - that's really all there is to it. So who's it gonna be?"

Ralph the french fry man brought them a heaping plate of cubed white cheddar sliced from a single block along with a basket of cellophane-wrapped Saltines. He looked like a heavyweight boxer on the downslide. "Fries will be out in five minutes," he said and shuffled back toward the rear of the bar.

Tommy Santucci speared a cube of cheese using a toothpick festooned with curlicues of red ribbon and popped it into his mouth. "We'll sit down on Tuesday when I get back from down the shore," he said. "I'll have it all worked out in my head by then."

The small saloon doors of the kitchen squeaked. They could smell the fries as they made their way to the booth. Just before they arrived Terry set three fresh beers down in front of them, the heavy glasses actively shedding small chips of ice.

Santucci grabbed a mug and hoisted it.

"Three dagos in an Irish bar on the Fourth of July weekend," he said with a smile. "God bless freakin' America."

Surf City, NJ

For a moment Mickey had trouble comprehending what she was seeing.

The woman behind Little Willie Wanamaker appeared to be what the city newspapers usually described as a Main Line society matron. Mickey figured her for about forty. She was wearing an expensive-looking summer outfit which Mickey knew did not come from any local boardwalk or beach town clothing store. Her hair was short and blonde with tendrils of gray at the temples. Patsy would say she looked "like she was made of money."

Charlie stood in the doorway, almost filling the opening with his athletic bulk. His sidearm was holstered, as was Mickey's. She hoped they could keep them that way. Outside, Dippolito was moving people away from the storefront and establishing a perimeter. She could see him through the plate glass windows, above the boxes, bottles and cans stacked on the large sills. On the way over she had thought about calling Ship Bottom for back up but was now glad she hadn't. Numbers weren't going to solve this problem, she knew.

"She's crazy," Little Willie said. "Plumb loco. Do something, Chief, before she shoots me."

"You shut the fuck up," the blonde woman said and poked Willie in the ribs with something unseen.

"You shut the fuck up, you bitch," Willie responded. Good old Willie, Mickey thought. If the woman didn't shoot him she just might.

"Willie," Mickey said. "No more from you for right now. Got it?"

Willie set his jaw but nodded in begrudged agreement.

"Ma'am," Mickey said. "I'm Chief Cleary and I really-"

"I know who you are," the woman almost spat the words at her. "Everybody knows who you are. Do I look stupid? How could you let this happen? You're a woman for God's sake."

"Could you at least tell me your name since you obviously know mine?"

The woman tossed her head and the short bangs cleared from her face which was a shade of red that didn't come from too much sun. It came, Mickey recognized, from unbridled fury.

The woman took several quick breaths in and out without opening her mouth. Then she spoke.

"Regina," she said. "Regina Dexter."

Mickey did her best to assume what she hoped was a non-confrontational body posture.

"Okay. That's a place to start at least. I had a girlfriend in high school named Regina. She went by Gina. Do you li-

"I just told you. My name is Regina. Do I look like some South Philly Guido tart to you?"

"No, ma'am, you do not. Just looking for common ground here."

"There is no common ground here," Regina said. Mickey could see she was beginning to perspire more heavily.

"Well then we need to find some," Mickey said, "before things get any worse."

"I seriously doubt they could get any worse," Regina replied. Mickey noticed there was now the barest of quaver in her voice. "I came here to make things better. That was supposed to be your job, I thought."

"Could you tell me the nature of your grievance here and maybe you and I can find a way out."

"The way out is I pull this trigger. That's the fucking way out. If I have to spend the rest of my life in jail it will be worth it."

Mickey thought back to what she had told Candy. Stupidity and desperation. This woman was clearly not stupid, she could tell. But if she was desperate, why was she desperate? Mickey struggled to find a connection between Willie and the seething, almost animal rage that was about to boil over right in front of her.

"Regina?" Mickey asked. "What has Mr. Wanamaker done to cause you to choose this rather drastic course of action?"

"What has he done?" The question came out with a laugh.

Mickey watched Charlie moving almost imperceptibly toward the counter.

"Hey. Timmy Brown. You stay right there," Regina said, referencing the Eagles' newly drafted running back.

Mickey tried again. "Help me out here, Regina. What did Willie do to earn what I assume is a loaded gun in his back?"

Regina turned her body slightly so that she was now further behind Willie. Mickey considered the possibility that the gun might not be loaded but it was a chance she had been trained never to take.

"This lowlife scumbag sold hard liquor to some boys last night. My daughter was with them. None of them were of legal age but he sold it to them anyway. I doubt he even bothered to ID them."

Willy began to speak but Mickey shook her head at him.

"What's your daughter's name?" Mickey asked, playing for time.

"Betsy," Regina said. "Betsy Ann Dexter. And she's only fourteen years old."

An entire sequence of events unfolded in Mickey's head like she was watching a stage play. She knew where this plot was going and it scared her. This wasn't just anger, Mickey now understood. This was something much more dangerous and unpredictable. This was the maternal protective instinct – which meant an emotional atom bomb that was possibly about to detonate. She knew things could go south in a heartbeat.

"Did these boys, Regina, did they hurt Betsy?"

Regina's head shook as she tried to get the words out. "Hurt her? Yes they hurt her. They took turns hurting her after she passed out from the liquor they gave her. The liquor that this asshole sold them. That was the idea all along. They knew her. They knew she never drank before."

"Where is Betsy now?" Mickey asked as gently as she could.

"She's with her father. He took her to the hospital over the bridge somewhere. In Somers Point I think. He took her as soon as Betsy told us what she remembered."

Mickey figured things were going to go one way or the other in the next few seconds depending on how she handled the distraught woman.

"Where are the boys she was with now?" Mickey asked. "We need to pick them up as soon as possible."

"Hah!" Regina said. "Good question, Chief. Gone. Gone! It was the son of one of our friends – our fucking *friends* for God's sake – and some of his high school buddies. We've known that kid for years. And this morning they're all mysteriously gone. Vanished into thin air. Their house is locked up tighter than Alcatraz on a Tuesday. No cars in the driveway. They could be halfway to Canada by now. And none of this would have happened, none of it, if this lowlife piece of shit had just fucking carded them. Like the law in your cozy little town says he is required to do." She jammed the gun tighter. "I read all about you. In the Philly paper. It said you don't have kids so you wouldn't know how this feels."

A little wave of nausea passed through Mickey. She swallowed hard to push it back down. "I know how it would feel if anyone hurt someone that I loved more than anything else in the world," Mickey said. "I do know how that feels. When they shot my dad. I wanted to do exactly what you're doing." Mickey paused. "But I didn't."

"They took *turns*," Regina cried, tears visible on her face now, her cheeks getting splotchier by the second. "They took turns hurting a child. Hurting my baby. They hurt my baby. If they'd been home this morning you'd already have three dead bodies by now. Nobody hurts my baby girl."

There was a loud sound and everyone flinched. Charlie's hand went for his weapon. But it wasn't a gunshot, Mickey knew immediately. It was the gun, dropping to the floor behind the counter. Regina was sobbing uncontrollably now, almost convulsing. Charlie flashed across the counter and pulled Little Willie up and over it by his belt. Mickey vaulted across it and slid down next to Regina, cradling the broken woman in her arms. She looked down at the weapon on the floor first in disbelief and then in relief. It was a starter's pistol, the kind hunters use in the field to prevent young dogs from becoming gun shy. It couldn't be loaded, she knew, with anything but harmless blanks. Mickey was fairly certain Regina did not know that it was not a deadly weapon. The gears in the procedural part of Mickey's brain started turning. She wondered if she could possibly salvage what was left of Regina's life on a technicality.

Dippolito came through the door. Charlie had Little Willie on the ground and was cuffing him behind his back. Dip leaned over the counter, his eyes wide.

"Bag the pistol," Mickey said. "Take Willie to the station and stick him in a cell until I can figure this out."

Willie squirmed. "Wait –what? You're takin' me in? Are you crazy? I'll sue this town for-"

Charlie pushed Willie's face into the dirty floor until he stopped yapping

"What about her?" Dip asked.

Regina was now almost incoherent, Mickey realized. She looked at Charlie.

"Charlie, you are going to drive Mrs. Dexter to Mainland Memorial to be with her husband and daughter. Lights and siren, OK?" Charlie nodded his understanding. "Make sure Mr. Dexter isn't carrying and that any guns he owns are accounted for and turned in. Her weapon here only loads blanks." Mickey paused and decided to add, "A fact I'm sure she was aware of when she came in here. Make sure the ER at Mainland documents everything – I want hair, fibers, fluids, skin cells, the whole nine yards. Alert the shop in Somers Point – as soon as you get ID on the neighbors, their kid and his friends have them put out a BOLO and an APB if they can. Same goes for the Island – call Davey on your way and ask him to handle it personally. See if Somers Point can spare an officer to stay with the family at the hospital. Let the Staties know. I'll call Major Joo and ask for a favor. I want the boys and the parents, all of them, in the tank by suppertime. But I really want the kids. Tell everybody I know it's the Fourth of July. But these people have money – the first thing they're going to do is try to buy a way out. This shit is not going to stand in my town, that's for goddamned sure."

Mickey turned to Regina.

"Deputy Higgins is going to take you to Betsy right now. But we'll need to talk to you later. Don't make any kind of a statement unless it's to me. Do you understand? Regina, look at me." Incoherence, Mickey thought, might have already given way to catatonia. "Regina," she repeated," Do you understand?" The woman sniffled and nodded. Mickey helped her up and supported her as they shuffled out from behind the store counter. Charlie put a beefy arm around her. She seemed completely oblivious. They moved her toward the door.

"Wait," Mickey said. "Do we have a blanket?"

"I do," replied Dippolito.

"Go get it," Mickey instructed. "Pull Charlie's cruiser around back. We'll take her out that way. Willie can do the perp walk."

She turned to Charlie as he flipped Dippolito his keys. "Full Mafia witness protocol. Here and at Shore Memorial. You know what to do."

Dip hustled out the door and quickly returned with the blanket. Charlie unfolded it and slipped it over Regina's shoulders first and then over her head like a hood. She seemed beyond knowing or caring.

"Get him up," Mickey said and kicked Willie in the ribs.

Dippolito hauled him upright. "Easy, Chief," Dip said. "He isn't going anywhere."

"I carded 'em, Chief. I did. Swear to Christ. All three of 'em. They got proper ID I can't refuse them. I didn't break no law."

"Twenty one, Willie? Did they look twenty one to you? I know the legislature wants to drop it to eighteen but it's still twenty one. And you better hope the fake ID's were done by a mob forger. I've given you a lot of leeway over the years. Maybe too much. But they had a fourteen year old girl with them, Willie. What the fuck did you think was going to happen?"

"I sell booze, Chief," Willie said. "Not morality."

Mickey almost punched him but held back. "Where's the reporter kid? Candy?" she asked Dippolito. "I told her to wait in the cruiser."

Dippolito's gaze moved behind her. Candy Catanzariti stood in the back of the store near the big cooler. The young girl wore a stunned expression. Mickey approached her. "Not one word gets written about this. Not one word gets spoken. Understood."

"Understood, Chief," Candy replied. "Totally understood."

Charlie led Regina Dexter past them, talking softly to her as he did.

"Jesus, girl," Mickey said. "You sure picked a hell of a day to tag along."

-12-

Paramount Air Service
Rio Grande, NJ

IT SEEMED TO BRAD like the planes were buzzing in and out every two minutes. The day was so hot that the field help was switching assignments on the fly just to get out of the pitiless sun for a few minutes. Mr. Tomalino had ordered boxes of burgers and cases of Cokes brought down to them but now the Cokes were almost gone along with half the burgers. Brad remembered days on the farm when it was just too hot to eat anything.

Mike Quinlan walked in holding a Masonite clipboard that was missing both bottom corners.

"Need the Zaberer's banner," he said. "Is it ready?"

"Just about," Brad said. He was on his knees and working feverishly. When he started at Paramount he thought there would be actual physical banners trailing behind the planes with letters attached to them. He was surprised to find out that there were none – just the five foot high nylon letters attached to one another in a long string. At the moment Brad was one of two people working on the aerial advertisement for the venerable Atlantic City restaurant. Across the hangar two other boys were working on one for The Latin Casino and near the door two more were busily creating a sign shilling Noxzema sunburn cream. The "Dunes 'Til Dawn" banner flew so often they never bothered to take it apart unless they were running short on letters.

To Brad's right was Jimmy Anderson, a high school buddy,

Brad knew, as well as a wrestling teammate of Quinlan's. They were all mostly college-age kids although the Tomalino's had hired a few Catholic kids out of Holy Spirit High School in Absecon as a favor to one of the local parish priests, Fr. Angelo from Hammonton. The priest had come out on Mother's Day to bless the planes, a ritual Brad didn't fully understand but he'd bowed his head and said "Amen" when it was over. The high school kids worked hard but still seemed to be intimated by the older group and so kept to themselves as much as they could.

"Anderson," Quinlan yelled. "Short time, short time, let's go. Green Jeans is kicking your ass. Short time."

Each letter was supported by a bamboo rod to hold it straight and a combination of eight straps and eight hooks to attach it to the preceding or next letter. The banner they were working on was to read: "Zaberer's Minutes Away!" Anderson was trying to get the exclamation point clipped on when Quinlan started laughing.

"Anderson, you moron," Quinlan said, pointing to the middle of the sign. "Can't you spell?"

Brad looked over. The black ripstop nylon said: "Mininuts Away!"

"Mini-nuts?" Quinlan cackled. "That's you, boy. Jimmy Mini-nuts Anderson."

Anderson looked on in disbelief. "Ah, shit," he said and started unhitch the scrambled letters.

"I'm done here," Brad yelled down to him. "I'll help you. We'll fix it from either end."

Quinlan was still howling. "Mini-nuts," said. "Christ, Anderson, you are dumber than rocks and half as useful, boy." Brad knew from their banter that Anderson had wrestled at least two if not three weight classes above Quinlan and so could probably put him on his back at will. But Jimmy Anderson was possessed of the quieter personality and so he just gave Quinlan the finger and went back to work.

The two other completed banners were already on their way out the door headed to the airfield. There each one would be strung between two poles so the pilots could hook the loop and tow bar with their trailing grapple. Brad thought it was like an aircraft carrier landing except in reverse.

The Zaberer's sign was corrected. Brad and Jimmy Anderson checked it one more time.

"Who's picking this one up?" Anderson asked.

"Yates," Quinlan replied with a wicked smile. "I think he's buzzed once already so he might not be too happy to see you when he lands. Better hope he doesn't run dry because of you." Brad and Jimmy Anderson exchanged glances. Barry Yates was six-foot-seven and built like, Gumby once said, a brick skyscraper. He had played two seasons at the University of Maryland and then been drafted by the hometown NBA team, the Philadelphia Seventy-Sixers. Although Brad had watched him do it, he still couldn't figure out how the big power forward folded himself in and out of the tiny cockpits. Yates hadn't even made a layup as a pro yet but he was already looking past basketball. The job at Paramount allowed him to log a slew of bankable flight-time hours in just a few months. Once he had enough he could apply for a commercial pilot's license. It was why most of the pilots at Paramount stayed there all summer and why they returned year after year.

Quinlan was still laughing as Brad and Anderson struggled to run with the long string of letters through the door and out into the blistering heat.

When they returned Quinlan was sitting on an old engine cowling drinking water straight from a small plastic pail.

"Did he have to go around again," he asked.

"Nah," Anderson said. "But it was close. The grappling hook almost grappled our boy Eb here again." Anderson shook his head sadly. "He'd have never gotten to go to Barber College."

Brad nodded in the affirmative. "Damn near snagged me," he said. "Still better than having Yates mad at us, though."

"Ahh, he's a really good guy," Quinlan added. "He'll beat out Bailey Howell at forward no problem. Shoot, Bailey Howell's gotta be about fifty already, I think." They all laughed.

"Hey, Green Jeans," Quinlan said. "We're going to Tony Marts Saturday night. A band called Tomorrow is playing – supposed to sound just like Chicago, horns and everything. Yates knows the guy working the door and says he'll get us in without a cover. You want to go? Bring your girlfriend, too. She is a major fox. Way too good for you, that's for sure."

Saturday night, Brad thought. That was tomorrow night. "Sure," he said. "Count me in." He knew they would barely notice if he wasn't there. Which he wouldn't be. He thought about his appointment in Hammonton. He wondered what the repercussions would be if he changed his mind. He wondered how far their reach extended, how big their underground network really was. He wondered mostly if they could somehow find him if he ran.

Surf City

The station house seemed smaller than when they had left it, Mickey thought. Candy had excused herself to use the bathroom and Mickey used her absence to call the mayor. She promised she would stop by his office and brief him on the events at Little Willie's. Willie's main concern seemed to be with finding replacement help to mind the store and keep the wine and spirits flowing to the thirsty populace and the cash flowing into the register. Candy returned and took the seat next to Mickey's desk once again.

"Had enough for one day?" Mickey asked, not completely in jest.

"Do you want me to make myself scarce, as they say?" Candy replied.

"No," Mickey said. "But it was a lot to take in. You're still welcome to spend the day as planned. I just want you to know you don't have to. That's all I'm saying."

"I'm OK," Candy answered. "I'd like to finish the day with you."

"Well, I don't think it could get worse," Mickey said.

"How are *you*?" Candy asked her. Direct as always, Mickey mused.

"I'm a trained professional doing my job. So I'm fine. I wish I could tell you it was the worst thing I've ever seen."

"The little girls in North Philly," Candy said. "It was in Gannon's article. I just can't imagine."

Mickey looked at her. "Do you still have all your Barbie dolls? Like at your mom's house? Did you keep them or did you throw them out or give them away?"

"I have every one of them," Candy replied. "And three Tupperware containers full of accessories. Why?"

"I'll tell you some other time," Mickey said.

"A man would have handled that differently today, I think."

The statement caught Mickey by surprise. She paused before replying.

"What do you mean, 'differently'?" Mickey said. "Like differently better or differently worse?"

"Oh, I mean worse," Candy said without hesitation. "Definitely worse. Like a lot worse. Like somebody dead on the floor worse."

Mickey shifted in her seat. It was not a conversation she would normally consider having if Charlie and Dip were there. But, Mickey considered, they weren't. And this girl, this young woman, Mickey was coming to believe, was what Eileen Cleary would have characterized approvingly as "wise beyond her years."

"OK," Mickey said. "Since it's just us here, let me set a few ground rules. One, you're not a real reporter, no offense, so I don't expect anything I say, do or tell you to appear in print without the expressed, written consent of the Commissioner of Major League Baseball, which, in case you're wondering, is me."

Candy nodded.

"Two, you will not repeat or share anything I tell you with friends, acquaintances, colleagues and especially not with either of my deputies even and especially if they ask you what I said. Agreed?"

Another nod.

"Three. You will tell me exactly what you think a man or, rather, what a male law enforcement officer would have done in that store today."

Mickey cocked an ear and listened for the sound of either deputy's patrol car outside. Hearing nothing she motioned for Candy to speak.

"Um, well, the whole, um, the whole *tenor* of the encounter would have been different. It would have had that 'Up against the wall, motherfucker' vibe to it right from the beginning, I think." Mickey noted her use of the term "vibe." "That woman," Candy continued, "Regina I think she said, she came there because a man, because men, had hurt her daughter. Raped her maybe from what I could hear. And yeah, she was angry at the liquor store guy but who she was really furious at were the boys and probably with all men in general at that moment. The last person on earth she would want to deal with in that situation would be another man."

Mickey thought about the idea. She started to speak but then decided to listen some more.

Candy continued. "You made the conversation about her and her daughter, not about her and the gun or that Willie guy. That was the whole difference if you ask me. If you had made it about the gun she would have shot him and then somebody would have shot her-"

"Probably me," interjected. "I would have had to shoot her."

"OK, yeah, so you obviously knew that and you obviously didn't want to do that. Men think differently – everything is a power struggle with them from why isn't dinner ready to an armed standoff. You let her keep her power until she was ready to surrender it and everybody walked away alive. Nobody will give you credit for it but you're a hero. Or a heroine, take your pick. You saved at least one life and probably two in there."

What surprised Mickey is that none of what Candy was saying had occurred to her in the heat of the moment.

"Where do you get all this?" Mickey asked. "I mean, I've always had to prove myself in a man's job but is this something you've been taught? And, before we go any further, is Grinnell in Indiana or Iowa? I-A could be either one you know."

Candy laughed. "Iowa," she said.

"Potatoes, right?" Mickey asked.

"Nope. That's Idaho."

Mickey exhaled. "Sorry. My geography gets a little hazy west of Conshohocken."

Candy pulled her skirt hem to her knees. "My major is Women's Studies and Grinnell is a pretty liberal place so I'm around a lot of women who are taking feminism and so-called women's liberation pretty seriously."

"Women's lib?" Mickey asked.

"We like to call it the Feminist Movement and, if anyone asks, we aren't all Sapphic."

"Sapphic?"

"You know, Lesbians," Candy said. "Or as every douche bag male says, 'lez-be friends.' Morons. Yes, I do know girls who date other girls. But I'd rather sit around with them than go to some bacchanal at a frat house where I can get groped, have beer spilled on me and get puked on all at the same time."

Mickey put her elbow on the table and her chin in her hand. "So back to this morning," she said. "Do you really believe-"

"I'd bet my non-existent paycheck that, like I said, at least two people are dead and one person is wounded. The liquor store guy, Regina and either you or your deputy. Charlie I think is his name."

"Charlie Higgins," Mickey added.

Candy chuckled. "Well if you're Little Black Irish then I guess he should be Big Black Irish."

Mickey put both arms on the desk and folded her hands.

"Feet together and no talking," Candy said with a little grin.

"You obviously went to Catholic school, too," Mickey replied.

"Until I went to Grinnell," Candy said. "First time in my life I was a minority. So what is going to happen to Regina? I was surprised you didn't arrest her."

"Yet. I haven't arrested her yet," Mickey clarified. "I don't think she's what we call a flight risk and technically she's sort of in police custody. Betsy Dexter needs her mom right now, not her dad and a bunch of male doctors poking at her."

The back door rattled and Mickey heard Dippolito and Little Willie shuffling in.

"You can stay," Mickey said to Candy. "But go be a fly on the wall." She pointed to the front of the station house where a picture of Mickey Mantle hung near the door Candy got up and complied.

Dippolito walked Willie toward the open jail cell door.

"Dip," Mickey said. "Take the cuffs off and bring him over here."

"Yeah, Dip," Willie said with as much contempt as he could muster under the circumstances. "Iz'at short for Diputy?"

Dippolito ignored the comment and roughly uncuffed the diminutive store-owner. Willie theatrically rubbed his wrists. "I got rights. I'm a citizen. This is police brutality."

The deputy led Willie to the chair next to Mickey's desk.

"Have a seat, Citizen Wanamaker," she said.

Willie looked around. "Where's the crazy bitch? Why ain't she locked up?"

Mickey made a loose fist and used the knuckle on her third finger to pop Willie right in the middle of his forehead.

"Hey," he cried. "Take it easy, Chief."

"Say 'bitch' again and next time I'll use my nightstick," Mickey told him. She reached into the desk's large bottom drawer and withdrew a thick file folder which she slapped down on her blotter. "You know what's in here?"

"Nah," Willie replied. "How would I?"

Mickey leaned back in her swivel chair, placed the file in her lap and opened it.

"Let's see," she said, thumbing the papers inside. "I got here in 1967 but these violations, Willie, they go back a long way before that. Looks like Chief Pete was even nicer to you than I've been."

Willie leaned forward trying to peek. Dippolito nudged him back.

"Now," Mickey said, "I'm not excusing what Mrs. Dexter did today. But she was distraught. You can understand that. And she was angry."

"She would'a killed me. She had a gun for Chrissakes," Willie complained.

"It was a cap gun," Mickey said.

"Didn't look like no cap gun to me, Chief."

"It is pretty realistic," Mickey replied, "but you couldn't load a real bullet into if you tried. Just blanks. You know what blanks are, right?"

Willie nodded.

"So, we can agree she had no intention of actually shooting you. If she did, why didn't she grab the gun you keep under the counter?"

Willie made a face.

"Right," Mickey continued, "because she had no intention of killing you. Agreed?"

"I guess," Willie said.

Mickey closed the folder. "Good. So you can press charges or file a complaint if you want, that's your right as a citizen. But if you choose to do that then my department will have to investigate Mrs. Dexter's grievance. And that means," she tapped the folder, "Everything in here comes out of my nice, private drawer and goes into the public record. And don't you think the boys at the ABC up in Trenton would find the contents interesting?"

Willie squirmed a little at the mention of the Division of Alcoholic Beverage Control which was headquartered in the state's capital. Mickey glanced up at Dippolito who was suppressing a smile. She turned back to Willie.

"They might see your side of it but they also might pull your Liquor License and good luck ever getting that back with even half of what's in here."

"What about the b-" Willie stopped himself. "What about the crazy broad?"

Mickey leaned forward. "You let me worry about Mrs. Dexter. But I might be able to convince her not to file a complaint that puts you out of business permanently. I can't promise that, but I can try." Mickey tried to look as sympathetic as possible although it was becoming increasingly difficult.

"I still ain't seen a check for the damages to my cooler," Willie said in a petulant tone. "Four years it's been already." It was a low hole card, Mickey knew, but maybe it was time to let him play it. "You was the one who asked me to put the Ragone kid's body in there. I helped you out, remember?"

Mickey let the question hang. In such a small town, she thought, events of the past never really went away.

"I can talk to Mayor Tunell and see if he would be willing to expedite reimbursement. How does that sound?"

"Two hundred bucks it cost me in repairs and lost inventory. That's a friggin' fortune. Plus interest." Willie looked up at Dippolito. "Sorry for what I said. No offense, huh?"

Dip clamped a hand on Willie's shoulder. "No offense, Willie," he said and returned to his desk.

Mickey held the folder over the open desk drawer and looked at Willie.

"In our out?" she asked. "Your choice."

"In," Willie said in a resigned tone. Mickey replaced the folder and slammed the drawer shut. She could see Candy over Willie's head standing motionless by the door. The girl was right, Mickey decided. Everything was a power struggle.

"Is your store locked up?" she asked.

"Yeah. You know how much money I'm losin' right now? With this heat?"

Mickey looked at her watch. "Deputy Dippolito will drop you back at your store," she said. "Put up a sign that says you'll reopen at four p.m. today. We need to let the hubbub die down for a while."

"People are gonna ask me-"

Mickey cut him off. "And you're going to say it was just a misunderstanding. And that is all you are going to say. *Capisce*?"

Willie snorted. "You been hangin' around too many wops, Chief. You're startin' to sound like one."

Mickey motioned to Dippolito. Willie stood up and the deputy led him out. Candy returned and took Willie's seat.

"Was that really his folder?" Candy asked.

Mickey waited until she heard the door close and Dippolito's cruiser start up. "God, no," she said. "It's six years worth of time sheets. But Willie didn't know that."

"Are you allowed to-"

"I'm allowed to use my discretion to obtain the best possible outcome," Mickey said. She thought back to when she'd told Kaylen Fairbrother, her first deputy, to use his discretion and how that had worked out. His smiling picture hung next to Mantle's, the only active SCPD officer to die in anyone's memory.

"What happened to the deputy?" Candy asked as if reading her mind. "The one in the picture. He was really young. Gannon didn't mention him in his article."

"Accident when he was off-duty," Mickey lied. "I still miss him." At least that was the truth, she told herself. Gannon had left that part of the story out because Mickey had asked him to. The squad radio crackled and popped.

"SCPD 2 to Base. Over." Charlie's deep voice rumbled out of the speaker.

"SCPD Base, Cleary here. Over. What's up, Charlie?"

A static squawk and then, "Chief, can you meet me – beach at North 3rd Street. I'm on my way back from Mainland Memorial – will wait for you at the dunes access."

"Copy," Mickey replied. "Beach at North 3rd. On our way." Mickey paused and hit the talk button again. "Any helpful details?"

Another burst of static. "Overtones," Charlie said. "Repeat. Overtones."

"Copy that," Mickey replied rising from her chair. "Overtones. Base out."

"What are overtones?" Candy asked. She scooped up her pad and camera.

"We'll go and see," Mickey said, intentionally not answering the question. "But you can probably forget what I said about things not getting any worse."

-13-

Merion Station, PA

DIANE SANTUCCI WAS TRYING to corral her four daughters when Tommy pulled his Corvette up the circular cobblestone driveway. The Mille Miglia Red paint job fairly glowed in the sunlight, Tommy having killed an extra half-hour at a Wash n' Wax in Ardmore.

"Timed that just right," Diane said as she grabbed the youngest girl by the waistband of her OshKosh B'gosh romper. The Pontiac Safari station wagon was loaded to the gills, Tommy noticed.

"Anything I can do the help you?" Tommy asked.

Diane flipped him the keys. "I packed it, Tommy Boy. You can drive it."

"I thought we'd take two cars this time," Tommy replied.

"Then you thought wrong," Diane said. She began loading the little girls into the back seats one by one and buckling their lap belts. "Unless," she said between daughters two and three, "You want me to drive the Corvette. Then you've got a deal."

Tommy considered the prospect of driving the tank-like wagon and tending to the four girls by himself and smiled amiably. "Let me run in and empty my bladder and we'll hit the road." He leaned his head into the car. "Are you ready, my four little princesses?"

The girls squealed in delight. Tommy flipped the keys back to Diane.

"Fire it up and get the AC going," he said. "It's hotter than bejeezus."

Diane gave him a sideways look. "Hey, after you've finished getting rid of all the rented beer," she said. "Carlton Dexter wants you to call him. The number is taped to the phone on the little secretary's desk in the hall. He said it was important. And he sounded pretty uptight, I thought."

"Did he say what it was about?"

"No, but like I said, he sounded pretty stressed out."

"They live closer to us now in Surf City than they do here. I'm sure whatever it is it can wait," Tommy replied.

"Tommy," Diane said. "Listen to me. He really didn't sound like it could wait. Just call him before we go, OK. This puke-green monster you insisted on buying has every goddamn bell and whistle along with wood panels on the side but one thing it does not have is a telephone. Call him before we leave."

Tommy wanted to mention that the wagon's color was actually called LimeKist Green by PPG but his bladder was fast approaching basketball proportions. He hurried into the six-bedroom wood and stone mansion to relieve himself in the ornate guest bathroom with the weird M.C. Escher drawings on the wall.

▲▲▲

Diane was already buckled into the passenger seat when he pulled the front door shut and keyed the deadbolt. Tommy walked around the car's huge hood and slipped behind the wheel without looking at her.

"Trouble?" Diane asked. She never asked Tommy about business but the Dexter's lived two streets over and had become good friends, welcoming the Santucci's into a neighborhood that Tommy thought might as well have a giant Wasp painted over the door of every home.

Tommy knew one corner of his mouth was twitching involuntarily. "Some minor legal thing he wants help with. Once we get there I'll run over while you and the kids are unpacking the car."

Diane gave him a look of astonishment as he pulled the big wagon to the end of the driveway. "Are you OK?" she asked.

"I'm fine," Tommy answered. He willed the twitch to stop.

"You're not upset that he asked for some free legal advice, are you? Remember, dear boy, they're the ones who gave us the heads up on the beach house coming up for sale. Without them we woul-"

"I'm not upset," Tommy answered. "I just want to get going. Traffic is going to be a nightmare the whole way."

"Well, we could have left a lot earlier if you'd been here to help pack."

Tommy didn't answer and he was thankful that Diane let it go.

They weaved their way through the swept streets and past the gates and the fine trimmed lawns toward Route 1. After several minutes Tommy turned to Diane. "How old is their daughter?" he asked.

"Whose daughter? The Dexter's?"

Tommy nodded.

"Goodness, Betsy has to be, oh, I don't know, thirteen, maybe fourteen I guess," Diane answered. "Why? Is she in some kind of trouble?"

"No," Tommy said. After a pause he continued, "No. Carlton wants to fund a revocable trust in her name. I can't do it but I'll outline the steps and give him Dave Silverman's name. Dave always does such good work."

"And he'd be the first to tell you that," Diane said. "Does he still wear that 'Damn I'm Good' gold bracelet?"

"I believe he does," Tommy answered. He looked in the rearview mirror at the four girls chattering happily in the back seats. He could have told her the truth, he knew. But he had to think. And he didn't want Regina Dexter to be a topic of conversation for the entire drive until he knew more. He didn't even want to think about Betsy.

The corner of his mouth started twitching again.

Surf City

The phone rang and Ronnie picked it up.

"Jesus, I tried you three times already today. Where've you been?"

"Sorry, honey," Stellwag replied. "I didn't know you cared."

"Shit," Ronnie said. "I thought it was Mickey. What the fuck do you want?"

"Well if you're gonna be like that. I don't want anything."

"Yes you do," Ronnie shot back. "What's the sit rep?"

"The boys have reconsidered. They want to be in on your

ballgame. Still interested?"

"What about their 201's?" Ronnie asked.

"Reenlistment, we decided, is not an option," Stellwag replied. "So screw the 201's. Meet me at the Pick-a Lily in an hour."

"Isn't there someplace closer?"

"Not for me there isn't," Stellwag replied. "But there is someplace farther." Ronnie jotted down the information. Then he hung up and tapped on Yossarian's bowl. The fish ignored him.

"Fine," Ronnie said. "Have it your way." He decided he needed some air even it was hot and headed outside.

▲▲▲

Charlie turned to Candy as they made their way from the cruisers toward the pilings that demarcated the beach access path. "Are you enjoying your day with Chief Cleary so far?" he asked.

"Don't answer that," Mickey instructed. "Who called this in?"

"One of the lovely beach tag girls," Charlie replied. "Those walkie-talkies were a great idea. Visionary, one might say." Mickey rolled her eyes at him.

They passed by the wooden pilings and the decaying wood snow-fence past the dunes and headed down onto the beach. At least there was no active hand-to-hand combat going on Mickey noted with relief.

"All quiet on the western front," she said to Charlie over her shoulder.

"Down by the water," Charlie answered. They kept walking.

On the otherwise packed beach Mickey noticed an odd open spot near where the high tide was inching out. There were two black families with small children to the right. One of the mothers was crying, she saw and the children were huddled tight together under a large pink beach umbrella with radial black stripes. Two men, the fathers and husbands Mickey assumed, were standing at the edge of the cleared space glaring at a group of white teenagers. Mickey's hopes for a simple argument over a loud radio or a poor choice of station vanished.

"You can wait here," she told Candy. Mickey approached the two men. "I'm Chief Cleary," she said. "Is there something going on here I should know about." Both of the men appeared to be in their late twenties. One was slightly taller, the other noticeably

more compact and heavily muscled. The taller one pointed to the
sand without looking at her. A message had been carved into the
flat, wet sand at the waterline, probably with a stick or a piece of
driftwood. Part of it had been rubbed out with a foot but filling in
the blanks was not difficult.

GO HOME N   S

Charlie came up behind her. "Did they at least bother to spell
it right?" he asked.

The two men turned, surprised at Charlie's presence and,
Mickey assumed, his complexion.

"Did you see who wrote it?" Mickey asked.

The taller man spoke. "We were in the ocean with the kids
and the moms were down at the edge of the water taking some
pictures. We all came back up the beach to find this." He nodded
toward the scrawled message. "Cheryl, my wife, she took a picture
of it. Something for the scrapbook, right?"

"Well, on behalf of the Borough of Surf City let me be the first
to apologize," Mickey said. She walked over to a group of smirking
teenagers. "Get your towels, get down on your knees and erase it,"
she said.

"We didn't do it," one of them said indignantly. "So we ain't
erasing nothing."

Mickey kicked at the corner of their tattered beach blanket.
Then she reached down and lifted it up, making certain she sent
sand spraying on them. When she had it to shoulder level she
spotted the driftwood stick. "First rule of crime – always get rid of
the weapon right away."

Charlie stood next to her. "Something you young gentleman
would like to say?"

They were starting to look a little nervous, Mickey thought.
"Deputy Higgins asked you a question," she said. She looked at
Charlie. "Cat's got their tongues, apparently."

An older woman sitting near them spoke up. She had blotchy
pale skin and wore a floppy flowered sun hat. "I'm sorry, Chief,"
she said. "We didn't see what they wrote."

Mickey reached down, picked up the stick and handed it to
Charlie. "Would you do the honors?"

Charlie took it and made a few lines in the sand next to the slowly eroding slur. "Looks like the ballistics are a perfect match, Chief," he said.

"So, gentlemen," Mickey said. "We have photographic evidence, forensic evidence and we also have an eyewitness who's willingly come forward. Are you sure you still want to test my rapidly dwindling patience?"

"It's free speech," one the teens said. "It's protected by the Statutes of Liberty." The others nodded self-righteously. "Yeah, and the Bill of Freedoms," another chirped.

"Afraid not, fellas," Mickey replied. "To me it reads like a threat. And I'm sure these good people took it that way. Threats are definitely not protected. But they are prosecuted. Now, like I said, get your towels, get down on your knees and erase every single bit of it. Let's go. All I want to see next are asses and elbows." Mickey smiled, thinking of how often she now mixed in Ronnie's rich vocabulary of military slang and phrases.

The small group muttered and mumbled but crabbed over and rubbed at the sand until all traces of the offending letters were gone. In the immediate vicinity, Mickey noticed, there was almost complete quiet. Again, the people on the crowded beach appeared spellbound by the goings-on.

"Now go apologize to these nice people," Mickey said when all that remained was a shallow trench.

The boys looked at each other.

"You heard me," Mickey added. "Go apologize right now. Deputy Higgins will escort you. For your own protection."

Charlie herded the group across the open space. Incoherent words were said with lowered heads and shuffled feet. "Not bad for a first try," Charlie said. "Now look these people in the eye like men and say you're sorry, not to mention stupid."

The boy who had spoken first looked at him. "Say it," Charlie told him.

"We're sorry," the boy said.

"And?" Charlie prodded.

"And we're stupid," the boy added. The others chimed in late and half-heartedly.

The two families looked at them stone-faced. "Yeah. Y'all are really stupid. And ugly, too," one of their older girls said before her mother could shush her.

"All right," Mickey said. "Get your stuff packed up and start walking that way," she pointed to her right. "You're no longer welcome in my town or on my beach. Ship Bottom is three blocks down. And that means you'll have to buy new beach tags."

The boys decided not to argue and glumly picked up their beach gear, trudging away with the insolence, Mickey mused, only adolescence and ignorance confer.

"Thank you for speaking up," Mickey said to the pale woman.

"I'm sorry we didn't stop them," the woman said. "I'm ashamed, actually, that we didn't stop them." Mickey watched as she got up and walked over to the two mothers and apologized again, this time to them and their children. Mickey thought there might be hope for humanity yet. Charlie conversed with the men and then nodded to Mickey.

"Let us know if there is anything else we can do," Mickey said to the two fathers. "Try not to let this spoil the holiday for you and your families."

Charlie handed one of them the driftwood stick. "Souvenir," he said with a grin. Both men laughed. Mickey snapped off a salute. The taller man returned it with what Mickey recognized as practiced military precision. Then she and Charlie headed for the cruisers.

"Do you want me to call Ship Bottom or is the honor yours?" Charlie asked.

"You can do it," Mickey replied, "Tell Davey to wait until they all pay for new beach tags and then hustle them down to Beach Haven. Pass the word to keep moving them south until they hit the pilings at the old lifesaving station."

"And then?"

"Then they're off the island and I don't care," Mickey said.

"Hmmm. Looks to me like some squirming dogs just had their day," Charlie replied. Mickey held up her thumb. Then she turned it down and wiggled it causing Charlie to laugh loudly. "Damn straight they are," he added.

Candy caught up with them. "Wow, that was amazing," she bubbled.

"Hail to the Chief," Charlie said as they crossed the dunes.

"It was a team effort," Mickey tacked on.

"Did you see their faces when Deputy Higgins walked up?" Candy asked. "I thought they were going to shit their pants, I mean shit their bathing suits right there."

Mickey looked at Charlie. "I told you she was direct," she said.

"Did I say something wrong?"

"No, child," Charlie answered. "Good for a woman to speak her mind. Refreshing, actually."

They arrived at the cruisers. Charlie opened Mickey's passenger door and let Candy slip in. He closed the door and motioned Mickey over.

"How were things at the hospital?" Mickey asked him.

"Pretty tense," Charlie replied. "The mom, Regina, she got bad again. The doc there had to give her something. Sedative, I suppose. The dad is pretty buttoned-up but I did get the names from him. I passed along like you said. He worries me, though."

"The dad? Why?"

"He said more than once that if we couldn't handle this he knew people that could."

"Meaning-"

"Meaning, might be better for these boys and their parents if we find them first."

"Dexter," Mickey said. "Not exactly a goombah name. Did he look like a mook?"

"No," Charlie answered. "Just the opposite."

Mickey chewed on the thought. Then she asked, "Was the girl, Betsy, was she-"

"Penetrated? They weren't sure. But maybe not. These boys were only fifteen or sixteen themselves. Probably not big drinkers yet. Quite possible they got drunk pretty quick. Too drunk to, how can I put this, do any actual damage."

"Jesus, let's hope so," Mickey said. "What were they drinking, anyway?"

"They walked out of the store with fifth of Nikolai Vodka. Mixed it with Tang. Classy guys. Looks like they drank the whole thing, though."

"Oooohhh," Mickey said. "It gives you a headache just thinking about it. Maybe we should interview them, the Dexters, all together. Are they going to keep the girl at Mainland?"

"Didn't sound like it," Charlie replied. "Maybe you should be the one to talk to the mom and the kid. They'd be more likely to tell you something than me or Dip. I'll talk to the dad since were acquainted now."

"OK. Does Somers Point PD have someone with them at the hospital?"

Charlie nodded.

"See if they can escort them back here then. And let us know when they're rolling this way. I might try to arrive just as they get home. I'm not bringing a girl that age down to the station after what she's been through. Allegedly been through."

"Copy that, Chief," Charlie said. "Just be glad Rich isn't here to catch this one."

"Why?" Mickey asked.

"He's the father of three daughters, Chief. And an *hombre*`. He'd make this one personal. Real personal."

"Got it," Mickey answered. "Is Mainland Memorial going to contact you?"

"As soon as they can say something definitively," Charlie said. "What did you do with Little Willie?"

"I cut him loose for now," Mickey replied. "But I really want to eyeball those fake ID's myself. He's a long, long way from being off the hook. I'll head back to the shop with Lois Lane here. When you get back we have some other business to go over. FBI type business."

"Don't tell me – Russian submarines have Crab Island and the Stink House surrounded?"

"Close," Mickey answered. "But you might find that more believable than what I'm going to tell you." Charlie's radio squawked. "You better get that," Mickey said and tapped on Candy's window as she made her way to the Barracuda's driver's side.

"Wow," Candy said, "You were right about me picking the right day." She was scribbling on her note pad.

"Remember our agreement," Mickey said as she keyed the 'Cuda's ignition.

"Oh, this is for me," Candy replied. "I have to do what they call a capstone project before I can graduate. I think I might do it on you."

Mickey shifted the big Plymouth engine into gear and the chassis vibrated with the power. She didn't want to dampen the girl's obvious enthusiasm but she had hoped Gannon's newspaper article would be the pinnacle of her fame.

"Who sees your, what did you just call it, your capstone project?" Mickey asked

"Oh, just my professors," Candy said, still writing.

"You might want to wait until the excitement wears off before you make a final decision on that," Mickey advised.

"Are you kidding? This will blow their doors off," Candy answered. "And it's barely noon."

Barely noon, Mickey thought as she headed the cruiser up 3rd Avenue toward Long Beach Boulevard. The big weekend hadn't even really begun yet and already she was wishing it were over.

14

Mae's Seabreeze Tavern
Sea Breeze, NJ

THE OLD WOMAN WAS at their table before they knew it. Despite the heat she had a thin sweater draped across her bony shoulders. In her left hand she held a drink.

"Y'aint locals," she said with a faint whiskey tenor. "So if you're here 'cause you're thinkin' you'd like to buy the place I'd be willin' to sell it to ya. You two boys look like you could be the saloon-runnin' types." She pointed at Ronnie. "You'd tend bar and keep the books." Then she looked at Stellwag. "You'd be the bouncer and do all the public relations." She drained the little bit of turbid liquid left in her glass. "Order me a scotch and soda," she said "and whatever you're drinkin' is on me."

"Two beers," Stellwag said. "Owner's choice."

"Pabst'll do for the likes of you two scurvy scoundrels," she said. "Feel free to look around. I ain't much for tours." The old woman walked back to her little table next to the bar and lit up a cigarette.

"Mae, I assume," Ronnie said.

"In what's left of the flesh," Stellwag replied. "Her old man built the original place on a barge. She's the one added food and it's been here ever since. She's run it all by herself since the old man croaked."

Ronnie looked across the blue-green expanse of Delaware Bay. "The lighthouse still out there?" he asked.

Stellwag squinted although the light was over three miles away. "Ship John Shoal Lighthouse is still there," he said. "And it still has three keepers as far as I know, although only two of them are on-station at a time I think." A middle-aged bartender brought the Blue Ribbons. They both nodded to Mae who raised her fresh scotch and soda to them in reply. "Coast Guard keeps threatening to automate it but they haven't gotten around to it yet. Tough job being a keeper." He took a long sip of the beer. Ronnie did the same.

"What changed the boys' minds?" Ronnie asked, wiping a trickle from the corner of his mouth.

"Boredom. The heat. An awakened sense of duty. Fuck if I know."

"Calhoun on board?" Ronnie asked, referring to the Sons of Stan's massive sergeant-at-arms Everett C. Calhoun who everyone usually just called Haystacks after the professional wrestler. Stellwag took another drink.

"The boys respect what I think but Haystacks, they respect him for what he does. He had a cousin, kid a bit younger than him that grew up almost next door his family. Haystacks was like a big brother to him, I guess. He just found out the kid was KIA evac'ing wounded ARVN out of Cambodia on a chopper crew. Bastards at MACV didn't tell anyone for almost three months." Stellwag finished his beer and looked over to the bar. "Did you know they were five klicks from the big NVA base when Nixon told them to stand down? Now, Everett is the most patriotic motherfucker on earth but he's done with the bullshit they're selling. He needs to do something otherwise it'll eat him alive twice as fast as it already is."

Ronnie finished his Blue Ribbon just as the bartender brought over two more.

"People aren't going to like it," Ronnie said. "Or us."

"Fuck'em if they can't take a joke," Stellwag replied. "I got a Prospect right now was in the shit for two tours. Got back in May. Says ninety-percent of the grunts are stoned from the time they wake up. Nobody's fighting, they're all just tryin' to stay alive 'til they call it off or they get shipped home. He swears the minute the last G.I. choppers out of Saigon it'll be like we were never there."

Ronnie looked across the Bay. The Delaware shoreline was just visible through the haze. "Remind you of anyplace?" he asked.

"Swap the scrub pines for palm trees add a stone-age village or two and you got the Mekong Delta," Stellwag said.

"My dad said Guadalcanal and the Pacific islands they took were just little patches of Hell even when there wasn't a fight," Ronnie replied. "Nam was almost too beautiful for a war."

"Brother, you should'a seen it from the air." Stellwag said.

"We need people to take notice," Ronnie continued. "I don't mean guys like us. I mean everybody else. We need to wake them up."

"What are you telling my favorite police chief about this ballgame?" Stellwag asked.

"Nothing," Ronnie said. "She won't be happy either."

"You can shack with us when she tosses you out," Stellwag said with a smile.

"Is that before or after she shoots me?" Ronnie asked.

"Have to be before," Stellwag answered. "She won't miss."

"The Pic-a-Lilli would have been a lot closer," Ronnie said. "Why this place?"

"We both needed the road miles," Stellwag replied. "Clears the mind. You ever been to Sea Breeze before?" Ronnie shook his head. "See it while it lasts. Sooner or later the Bay will be right here where we're sitting. If a hurricane doesn't get it first."

They didn't see her approach but Mae Griffith had walked back over. "So, got a price in mind?" she asked. "I'll give you a bargain. Maybe even a roll in the hay with the owner instead of a commission." She winked.

"Just the beers today, Mae," Stellwag answered. "We need to talk to our accountant."

"'Pshaw," Mae said. "Don't come back 'til you're totin' a fat check." She turned around and headed for her table.

"Tomorrow night," Ronnie said. "I'll let you know when to saddle up."

They grabbed their bottles, clinked them together and sucked down the last lukewarm drops.

Penn Station
New York City

Mary Kathleen Browne sat on the bench with her legs crossed. She sensed his presence even before he spoke.

"I have to ask," he said. "Which modeling agency are you with?"

"Excuse me?" she replied.

The man next to her smelled of expensive cologne. His clothes were flashy in what she assumed was a very "New York" way. His skin was the color of the double-scoop hot chocolate her mother had made for her on freezing North Dakota mornings. She put down the bus and train schedules and in that instant he was handing her a card.

"You," he said in a voice like an FM deejay, "are exactly what the industry is looking for right now. If you're not already signed, I would be happy to do some portfolio pictures for you at my studio."

Mary Kathleen looked at the card. She knew the pitch. She'd heard it outside the O'Farrell Brothers Theater in The Tenderloin when she'd first arrived in San Francisco. That "agent" had been white but she knew the game was the same – prostitution and pornography in equal measures. She handed back the card.

"I'm flattered," she replied. "But I'm actually on my way to Philadelphia."

"That's not where it's at, sweet thing," he cooed. His smile was dazzling she thought. "Mmm, mmm, my goodness, no. All they got there is brotherly love – and this brother has something very different in mind for you."

"I'm sure you do," Mary Kathleen said and reached for her bag. "And I'm sure you'll find what you're looking for on another bench." She got up and walked away.

She smiled, thinking to herself that at twenty-three she could still be mistaken for a Midwestern innocent or a runaway. That impression would be very helpful in the days to come. She ducked into the little automat and sat at the battered counter. She had to first make the train to Philly and then find a local line that would take her into the New Jersey hinterlands. Her instructions were to make sure he carried out the plan – the fact that she didn't actually know what the plan was didn't seem to faze anyone. "The less you know," they told her.

She ordered a cup of coffee and a slice of pie, deciding she'd smoke the joint when she got to New Jersey. She had never been east of the Mississippi River and this little jaunt was turning out to be something of an adventure. The coffee was hot and tasted good. The pie was stale but she wolfed it down like a starving person anyway.

When she went to pick up her bag she saw that he had

slipped his card in the little slot meant for the name and address identification paper. She pulled it out.

Cherchez La Chatte
Modeling & Talent Agency
[212] 555- 2868

Her French was rusty but she got it almost right away. Look at the Cat, she thought at first but then it hit her. Looking for Pussy. She decided she had to at least give him points for truth in advertising.

Mary Kathleen Browne lit up a Virginia Slim and stared at the wall clock hanging above the five-gallon coffee urns and the Hamilton Beach milkshake makers. It was a smiling black plastic cat whose eyes and tail moved to-and-fro with metronomic precision. She had forty minutes. *Cherchez la chatte* – look at the cat, she thought as she gathered up her things and left. Her pilgrimage to the Blessed Virgin was halfway over.

15

Surf City

"WHERE'S YOUR GAL FRIDAY?" Charlie Higgins asked with a chuckle.

Mickey was at her desk, shuffling folders and notes on her desk. "She had to run back to the newspaper office for a little while. She'll be back."

"Seems nice. Smart. And no Shrinking Violet, either."

"You got that right," Mickey said. "As Patsy would say, she's about as subtle as a thrown brick."

"I suspect she'll grow into someone to be reckoned with," Charlie replied.

Mickey looked up. "Where's Dip?"

"Dip got a call from the Polish Temptress."

Mickey rubbed her palm over her face. "What is it this time? He's found her dog twice already this year. I just hope he hasn't finally found her-"

"Uh, uh. Don't say it," Charlie chided.

"I was going to say cat," Mickey replied. "So what's the call?"

"Strange man lurking about. I wouldn't worry about him, Chief." He held up the paper with the zigzag line again.

"Yeah," Mickey said. "What is that all about?"

Charlie gave out with a deep, rumbling laugh. "The Thunderbolt."

"Charlie, the only Thunderbolt I know of is the big roller coaster at Willow Grove Park."

"How about *The Godfather*,'" Charlie replied. "When Michael Corleone goes to Sicily and sees Appollonia for the first time. Our boy Dip has done been struck by lightning. You didn't see that?"

"Candy?" Mickey asked with no lack of incredulity.

Charlie nodded.

"I mean I saw that he noticed her but she's cute and built and," she paused and then continued. "Oh, man I have bad news for him," Mickey said. "She's down here this summer with her farm boy college boyfriend. They're living in sin and probably screwing like rabbits in the little rooms Mary T. rents out over her store. Poor Dip. Although...I have to say I did get the sense she may not be in it for the long haul. They sound like an odd pairing."

"See? Don't count our boy Dip out just yet, Chief," Charlie said.

"Remember when Rich thought he might be-"

"Flamboyant?" Charlie said.

"Yeah," Charlie replied. "Flamboyant. But the only evidence was that he had no steady girlfriend and at least one Liberace record. Circumstantial at best I'd say."

"How long has he been at Miss Skotnicki's house?"

"Just a few minutes," Charlie answered. "His mind will be on other things. Trust me on this one."

"Hey," Mickey said. "Anything new in Darnell's investigation?"

Charlie pursed his lips. "Cole Prejean was promoted but he's still in charge of it," he said. "I get the sense his hands are tied at the moment. He says nothing will happen to any of the higher-ups while they're in-country or as long as there's an active theatre of war. I may need to look elsewhere for help."

"Justice delayed is justice denied," Mickey replied.

"Revenge is a dish best served cold," Charlie shot back.

"Vengeance is mine says the Lord."

"Sayeth the Lord," Charlie corrected. "And He helps those who help themselves."

"So how high does it go? Do they know?" Mickey asked.

Charlie interlaced his fingers in front of him. "Criminal perpetration goes high. Knowledge of the perpetration goes even higher." He unlocked his hands and rubbed his chin. "I'm willing to wait. Prejean says if Nixon is going to let the massacre at *My Lai* slide then we may have to wait until after Nixon is out of office or the war ends abruptly."

"Neither seems very likely," Mickey said and considered the timeline. "Charlie, why didn't you take the North Carolina job, if I may ask?"

"You may," Charlie replied. "Because I have work to do here, Chief. *We* have work to do here. A position like that will always be an option. I am exactly where I am supposed to be right now."

The back door rattled. A few seconds later Dennis Dippolito walked in shaking his head.

"No arrest, I see," Mickey said as he plopped down at his desk. "Any likely suspects?"

"Where's Candy?" Dippolito asked ignoring her question. Charlie cleared his throat loudly and went back to working at his desk.

"Running a few errands at *The SandPaper*. She'll be back in a little while."

Dip set his hat down on his desk. "You know, Chief, if you're busy she's welcome to ride with me."

Charlie held up the piece of paper with the jagged line again.

"Thank you, Deputy," Mickey replied. "I'll consider that our Plan B." This seemed to satisfy Dippolito who busied himself with a sheaf of papers. "Charlie, did Ronnie happen to call while I was out?"

Charlie shook his head.

"Then I may just run home for a minute," Mickey said. She smiled at Charlie. "Dip, if Miss Catanzariti comes back while I'm gone can you fill in for a little bit? Maybe give her some background on the problems we face on a big holiday weekend like this."

"You bet, Chief," Dippolito chirped.

Mickey winked at Charlie. "I won't be long. Check again with Mainland Memorial and see what the status of the Dexter girl is. That's one interview I may need to do alone."

"On it, Chief," Charlie said and picked up his phone.

▲▲▲

Mickey started up the Barracuda and turned the AC up to Maximum. Candy surprised her by tapping on her window.

"Something exciting?" she asked as the window glided down.

"Afraid not," Mickey said. "I'm just going to run home and check on my b- , on my better half. I won't be a long time. I asked Dennis to give you some background info you can use for your story." The girl looked disappointed.

"Um," Candy said. "Brad, my boyfriend, he called the newspaper office and left a message. He won't be home until late – they have to set up all the banners for tomorrow he said. Would it be OK if I hung around to watch what happens when the sun goes down?"

"Sure," Mickey said. "Dinner won't be much. Probably just burgers and Cokes at our desks."

"That's great," Candy bubbled. "It gets so hot in that little apartment."

"Where does your boyfriend – Brad, right? Where does he work again?"

"Paramount Air over in Cape May County. I'm not exactly sure where it is. I haven't been there. Kind of in the middle of nowhere it sounds like."

"OK," Mickey said. "Maybe I'll get to meet him before the weekend is over."

"He said this is the busiest weekend of the whole summer so I may not see much of him either. Maybe just a fly-by, you know?"

"Yeah," Mickey replied. "I know how that is. I'll see you when I get back."   Candy gave a finger wave and Mickey raised the window. She hoped if Ronnie wasn't there that he had at least left a note. But she wasn't counting on it.

Atlantic City Expressway
Outside Hamilton Township

Tommy Santucci had stood all he could stand.

"Time for a new plan," he said. The big wagon was inching along in what looked like a march of squirming caterpillars all farting blue smoke. Tommy poked the Safari's prow-like grill towards the right-hand lane eliciting horns and curses as he maneuvered.   He took the next jughandle for County Road 50 toward Egg Harbor Township.

"This isn't going to be any faster," Diane said. She had a copy of *Cosmopolitan* magazine on her lap.

"As long as it seems faster, I don't care," Tommy said. "We'll take 50 until we hit the White Horse Pike. Then we'll take that to old Highway 9 – it's the way my dad took us in his big old Buick when we were little." He checked the rearview mirror. "We're taking the White Horse Pike, my little princesses. First one to spot a white horse gets extra pizza." The three older girls squealed and began looking out the windows. Abigail, the youngest, snoozed in her seat.

"You haven't said two words," Diane chided him. "What are you upset about?"

"I told you, Diane, I'm not upset." Tommy checked the girls in the mirror and lowered his voice. "That phone call from Carlton. It was about his daughter. Apparently some older neighbor boys got her drunk and – well you take it from there.

Diane's magazine slipped to her feet and her hand went to her mouth. She instinctively swiveled her head around to check on the four little girls who were busy looking for magical white horses.

"Did they-?"

"They aren't sure," Tommy said. "That number was a pay phone at the hospital in Somers Point and they were still checking her out. He said they're treating her like it was her fault and like maybe she deserved it or asked for it."

"Oh my God," Diane said, trying to control her emotions. "Oh, the poor thing. Did they arrest the boys?"

As Tommy began to speak Diane gave him a hand signal to talk softer. "When they figured out what happened this morning the boys and the parents had already hightailed it out of town. The local cops are looking but Carlton said they're about one step up from the Keystone Kops."

"How is Regina?"

Tommy braked for a deer. "How would you be?"

Diane covered her mouth with her hand. Tommy knew she was struggling not to cry. "First I'd castrate the fuckers and then I'd kill them," she said quietly.

"Yeah, well they weren't around for that so Regina did the next best thing."

Diane looked over.

"She put a gun in the back of the liquor store clerk who sold the boys the booze."

"Did she…?"

"No," Tommy said, easing up on the brake pedal. "Fortunately it was a starter's pistol – a glorified cap gun loaded with blanks. The police chief – the girl that was in the Philly paper-"

"The woman," Diane corrected.

"OK, sure," Tommy said as the wagon picked up speed. "The woman. The chief, she had one of her officers take Regina to the hospital over the causeway so she could be with the girl. She's going to interview them at the house when they're released. Carlton wants me to be there when she does."

"Should we stop there on the way in?

Tommy shook his head. "I can't be his attorney on this so I'll just listen to make sure she, the woman police chief, follows protocol. Regina could be in some deep shit if this Chief wants to be a prick about it."

"I doubt a woman can be a prick, dear."

"You know what I mean," Tommy replied. "Do you want me to use a more anatomically correct term?"

"No, I most certainly do not," Diane answered. "I get the picture. But it wasn't a real gun. Doesn't that change things?"

"Not necessarily," Tommy said. He readjusted the sun visor. "What counts is if the clerk *believed* it was a real gun. Then she could be charged with assault with a deadly weapon. It really kind of surprises me that they didn't charge her and lock her up. This chief must have an angle she's playing."

"I read that story," Diane said. "She didn't strike me as a Keystone Kop, Tommy. I wouldn't make any assumptions and I would not underestimate her just because she's a woman."

"Thank you, counsellor," Tommy said. "I'll take that under advisement."

"And don't call Rusty Pandola."

Tommy looked at her.

"You heard right," Diane said. "Don't play dumb with me, Thomas Francis Santucci."

"I think Rusty's on vacation."

"Goombah enforcers don't take vacations," Diane shot back. "They take orders. I believe you told me that one time."

"Strong words from someone whose maiden name is Biancone," Tommy replied. "And whose father was Angelo 'Tony Angels' Biancone, a doting dad who taught his daughter everything she knows," Diane said.

"So noted," Tommy said. He looked at his watch. "We can stop at Emil's for supper. Give the causeway bridge time to empty out. The girls can play that shuffleboard game they like."

"Never too early to start developing bar athletes," Diane said.

"Maybe they'll get scholarships." She retrieved her *Cosmopolitan* from the plastic floor mat in the carpeted foot well. "Let's skip Emil's this time. I want to be there when Regina and Betsy get home. Strength in numbers." She absent-mindedly flipped a few pages of the magazine. "I just cannot imagine," she said. "All I can say is I would not have brought a cap gun."

Paramount Air Service
Rio Grande, NJ

Quinlan and Anderson tracked Brad down while he was in the field's rickety outhouse. They were together so often he began to think of them as one entity and nicknamed them Q & A.

"Farm boy," Quinlan called through a space in the boards. "Von Don wants to see you when you're done laying cable."

Brad Vreeland finished his business and the requisite paperwork and pushed open the door. Q & A were already walking back to the banner shed, punching each other as they went. "Von Don" was Gerrit von Donnersmark, one of the pilots Brad had been bugging for a ride. Von Don's father had been a Messerschmitt fighter pilot in the war and there was talk that he and Mr. Tomalino might have crossed flight paths in the skies over Europe. Yates was by far the best pilot but between his height and his power forward bulk he only flew the single seat aircraft. There were several biplanes and two of them were painted to look like an RAF Sopwith Camel and a German Fokker. But America was rapidly losing its fascination with Snoopy and the Red Baron, much to the chagrin of The Royal Guardsmen. Barbara, the Tomalino's beautiful teenage daughter let it slip that both would be repainted over the winter. Von Don, naturally, always flew as the Red Baron while Bobby Gilmore flew the Camel. Like several of the other pilots, Von Don was attending the Aviation School at Purdue University in Indiana pursuing first a degree and then a career as an airline or a corporate pilot. Paramount provided him and the others a huge number of flight-hours in an enjoyable atmosphere.

Brad found Von Don talking to Gumby in the mechanic's shed. There were three full-time aviation mechanics during the summer. Normally only two worked at a time, rotating their days off. But on the summer's busiest flying weekend all were elbow deep in grease and the horizontally arrayed pistons of the Lycoming engines.

Von Don greeted brad with a crisp American military salute. Brad retuned it with a "Heil Hitler" outstretched arm. Von Don countered with his middle finger. It had become almost a ritual.

"Tomorrow," Von Don said with a big smile. "I take you flying tomorrow." He spoke perfect English but still maintained a trace of his Teutonic ancestry. "Tomorrow, Samstag is *gut*, yes?"

"*Sehr gut*," Brad replied. After Scandinavians, Germans made up the largest demographic of descendants in his home state. Several of the hired men on the family farm had come from West Germany. Brad knew Von Don's parents had been trapped when the Berlin Wall went up almost overnight. Only a daring plot involving a Trabant with a false boot had allowed him and his sister Birte to escape to the West. Helmut von Donnersmark had died without ever seeing his children again.

"That would be great," Brad replied. "Thanks."

"We'll take the trainer," Von Don said. "Maybe I even let you fly a little on the way back. But promise you won't crash into anything." Although all the seasonal pilots arrived with significant flying experience, those who had never towed a banner before had to go through a training period overseen by the returning pilots and Mr. Tomalino himself. With the exception of the Piper Super Cub trainer, all the other planes had their passenger seats torn out to lighten them. New tow pilots would spend most of late April and early May learning the routes and, more importantly, the occasionally dicey crosswinds that grabbed the banners in the trainer with a more seasoned pilot in the right seat. Paramount had never had a fatal accident or serious injury and safety was a Tomalino trademark, strictly enforced by the owner himself and reinforced by the veterans who often returned summer after summer. The first banners started flying around Mother's Day on weekends and then every day from Memorial to Labor Day.

Calls from the shed fell on Brad's ears. He trotted back to finish piecing together an updated banner for a Gary Puckett and the Union Gap concert at the Steel Pier. He still had a package to pick up and the way the day was shaping up this was, he knew, going to be a problem if he still wanted to keep that appointment. He had less than thirty-six hours left to get everything ready.

-16-

Route 49
Millville, Cumberland County, NJ

RONNIE REFOLDED THE SUNOCO map of New Jersey and stuffed it in his waistband. Neither he nor Stellwag needed to refer to it but a State Police cruiser had been tailing them since not far outside of Bridgeton. They made a show of consulting the ancient paper which on which every fold had been taped to prevent it from separating completely.

"Where's our rally point?" Stellwag asked.

"You guys can rally off island. I'll make my own way to the objective." Ronnie replied. "It needs to be secured by no later than twenty-two hundred hours. And no sidearms, knives, chains or monkey wrenches, agreed?"

Stellwag laughed. "You're asking a lot."

"I'll bring what we need," Ronnie said. "The perimeter you have to establish is pretty small."

"Can we at least bring the smoke?" Stellwag asked.

"Sure," Ronnie answered. "I'll even let you pick the color."

"You know this could go south, right? All it takes is one nervous cop to overreact or play hero."

"I know," Ronnie said. "But we'll be at the northernmost point so that gives us eighteen miles of south to work with."

"I told the boys who are already on parole to sit this one out," Stellwag replied and rubbed the blond stubble on his chin. "You got a name for this little party?"

Ronnie put on his sunglasses. "I was thinking Operation Tea Party."

Stellwag took a final puff on his Lucky Strike and flicked it to the pavement. "I just hope it's not the Boston Massacre," he said. "But I got a better one."

"Shoot," Ronnie replied.

Stellwag flipped his aviators off the crown of his forehead and down onto the bridge of his nose.

"From now on this here ballgame is officially Operation Dark Light."

Ronnie recalled their discussion at the Pic-a-Lilly about MVAC's Operation Arc Light. "Fuckin' A," Ronnie said. "Operation Dark Light it is." He kicked the Royal Enfield into life.

"Fuckin' A, Bubba," Stellwag replied. He gave a two finger salute morphed it into a Peace Sign and roared off.

Ronnie clutched the Enfield and peeled out in a hail of stones, sand and hydrocarbon vapor. He hoped Mickey would be home when he got there.

Surf City

Mickey tapped on Yossarian's glass. "Did you get fed today?" she asked.

The little fish darted around the bowl and took refuge in the medieval castle. The phone rang as she was heading for the shower. It was Charlie.

"The Dexter's left the hospital about forty minutes ago," he said. Traffic is heavy but you might want to swing by."

"Did you talk to the doc?"

"No, but the doc talked to the Point patrolman and he talked to me. Apparently there's no such thing as privacy when it comes to your medical information. I sure hope the newspapers don't call – they'll tell anybody anything it would appear."

"Shit," Mickey said. "This girl's a minor for Christ's sake." She drummed her fingers on the wall. "How bad was it?"

"Not so bad," Charlie said. "No evidence of forcible penetration or trauma. No semen and the maidenhead remains intact."

"The maiden-what?"

"The hymen. The thing that makes you officially a virgin. If anyone wants to check, that is. Come on, Chief, don't make this any harder on me."

"So what do they think happened?" Mickey asked.

"The doc said it's likely they just looked around down there. At their ages those boys probably had no idea what they were even seeing."

"They could'a just checked out the Collier's Encyclopedia, the one with the clear plates," Mickey replied. "At least it has labels on the parts. What were they drinking again?"

"Nikolai Vodka and Tang. Nasty ass stuff."

"Yeah," Mickey said. "That is nasty. Any hits on the APB or the BOLO?"

"Nothing yet," Charlie answered. "If they were smart they'd be checked in at some no-tell motel in Winslow Township under assumed names."

"Anything else?"

"Ronnie called here," Charlie reported. "Said he was heading home from a meeting in Sea Breeze."

"Where the hell is Sea Breeze?" Mickey asked.

"A ways from here," Charlie said. "Out past Bridgeton on the Delaware Bay. There's a little lighthouse out there that marks the channel."

"Yeah, well the last thing I'm worried about at the moment is a lighthouse," Mickey answered. "I'll swing by the Dexter's and see if I can catch them before they have time to start concocting a different story. You have the address?" Mickey slipped a light green Papermate pen from her pocket and wrote it down. "Call me right away if anyone snags the boys or the parents. And I want to see the ID's they used myself. Little Willie's a pain in the ass but he's our pain in the ass. He has a few rights, too."

"Copy that, Chief Cleary," Charlie said. Mickey replaced the phone in its silver receiver, wondering what Ronnie was doing in Sea Breeze. Her stomach had been upset all day and none of the new information was helping to settle it. She had a bad feeling about Ronnie's new focus and his new friends. There was enough going on inside her already, she decided. She did not need to be feeling the vibe right now. She dialed Dr. Harman's office.

No one answered but she knew the office had gotten something called a PhoneMate 400. Dr. Harman had showed it to her on her last stealth visit and thought it would be something the PD might want to consider. "For anonymous tips," she had suggested with a laugh. Mickey waited for the little hum to stop and then a mechanical voice said, "Please leave your message now."

Mickey was unsure who actually listened to the recordings. She hung up without speaking.

Paramount Air Service
Rio Grande, NJ

Barbara Tomalino was eyeing Brad suspiciously so he tried to end the phone call as quickly as possible. She was eighteen but looked older to Brad. Her dark hair and eyes intrigued him. He wondered if his penchant for girls his mother often referred to dismissively as "southern" was a result of growing up in a land of light-haired, blue-eyed Scandinavians.

"Was it a toll call?" Barbara asked him. "Or a long distance one?"

"Hammonton," Brad answered. "I'm not from around here. Is that a toll call?"

Barbara sized him up. "I don't think so. But if it was it has to come out of your wages. That's the policy. Where are you from?"

Brad knew she already had the answer.

"Minnesota," he replied.

"Never been there," Barbara said. "Don't plan on going, either."

"Too bad," he answered. "You'd like it. It's pretty. Lot of lakes."

"No beach? No ocean? No thanks," Barbara said and went back to stamping invoices. "Anything else I can assist you with before you get back to work?"

Brad understood he was being dismissed. She was her father's daughter he decided so he smiled, shook his head and let himself out of the air-conditioned office and back out into the sweltering late afternoon heat. The supplier had been a little miffed but Brad promised he would be there early in the morning to pick up the merchandise. The man wanted to know why someone else had mailed the check and why it was drawn on a California bank. He complained that it had taken a week to clear. "I just do what I'm told," Brad had replied, which was not far from the truth.

Several things still needed to fall into place, he realized. But he still thought he could pull it off. As the small planes buzzed overhead he wondered why what had seemed only a month ago to be his destiny was starting to feel like the last few stops on the Stations of the Cross.

Intersection of Hwys 55 & 347
Cumberland County, NJ

Ronnie pulled the Enfield onto the gravel shoulder. He looked at his military issue watch but only out of habit. The crystal had permanently fogged the night he took out Billy Bowker with an M3 white phosphorous grenade. Portions of the plastic case were bent from having melted in the heat and then warped when they cooled. He knew the watch was a trophy but it didn't bother him anymore. His father told him tales when he was growing up of the battle for Guadalcanal and the "souvenirs" the GI's had taken from Japanese soldiers living, dead and dying in the aftermath of the fighting. His father kept his own stash in a coffee can in his parents' bedroom closet – a few teeth, a neck chain and part of a scorched jawbone with a single embedded molar. In his teens Ronnie was ashamed to know his father had done these things. When he'd gotten home from Vietnam he was thankful to think that was all he'd done.

The sun was getting lower but night was still several hours away. Ronnie had never been to the little airfield in Rio Grande but figured it couldn't be that hard to find. He'd lost the old Sunoco map somewhere since leaving Stellwag but his dead reckoning skills were so good he wasn't really worried. He needed to pick up the package but if he made the trip now, he realized, he might not see Mickey at all before it all went down.

Assuming his contact would understand and adjust Ronnie gunned the bike's engine and peeled out, the knobby rear tire skidding in the soft sand and stones. He needed to see Mickey. He couldn't tell her what was coming without jeopardizing her. But if it went really South he might not be able to explain himself afterwards. He knew she could live without him. They had no kids to worry about and marriage always seemed like the Sherman tank in the room neither of them wanted to talk about. Ronnie shifted gears and pushed the motorcycle to its limits. The wind screaming in his ears helped to blow what should have, he knew, been serious considerations and calculations out of his mind. Why had he chosen the target he'd chosen, he wondered? Whenever the question reared its head he answered it with mountaineer George Mallory's quote about Everest.

"Because it's there."

17

Surf City

IT WAS ONLY A quick shower but Mickey felt immeasurably better. She pulled a new uniform blouse from the closet. Her summer uniform shorts looked clean and the pockets held all her essentials so she slipped them back on and cinched up the web belt with the brass buckle. Her new, shorter hairstyle was essentially no-maintenance but she brushed it anyway. She had stopped worrying about covering her bullet-nicked ear. When anyone asked, and she was surprised at how many people did, she simply told them the story of her rookie patrolwoman year. When she got to the part where the three little girls were shot the questioners' curiosity usually and immediately evaporated. She grabbed the cobalt blue-and-silver bottle of *Rive Gauche* perfume Loretta had given her at Christmas and dabbed some on. She still couldn't remember how to properly pronounce Yves St. Laurent. Mickey thought accentuating her femininity was going to be important when she sat down with the Dexters. She pulled on and buckled up her gunbelt, laughing at the thought that the hand-tooled leather holster had been Ronnie's notion of a romantic Christmas gift to her and that she had understood the sentiment. She slid the Smith & Wesson Model 59 pistol off the dresser and made sure the manual safety was engaged. Then she slipped it into the holster and snapped it up. She wanted *Mister* Dexter to understand that her femininity was still paired with the threat of lethal force. She really liked the new sidearm, a 9 mm double-action that had originally been designed for Navy commandos and demolition teams. It had a blued steel slide and nylon grips which, although not as pretty as the knurled wood ones, held up better in the salt air. Other than to check the sights and do some monthly target practice, she had yet to have to discharge with lethal intent - a fact for which she was grateful. Ronnie faithfully cleaned and oiled the weapon once a week for her, a ritual that dated back to the morning after their first night together.

Mickey walked to the kitchen and scribbled a note to him.

Fed Y
Call or come by PD
Long time no see - - -

She stuck it to the refrigerator with the watermelon slice magnet and headed out the door.

Paramount Air Service
Rio Grande, NJ

Brad wasn't sure how many advertising banners he'd hooked together and hung on the poles for the grapple but it seemed like at least a hundred. The heat, the work and the unavoidable inhalation of avgas fumes were making him woozy. So was the constant whine and buzz of the Lycoming engines. The tow cable on the banner advertising the latest Steel Pier concert looked slightly askew for some reason so Brad decided he would straighten it.

In the next instant he felt himself being hurled to the ground. Something heavy was right on top of him making it hard to breathe. He heard the roar of an airplane engine in close proximity and something whooshed by the side of his head. His face was in the dry, packed dirt and it took him a second to realize it was because a hand was pushing it there.

"Shit, white boy," said a voice close to his ear. "That was too damn close."

The pressure on the back of his skull eased up and he turned his head. A black face was an inch from his, eyes wide, a wicked smile curling on the cracked lips.

"Damn near took a ride, there, Paleface."

It was Paxton Flournoy, one of the senior pilots and one of the several black employees at Paramount.

Things were still moving in slow-motion. Brad watched as the banner he'd gone to adjust lifted off from the ground. Flournoy rolled off of him.

"Another second and Yates would have hooked you," he said. "And no guarantee he would have cut you loose, neither." Flournoy laughed.

Brad watched as Barry Yates' Piper Cub throttled up and climbed smoothly, the Steel Pier banner straightening out and then snapping behind it. "Shit, if not for the drag I doubt he would have known you was even along for the ride."

Flournoy got up, brushed himself off and extended a hand to Brad who was still trying to process what had just happened.

"Yeah. Shoot. Thanks, man," Brad said, struggling to get to his feet even with the tug from Flournoy. "I guess I just lost track of where I was."

Flournoy looked around. "I don't think anybody seen it," he said. "So as long as you OK let's not say anything. Mr. Tomalino, he finds out about this and he'll fire your white ass double-quick. That's a natural fact, Jack."

Brad brushed grass and dirt from his coveralls. "OK, yeah. Like I said, thanks, man."

"Don't thank me, thank God in his wisdom," Flournoy replied. "My engine sounded like it was missin' so I got Dumby Gumby takin' a look at it right now. Otherwise I wouldn't have been nowhere near here and you'd be," Flournoy pointed to the bright blue sky, "Up there."

The world was starting to come back into focus and the immediacy of the near-miss was slowly seeping in. "Holy shit," Brad said as the cobwebs cleared. "I mean, ho-lee shit."

"Yeah, you got that right," Flournoy answered. "You the dude say he don't agree with the war, aren't you?"

Brad hesitated. As the days had worn on he'd felt less inhibited about sharing his sentiments, but only to the other guys on the field crew. And Brad knew Flournoy's story. Gumby had told him. Flournoy had been in Vietnam. He'd flown something Gumby called Forward Air Control in a Cessna Skymaster. Brad knew the specs of every light plane in existence and their farming operation had actually looked at the civilian 337 Super Skymaster as a possible duster. Brad had been especially intrigued by the split tail and the front and rear propellers on the fuselage.

"I just think maybe it's gone on long enough is all," he replied, trying to strike a conciliatory tone now that he was face-to-face with a real veteran. "I just think enough people have died. If we don't say something – if we don't *do* something, it won't stop. Maybe ever."

Flournoy chuckled. "All wars eventually stop," he said, "but only for a while. World War II was nothin' but the continuation of World War I after intermission. Like a double feature at the Manahawkin Drive-In. Shit, might as well have run 'em right together. The U.S. is fightin' the same war the French fought and the French was fightin' the same war somebody else was fightin' before them. Thing is, it ain't nobody's war but the Vietnamese. But I guess ain't no use in havin' a military if you can't use it to shoot people and bomb shit, right?"

Brad got the sense he was not going to be lambasted for his political opinions as he had been expecting. "So, are you *against* the war, then?" he asked.

"I fought in the war, boy," Flournoy replied. "I saved air crews' asses and I brought down hellfire on enemy soldiers I had no personal quarrel with. I got shot down more times than I got laid. I ate snakes and bugs in the jungle 'til I got picked up. I did my job. But I come to realize there wasn't anything to win. You get what I mean? There wasn't no Hitler, no Stalin, no He-ro-he-toe to defeat. And Ho Chi Minh? Shit, he's like Robert E. Lee over there – you can't never beat a ghost. It's just politics now – and the politicians, man, they don't send white boys like you to get shot up. No, sir. They be sending the brothers like me. Long as rich white dudes are making money selling shit to the government they'll keep it going. But you crazy if you think you can stop it. You like a bug to them, boy. Squash you without givin' it a second thought."

They began walking toward the shed.

"So would you do anything to try to stop it?" Brad asked.

Flournoy spit on the ground. "I would rather channel my anger and my frustration into improving the situation for African-Americans in this country and this society," he replied. "That's my war now. And when it comes to that, best stay out of my way."

"But what about people who do things to try to stop the war?" Brad asked.

"That's they thing, boy. I got no quarrel. I help if I can and I wouldn't stand in nobody's way, that's all I'm sayin'. People, they will eventually forget about the war. But they ain't never gonna forget I'm black. You dig me? You plannin' a protest march or somethin'?"

"No," Brad said. He was concerned that maybe Flournoy knew more than he was letting on. "I don't think marches are going to do any good at this point. Nobody pays attention to a march."

"So then, what?" Flournoy replied. "You want to blow up a Post Office or a Marine Recruiting Station – you think that'll get their attention and then they'll say –'OK. Now we get it. War's over.'" He looked hard at Brad. "Let me tell you somethin'. War is only about one thing - hurtin' people. That's all it is. You hurt enough people, you win. You willing to hurt enough people to make your point? That's the question you need to be askin' yourself. If you're not, then just go back to your fancy college, screw as many white girls as humanly possible and shut the fuck up." Flournoy let out a big laugh.

"What did you think of the Skymaster?" Brad asked, switching gears.

"It ain't no plane," Flournoy said. "It is a magical being that lets you fly it. I grieved over every one that I got shot down in. Someday, I'm a get me a little airstrip of my own and I'll have one – Army surplus. Fly it just for the pure joy of flyin' it. That's when I'll know I've won."

Brad could hear Gumby banging wrenches and cursing.

"Are you planning a protest?" he asked Flournoy. The pilot looked at him.

"My fightin' days are behind me, Farm Boy," he replied. "Why don't we just leave it at that." He turned. "Gumby. I got time to do one more run. You got me ready to take off." The mechanic gave him a thumbs up. Flournoy walked away without another word.

Surf City

Mickey got out of the cruiser and approached the neat little bungalow. The crushed and bleached shells that stood in for grass in the front yard still had a few dandelions poking through but even they looked ready to give up the ghost in the heat and drought. A wooden sign on the front door, festooned with miniature life rings and braided boat line exclaimed "The Dexters Welcome You to the Beach!" She placed her palm on the hood of the car parked in the cement driveway. It was a new model Mercedes-Benz. The paint job was a cream color Mickey didn't think was even available on American cars. The hood was still warm. They hadn't been home long.

Mickey took a deep breath and approached the door. She looked for a knocker or a doorbell but saw neither. She paused, trying to decide how loud was too loud. It wasn't a raid, she thought to herself. She finally rapped firmly with her knuckles four times and waited.

She heard shuffling inside and then a face appeared in the four glass pizza-slice windows at head-level. Carlton Dexter, she assumed. The brass knob turned and the door swung inward.

"Can I help you, Officer?" Carlton asked.

"Chief, actually, Mr. Dexter," she replied. "Chief Mickey Cleary, Surf City Police Department. Are your wife and daughter at home?"

Carlton Dexter looked exhausted, Mickey thought.

"This is really not a good time," he said from behind the screen door.

"There's never really a good time, Mr. Dexter," Mickey replied. "I'm here to ask some questions of your wife and daughter and I thought it would be much better if I conducted that interview here in the comfort of your home than at the station. May I come in?"

Carlton did not move and appeared to be momentarily unsure of what to do.

"Is Betsy in some kind of trouble?"

Mickey exhaled sharply. "No, although I will need to speak with her about the incident with your neighbor boys."

"Well if she's not in trouble than I'm not sure what there is to talk about."

Mickey could not decide if he was still in some state of emotional shock or if he was just being an asshole.

"Mr. Dexter," she said. 'Mrs. Dexter, Regina, your wife, she held a gun in the back of one of our local shopkeepers earlier today. Were you not aware of this?"

Carlton looked befuddled. "A gun? I'd hardly call it a gun," he said. "A cap pistol maybe. A glorified toy is all it is. Are you sure this can't wait? We've all had a long day."

"Let me assure you it can't wait," Mickey said. She was starting to lose patience. "I understand this has been a long and also a difficult day for you and your family. But Regina threatened someone with what that someone believed to be a deadly firearm. I could be here to arrest her on an array of serious charges but I have chosen not to go that route just yet." Mickey put a hand on the butt of her gun for effect. "I am concerned about both Regina and Betsy. I have the matter of your wife's actions to consider but I also have the matter of the boys who Regina believes may have assaulted her."

"Have you found them? The degenerate boys and their scumbag parents I mean."

"Not yet but we will," Mickey replied. "Mr. Dexter, things will go a whole lot smoother if you invite me in and let me speak with your wife and daughter."

"Don't you need a court order for that? Or a writ or a warrant? Something."

"I could certainly get any of those but I don't need them if you invite me in."

Carlton Dexter looked like a man waking up from a dream. In what seemed like a heartbeat, his posture straightened and his facial expression hardened.

"Then I suggest you get them all," he said.

Mickey decided to give it one more try. "It won't take long to get a warrant and you won't be allowed to leave town before I have it, just so you know. But it will force me to have one of my deputies pick up your wife and Betsy in full view of your neighbors and take them down to the station for separate interviews in an unfamiliar and perhaps intimidating environment. Do you really want to put your daughter though that right now?"

Carlton's mouth twitched and Mickey could see the wheels turning.

"Do I need to have an attorney present?"

Mickey had anticipated the question. "It's certainly your choice," she replied. "But I'm willing to limit my questions to the incident involving your daughter and leaving your wife's armed hostage-taking for another time. If I were you I would consider that a rather generous offer under the circumstances."

Carlton's facial twitching subsided. He reached for the handle and pushed on the screen door. Mickey stepped back to let it swing out. He held it open for her and she stepped inside. The home smelled of lavender and cigar smoke. She followed Carlton toward the little living room where Regina and Betsy sat side-by-side on a gingham plaid loveseat.

"They didn't," Carlton said softly, turning his head back toward Mickey. "The doctors said they didn't, uh, *do* anything to Betsy. But it's still a crime right. They still go to prison so they can get fucked up the ass every day, right?"

Mickey let it slide. Under similar circumstances she knew her own father would have been prowling the streets, armed, dangerous and aiming for the testicles.

"We're going to investigate it as a crime for now," Mickey said. "Punishment will be up to the courts, not me."

"I know certain people," Carlton said as they neared Betsy and Regina. "I can handle this if you can't or if you won't."

Mickey leaned close to him. "I'm sure you do," she whispered. "Let me do my job and that won't be necessary."

Regina Dexter looked up pleadingly as Mickey approached. Mickey realized she probably thought she was about to be arrested. "Regina," Mickey said in a calm voice. "I need to ask Betsy some questions. And I'd like you to stay here with her while I do. Is that OK with you?"

Regina nodded.

"Betsy, is it OK with you if we talk with your mom right here?"

Betsy shook her head in assent. The two bore a striking resemblance despite their age difference, Mickey thought. And Betsy Dexter was clearly going to be a knockout. Mickey realized that what happened in the next few minutes would affect her for the rest of her life. She sat down in the chair next to the loveseat and slid it closer.

"I like your perfume," Betsy said. "What is it?"

"Rive Gauche," Mickey replied. "It was a gift from a good friend."

"It's by Yves St. Laurent," the girl answered, pronouncing it perfectly. "Mom says I can get it when I'm sixteen."

"What perfume do you wear now?" Mickey asked.

"Love's Baby Soft," Betsy said with a smile. "It's pink!"

"Yes it is," Mickey answered. "Are you feeling up to answering some questions about what you remember?"

The girl looked at Regina. "It's OK," her mother said.

"Sure," Betsy replied. "I guess so."

Mickey slipped out her pen and notebook. "Who's you favorite singer?" Mickey asked.

"David Cassidy," Betsy said without hesitation. "But I kind of like The Carpenters now, too. The girl one, Karen, she plays the drums. I read all about her in *Tiger Beat*."

"Was it the one with Davy Jones on the cover?"

Mickey had seen a copy of the teen gossip magazine in the rack by the register at Mary T's Notions, Lotions and Potions.

"No," Betsy said. "It had Donny Osmond, David Cassidy, Bobby Sherman and Laurie from The Partridge Family all on it."

"Hmmm, I haven't seen that one yet," Mickey replied. "Guess I'll have to keep an eye out for it." Now Mickey knew she needed to start asking the hard questions. The uncomfortable ones. She looked at the girl and tried to imagine how adolescent boys could possibly see anything beyond what Mickey saw. She was a child. A beautiful child but still a child. "Girl, you'll be a woman soon" popped into her head. For Regina and Carlton she was still their baby girl, mooning over pop heartthrobs but still sleeping every night with a beloved stuffed animal. She could understand their rage at even the hint of violation.

"I know certain people," Carlton had said.

What she had wanted to reply was, "Don't we all."

18

Surf City

CHARLIE HIGGINS WAS WATCHING with barely containable amusement as Dennis Dippolito did his best to be witty, charming, dashing, debonair as well as cool and laid back all at the same time. For the moment, he decided, Candy Catanzariti was buying it. Dip had his service pistol out on his desk. Charlie glanced to make sure the magazine was out. Dippolito was pointing out the firearms's various features. The Smith & Wesson Model 27 was a big, heavy gun which handled 0.357 Magnum cartridges. It had a five-inch barrel which, Charlie figured, probably outdid its owner's.

Dip started showing Candy the cartridges which were truly impressive. Charlie knew that the Dennis Dippolito who had come back to work after having his larynx crushed by Dickie Robichaux was a different person than the one who'd sat at the same desk two years earlier. It wasn't just the permanent rasp in his voice. Charlie saw a new bravado that he felt masked a deep core of fear and vulnerability. He'd been assigned to safeguard the little Vietnamese girl Bunny and he'd failed. Nobody blamed him, Charlie knew. Robichaux was a trained and experienced hand-to-hand killer. Dip never had a chance. The months in the hospital were not easy ones. He or Rick or Chief Mickey had visited him every day but when they welcomed him back to the station Charlie sensed the change. The Model 57 was a hand-held cannon and its makers proudly billed it as the most powerful handgun in the world. Charlie believed it would blow a perpetrator's head clean off if aimed properly. It was as if Dip was arming himself for Robichaux's return even though he knew Dickie had taken a flyer from the top of Old Barney rather than surrender to Mickey or the Army. Charlie always worried that a frightened cop was a dangerous cop and with the firepower Dip was holstering, the risks went up.

Charlie's reverie was broken by the ringing of Mickey's desk phone. He punched the blinking light below her line on his own phone and picked up. Dippolito was now letting Candy hold the weapon while he supported her ridiculously skinny forearm and wrist.

"OK. She's interviewing the young girl right now," Charlie said. "But I'm sure she'll be more than pleased. She or I will get back to you shortly. She should be pretty close to done. Yeah, Copy that *amigo*."

Dippolito was now standing behind Candy, his arms around hers, showing her how to level and sight the gun with both hands. Charlie decided he'd go out to his cruiser to make the call to his Chief.

▲▲▲

Mickey sat in the padded chair and looked at her notes. She probably had enough for at least statutory rape if she wanted. But the alleged perps were minors as well and she knew that the Juvie Court judge would be lenient as they were all first offenders from stable homes. The neighbor boy's father was a big-shot anesthesiologist at Misericordia Hospital and the mom was plugged in to Philly's society scene which meant receptions at the Peale Club and friends with money and power. She had them on aiding and abetting unlawful flight to avoid prosecution but the whole case was a house of cards and Mickey knew it. Betsy had not drunk any of the bargain basement liquor but rather had consumed at least half a bottle of Boone's Farm Strawberry Hill wine one of the boys had liberated from the parental cabinet. She fell asleep while they were watching a "That Girl" rerun. She woke up with her Maidenform bra pushed up to her shoulders and her panties around one ankle but had no memory of being touched anywhere. She said none of the boys had even tried to kiss her or feel her up.

It occurred to Mickey that the poor girl was probably assaulted far more heinously at the hospital than she was at her neighbor's house. Regina had made the unsettling revelation that not one but three young male doctors had done vaginal exams on Betsy and that they each seemed to spend an inordinate amount of time "poking around down there." With little to really glean from Betsy, Mickey had let her go off to her bedroom and she spent the last twenty minutes listening to Regina who seemed to have completely regained her composure.

"And the questions they were asking her," Regina said. She had made sure Carlton was out of earshot and she spoke barely above a whisper. "Insinuating that she must have teased them or led them on somehow and then freaked out afterward. Asking her what she was wearing or whether she had underwear on when she went with them. It was just, just, just...vile what they were suggesting. If Carlton had heard any of it he'd be in your jail right now for killing them." Mickey made notes of it all. It had the makings of a complete shit-show she realized. One where justice could not or would not be served, a young girl would be further and possibly irreparably traumatized if she wasn't already and where wealthy, connected parents would almost certainly take matters into their own hands with predictably disastrous results. Her head was beginning to hurt just imagining it.

"One of them wanted take a Polaroid," Regina was saying palpable horror. "Can you believe it? A fucking Polaroid for God's sake. I told him that if he tried I'd ram that camera so far up his ass he could pull the shutter with his teeth. They pretty much stopped talking to me after that."

"I imagine so," Mickey said. "Look. Once we've sorted this all out I promise I will pay a visit to the white coats. First things first, though."

"You arrest them, right? That's the first thing." Regina unsnapped a sequined clutch purse that held a pack of Vantage Menthols. She tapped out a cigarette and reached for the heavy lighter on the glass-top coffee table. Her hands were shaking, Mickey noticed.

"When we find them we can detain them," Mickey replied.

Regina fumbled with the silver lighter which was badly tarnished and in desperate need of a Blitz Cloth. "Can is different than will," she said before finally getting the wick to catch. A whiff of butane filled the air.

"There's a lot going on here, Regina," Mickey said. "And you're at the center of it, unfortunately."

"What does that mean?" Regina took a nervous puff.

"Look, right now you're the only one I can successfully charge with something that would stick. The docs, creepy and possibly perverted as they may be, found no signs of a sexual assault. You, on the other hand, held Little Willie Wanamaker at gunpoint in front of a crowd in his own store. He could decide to press charges. Anything from simple assault to attempted murder."

"Murder? It was a cap gun for Christ's sake. Besides, I'll cut his balls off if he does. Slowly. One at a time," Regina shot back.

"OK, fine," Mickey answered. "But hear me out. Let's say the ID's these boys had looked real enough to pass. Little Willie is technically off the hook. I can probably persuade him not to press charges and let it go as a heat-of-the-moment indiscretion. One that I, although not a mother but as a woman completely understand. So that solves Willie's problem and yours at the same time although you might have to buy your booze somewhere else for a while."

Regina continued to puff, quickly burning the cigarette down to nearly half its original length. She stubbed it out in an emerald-green glass ashtray and reached for another.

Mickey continued. "I can charge these boys. I can. But something tells when I do me there will be a Center City attorney in a khaki suit in my station within an hour walking them out and convincing them and their parents that they are the real victims here.. They call it lawyering up. Even if I could get the County Attorney to prosecute the case – which is not by any means guaranteed – your neighbors look like they have the resources to fight it and at least make it ugly for a long time. Plus, it raises the real possibility that Betsy would have to testify in open court about something she doesn't remember and which we don't have any hard evidence occurred. Trust me, you do not want that to happen."

"Are you shitting me? She woke up in a bedroom in their house with her bra all twisted around and her panties off. She might as well have been naked. What do you think occurred?" Regina's hands were shaking badly now. Mickey took the lighter from her.

"Regina," Mickey said, "It's not about what I think or you

think. It's about what we can prove if we have to."

"So what now? We just laugh it off and go back to having backyard barbecues with them? Pinochle nights or maybe family Scrabble tournaments. Sure – say, what's a four-letter word for what happened to Betsy – RAPE, oh and it's a Triple Word Score." Mickey leaned back in the chair.

"I'm not saying that, Regina. I'm not. I'm thinking we bring them in and use every trick I know short of charging them with a felony. We make the parents sweat, puke and pee their pants all at the same time. The boys will shit themselves the minute I swing the cell door shut. I'll tell them they are no longer welcome here or anywhere else on the Island and if they choose to stay we'll pursue sterner measures including publishing their names as Juvenile Sex Offenders."

Regina seemed to be listening now which Mickey thought was a small victory.

"Carlton knows people. And you know what kind of people I mean," Regina said.

"Yes. He told me as much. I know people as well. The people I know might know the people he knows. In fact, the people I know might *be* the people he knows. But that doesn't matter right now. It's a much smaller world than you realize, I'm afraid. And it's considerably more intertwined than you would believe."

"Tommy Santucci is a good friend of ours. *That* Tommy Santucci. The one in the papers all the time. You know who he works for. I know you do. He'll be here in a little while. Their beach house is-"

"About a block from mine," Mickey interjected. "I know all about him. And my advice to you and Carlton is to keep him out of this completely unless he's your personal attorney which I sincerely hope he is not."

"What do I tell Betsy?" Regina asked then. She was on the verge of tears. "What do I tell my baby girl?"

Mickey lit the Vantage for her, waited for Regina to exhale the blue smoke and answered.

"Regina, you have to tell her she's not a baby girl any more. She'll be a woman before you know it but she's not one yet. She's in-between. Tell her boys are stupid and selfish and think mostly with their dicks and because she's pretty they're going to start noticing her even if she's not ready to be noticed. You have to teach her how to handle that attention. You have to tell her that something really, really bad could have happened to her but as far as we know it didn't. You have to tell her it wasn't her fault. I'm sure she was thrilled that some older boys even paid attention to her. You remember what it's like. But you have to tell her she has something precious and she has to protect it. If you do this right, this will be a lesson learned and then tucked away, unless one of the dipshit boys decides to run for President someday. But if you go in with your guns blazing right now she could end up with a scar she'll carry with her forever."

Regina remained quiet.

"Just think about what I said," Mickey went on. "Right now your little girl needs her mom more than she needs anything else."

"What would your mom do?" Regina asked.

They question threw Mickey for a moment but she decided to answer it as honestly as possible.

"My mother, her name was Eileen. My mother committed suicide when I was about Betsy's age. I miss her every day and so many times I just have to wonder what she would have told me. I didn't have that and I never will. But Betsy does. She has you. And as much as you want to castrate Willie and these boys your job right now is to take care of Betsy. I'll do my best to take care of the rest."

"You're going to let them get away with it, aren't you?"

Mickey smiled. "That is exactly what I am not going to do, Regina," she said. "And five minutes after I leave here I think you'll believe me."

Mickey got up from the chair.

"Should we-" Regina paused

"Leave? No. But I'd stay close to home for a couple days. Maybe just the beach and take-out until I can get some things cleared up."

"But what if they come back?"

"Like I said," Mickey replied. "Give me five minutes." She tucked her notes and pen into her pocket and moved for the front door. Carlton came in from the kitchen, weaving slightly and smelling strongly of Scotch, and saw her out. He said nothing.

Mickey walked to the rear of the cruiser and popped the trunk. She rummaged in it for a few minutes and pulled out what she needed. She angled toward the locked and shuttered beach house next door to the Dexters. The square plastic and metal sign next to the the door said only "The Bretts" in neat block letters

Five minutes later a web of bright yellow "CRIME SCENE NO ENTRY BY ORDER OF POLICE" tape criss-crossed the dwelling's every portal. Mickey tossed the remainder of the roll back into the trunk and slammed it down. She could see Regina at the Dexter's front window mouthing "thank you." Mickey nodded and hopped into the Barracuda just as the radio crackled.

"SCPD Base to SCPD 1. Chief Cleary, you there?"

"Roger, Charlie," Mickey answered, microphone in her hand.

"We found them."

"Where?" Mickey asked.

"Rehoboth Beach. Rich has them all on ice. Awaiting further instructions."

"Copy that. Let me think about it on the ride back. ETA about ten minutes."

Mickey replaced the microphone and started the Barracuda's big 8-Cylinder engine. She revved the motor a couple of times. She knew she'd just told Charlie ten minutes but there was something she wanted to do first. She waited to let a big station wagon with little girls bouncing in the back seat and a couple bickering in the front seat pass by.

Then she slowly rolled out.

-19-

The Pine Barrens

STELLWAG WATCHED AS MIKE Garufi, the best bike mechanic in the Sons of Satan, deftly tapped the aluminum keg. A pitcher was handed up and Garufi manipulated the apparatus like a safecracker until the first of the sixty-four quarts of Miller issued fourth. The thinnest layer of foam floated at the top. Garufi inspected it and led the incantation they all knew:

"You buy f'in meat?" he said.

"You get f'in bone," the assembled members replied.

"You buy f'in land?" Garufi continued.

"You get f'in stone."

"You pour f'in beer?"

"You get fuckin' foam!" they all yelled.

"Fuckin' A, Sons," Garufi said, handing off the pitcher and taking another empty one. "Fuckin' A right."

Stellwag knew that Garufi had been a Navy commando in-country and had specialized in underwater demolition. He partied like a madman but when there was work to be done or an assignment to be handled, Garufi never let the club down and Stellwag's Electra Glide sounded the way it did due to Garufi's magic touch.

The LT couldn't remember when the group had been in a better overall frame of mind. The ball game they were playing tomorrow was the only explanation. They were all still soldiers at heart and finally they had a mission. Stellwag wasn't worried about hangovers this time. The clock on Dunn's plan didn't start winding until 1700 hours a day hence and even that gave them a generous time pad.

Haystacks got up and said he'd reveal details of the mission tomorrow so nobody needed to worry about anything tonight. Except maybe one thing, he added. On cue, Stellwag popped a red smoke grenade and the front door opened. Ten agreeable and generously remunerated ladies from Atlantic City sauntered in to wild cheering. Jimmy "Frisky" Filisky cranked up the music and the debauch began. Stellwag slipped out the side door and into the night. He cast an eye in the direction of the Druid's property but saw nothing. He laughed at the irony of the situation. What drew these men together were the shared and unshakeable horrors of the war they'd fought in – and soon they'd use the same training and skills that war had taught and honed to oppose it.

The gibbous moon was waxing and Stellwag took a moment to regard it and listen to the sounds of the nocturnal inhabitants of the Pine Barrens with four legs going about their business. Dunn was point on this and even Stellwag didn't know the true endgame. But Dunn had promised him none of them would do any time and he would take full responsibility when the shit hit the fan. Stellwag envied Dunn the strength of his convictions even if he didn't fully understand them. Ronnie Dunn acted like things that happened thousands of miles away in a steaming, stinking jungle and in a Fort Benning courtroom were somehow his fault. Stellwag didn't believe in penance but if Dunn needed absolution, he and the Sons were happy to help. He thought that Dunn had the Rolling Stones take on things backward – what he wanted was sympathy *from* the Devil. But the LT knew, even if his comrade Ronnie didn't, that the Devil had none to give.

Paramount Air Service
Rio Grande, NJ

Brad was surprised to see Paxton Flournoy in the banner shed. He was bending over something in the far corner where the aerial ads for the next morning's first run were lined up. In the waning daylight Flournoy was as much silhouette as man. He apparently sensed Brad's presence and turned around.

"Need a hand with something, Mr. Flournoy?" Brad asked.

Flournoy scraped his hands together. A small cloud of dust motes appeared, suspended in the fractured rays of sunlight sneaking between the shed's boards like tiny planets in a vast universe.

"Don't need nothin' from you, Farm Boy. You can go on home now," Flournoy said. "I heard Don Von say he's takin' you up in the trainer tomorrow."

"You mean Von Don?"

"I call him Don Von 'cause I swear that sumbitch gets his self laid about every night. I think maybe it's that little bit of German accent or maybe he just has a big ol' johnson. Last summer he was tappin' all three girls that made the banner letters – Mr. Tomalino about fit to kill him for that. So now I call him Don Von – like Don Juan, you dig?"

"Got it," Brad replied.

"Your pale ass got a girlfriend?" Flournoy asked. He took a step forward and emerged from the shadows.

"Yeah," Brad replied. "She works in Surf City. For the newspaper. She's eye-talian."

"Ih-talian," Flournoy said stressing the short opening vowel sound. "She be a spitfire then I bet. You can't tame no Italian girl. No sir. She a reporter?"

"Kind of," Brad said. "She does a lot of stuff around the office and they let her write a story once a week."

"What does she write about? Sports, politics? Sex and the single girl?" Flournoy arched his eyebrows. "White guys with small dicks?"

"Nah. She does stories like what's the secret ingredient in the hamburgers at Bill's Luncheonette. Or if you can really cramp up and die if you go swimming right after you eat."

"Can you?"

"Well, yeah but only if you eat like a five-course meal and then try to swim a mile offshore."

Flournoy laughed. "So, she's not exactly an investigative reporter then."

It was Brad's turn to laugh. "No. Besides, what's there to investigate? How much saltwater there really is in saltwater taffy?"

Flournoy began walking. "Maybe you tell her to keep her eyes open. That's what a good reporter does. Never know where that big story gonna come from. Maybe she writin' a story about you right now and your dumb ass don't even know it. Like what's a corn-fed motherfucker like you really doin' at the Jersey shore? Steamin' open your mail before you read it like they do in the movies."

Brad was sure that Flournoy was just messing with him but an uneasy feeling was starting to creep in.

"You best catch some Z's tonight and put a little something in your stomach 'fore you get here in the morning," Flournoy said. "Don Von, he probably thinkin' it'd be pretty funny if he was to get you to puke on the first barrel roll or loop-de-loop. I give you a little intel to help you out – he like to pretend that he's passed out and you be heading right for the top of the lighthouse fixin' to crash right into it. You want to earn some stripes you just sit there like you was on a Sunday drive. Kind of like playing chicken. Just don't tell him I told you or he'll rag my ass until Labor Day."

"OK," Brad answered. "Thanks for the heads-up."

"You planning on watchin' the fireworks?" Flournoy said.

That uneasy feeling inched closer to dread. Brad wondered just how much Flournoy was teasing him and how much he really knew about Brad's assignment.

"Which fireworks are you talking about?" Brad queried, trying to act as laid-back as possible.

"In case you haven't noticed, Minnie Mouse, it's still the 4th of July weekend in this here U.S of A. and we don't fly no banners at night. I'm talkin' 'bout the big fireworks show up the North end of the Island. Tomorrow night. You best be planning on takin' your girlfriend to it or I guarantee you won't be eating Italian later on. I always wanted to see them fireworks from the air but I'm afraid it might take me back to a different state of mind. I already been shot at by tracers and rockets – I really don't need to go through it again. Dig?"

"Dig," Brad said. It seemed that Flournoy was not going to leave until Brad did, so he turned and headed toward the patch of gravel where they all parked their cars. Flournoy's matte black Dodge Challenger and Candy's white Camaro were the only cars left. Brad thought to himself that getting his package in the morning might not be the best idea now since he was going to ask Candy to drive him to the airfield. When he got to the car he pulled out his wallet and dug until he found the multiply folded square of note paper with the phone number on it. The office would be locked so he'd have to use one of the New Jersey Bell Telephone booths that dotted Highway 9 at irregular intervals. He just hoped he could find the place in the dark.

30th Street Station
Philadelphia, PA

The big and newly installed split-flap Solari Board display clicked and clattered above her but after watching for five solid minutes Mary Kathleen Browne did not see anything that said Atlantic City. She put on her glasses. Unfolding the pages, she studied the minute print in the Train & Trolley Schedule she'd pulled from a dirty holder at the Information kiosk. She looked around to see if there were any other overhead boards she should be looking at but didn't see any. Barely intelligible announcements of trains and tracks, arrivals and departures and various behavioral admonitions echoed in the giant atrium. When she felt someone sit down next to her on the long and otherwise empty wooden bench she twisted her torso in the opposite direction.

"Can I help you navigate this mess?" a polite voice asked her. It sounded like an older man and the tone struck her as paternal. Her frustration at getting where she needed to go was now at the tipping point. She told herself "fuck it," straightened her shoulders and turned toward the source of the question.

A bit to her surprise it had come from an impeccably dressed gentlemen who she guessed was in his late forties if not yet fifty. He had silver hair with persisting strands of blonde, a strong jaw and a disarming smile. The blue blazer, khaki pants and button-down blue pinstripe shirt made her think he might an Amtrak supervisor.

"It can be very confusing if you're not used to it," he said.

Kathleen handed him the schedule.

"Where is it you wish to go?" he asked as he thumbed the creased and wrinkled paper.

"Atlantic City," Kathleen replied.

"Ahh, America's Playground," the man replied. "Business or pleasure? Wait, pleasure I assume."

"Yes, pleasure. I'm going to the beach."

"You're not from around here, I gather." He folded the schedule once and continued to peruse it.

"I am, actually," Kathleen lied. "I've just been away for some time."

"California?" the man asked. "Why do I think California?"

"No," Kathleen said with a laugh. "Definitely not California. If you don't surf they don't let you into California."

The man laughed and folded the schedule again.

"Nebraska?" he asked. "Just a long shot hunch. Plus it's almost exactly halfway between New Jersey and California. Of course, so is North Dakota."

The seemingly offhand geographical references were starting to unnerve her. Kathleen shifted and reached for her bag. She no longer thought he worked for the railroad.

"Atlantic City, you said?"

"Yes," Kathleen replied."My aunt lives on Long Beach Island but I'm sure there still aren't any trains that run all the way out to an island. She said Atlantic City would be the closest now and that I could get a bus from there." It was a risky gambit but experience had taught her the small details were what kept the cover story from blowing up.

"Indeed you could. Indeed you could. Your aunt, does she have a name?" the man asked. "I'm inquiring because I have a summer house not far from there."

He had a deep tan and Mary Kathleen thought maybe he just might be playing it straight.

"Fitzpatrick," Kathleen answered. "Rosemary Fitzpatrick."

"Ah, a daughter of Ireland. Or is that a married name."

"No," Kathleen answered. She noticed two men in dark suits loitering near them reading newspapers. "That's her name. She never married."

"A maiden aunt then. Very good. Well, I'm sure she must dote on you, having no daughter of her own."

"I have to use the Ladies' Room," Mary Kathleen said. "So if you'll excuse me."

"I'm an Irishman myself," the man said. "John is my name. Although most people call me J.J. You can feel free to call me that if you wish."

"Thank you, John, did you say? But I do really need to pee, if you'll excuse my French."

"I imagine you do," J.J. replied. "Sara, isn't it?"

"Excuse me?"

"Sara. That's your name, isn't it?"

"I'm afraid you must have me confused with someone else. My name is Ingrid. Ingrid Olafson. Now like I said I really do have to-"

"Oh, you're absolutely right. Sara was a couple of productions ago. Having a theatre background must be of great benefit. Roling and deroling, isn't that what they call it? Henrik Ibsen was your forte if I'm not mistaken."

Now Mary Kathleen Browne really did need to pee. And perhaps upchuck as well, she realized. The men with newspapers sidled closer. John or J.J. or whoever the hell he really was had the Train & Trolley Schedule folded back down to its original dimensions and was methodically creasing its edges.

"I am going to scream and tell the police who come running that you were trying to proposition me to give you a blow job in the Men's Room," Mary Kathleen said in an even tone.

"Go ahead," John said. "They know who *we* are. And *we* know who you are. And we also know who you were. What I'm most curious about is who you were planning to be and what you were planning to do."

"Curiosity is what killed the cat," Mary Kathleen replied with a sigh of resignation.

"That's only because the cat was careless with the C-4," John said with a smile. "Or should I say the Chanel Number Four. We really like that, I have to tell you. Our agency has pretty much adopted it. So, you've made a lasting contribution to the Intelligence Community lexicon. Not exactly something the everyday anarchist can claim." He laid the schedule on the bench beside him. "We're going to become good friends, Mary Kathleen. I know you think that's an absurd idea at the moment but you'll come to realize at some point that it's true. I see you someday back doing community theatre in a snowy Midwestern suburb with a couple of kids and a split-level ranch to look after, heading up bake sales, meals-on-wheels and trick-or-treat for UNICEF."

"You FBI guys, you always think you can turn us," Mary Kathleen replied. "I'd rather sit in solitary than live the life you just described."

"I'm sure you would – right now," John said. "Baby steps, Mary Kathleen. Baby steps. And as for the FBI, let me assure you that I share your sentiments completely. They wouldn't have found you even if you'd showed up on Pennsylvania Avenue knocking on their door with a sign around your neck and waving a gun. And as for turning you, that's just not our bag as your compatriots might say. We simply wish to show you a path that's in your ultimate best interests."

"*Va te faire foutre*," Mary Kathleen replied.

"Once again, I will pardon your French," John said. "It's completely understandable. You're under a tremendous amount of stress at the moment. And isn't it so often just the perfect retort – go fuck yourself? I actually used it myself in my last conversation with that dolt Hoover. Quite satisfying, I have to admit."

Mary Kathleen realized she was about to cry. She'd never failed on a mission before and now she had done so much more than fail. There would be no joy in Jingletown. They were ruthless, that she knew all too well. They would track her down and they would kill her, trussed up in a rat-infested loft somewhere or left to rot in a dumpster.

"You don't have to decide right now," John said in a soothing voice. "There's a train departing for the District in twenty minutes. You and I, accompanied by several well-dressed and heavily armed fellow commuters will be on it."

Mary Kathleen reached for her bag. "I still need to pee," she said.

A cleaning woman pushed her cart close to them. For a second Mary Kathleen mused that she was the prettiest, most well-groomed cleaning woman she had ever seen. Then the woman deftly slipped a handcuff over her wrist. The connected half was around her own. The ersatz housekeeper grabbed a "RESTROOM CLOSED FOR CLEANING" sign from the cart and motioned for Mary Kathleen to stand.

John stood with her.

"J.J. Durkin," he said. "Central Intelligence Agency. Agent Gann here will accompany you to relieve yourself. I should tell you now that she garnered top marks in both firearms and close-quarters confrontation. Let's just say Lethal is her middle name." Gann gave a confirmatory nod.

"What if I can't go with someone watching me?"

"Oh, gosh, got a bashful kidney as they say? Well, then I'm afraid it's going to be a very uncomfortable train ride to Washington." Agent Gann gave a discreet tug.

"We'll never be friends," Mary Kathleen said to Durkin. "I'm not going to help you. Ever."

Durkin chuckled. "On the contrary, Mary Kathleen. As Bogart says at the end of *Casablanca*, I think this is going to be the start of a beautiful friendship. And, just so you know, you're not the first of the usual suspects we've managed to round up."

A chill rippled through Mary Kathleen's entire being.

Then a trickle of urine ran down her leg.

20

Surf City

MICKEY DID NOT SEE the Royal Enfield motorcycle parked behind their bungalow and so was surprised when she heard noises coming from their bedroom. She didn't really believe anyone would be moronic enough to try to burglarize the Chief of Police's home in broad daylight but she dropped her hand to her holster anyway.

"That you, soldier boy?" she called.

"Out in a minute," Ronnie called back. She realized she hadn't heard the sound of his voice for nearly a day.

"You decent?" Mickey asked.

Ronnie emerged from the bedroom with a pink terrycloth towel cinched around his waist. "No more than usual," he said with a grin. "Where you been?"

"Me?" Mickey said. "Where've you been? I'm not the one enjoying a week's paid vacation."

"I tried to call you a couple times," Ronnie said.

"Must not'a tried very hard," Mickey replied.

"Maybe we should put a Police Band radio in the house. I'd at least know where to look for you."

Mickey unbuckled her gun belt and laid it on the counter. "Just what I need," she said, "This job to follow me home more than it already does." She went to the refrigerator and pulled open the door which made a sucking sound as the rubber seals parted. "Hey," she said, "Did you drink my last bottle of Tab?"

Ronnie tousled his hair with his right hand. "If I did I sure don't remember doing it," he said.

Mickey poked among the fridge's contents. "How was Sea Breeze?"

"It's pretty-"

"Oh wait, here it is," Mickey said. "OK. I'm dropping the charges."

"Good," Ronnie replied, "Because that was my best and only defense. And Sea Breeze was...um, Sea Breeze was interesting. I didn't even know it existed before today. And I was born down here." He peeked over her shoulder and into the foggy Frigidaire. "Hey, are you wearing perfume?" he asked.

Mickey took the Tab to the counter. She pulled the magnetic bottle opener from the side of the refrigerator and popped it open. "Yes, I'm wearing perfume. Rive Gauche, the pricey one Loretta gave me for Christmas."

"Something you want to tell me?" Ronnie asked. His left hand was on the rolled and tucked portion of the towel.

Mickey pondered the question and decided to wait. "Well, you were going to find out sooner or later, so, here it is." She took a long sip of the Tab. "Mayor Billy and I are having an affair, have been having an affair. I'm surprised it took you this long to find out, frankly."

Ronnie stared at the floor. "I know," he said. "I've known since the beginning."

"How?" Mickey asked.

"Well, this is awkward but you might as well hear it from me. Margaret and I have been doing the horizontal mambo for some time now."

"Margaret," Mickey said solemnly. "Let me get this straight. You've been doing Double D's mother?"

"And the mayor's trusted secretary. Who better to know what's really going on around here than her? Not to mention discreet."

"Isn't Margaret about sixty?"

"Sixty three. But you have to admit – that Maggie May, she still has it going on."

Mickey paused. She knew it was now a contest to see who would break first.

"Didn't know about the older woman thing. That's a surprise."

"Ever since I saw *The Graduate*. It was just kind of an awakening,

I guess."

"So that's why you're listening to the new Rod Stewart album all the time now," Mickey said.

"Yep," Ronnie replied. "I've been trying to tell you."

Mickey thought about her Carole King album and her conversation with Loretta at the lighthouse. She walked toward him.

"So what does Maggie May have that I don't?"

"Bifocals, for one thing," Ronnie said. Oh my, those big, round, beautiful…bifocals."

Mickey couldn't take it anymore and burst our laughing. Ronnie held out for only a few seconds longer. She pressed herself against him.

"I should get back to work."

"You really should," Ronnie said. He wrapped his arms around her.

"Are soldiers always at full attention?" she asked and pushed her hips forward.

Ronnie pushed his back.

"This didn't seem like the appropriate time for Parade Rest," he said.

"Oh, I completely agree," Mickey said and dropped her hands to his hipbones. "So now that we've both made sincere Acts of Confession do you think we can drop the um," she tugged on the rolled cinch in the towel, "pretenses?"

"Ma'am, yes ma'am," he said. The towel fell with one quick pull.

Mickey moved her hands front and center and put her lips to his ear. "The manual says you should discharge your gun regularly to avoid having it fail when you really need it."

"Uh huh," Ronnie half-said, half grunted. "I can see how that would be a good idea."

"Yes," Mickey said. She lowered her voice to a whisper and began walking forward, pushing him backwards as she went. "Yours has been in the holster for a while, right?" Her ministrations became slow and rhythmic.

"Uh huh," Ronnie said again. This time it was almost all a grunt.

"Well what do you say we make sure it's in proper working order? Are you up for that, soldier boy?"

They were almost to the bed.

"I am definitely up for that," he managed to groan. "I am fully up for that, in fact."

"Good," Mickey replied. "But I don't think only one of us should be out of uniform for this exercise, do you?"

"No, ma'am, I do not," Ronnie said. He arched back toward the bed. Mickey slowly released her grip and started unbuttoning her uniform blouse. Ronnie went to work on her belt and khaki shorts. In less than thirty seconds they were naked on the mattress.

"Where you been lately?" Mickey asked him as he kissed her neck. "I don't want you drifting away from me."

"I'm here now," he answered and eased himself on top of her.

The last thought Mickey had before she lost track of thinking anything was that she wasn't letting go of the rope.

▲▲▲

Charlie Higgins stood up when he heard the door open.

"Thought maybe you got-" He stopped speaking when he saw it was not Mickey who had entered but Davey Johnson, Ship Bottom's young Chief of Police.

"Did you see the Chief's – our Chief's cruiser out there when you parked?" Charlie asked him.

Davey took off his hat. His white-blonde hair was parted in the middle and a little longer, Charlie thought, than strict departmental regulations would probably recommend. Mickey had once joked that he looked like a Nordic version of Jackson Browne.

"No," Davey replied. "And I need to speak with her. Can you get her on the horn?"

"Believe me, I've been trying," Charlie said. "She was doing an interview with a possible victim but she finished that up and gave me an ETA of ten minutes. That was forty minutes ago."

"Just have Dip drive by her house and see if she's there," Davey said. "Or I can do it on my way back, I suppose."

"Dip's out on a call – along with Lois Lane, our PD's own personal newspaper reporter."

Davey gave him a funny look.

"Nice young girl from *The SandPaper*. S'posed to be tailing Chief Cleary for a story but Dip seems to have taken a special interest in her so she's out and about with him at the moment."

"She cute?" Davey asked.

"She's adorable," Charlie replied. "But with a fair dose of piss and vinegar, I'd have to say."

"That's not all bad," Davey said. "It seems like they used to say the same thing about Chief Cleary."

"Indeed they did," Charlie said. "Now is this something maybe I could help you with until she gets here?"

"Maybe you can," Davey answered. "In fact, maybe you can help in a way nobody else can."

Charlie looked perplexed. "What have you got?"

"An assault, a fairly bad one. Wait, did you say this girl works for the newspaper?"

"Yeah. The little folded one with all the ads and the local scuttlebutt. I think she's a summer intern or something."

"What's her name?"

"You aren't going to get into a fight with Dip over this, now are you?" Charlie said.

Davey shook him off. "No, seriously, what's her name?" He reached into his pocket, pulled out his leather-bound notebook and flipped it open, thumbing through several pages.

"Candace," Charlie said. "But she goes by Candy. Long Italian last name – sounds like a pizza or maybe one of those mushy desserts they seem to like."

Davey Johnson stopped at a page. "Begin with a C? Like cannoli?"

"I believe it does. What do you have?"

"This assault. The vic is a young Negro kid. Wait, did I say that right?"

"We would prefer you use Black or African-American these days but forget that for now. What's going on?"

"Young black kid," Davey answered. "Beat pretty badly. Probably by more than one guy. They left him at the foot of the causeway down in the weeds. Was probably there an hour before someone spotted him. The ambulance boys took him to Mainland Memorial over in the Point. Said they were talking about maybe having to transfer him to AC depending on how his X-Ray tests came back."

"What's this got to do with the girl?"

"Whoever stomped him took his wallet and any cash or other identification he might have been carrying so we don't have a name yet and he's not up to talking. They did find a note in his pocket, though." Davey flipped a page in his notebook. "Yep. Didn't have but a few scribbles on it but it did say 'Candy C. paper S. City'.

Sounds like it might be your Lois Lane to me."

"That it does," Charlie said. He sat back down in his chair and punched the radio button. "SCPD Base to SCPD 3. Dip, do you copy." When he released the Talk button only static returned. He tried it again three more times with the same result.

Davey looked at Charlie. "Would you be willing to talk to the kid?"

"Me? Why me?"

Davey gave him an exaggerated eye roll. "I don't know. Because you're Irish? Why the fuck do you think, Charlie?"

Charlie grimaced. "Black folk don't all know each other, Davey. You realize that right?"

"Hey now," Davey said. "Come on. This poor kid didn't get the shit kicked out of him by a band of marauding African-Americans. It was at least two, three, who knows, maybe more white motherfucking assholes that did this. Every face at that hospital is white or whiter than mine. What would you do? Shit, Charlie, if this kid were Chinese I'd be looking for someone named Hop Sing. Help me out here?"

"And you came looking for Chief Cleary because-"

"Because my first thought was that with her time on the North Philly streets she might have some, some, you know, insight. However, you just became my top draft pick. But we need to go before this kid, if he's even able to, before he signs himself out and disappears. Charlie, I guarantee the white trash that did this is still on the Island, probably drinking and shooting their mouths off about it right now. Just get me a head count and a description and I'll do the rest. And I'll do it with pleasure."

Charlie looked around the empty station house. Both his Chief and his junior deputy were MIA and now Davey wanted him to go AWOL. He thought about how all the local law officers had come screaming to his house in Beach Haven two years before when another group of race-baiting punks had showed up to threaten him. Davey had been one of the first to arrive.

"OK, let's roll," Charlie said almost jumping up from his seat."I'll take my cruiser and follow you. I'll keep trying Chief Cleary and Dip on the radio on the way."

"See you there, then," Davey said and started to turn.

"Hey, Chief Johnson," Charlie said.

"Yeah, Charlie."

"Just so we're clear. There is not a face on God's whole earth whiter than yours."

▲▲▲

Mickey was curled around Ronnie, her right leg slung over his right hip.

"How does it go again?"

Ronnie twisted his head off the pillow. "You know how it goes. This is my weapon, this is my Gun. One is for fighting, one is for fun."

"Just checking," Mickey said and bit him lightly on the shoulder. "Because that was definitely fun."

Ronnie let out a satisfied sigh. "I think that's an understatement. Hey, did I tell you Dr. Harman called?"

Mickey had to resist the urge to stiffen up. She took a quick breath and answered as calmly as she could.

"No, you didn't," Mickey said. "Although I'm sure you were going to before you got-"

"Waylaid?"

"Well, you're half right, anyway. What did she want?"

Ronnie turned toward her. "Just that the laboratory offices were closed until Tuesday so she didn't have any results. Her office, she said, would be open on Monday if you needed to see her. Make sense to you?"

"Yeah. I have to have a physical and some lab tests done every year according to my contract with the Borough. That's all. I'll stop by on Monday while all the shoobies are packing their trunks. If they don't leave on Sunday, that is. I think most people got today off for the holiday. That's why the fireworks are tomorrow night and not on the actual Fourth."

Mickey looked at her watch, the one item that had not been shed.

"I radioed Charlie I'd be there in ten minutes close to an hour ago. What should I tell him?"

"Tell him the truth."

"Can I say I got way laid?" Mickey asked.

"That would be the truth," Ronnie answered.

"What if I say I got way, way, way laid?"

"That would still be the truth," Ronnie said. "But like you always say, the simplest answer is usually the best."

"Then I'll just say I was de-laid and leave it at that." Ronnie laughed as she pushed herself away. "I better jump in the shower real quick," she said.

"Do anything to help you while you're hosing down?" Ronnie asked.

"Clean my gun, maybe?"

"Happy to return the favor," Ronnie chuckled. He wiggled to the opposite side of the bed.

Mickey shook her head. "Soldier boy," she said. "You are incorrigible."

"Ha," Ronnie shot back. "Incorrigible. I'm not so sure Charlie Higgins has been a good influence on you. You used to talk like a regular person."

"I still talk like a regular person," Mickey said as she headed for the bathroom. "Just a smarter regular person. Now go get to work on my weapon. The one that's not for fun."

"Copy that, Chief," Ronnie said and reached for his boxers.

21

Somewhere off Route 206
Hammonton, NJ

COWBOY BARSTOW DRANK HIS coffee and waited for the sound of rubber on gravel and the glare of headlights hitting his front window. He'd been studying up on "bloop gun" grenade launchers when he got the phone call pleading to change the merchandise pick up time yet again. Cowboy figured he was going to be up for a while anyway and although he was not a late sleeper, he could avoid the crack-of-dawn transaction. The bloop gun research was for a different customer who, to Cowboy's mild surprise, seemed to have already his own supply of grenades. Cowboy had four of the weapons in the bunker but the customer only wanted one. He was researching the fair market price. He knew all of the specs by heart.

As he was going to the kitchen to refill his mug he heard the sound of an engine approaching. The headlight beams swung with the arc of the vehicle's turning radius and cast revolving, fenestrated shadows that reminded Cowboy of the big aerial searchlights in old war movies.

Cowboy grabbed his Big Jim flashlight and tucked the Bauer Automatic 0.25 pistol into the holster sewn in his boot. He headed outside into the fading twilight. The small, easily concealable sidearm wasn't in commercial production yet but he'd gotten his hands on a prototype from the Michigan manufacturer by trading him for an out-of-production flamethrower. The thick canopy of his heavily wooded property effectively brought on night a full hour before sunset. Cowboy liked it that way.

He stood on the crumbling cement front step and pointed the flashlight at the car, a several-year old Chevy Camaro. Its white paint job reflected the Big Jim's light onto the gnarled trunks of the big oaks giving them the look of the ones in the Haunted Forest from *The Wizard of Oz*.

The Camaro slowed, the brake lights adding a blood-red component to the lightshow effect in the little grove. Cowboy approached the passenger-side door and tapped on the window. The unbelted driver reached across and rolled down the window half way. Cowboy motioned for him to complete the action and the window squeaked and shimmied into its pocket in the door. He shined the big light into the driver's face causing him to shield his eyes. Cowboy didn't see a weapon and when his eyes adjusted he was surprised at the youth of the customer.

"You sounded older on the phone," Cowboy said.

"Does my age matter?" the driver asked.

"Not really," Cowboy replied. "Maybe if school was in session I'd have second thoughts but no, it doesn't matter." Cowboy pulled up on the lock, opened the door and slid himself in. "I'll ride shotgun if you don't mind," he said. "We're headed for the barn. About a thousand yards up the path. You'll see it when we crest the hill. You bring the money?"

"You said an extra two hundred. Because I changed the time twice." the driver said. ""It's in the glove compartment."

"Just checking," Cowboy said. "Now, before we go you might be thinking that in the dead of night as it might as well be, you might be able to leave with both your merchandise and your money." He shone the light around the back seat and then in the driver's face again. "And maybe you could. You're bigger'n me. Probably stronger. Maybe you could do it. Not like I'm in a position to call the police, now is it?" Cowboy shifted in the bucket seat. "Nice car – rode hard and put away wet, though. You can tell. Yours?'

The driver shook his head and looked confused. Then he said, "It's my girlfriend's."

"Fair enough," Cowboy replied. "Reason I ask is, going back to the recent conversation, that if you weren't successful in neutralizing me then I would use a backhoe I own and dig a trench with a little ramp leading down into it. Then I would roll your girlfriend's car down the ramp and into the trench. Next I would back fill the trench and plant something over the top. I don't know, maybe sweet corn or Jersey tomatoes. Did I mention that you would be in the car when I rolled it in? Maybe you'd be dead but more'n likely you'd still be breathing. I like to leave the windows open so you can feel that dirt pouring in, like water rising around your neck. But trust me, downing's better."

"OK, I get it," the driver said. "I don't want trouble. We had a deal. I just want what I asked for. Do you want more money?" The kid looked petrified.

"Nah," Cowboy said. "I'm a fair judge of people. Let's head over to the barn so you can get on home to your girl. I imagine she's wonderin' where you are. She know anything about your little project?"

The kid put the car in gear and they rolled slowly forward. "No. Nothing. She's not a part of it."

"She's not the one from California then I take it?"

"No," the kid replied, "She's from here. From New Jersey, I mean."

"Then you have very generous West Coast patrons," Cowboy said. "Now, just out your window over there is my newest patch of sweet corn." He pointed to his left. "Didn't get the ground as level as I would've liked though. But that's OK. It'll compact down over time." He watched the kid grip the wheel until his knuckles went white.

Surf City

Mickey hung up the phone. She looked at Charlie who was drumming his fingers on his desktop. Candy was sitting on one of the cell bunks crying Dippolito was sitting next to her awkwardly trying to be of comfort.

"Davey says they're bird-dogging some possible shitheads, waiting for them to flash cash or use the kid's ID or something that would tie them to him."

"They beat that boy in broad daylight while carloads of tourists crossed the bridge twenty yards away," Charlie said. "You really think nobody saw that going on? But, nah, wasn't any of their business and they were missing out on beach time."

Mickey got up and went over to the open cell where Candy sat with Dippolito, She motioned for the deputy to excuse himself. "I won't be far," Dip said to Candy.

Mickey handed her a fresh personal pack of Kleenex. "They said he's going to be OK," she told the girl. "No fractures, no internal bleeding, just cuts, scrapes and a lot of bruises. Now I have to ask – your boyfriend, he couldn't have-"

Candy shook her head. "Even if he could he wouldn't," she said, her words mixing with sniffles. "He says he's a devoted pacifist. If I screwed the guy right in front of him I don't think he'd care. So, no, he didn't have anything to do with this."

"When was the last time you talked to him?" Mickey asked.

"This morning when he went to work."

"Which is where again?" Mickey probed.

"Paramount Air Service. It's way out in some little town in Cape May County. They're the ones who pull those big banners that fly over the beach all day."

"Right. Zaberer's and Dunes til Dawn?"

"Yeah, those," Candy replied. "He and the other guys he works with put them together and set them out so the planes can pick them up."

Mickey nodded. "OK. He ever make any remarks about black people or, you know, that kind of thing?"

Candy laughed. "Honestly Chief, I don't think Brad ever actually met a black person until he got to Grinnell. And no, he never said anything about anybody's race being a problem. Except maybe the Vietnamese?"

"He didn't like them?" Mickey asked.

"No, just the opposite in fact," Candy replied. "I think he'd rather be Vietnamese. He's always talking about how they suffer and how they're the ultimate casualties of the war. That's why he wants to stop it so badly. He said to me one time that if American citizens had to endure for an hour what the Vietnamese people have endured for decades the war would be over tomorrow at noon."

"Is he home from work yet?" Mickey asked. "Just in case we need to ask him anything."

"I don't think so," Candy said. Her sniffles had dried up along with her eyes. "This is the busiest weekend of the whole summer for them he said."

"OK," Mickey said and patted her on the knee. "I had to ask. Jealous boyfriend and all that. You understand?"

"I understand but you don't need to worry about Brad. I don't think he really cares enough about me to be jealous."

Mickey got up from the bunk just as Dippolito swooped back in.

▲▲▲

Diane Santucci was still steaming mad when Tommy came through the backdoor sliders.

"I know, I know," he said, holding up his hands in surrender.

"Fuck you, you know," Diane spat back. "You left me with the girls and the car to unpack after leaving me to pack it by myself this morning and get them all ready. So, like I said, fuck you, you know. You know shit."

Tommy pleaded his case, "Diane, come on. These are really extenuating circumstances."

She slammed a plastic tumbler on the kitchen table. "Save your crap for the courtroom, Tommy," she said. "You put someone else's family ahead of your own. Again." She opened the cupboard and pulled out a bottle of Dewar's Scotch."I'm sorry if something bad happened to Betsy. I really am. They have one daughter to worry about. You have four. Four. Can you even say their names and ages? Can you?" She poured three fingers of the Dewar's into the tumbler then went to the freezer for ice.

"Diane," Tommy said, "What was I supposed to do?"

She grabbed a handful of ice from the tray. Several stray cubes bit the tiled floor with a clatter. She plopped the ones in her hand into the tumbler and stirred it with her index finger. Then she took a drink.

"You were supposed to carry the suitcases in while I got the girls settled. You were supposed to help feed the baby. You were supposed to read them a story. You were supposed to help me unpack. You were supposed to go to the Acme so I didn't have to lug the kids and the bags in and out. Jesus, Tommy, quit acting like this is Day One of our life. For fuck's sake."

Diane sat down and took another gulp of the Scotch.

"OK, I'm sorry," Tommy said. "You're right about it all. Won't happen again."

Diane gave a derisive laugh. "Yes it will," she said. "You know it and I know it. It's this way because you like it this way. Stop kidding yourself."

Tommy grabbed a glass. "OK if I join you?"

"Sure," Diane replied. "Misery adores company."

He poured himself two fingers and sipped. "I don't think they raped her," he said. "Betsy. They might not have done anything but look. If it weren't for Regina's *molto pazzo* reaction we'd have a pretty strong chance of nailing the little perverts with something."

"Can you really threaten someone's life with a cap gun?" Diane asked, starting to come down from a rolling boil to a rapid simmer.

"We talked about this in the car. If the person threatened thinks it's a real gun, then it's the same as if it were a real gun. And a starter's pistol is not a cap gun. If you pulled one on a cop he - or she, given the town we're in - would shoot you first and ask questions after."

"How's Betsy?"

Tommy cocked his head. "She was passed out for whatever happened, if anything. So other than some general embarrassment and a tummy ache from the Boone's Farm I think she's OK."

"Tell me it wasn't the strawberry wine," Diane said.

"You guessed it," Tommy replied.

Diane made a face. "That stuff is vile. Yuck. Making and selling it should be the crime."

"Anyway," Tommy continued, "The Police Chief had been there already. Regina said she did a really good job with Betsy but she and Carlton are getting the strong sense that the little fuckers are going to get away with whatever they did, even if was only undress an unconscious female minor and gawk at her privates."

"Which means what?" Diane asked.

Tommy took a longer drink. "Which means Carlton is going to want something approaching justice no matter what."

"You can't be invol-"

"I told him that," Tommy said. "I made that very clear. But everybody and their brother's uncle has read *The Godfather* by now, including Carlton, so they and he all think it's some kind of new playbook. I told him he needed to focus on the family for the moment and we'd talk more this weekend."

Diane took a slug and poured herself another. "I don't want to hear Rusty Pandola's name even mentioned. Promise me that."

"Diane," Tommy said. "Rusty's a driver, a gofer, a guy who takes your shoes to get them shined one at a time."

"Right. And if Rusty Pandola is just a gofer then I am Tallulah Fucking Bankhead. Don't give me that shit."

Tommy didn't answer. They both heard the sound of footy pajamas approaching.

"Are you guys fighting?" their second oldest daughter Francesca asked.

"We are not fighting," Tommy answered her. "We're having a loud discussion. It's totally different than fighting."

"I want a story," Francesca said. "And a Yoo-Hoo"

"Yes to the story," Diane said. "No to the Yoo-Hoo. Daddy will read it to you."

"How about *Goodnight, Moon*, you like that one. Or *The Velveteen Rabbit?*"

Francesca shook her head. "*Little Red Riding Hood*," she said. "But the one from the real old storybook where they cut the wolf open at the end."

Diane arched her eyebrows. Tommy got up. As he passed Diane he bent to whisper in her ear. "If somebody tried to hurt her the first thing you'd do is ask for Rusty."

Diane picked up the tumbler, swirled the Scotch and the ice contained within and then drained it all in one swallow.

Outside Egg Harbor City, NJ

Brad knew he was on U.S. Route 30 and that he was heading in a generally southwesterly direction. He wanted to call Candy and let her know he was on his way back but he hadn't seen a phone booth in a while. He thought if he kept going he could get to what the locals now called "old" Highway 9. He didn't want any State Troopers snooping in his trunk so he would avoid the Garden State Parkway. He also knew that having long hair would be enough to get him pulled over. He'd made sure to check the headlamps, taillights, brake lights and turn signal before he left Hammonton.

Brad was beginning to think maybe he should just leave the car on the mainland side of the causeway bridge and thumb his way out of town. He had a wad of cash in his pocket, insurance against being stuck for more money at the exchange.

The whole plan had gone to shit, he realized. The funny little man in the cowboy hat looked at him like he was a moron when he asked how the little bombs exploded.

"They don't explode," he'd said and then went on to explain that Lazy Dog Bombs, that's what he said they were called, did their damage strictly by mass and velocity. The problem was their mass was so small that to attain anything near really damaging velocity they needed to be dropped from a few thousand feet in the air, not the few hundred the tow planes flew at. Brad had concealed the box of projectiles in the trunk under a blanket and some jumper cables. All but one, which was on the seat next to him.

As he neared a streetlight perched high on a telephone pole he picked it up and inspected it again. It looked like a little boy's toy. It was shaped to look like the bombs he saw dropping from B-17's on the TV show *12 O'Clock High* only in miniature. It was shaped like a missile and had four little tail fins so it would fall nose-first. The little man said if a plane dropped it from three thousand feet it would pierce armor and put hole in sold concrete nine inches deep. "You don't want to even imagine what it does to flesh and bone," the little man said. "If it landed atop your head it'd punch a hole in your skull and wouldn't stop until it came out your toes. And maybe not even then."

Brad knew the service ceiling on a Piper Cub or a Cessna was upwards of ten thousand feet so that wasn't the problem. His plan was to target a very small area but from anything more than several hundred feet he'd have no control and no accuracy, especially with offshore winds to contend with. When he thought that anything called a bomb must by definition explode it hadn't seemed much of a problem. But things had changed. He'd left the dispersal canister with the man after immediately realizing it would be of no use. When Brad had asked him what else he could use instead his only suggestion was, "I dunno. Maybe a big bucket."

He looked at the little "bomb" again. It fit neatly in the palm of his hand and was only about the length of his thumb. It felt like it weighed less than an ounce. Brad knew he had used a heavier sinker on fishing lures he'd dropped into Lake Minnetonka. But the little man assured him that even from low altitude there would be some destruction, damage and injury. He assumed those were Brad's objectives.

"I want people to know what it's like for the Vietnamese civilians every day of their lives." It was a good answer, he thought. "That's the message I'm trying to send."

The little man in the cowboy hat had just smiled. "Dump a bucket full of these and I suspect people will get your message," he'd said. And little else after that.

Brad set the Lazy Dog next to his leg. He had to get a decent night's sleep and he could not be late to the field in the morning. If Von Don didn't take him up first thing he'd have to figure out the dashboard, gauges and controls of an unfamiliar aircraft in the dark. He spied a phone booth in the far reach of the headlights and started to brake. There had been no follow-up messages to the Blessed Virgin in any of the target newspapers. The mission was still on. Sara or Ingrid or whatever her name really was had cautioned him about what happened to people who backed out. The dark haired woman, the one they called "the general," had said they'd try to have someone local to help him leave the country for a while but couldn't promise it.

"In the end," she'd told him, "We're all on our own. Deal with it."

Surf City

Candy was cleaning up the detritus and debris from their take-out dinner. Bill Kuriakos had been kind enough to deliver the small feast himself. He'd included more items than they'd ordered and hadn't charged them a penny.

"You don't have to do that," Mickey said. "We can mop up after ourselves. We're adults you know."

"Tell that to the guys at *The SandPaper*," Candy replied. "One of them went so far as to say he didn't pick up trash because he considered it WW. Women's Work."

"That would be a good title for your story on Chief Cleary," Charlie interjected from his desk.

Candy stopped. "Yeah – may be. I like that. Wait. How about this for the headline: Women's Work? Think Again! With a picture of the Chief with her gun drawn."

"Or putting the cuffs on somebody," Dippolito chimed in. "Yeah, that's a great idea,"

"Whoa, easy guys," Mickey said. "Let's not get ahead of ourselves. I'm not Calamity Jane, you know. And this is a PD, not a Wild West Show."

"Hard to see the difference last couple'a days," Charlie added

"What's our plan for the night, Chief Cleary?"

"I've been home, gotten a shower and now I've had supper so I'm fired up and ready to go. Charlie?"

"Not to mention getting unavoidably de-layed," Charlie said and winked. "Me, I'm all set. Christine is out of town at her mother's up in Blackwood until Thursday so I'd rather be around my comrades-in-arms than sitting in an empty house."

"Hows that going?" Dippolito asked. He turned to Candy. "Charlie and Chris are-"

"We are from different backgrounds," Charlie interrupted. "She tans well and I do not." Candy looked at him with interest. "And no, Miss Candace, you may not do a story on Long Beach Island's only mixed-race couple. You put that thought out of your head right now." He smiled broadly but Mickey and Dippolito understood he meant business.

"Candy?" Mickey asked. "Big plans with your boyfriend?"

"None that I know of," Candy replied. "I haven't heard from him all day. I would like to go home and get cleaned up if that's OK? I can come back later though, right?"

"I'd say the fact that you don't work here makes that OK," Mickey said with a smile."Doesn't the newspaper need you back?"

"Not 'til Monday," Candy answered. "I'm expanding the story to include what the whole PD has to deal with on the biggest summer weekend of the season. I think it could be really good."

"OK," Mickey said. "You're dismissed then." Candy began to gather up her belongings. "Dennis?" Mickey asked.

"I could use an hour Chief, if it's convenient. Get cleaned up, check in with the folks, you know." Mickey nodded. "I can drop Miss Catanzariti off on my way. I go right by Mary T's shop."

Mickey and Charlie exchanged a quick glance.

"Only if Miss Catanzariti agrees," Mickey said.

"Sure. That'd be great. Thank you, Dennis," Candy replied.

Dippolito waited and then followed the young girl out. When the door shut Charlie cleared his throat. "I see that bad moon rising Creedence Clearwater talks about," he said.

Mickey inhaled deeply then exhaled sharply. "They're young. It's hot and it's summer down the shore. At least they're both Italian. That's good, right?"

Charlie laughed. "Let's hope so." He pushed back from his desk. "I didn't want to get Miss Candy going again but I heard from Chief Johnson."

Mickey leaned forward.

"Did he?"

"He did," Charlie said. "Three of them. You'll love this. One of them tried to buy booze on the kid's ID. That young man has darker skin than mine."

"Well thank God for stupidly and arrogance," Mickey said. "Certainly makes our job easier. Let me guess – shitheads from South Philly again, right?"

"You are most definitely…wrong." Charlie paused. "Sorry. And you need to let up on South Philly. In know it's a rocky part of town but it's a workingman's part of town. Cut it some slack."

"OK," Mickey said with a shrug. "So who were they? Are they?"

"Three college kids from – ready? Haddonfield. Country clubbers. The things they teach in college I don't understand."

"Motive?" Mickey asked.

"Young Andrew made the mistake of telling them he was looking for a white girl. This, apparently, so deeply offended their delicate sensibilities that it provoked them to unconscionable violence."

"She thinks it's her fault," Mickey said.

"Yes, she does," Charlie replied.

"But It's not her fault," Mickey offered.

"No, it is not," Charlie answered. "But guilt is a gift that keeps on giving. How many times have you said Ronnie Dunn thinks the *My Lai* Massacre and basically the whole Vietnam War are his fault?"

"More than once," Mickey admitted.

"Some people just feel too much. You know?" Charlie rubbed his forehead. "They're full of compassion and they can actually feel the suffering of others. So they want to alleviate that suffering or they want to stop whoever or whatever is causing it. Which doesn't always turn out the way they think."

"Wrong things for the right reasons?"

"Chief Cleary, you are a wise woman. That's what WW should really stand for."

"How is it going with Christine? Now that it's just us."

Charlie interlaced his fingers on his lap. "Good. We've decided we're pioneers and all pioneers face hardships. I'm big and imposing and I carry a gun so she ends up taking the brunt of it. It's not fair but it's how things are. They say that someday couples of all kinds of mixtures will go completely unnoticed by society. But not yet. Christine has really good friends who support her – and me. This was a good weekend for her to feel some of that love."

"What do we do if Dip doesn't come back in an hour?" Mickey asked.

"I just hope Miss Candace's boyfriend is the pacifist she says he is. And that Dip can't get to that Magnum if he's not."

▲▲▲

It was dark when Brad Vreeland finally pulled in to Surf City. Traffic on Long Beach Boulevard was still only crawling but eventually he found a parking spot on a back street when someone fortuitously vacated it just as he approached. There was a police cruiser parked further up the block but Brad didn't see any activity anywhere near it. He checked the sidewalks for onlookers and the street for traffic. He waited for a couple of slow-moving cars to pass and then got out and walked around to the trunk. He fumbled with the key momentarily but slipped it and lifted it open. He looked at the contents from several angles and even in the unlikely event that Candy would open it he didn't see anything that would attract her attention. He decided that when she dropped him at the airfield in the morning his story would be that he'd picked up some hardware that Mr. Tomalino needed for the banners which would explain carrying the box from the trunk. He thought he could still salvage the spirit of the protest even if the details were different. It would still garner significant attention which was the prime objective. Whether or not Sara was there or not to coordinate it the movement would still claim responsibility and get the credit.

Brad closed the trunk. He walked to the narrow alley that separated Mary T's from the shops in the building next door. He began the climb up the outside wooden stairs. When he reached the tiny landing at the top he hesitated. The door was open and he heard voices inside. He pushed on the door and the voices became more distinct.

Too distinct.

He was certain for a few seconds that he was hallucinating. But he quickly came to grips with the fact that he was not and what he thought he imagined was happening was indeed actually happening.

The years of being told to he was "Minnesota-Nice" were being sorely tested. He kept his hand on the door feeling almost paralyzed. Then he opened it slowly and stepped inside. The moans and groans coming from the bedroom persisted. On the table he spied an unfamiliar shape. With one more step he saw it was a gun and holster.

He crept closer.

In the weak light from the streetlamp outside he could make out its details as his eyes slowly adjusted. It was not just a handgun. It was the biggest handgun he had ever seen. He moved a step closer and put his hand on it. The bedroom noise seemed to fade away and he developed a kind of tunnel vision. He slid the gun silently from the holster. It was ridiculously heavy. But it was manageable. And he could see something else.

It was loaded.

SATURDAY
JULY 3rd, 1971

-22-

Over Wharton State Forest, NJ
Heading SSE   Altitude 500 ft

IT WAS THE PART of the flight Paxton Flournoy liked best. Looking down over the dense green canopy and knowing that nothing lurked in there that wished him ill. In more than three hundred missions as a Forward Air Controller in Vietnam he'd been shot down eleven times, been rescued nine times and twice made his own way out of the jungle to safety. He had a bagful of medals, ribbons and commendations. His hearing was mildly diminished, the result of an RPG that hit the rear-mounted engine of his Cessna Skymaster over the *A Shau* Valley but other than that he had somehow escaped the war physically unscathed.

He also enjoyed occasionally being able to fly without the lead-weight drag of a tow banner. Of the ten summer pilots, Mr. Tomalino allowed only he, Yates and von Donnersmark the privilege of the occasional milk run. The sun was just cresting the eastern horizon and the soft light on the vast forest was almost mesmerizing but Flournoy's attention was on finding a suitable spot for a quick touch-and-go. He was looking for a tiny, one-runway asphalt strip just on the back edge of the vast Pine Barrens. He knew it was just south of Route 206 and short of U.S. Route

30, the White Horse Pike. There was some patchy ground fog but visibility was good.

Flournoy eased up on the throttle and the Super Cub gently descended. In the distance he could see the wide gray ribbon of the Atlantic City Expressway. The airfield windsock hung dejectedly straight down. Like a limp orange dick, Flournoy thought and laughed at the idea. Still descending, he executed two left turns. He was now facing the vast pine forest and the black strip came into view. The little municipal airfield had no tower, no lights and no attendants. It would almost certainly be completely deserted at this hour of the morning.

The package rested against the door where the right seat would normally be. The seat had been removed to reduce weight and drag when towing. Flournoy had rigged a doubled-up length of parachute cord to the door's handle. He also had a length of 2 x 6 lumber to push the door open once it was unlatched. The package was positioned so that when the door opened it would drop out as soon as the door aperture exceeded its width. The package was just large enough and heavy enough that he didn't want to try heaving it out the left-seat door. He could land if he had to but thought it was better if he didn't.

He worked the trim wheel and the flaps and eased up even further on the throttle. He saw a lone figure in the trees that ringed the strip and did a quick wing-tilt. The figure raised an arm and waved. Flournoy glided in. The wheels grazed the asphalt as he worked the door open. The package dropped out. Flournoy pushed the throttle and pulled back on the yoke. The little plane angled skyward and the door slammed shut with the slipstream. The tall pines loomed in front of him but the Lycoming radial engine's pistons roared their defiance and carried him up and over the tree-tops.

Once he leveled off, Flournoy executed two right turns, returning him to his original SSE heading. This would carry him over Hammonton, Millville and then over the bedroom community of Vineland. When he passed the Maurice River he would angle further south a few degrees. Then the sparkling blue-green water of the Delaware Bay would open up before him. Flournoy liked to buzz the squat little lighthouse that sat in the middle. It still had keepers on-station and sometimes they would sound the foghorn as a return gesture. Paramount had received a few "advisories" from the U.S. Lighthouse Service over the years that discouraged the practice but he knew they were only formalities. Flournoy was still amazed at how close he could get. Close enough to see clearly the expressions on the faces of the two working keepers who often stepped outside the lamp room to greet him. The light itself was a little over forty-five feet tall and so low enough that the wind wrapping around it didn't affect him on his close passes. Barnegat Light, he knew, was a different ballgame.

As the New Jersey coastline appeared before him he thought about his role in Ronnie Dunn's plan and what he'd said when Dunn asked him.

"You bet, brother. We all in this together."

Paramount Air Service
Rio Grande, NJ

Brad was not particularly good at acting dumb. But fortunately, he thought, Gerrit von Donnersmark was exceedingly good at being condescending. It took everything in Brad to appear interested and awed as they did the mandatory pre-flight inspection of the plane's exterior surfaces, propeller and engine.

"*Sehr gut,*" Von Don said finally after an interminable planeside lecture on the differences between flaps, rudders, stabilizers, trim tabs and ailerons. Brad's neck was sore from nodding. "Now we fly. You know the term *Luftwaffe*, yes?" Brad indicated that he did. "So you know what it means then?"

"It means Air Wing, I think. Like we say Air Force in America."

"Ah," Von Don said, "But see here you are wrong. Or half-wrong anyway. Yes, *luft* means air, like we say *luftballon*. Those little balloons you have at parties. But *waffe*, this is not wing or force. It means weapon. The plane, it is not just a plane with weapons, then. The plane *is* the weapon."

"You learn something every day," Brad replied with a smile.

"We go," Von Don said.

"Do we need parachutes?" Brad asked hoping he wasn't taking the stupid act one step too far.

Von Don burst out laughing. "We only fly the tow route today. A hundred meters of altitude at most. No time for a parachute to open. Don't worry, Farm Boy. I bring you back safe. You will live to *Fick deine Freundin* again. Your girl, *sie fickt gut* I bet." Brad shook his head in agreement pretending he had no idea what he'd just heard.

They clambered into the Piper Cub trainer. Again Brad feigned ignorance of how anything worked or where anything was. He put on a dumb look when Von Don handed him the pale green headset and microphone. "So we can talk and listen," he said pointing to himself. "I will talk and you will listen. I make a pilot out of you in two hours. You'll see." Brad gave him a thumbs up and watched him go through the pre-flight checklist. He noticed that Von Don missed one or two small things or did them in the wrong order but Brad tried to look like he was paying rapt attention. Glancing at his watch Brad saw it was just edging past six-thirty. The field and banner crew were expected to be ready to go at eight every morning. The pilots reported at nine and the first banner pick up was supposed to be no later than ten. Perhaps, Brad thought, last night had not been a "Don Von" night as von Donnersmark had gotten up much earlier than he needed to just to accommodate Brad. It also meant they could fly for more than an hour. Plenty of time for him to acquaint himself with this particular aircraft and its nuances, he knew.

As Von Don started their roll Brad tried to push the previous evening out of his mind. In less than eighteen hours none of it would matter anyway. He didn't even feel bad about Candy or the Negro kid.

Eventually, everybody got what they deserved he figured.

-23-

Central Intelligence Agency
Langley, VA

THEY WEREN'T LETTING HER sleep.

And it was working, she knew. Mary Kathleen Browne had long ago realized she was not cut out to be a soldier in the Revolution. A correspondent or a courier perhaps.

But not a soldier.

The conference room was small and well appointed. Like the waiting room of a law firm she had once interned at in Fargo. She didn't see any cameras or microphones or two-way mirrors like in the movies. The meal they brought her was warm and had come from a local Italian restaurant and even included a large helping of Tiramisu for dessert. She asked for Fresca and got it. There was no clock, though, and they'd relieved her of the pretty Speidel wristwatch her mother had given her at her high school graduation. The pairs of interrogators, if that's what they were called, were different every time. One was always a woman and sometimes both were. Sisterhood and solidarity she assumed is what they were going for. Maybe they thought they could get her to bond with them over discussions about Kotex and Summer's Eve.

They never asked direct questions. Never asked who she was meeting or what they were planning. It was like they already knew or like they really didn't care. And, she wondered, what had Durkin meant about the usual suspects? She got the movie reference right away. She hadn't seen a newspaper or looked at a television since she had left Chicago. Maybe it was all over. Maybe they had everyone, including the general.

Mary Kathleen realized, in retrospect, that she'd slipped up by mentioning Long Beach Island. A small detail was good but not an accurate one. Brad, the Blessed Virgin, was now all on his own. She wasn't sure he was really a soldier either. Had she made it she was going to give him the option of bailing out with her and going even further underground than the Weather Underground.

She wanted to take a shower. More than anything she wanted to wash her hair. The thought of having to do either in the presence of and perhaps cuffed to a female agent was not appealing but she knew she was ripening rapidly. She could hear nothing outside of the door or through the walls. A subtle form of sensory deprivation she figured. The lighting was subdued but it was still cold and fluorescent. At least they weren't piping in Muzak. Not yet anyway.

She decided she needed to do something self-assertive. There was nothing to break, nothing to damage. The chairs were so heavy she knew she couldn't possibly lift one. Likewise with the table. But she needed to do something before she herself became just another piece of the room's furniture.

Mary Kathleen Browne stood up and began taking off her clothes.

Surf City

Mickey was groggy and momentarily disoriented. It took her a few seconds to realize she was on one of the cell cots and not in her own bed. The smell of strong coffee was coming closer.

"Good morning, Chief Cleary," Charlie said. He held a steaming ceramic mug in his large hands.

Mickey swung her legs over and sat on the bunk rubbing her eyes.

"Five after seven," Charlie said before she could ask.

"Anything cooking?" Mickey queried.

"Bill is bringing over some eggs and bacon with a mess of toast. Otherwise it's been unusually quiet on my watch."

"Mmmmmh," Mickey said stretching her arms. She pushed herself up from the cot. "Where's Dip?"

"Cruising the loop as we speak," Charlie replied. "He is in quite a good mood, I have to say. Chipper almost."

"I bet," Mickey said. "Why does that song 'Angel of the Morning' come to mind?"

Charlie laughed. "Ah. Merilee Rush and the Turnabouts."

"Have we accounted for Candy and her boyfriend yet? They only thing I need to hit for the cycle is a crime of passion."

Charlie handed her the mug. "They're not on our Watch List so I really can't say. I'd send Dip to do a welfare check but-"

"Yeah, let's not do that," Mickey shot back and took a slug of the brew."Hey, that's really good."

"Miss Candace taught me the right way to do it so you can thank her."

"When she gets here I will," Mickey said. The radio lit up with a burst of static.

"SCPD 3 to Base. Copy?"

"I got it," Charlie said. He walked out of the cell and sat down at his desk. Mickey followed him and went to hers. "SCPD 3 this is Base. What's up, Deputy?"

"Has Candy – I mean, has Miss Catanzariti come in yet?"

"That's a negative," Charlie said. "Copy?"

"Copy that. SCPD3 Out."

Charlie glanced at Mickey. "I think she said something about having to take the boyfriend to work early this morning. That airfield in Cape May. She's probably on the road there or back."

"Probably," Mickey said mulling over the situation and its possible permutations.

"You can over-think it, if you don't mind me sharing my opinion," Charlie said.

"Dip say anything to you about last night?" Mickey asked.

"He did not," Charlie answered. "And I did not ask. But I'd venture a guess that he's pulling up outside Mary T's right about now. You want me to call off the law dog?"

Mickey pondered the question. "No. Let him check. It's probably not an issue. If anything happened it would have happened last night and we'd have heard about it by now."

"True," Charlie said. "Heard anymore from Rich?"

"He had them on a 24 hour hold," Mickey answered. "So we've got a few hours to maneuver yet. Let's check in with Davey and see what he's doing with his country club perps and if he's heard any more on how young Andrew is recovering." She took another healthy gulp of the coffee. "I'm going to go accidentally roll by Mary T's." She got up and patted her pockets for her keys.

"Notions, lotions or potions?" Charlie asked, smiling.

"I'll see if she has any Love Potion Number Nine. My bet is she's fresh out."

Over Long Beach Island, NJ
Heading NNE   Altitude 200 ft

Brad had the cockpit controls and instrument layout memorized in the first fifteen minutes. Now he was learning the landmarks. They had made a beeline from the airfield straight out over Delaware Bay. Von Don had pointed out a small lighthouse in the mid-channel which he said was named after a ship that shoaled there once. They turned left twice and then followed the coastline north starting at Cape May. Beneath them passed the towns Brad had memorized from the map in order. Wildwood, Sea Isle City, Ocean City and the sprawl of Atlantic City reaching its long finger out into the Atlantic. Brad could see clearly the gantry tower of the Diving Bell and the tower from where the Diving Horse took its plunge. He made note of the gap north of Atlantic City and the southern tip of Long Beach Island.

"It's very pretty at night if you ever get to see it from up here," Von Don said into the headset. "Like a long string of Christmas lights." Brad did not doubt him.

When they passed over the causeway bridge Brad asked, "Do you do your turnaround at the lighthouse?"

Von Don shook his head. "We'll go farther north. I'll show you."

The conditions were CAVU Brad thought - Ceiling And Visibility Unlimited. The last weather forecast he'd seen had no clouds and no precipitation for the next twenty-four hours. Winds aloft would be his only worry.

"There. You see?" Von Don asked. "The lighthouse. Can't miss it, really, can you?"

"Not even if you tried," Brad replied.

"You have to stay at least hundred meters from it," Von Don said. "Otherwise you get a nasty letter from the Lighthouse Service and the U.S. Park Service. Mr. Tomalino, he gets very angry when he gets those letters."

"Got it," Brad said.

"You should learn to fly," Von Don went on. "Nothing in the world like being up here. You can transfer your college to Purdue. That's what I did. I am going to fly for a living. Even Yates knows he can't play the basketball forever. "

"I'll think about it," Brad replied.

They gave Barnegat Light a wide berth but still it was a beautiful sight. The Cub rocked and rolled as they made their pass."

"Turbulence, yes, always," Von Don said as he gripped the yoke. "From the wind wrapping around the structure on both sides. It is worse the closer you are. Another reason to go wide if you can."

They passed the light and the tip of Long Beach Island. The sun glinted off the glass of its lamp room. Brad pointed down.

"What's that?"

"Island Beach," Von Don replied. "It's a State Park. No houses allowed. Only the Governor has one. Not many people on the beach. We fly banners over it just because it's there." Brad noticed a few bodies walking on the long strand. Looking for shells he assumed.

"That's Toms River below," Von Don said. "Now we turn around."

Two more left turns perfectly executed took them south again. They flew directly over Highway 9 which despite the hour was still heavy with traffic. Brad closed his eyes.

The return trip didn't really interest him.

Surf City

Dippolito was descending the outside stairs in the alley next to Mary T's when Mickey rolled up. He gave her a quick wave and walked over.

"Is there a problem, Officer?" she said, parroting every traffic stop in police history.

"That's funny, Chief, but no, I don't think so."

"Candy sleeping late I presume?"

"I guess," Dippolito replied with a shrug. "No answer when I knocked and I don't see her car but I know her boyfriend uses it to get to his job out in Cape May somewhere."

"Charlie said she may have driven him to work this morning," Mickey replied.

A frown crossed the deputy's face. "I guess that's a memo I didn't get." He seemed to have a quick conversation in his head and then said, "But that would explain the situation. I might just check back later."

"OK," Mickey answered. "Dennis?"

"Yes, Chief?"

"While we're on the subject of situations." She paused. "I assume this, um, situation isn't going to be a problem. Am I correct in that assumption?"

"Not sure I foll-"

"Dennis," Mickey continued. "Now is not the time for blanket denials or pleading the Fifth. What you do and who you do it with is your business. I don't have to tell you this is a small town. She's a very nice girl and she is smarter than I will ever be. Just be discreet and exercise exquisitely good judgment here. You have a reputation and so does she. And cuckolded boyfriends are like bombs just waiting to explode. It becomes especially worrisome when one of you has a .357 Magnum on his hip. I'm talking about protecting yourself as much as I am protecting her. And speaking of protection."

"I got it covered, Chief," Dippolito replied. "Literally...covered."

Mickey laughed and shifted the Barracuda into Drive. "One more thing."

Dippolito let out an exaggerated sigh. "Yes, Chief."

"First time she calls you snookums in my shop consider your ass terminated. On the spot."

Now it was Dippolito's turn to laugh. "Copy that, Chief Cleary. Message received loud and clear."

Mickey eased up on the brake and rolled forward. She did not have time to be a Den Mother and she certainly hoped Candy Catanzariti was on her way to or from Cape May. She had never met "the boyfriend" as Candy referred to him but he didn't sound like the hot-tempered type. More like the opposite. Mickey didn't know whether that was better or worse for Dippolito. That thought was interrupted by the radio.

"SCPD Base to SCPD1. Chief, do you copy?"

"SCPD1. Copy. What do you have, Charlie?"

"Stop by the shop when it's convenient. Copy?

"Copy that. ETA five minutes." Mickey knew that "when it's convenient" really meant "as soon as possible." She was surprised when the radio squawked again.

"Is that five minutes five minutes or a de-layed five minutes?"

"SCPD1 out," was all she said before switching on the light bar and speeding off down Long Beach Boulevard.

Paramount Air Service
Rio Grande, NJ

The barrel roll and the death dive had both come on the return flight. Brad had been lightly dozing and so his shock and his yelp was at least partly real when it happened. Von Don had even tried the old instructor's trick of shutting off the engine in flight and pretending he was unsure of how to restart it. Brad played along as best he could having pulled the same trick a dozen times on unsuspecting ride-alongs. He did not throw up which seemed to disappoint Von Don immensely.

Back at the field they were met by Barry Yates who had come in early.

"No puke to clean up?" he asked. Brad shook his head. "Damn, Von Don. You must be losing your touch."

"*Ach,*" Von Don said. "He still screamed like a little girl. It was pitiful to hear. Pitiful."

Brad shrugged. "Guilty," he said. "I figured it was payback for losing World War II. And also for losing World War I."

Yates belly-laughed at that. Von Don gave him the finger and walked off towards the pilots' lounge. "Big day today," Yates said to him. "Hope you ate your Wheaties this morning and got laid last night. You won't be worth squat when today is over."

"Hey, Yates," Brad said. He had to tilt his head back to catch the big man's eye. "You almost hooked me with the grapple yesterday."

"Yeah, well," Yates replied with a smile. "Guess I'll just have to try harder next time." Then he followed after Von Don.

Brad began walking toward the banner shed. He'd put the box from the Camaro's trunk in a far corner and thrown some burlap over it. In the darkness it had all but disappeared. He could hear Quinlan and Anderson jawing at each other already – one of them was loudly accusing the other of being a "homo." He knew they'd start tag-teaming him the minute they saw him.

"Hey, homos," he said when he rounded the corner deciding

to get his shot in while he could.

They both tackled him.

Surf City

"When?" Mickey said into the phone. Rich Rodriguez was on the other end of the line. "OK, Rich, *muchas gracias* for trying. I'll call you back later." She hung up and looked over at Charlie. "They walked."

A thoughtful look passed over Charlie's face. "How did they manage that?"

"Same way I was afraid they would if we'd picked them up," Mickey replied. "The family attorney drove all the way from Chestnut Hill and got a judge's order to release them on their own recognizance."

"He play the not-a-flight-risk card?" Charlie asked.

"She," Mickey corrected. "And yes, she played that card along with several others, including false imprisonment. There wasn't anything Rich could really do. She walked in holding a Full House."

"Sounds more like a stacked deck to me."

"Shit," Mickey said. "Now I have to go explain to the Dexter's why their daughter's molesters are probably having Sno-Cones and Mister Softee while we speak."

"Not your fault," Charlie said.

"I know," Mickey said. "But now I think there's a very high likelihood the Dexter's are going to consider pursuing extra-judicial avenues of recompense."

"You really think they can find somebody to whack three teenagers and a white suburban couple?"

"No. Probably not," Mickey replied.

"Dip said you yellow-taped their house."

"That I did. Don't want them pulling up in the driveway and us having to respond to a domestic disturbance with shots fired."

"Starter pistol won't do much damage," Charlie joked.

"The dad's a hunter," Mickey said. "He's got more guns stashed somewhere."

"They don't look like the murder-for-hire type."

"Betsy's their only child. Their baby girl. This has just

completely unhinged them, I'm afraid," Mickey said.

"I can halfway understand that," Charlie replied. "But it's not like they can take out an ad in *The SandPaper* for a hit man."

"It gets worse," Mickey said. "Their friend and neighbor up on the Main Line *and* here in the borough is none other than Tommy Santucci."

"A mob lawyer," Charlie said and stroked his chin. "The plot thickens."

"The girl's dad told me he 'knows people' who can handle this so it's already crossed his mind."

"Maybe their lady lawyer will advise the perps and the parents that other parts of the country have both excellent schools and tax advantages," Charlie opined.

"I don't know that I'll have the chance but I might suggest that," Mickey replied. She tapped a tooth marked pencil on her desk as a hundred thoughts whirled in her head.

"You heard from Patsy?" Charlie asked.

"What? Oh, uh, no, I haven't. I figure he and the dog must be having a good time down in Fake Mexico. No news is good news, right?"

"Right," Charlie said. "And still nothing from Bunny or Yvette?"

"Nope," Mickey replied. "Radio silence. As soon as we put this weekend behind us they're first on my list to track down."

The phone rang and Charlie picked it up. After a few seconds of listening he said, "She's out on an urgent call right now. An armed robbery in progress, actually. But if you'll give me your name and a phone number I'll have her get back to you when it's convenient for her." He pulled a Bic from his holder and began writing on his blotter. "Uh huh. Yes. Yes, I'm sure it's of the utmost importance. I'll relay that to the Chief when she returns. Yes, thank you. My name? Certainly. Higgins. Deputy Charles Higgins. Yes. Yes. I understand. We will." He dropped the receiver back in the cradle. "One guess," he said looking at Mickey.

"Lady lawyer."

"Bingo," Charlie said. "Want to guess her name?"

"Are we playing Sympathy for the Devil now? I can't even-"

"Alex," Charlie answered looking down at his scribbles. "Short for Alexandra. Alexandra A. Hasapopoulos. Esquire." He exhaled slowly. "Hundred bucks says the A stands for Athena. But,

I guess if you want to play a man's game you need a man's name."

"Like Mickey?"

"Yeah," Charlie said. "Like Mickey."

24

The Pine Barrens

STELLWAG'S REMARKS WERE BRIEF. He yielded the briefing to Everett "Haystacks" Calhoun whom Stellwag hoped might someday succeed him if he were to ever consider leaving the club. Calhoun, despite his bulk and his penchant for torrents of profanity was all business. He stood in front of a large US Geological Survey map of Long Beach Island Ronnie Dunn had procured from the Forest Fire Service.

"Before Private Dunn talks I want to say that it's been a while for most of us since we've been on any kind of real mission. I don't think any of us will have any trouble remembering that it's still about doin' your job and not lettin' your buddies down while they do theirs. There's nobody in this room ain't served at least one tour, most of us two or more. This ballgame might be our last for a while so let's make it count."

Instead of whoops and hollers there was a ripple of murmuring assent.

"Y'all know Ronnie," Calhoun continued. "Y'all know his story. And ya'll know all he wants is for the war to end as soon as possible so more guys like us don't haf'ta see what we seen, don't haf'ta do what we was asked to do and don't haf'ta come back they way we came back. I ain't gonna try'n tell y'all that hearts and minds bullshit they fed us. This ain't about hearts and minds. This here is about evr'y regular American feelin' gut-sick 'bout what their government's doin' in Vietnam. Feelin' ashamed every time another box comes off the plane at Dover. Feelin' pissed off every time some asshole says peace with honor. It wadn't our war but still we fought it. Honorably, too. So's if we'all are against it now then every damn person in the country should be against it now. So let's do this one right and maybe people'll finally wake their dumb asses up and notice. Some are gonna say what we done is wrong. Well, you can tell'em we seen shit that's wrong. So fuck'em. This is all about right."

Again, Stellwag observed, no cheering or whoops. They all seemed to have reverted to what was drilled into them years before.

"Last thing a'fore Ronnie gets up here," Calhoun said, "He's the one willing to take all the risk here. Our job is to get him where he needs to get to. Ronnie?"

Ronnie walked to the front of the group. "How many guys were in-theatre during Tet?" he asked. A dozen hands went up. "Well, this is our version of Tet, I guess. We're using the biggest holiday of the year to make our point. Maybe the one day when everyone's guard is down. When they feel like whatever else is going on in the world it's not their problem. Tonight is just about telling them that's not true. There will be no civilian injuries if this goes off as planned. If executed properly there will be a lot of confusion and by midnight you all can be back here drinking beer and congratulating yourselves. I might, like Ricky Ricardo says, have a little splainin' to do but that's on me not you. I appreciate all the help and support from the LT here as well as you men. I'll turn the briefing back over to Everett."

Ronnie nodded to Stellwag and Calhoun, who stood front and center again.

"OK, listen up," the big man said. "Won't be saying this more'n once. Rally point is Mud City, three klicks west of the end of the causeway bridge in Ship Bottom at twenty-one hundred hours. Forbes and Slivka – you and your team will create the diversion in Long Beach a half-klick from the main intersection. Now Long Beach Boulevard is kind'a like the Ho Chi Minh Trail so we need you to jam it up pretty good to keep any cherry tops from the south from responding. Garufi and Filisky, you're the offshore diversion in Ship Bottom. You ready to go?"

Mike Garufi stood up. "We stole one of those little fishing boats from Mystic Islands. I'll have it rigged to go off as planned and we'll wade ashore and then fade into the crowd. From there we'll make our way to Long Beach and rally with Larry and Mike." Calhoun tapped his chest. "Mizener and Homan – you have Surf City covered?"

They both gave a thumbs up. "OK. Myself, the LT, Earl and Greg will ride together. We'll push north using either the Boulevard or the beach until we reach the objective and rendezvous with Ronnie, here. Wait until you see the white parachute flare and then commence your assignment. Now there's prob'ly gonna be a lot of people shootin' off their own little-dick fireworks before the big show s'posed to start. Don't get fooled or rambunctious and go premature ejaculatin'. Y'all know what a parachute flare looks like – ain't no tourists gonna be sendin' one of them up. That's the only signal you're gonna get. We'll secure the objective and Dunn will complete the mission. Any questions?"

There were none.

"Dismissed, then, you ugly sons of bitches." Calhoun said. The Sons of Satan milled around, exchanging bear hugs and handshakes with Ronnie Dunn. Stellwag greeted him last.

"Feels good to saddle up again, doesn't it?"

"I forgot how much I missed it," Ronnie replied. "I probably won't be here for the de-brief."

"We'll have one for you."

"Fuckin' A," said Ronnie.

"Fuckin A fuckin'A," Stellwag replied.

They tapped fists and Dunn was gone.

Surf City

Candy Catanzariti waltzed through the station house door at exactly four-thirty.

Mickey, Charlie and Dip all looked at her.

"What?" she said.

"Just wondered if we were going to be graced with your presence today," Charlie finally asked.

"Chief Cleary reminded me that I really don't work here," Candy replied, "So I guess that means I can't really be late, right?"

"I guess it does," said Mickey. "We just wanted to make sure you were alright."

"Why wouldn't I be alright?" Candy asked and went to check the coffee urn.

Mickey noticed that Dippolito appeared a little tentative on joining the conversation. "No reason," Mickey said. "No reason at all."

Candy was wearing jean shorts and a white sleeveless blouse. She brushed by Dippolito. "Deputy," she said.

"Miss Catanzariti," Dip replied.

Mickey thought they were both really bad at acting nonchalant. "Uh, we know you don't work here," Mickey said, "but we set you up with a little desk over in the corner. So you wouldn't have to lug your stuff every time. Charlie found an old Royal portable typewriter in the storage closet. It's in that blue plastic case. Probably needs a new ribbon, though."

"Well aren't you guys just a girl's best friends," Candy said.

"It was Deputy Dippolito's idea," Charlie said even though Mickey knew he had done it.

"Well, thank you Den...Deputy," Candy said.

Really, really bad at nonchalant, Mickey thought again.

"Did I miss anything?"

"Let me see. Two murders, an arson, a kidnapping, three armed robberies, and a bomb threat," Charlie joked. "So no, pretty much just an average day around here so far. Oh, and some pirates seized the *Lucy Evelyn* and killed several tourists but that's Beach Haven's problem."

Candy laughed and surveyed her little workspace. "Can I use a pillow from one of the cells for a chair pad?" she asked looking at the battered but serviceable straight-backed wooden one they'd found for her.

"Sure," Mickey said. "Make yourself and your backside right at home." She reached for her hat. "I have to make a quick visit to the Dexters and one of neighbors before it gets too late and we get busy. I won't be long."

"Can I ride along?" Candy chirped.

"Ah, not on this one. Bit of a delicate situation. Probably best if I go alone." Mickey said. "Maybe you could go with Charlie on his next call. Get a, you know, perspective how each of us deals with what we see."

"I also have a quick errand to run," Charlie said, "but when I get back I'd welcome your company, young lady. I'll only be about twenty minutes."

Mickey glanced at Dippolito who started straight at the papers on his desk.

"I'll walk out with you, Chief," Charlie rose from his chair. Mickey gave him an *are you serious?* look and grabbed her keys.

"Hey," Candy said, "Wait." She fished in the pocket of her jean shorts and withdrew a small object. "You said bomb threat and it reminded me. Any of you guys know what this is?"

She held out her palm as they crowded around her.

"May I?" Charlie asked and plucked it from her. He turned it in his hand.

"I found it in my car this morning when I was on my way back from taking the boyfriend to work," Candy added." Crimanee, that place is in the absolute middle of nowhere. I got lost coming back. Ended up at some tomato farm."

"Looks like a toy," Dip said.

"It's too heavy to be a toy," Charlie said. He grabbed it between his thumb and forefinger and held it up.

"It looks like a little bomb, though. Right?" Candy asked. "The ones they drop from B-12's or whatever those planes on TV are."

"That it does," Charlie said. "A perfect miniature of one, anyway."

"Is it, what are those things called, is it maybe a Lawn Dart?" Dip asked

"I think those are bigger," Mickey said. "And definitely more dangerous."

"But it's not a bomb, right?" asked Candy. "I mean it won't explode or anything. Will it?"

"It feels pretty solid," Charlie said and shook it gently. "I don't think there's anything inside it that would go boom."

"Let me show it to Ronnie," Mickey said and held out her hand. "If anybody knows what this is, it'll be him." Charlie handed her the little missile. She rubbed her fingers over its polished surface and tucked it in her uniform shorts. She made a mental note of relief that Dip had at least not shot "the boyfriend" which gave her one less thing to worry about. She and Charlie walked out. They stopped at her cruiser.

"Really?" Mickey said as she slipped on her Ray-Bans. "You first instinct is to leave those two rabbits alone in the hutch?"

Charlie flashed a big smile. "If they can manage to be romantic on a jail cell cot, who am I to interfere?"

Mickey shook her head. "OK," she said. "But if they do manage to you're taking the linen over to Mayor Billy's new Laundromat."

"Copy that," was all Charlie said as he walked to his patrol car.

Paramount Air Service
Rio Grande, NJ

Gumby Gambacorta took a long pull from his tin cup of water. Brad, Quinlan and Anderson were stretched out on the ground in the banner shed.

"Let's go boys," Gumby said. "We fly until six p.m. That means more banners."

The three groaned and pulled themselves up off the ground.

"I heard you didn't puke," Gumby said to Brad. "That's a first. Von Don is pretty nasty when it comes to that."

Brad dusted himself off. "He swears I screamed like a girl when he went into the dive but I don't remember it that way."

"Yeah, right," Gumby replied with a chuckle. "I bet you don't"

"Hey Gumby," Brad said. "I can't find my wallet. I think it might have dropped out of my pants in the trainer. Any way I can get back in it to check?"

"Gilmore has it in the air right now," Gumby said. "But he won't land until after the last run. I just tanked him up." Gumby thought for a second. "I'll leave it unlocked when I tuck all my beauties in tonight. Keys will be on the pilot's seat. You'll need the key to lock it up though when you're done looking around. I'll leave this cup on my workbench, right next to the big green vise. Just drop the keys in there before you go home. That way I'll see 'em first thing tomorrow when I get here."

"OK, thanks," Brad replied. "Hey, where's Von Don now?"

"He took the red biplane up again. Mr. T. says it's getting a new paint job when this season's over so this is von Donnersmark's last summer to be von Richtofen."

"He really thinks he's the Red Baron, doesn't he?" Brad said.

"I'm pretty sure he does," Gumby answered. "So just be glad all we got is an unarmed biplane. Can you imagine that crazy kraut in a Stuka?"

"*Luftwaffe*," Brad said with a clumsy German accent. "Ze plane *is* ze weapon."

25

Surf City

MICKEY'S DETOUR TO CITY Hall was taking more time than she had, she thought.

"You really put Crime Scene tape around one of our exorbitant property-tax paying citizen's homes?" Billy Tunell asked. His face was red. "Couldn't you have used, I don't know, red white and blue streamers or something?"

"What they did was not exactly a patriotic act," Mickey shot back.

"Well, according to Sam the Holy Ghost, they didn't officially do anything. You have no charges filed and no one in custody. Am I correct?"

"Yes, but-"

"But what?"

"Someone on that street is in touch with the parents of the perpa-, of the alleged perpetrators," Mickey said calmly. "I didn't want them coming back to town for fear there would be a confrontation with victim's parents that could get ugly."

"Alleged victim. How ugly?"

"Shotgun ugly," Mickey said. "And I don't think that's an exaggeration on my part."

"But you said a rape did not occur," Tunell replied.

"Mayor Billy," Mickey went on. "It doesn't matter. I mean, yes it matters in the strict legal sense. But these dipshits got a fourteen year old girl drunk and when she predictably passed out they undressed her and at least looked, maybe touched her where they shouldn't have. We'll probably never know exactly. But it was wrong. It was way wrong and they shouldn't get away with it scot-free."

"Bur Crime Scene tape? This isn't *Dragnet* for God's sake. Or, what's that one Loretta likes, *Adam-12*? The locals are in an uproar. Say they all have company for the holiday. And these boys, they have an attorney now?"

"Of course they do," Mickey said. "Everybody has an attorney these days. Even attorney's have attorney's. But at some point either I'm responsible for the safety of every one of our citizens or I'm not. And if I'm not, then I'm taking the rest of the weekend off and going to Ocean City."

"That was uncalled for," Tunell said. "You know how I feel about the blue-bloods of Ocean City."

"Look, Billy," Mickey said. "I'm headed over that way right now. I will take the tape down. I think it accomplished what I wanted it to."

Tunell appeared mollified but still unhappy.

"If these people are smart," Mickey went on, "they won't show their faces for the rest of the summer. And after Labor Day they'll call Sherry and put their house on the market. Best-case scenario at the moment."

"What about this lawyer. He's making a lot of noise. Lawsuits and the like."

"She," Mickey said. "She's making a lot of noise. Alex Hasapopoulos is just puffing up like a cat to scare us. She's got juvenile perverts for clients and parents who aided and abetted flight. She'll settle down as soon as we push back. I'll take care of her and get her teed up for Sam the Holy Ghost to finish off. And dollars to doughnuts her parents own a diner in Jersey."

"All right," Tunell said, now visibly calmer. "But you will remove the Crime Scene tape post-haste."

"As soon as I leave here," Mickey said. "Which I really need to do right now."

The chair legs scraped as she got up.

"I do understand," Tunell said. "I have a grown daughter as you know. I would be nothing short of apoplectic in the same situation. If you have a daughter you'll understand even more."

Mickey nodded. She knew Billy also saw Dr. Harman. She wondered if doctors ever gossiped about their patients.

▲▲▲

Diane Santucci cleaned up the lemonade glasses and set them in the sink. Tommy had just shown Chief Cleary out. He sat down at the table.

"So?" she asked.

Tommy looked pensive. "Well, she met with the Dexter's to let them know she was removing all that yellow tape from the Brett's home. They found the kids and the parents in Delaware and held them briefly but a lawyer they retained found a friendly judge and she sprung them this morning. If they're smart they won't come back here. Maybe ever."

"Who's the lawyer?" Diane asked. "Anyone we know?"

"Ohhhh, yeah," Tommy said. "Alex Hasapopoulos."

"The dragon lady?" Diane replied. "Ooooh, I don't like her. But if we ever get divorced I've got dibs on her."

"She's a barracuda not a dragon," Tommy said. "Never lets you forget she grew up blue-collar. Parents ran, in fact I think they still run a little diner up in Woodbridge. She worked there nights and weekends all through law school. Hamburgers, cheeseburgers and chips on both shoulders."

"What did the Chief want with you?"

"Same thing you do," Tommy said and dabbed at a water spot on the table. "Stay clear of it all."

"Which is exactly what you're going to do," Diane said firmly. "Poor Regina. She said what they put that little girl through at the hospital was just awful. They must feel like they're victims several times over."

"Yes, I'm certain they do," Tommy replied. "And they're probably right. And if Regina hadn't gone off the deep end they would have had a very good chance of nailing the little creeps. That scene at the liquor store has really screwed the pooch, legally speaking."

"Hard to argue with maternal instinct," Diane said. "I can't say that if somebody did that to one of our girls I wouldn't do the same thing. Except I own a real gun."

"So you've reminded me on multiple occasions."

"But you are going to stay out of it. I mean totally out of it. Right?" Diane pointed a finger at him.

"I am," Tommy replied. "I promise. I'm going to walk over and talk to Carlton right now and explain my forced non-interference if that's alright with you."

"Good. Supper will be ready in an hour. The fireworks start at around ten p.m. up at the lighthouse. I put the two little ones down for naps so they can stay awake for them. I'm making cheesesteaks. And I got that Hires Root Beer you and the girls like."

"Cheesesteaks wit Whiz?" Tommy asked. "Like from Larry's?"

"Yes," Diane said, "With Cheez Whiz. But I do also some have Provolone and the rolls are from Amoroso's so come back in time to help dish up."

"OK," Tommy said. He got up and walked toward the door, grabbing his red Phillies cap on the way.

Once outside he reached into his pocket. There was a phone booth two blocks away on Long Beach Boulevard. Tommy put on his sunglasses. He doubted Rusty Pandola would mind the call even it was the weekend.

▲▲▲

"How did it go?" Charlie asked.

Mickey took her shoes off and rubbed her feet. "As well as you might expect. They're upset but they're handling it better than they were, anyway. I did ask Carlton Dexter if he had any firearms on the premises. He assured me he did not."

"You believe him?"

"I think so," Mickey said. She slipped back into her shoes. "Had a nice chat with Mayor Billy."

"About?"

"Why I used yellow crime scene tape and not red, white and blue paper streamers," Mickey said. "I took it down, just so you and Dip know it was me. But I want us all cruising by that place every time we scoop the loop. Whoever is feeding information to the Brett's needs to know we're not kidding. Where are Romeo and Juliet?"

"Dip's out on a possible Public Intox call. She wanted to go along."

"Jesus. I just hope he doesn't bring a drunk back here." Mickey said. "I don't think I could take it right now."

"Hopefully it's just a local who can be escorted safely home,"

Charlie said.

"I pray to God you're right."

The front door of the station rattled and then opened. Ronnie Dunn walked through it.

"What brings you here, soldier boy?" Mickey asked.

"Social visit," he said. "Hey, Charlie."

Charlie snapped off a quick salute then said, "Chief. Show him that thing Candy gave you."

"Oh, yeah," Mickey said. She stood up and reached into her pocket. "Take a look at this. You're the expert on things that go boom in the night."

Ronnie took the small object from her and inspected it carefully.

"Is it a bomb?" Charlie asked.

"Yes and no," Ronnie said. "Shit, I haven't seen one of these since Nam."

"OK, then what is it?" Mickey asked.

"It's a Red Dot bomb. They also called them Yellow Dogs or Lazy Dogs. Strictly speaking it's a bomblet. Where'd you get this, anyway? Pretty sure they don't stock these at Woolworth's Five and Dime or Ricky's Army/Navy."

Mickey answered. "Candy, our faithful girl reporter. Said she found it in her car this morning. Is it dangerous? I mean, a bomb is meant to explode, isn't it?"

"Depends on your definition," Ronnie said holding it up to the light. "One says for something to be a bomb it has to detonate. Another says if you drop it on something or someone and it does damage it's a bomb."

"So which is this?" Charlie asked.

"The second one," Ronnie said. "Lazy Dog bombs are dropped from airplanes. Flying at maybe five thousand feet or higher. Usually they're in a dispersal canister that holds thousands of them. Like bees in a hive. They're little bombs inside a big bomb but there's no explosion. You release the canister at altitude. As it falls it opens and all these bomblets tumble out. See these four little fins? They're there so it drops straight down, nose first. And this thing is not a model or replica – this is military grade. Either it's a souvenir somebody brought home or it's from a larger cache someone managed to acquire somehow."

"But it's so small. How much damage could it really do?" Mickey asked.

"Depends on how far it falls," Ronnie said. "It doesn't have much mass but let it loose from a mile up and it's probably going five hundred feet per second when it hits the ground. Like throwing a penny from the top of the Empire State Building. From enough altitude this will punch through metal, concrete, you name it. It's traveling, like they say on that old Superman show, faster than a speeding bullet."

"What about people?" Charlie asked.

"Even one of these things could probably kill you if it hit you in the head or chest. It would go through flesh like a knife in butter. Shatter any bone it ran into. Try to imagine thousands of these things dropping out of the sky. No noise, no fire, no explosion but still absolute carnage on the ground." Ronnie handed it back to Mickey. "She said it was in her car?"

"Yep," Mickey replied. "Laying on the seat. Said it poked her in the butt when she sat down."

"I bet it did," Ronnie said. "Maybe her dad was a vet. Things like this have been around since the fifties. Let me know if you figure out where it came from. I wouldn't mind having a box of these babies myself."

Mickey laid the missile on her desk. "Big plans?" she asked Ronnie.

He gave her a funny look then said, "Nah. The Sons are riding over to take in the fireworks. I told Stellwag I'd hang with them. You know, give them an air of respectability."

"And vice-versa," Charlie added.

They all laughed. "OK. I'll try to stop home but it'll be probably be late," Mickey said. "I have something I need to tell you."

"Just tell me now," Ronnie said.

"Later will be better. It's good news so don't worry. And no going back to their little clubhouse in the woods with them."

"That's not going to happen," Ronnie said. "I'm sure of that." He kissed her on the cheek and grabbed her hand, "River deep, mountain high," he said and then walked out the door.

"Did I just witness a public display of affection from Ronnie Dunn?" Charlie asked.

"Yeah. I'm just glad I have a witness. Nobody would believe me otherwise."

The back door opened. Dippolito and Candy came in.

"No drunk?"

"No," Dip said. "The guy has the sugar diabetes and turns out his blood level was like zero. That's why he was acting so goofy. He hadn't eaten all day. The ambulance guys got some OJ in him and he was a little better but they're getting him checked out anyway." He went to his desk. Candy walked over to Mickey's desk and picked up the metal object.

"So," she said. "Do we know what this thing is?"

"We do," said Charlie.

"And maybe we should talk a little bit about where it might have come from," Mickey said.

"OK," Candy said. "My mouth is really dry, though." She reached into her purse. "Anybody want a lozenger?" They shook their heads.

"Bring your chair over," Mickey said. "This might take a minute."

26

Central Intelligence Agency
Langley, VA

"CAN I PLEASE, PLEASE, *please* just take a shower?" Mary Kathleen implored. "I'm gross and I'm disgusting and I'm pretty sure I'm getting my period."

She was also completely naked, a fact that neither J.J. Durkin nor the younger agent, a male this time, had made even passing mention of. She didn't really think she was getting her period but she was desperate. Experience had taught her that nothing petrified men more than the merest mention of menses.

"Certainly," Durkin said. "Give me something useful and I'll even have Calgon take you away if you'd like."

Thirty seconds after she had stripped off her clothes a female agent entered the room and scooped them up promising to get them washed for her. She'd lost track of how long ago that had occurred. All she knew was that the Muzak started playing right after. A bouncy *pizzicato* string version of "Tiptoe Through the Tulips" was in heavy rotation. That by itself was making her nearly insane.

"OK, OK, OK" she said. "The Steel Pier."

"The Steel Pier," J.J. Durkin repeated with an inflection that implied disbelief.

"Yes," Mary Kathleen said. "The Fucking Steel Pier. Or the Steel Fucking Pier if you like that better. That's the target."

"When?"

"Tonight," Mary Kathleen said. "Tonight when all the

people will be there for the big fireworks show. OK? Now can I get a shower?"

She noticed that the younger agent was staring at her breasts. Her nipples were erect from the chilly air and they seemed determined to remain so despite her exhaustion. She crossed one arm over to her opposite shoulder to cover them.

"Why did you say Long Beach Island, then?" Durkin asked. "In the train station. You said you were going to Long Beach Island." His face was expressionless. "Maybe the target actually is something on Long Beach Island."

"I said Long Beach Island because it gave me a plausible reason to be traveling to Atlantic City. And a plausible explanation for why it was not my final destination."

"And who is Rosemary Fitzpatrick? You do have a maiden aunt but her name is Rita and she lives in Jamestown, North Dakota. Is she a contact?"

"She was my college roommate. I think she's an accountant somewhere now."

"She's an actuary, actually. Works for an insurance company in Omaha." Durkin paused. "So tell me, Miss Browne. Why the Steel Pier of all places? Why not Independence Hall and the Liberty Bell? Why not the Art Museum? Why not Lucy the Elephant in Margate for that matter? The Steel Pier doesn't exactly scream Stick it to the Man now, does it?"

"C'mon, Durkin," Mary Kathleen said, "How much more American can you get than the Steel Pier on the Fourth of July weekend? Flags, fireworks - Ed Hurst broadcasting the explosions live on the radio. It's beautiful. It's, it's...inspired. Forget sticking it to the man, this is telling Uncle Sam to take Old Glory and stick it up his ass, flagpole and all. You have to hit people where they think they're the safest. That's what we learned. Nobody gives a crap about a Post Office or a Draft Board anymore. Nobody thinks you're striking a blow for freedom when their welfare check or their birthday money from grandma doesn't come."

"You said explosions, plural," Durkin continued in the same tone of voice and with the same subdued demeanor. "Unless you have some sort of underwater demolitions team – which you don't - you can't expect me to believe you thought you could destroy the Steel Pier with explosives."

Mary Kathleen groaned. "You know that it's really not made

out of steel, right? They just call it that. It's crappy old wood that would go up like matchsticks. All those panicked people trying to run to get off it? We figured the stampede would kill as many law-abiding citizens as the fire. You know, O, *the humanity* and all that shit. Like the fucking Hindenburg." Mary Kathleen began to think he was starting to buy it. The Steel Pier had been their original plan but after two quick arrests in Oakland they had decamped to Chicago on the run and now they just didn't have the manpower or the logistics to pull it off.

J.J. Durkin made some notes on the lined pad in his leather portfolio. "I'm going to need more," he said. "Something tangible. Something to prove you're not just spinning this yarn on the spot. Making it up as you go along. A receipt maybe? The name of a supplier?"

"I don't have any of that. I didn't come here to take part. My job was to make sure it happened and that we got the credit right away. I don't even know the ID of the person on the inside."

"Well, then you don't really have anything, do you? That window-dressing won't even get you a washcloth and a bar of soap, I'm afraid."

Mary Kathleen Browne looked at the younger agent. "Quit staring at my tits you little pervert," she said. Then she turned toward Durkin. "OK, how's this? We used newspapers to leave coded messages. One in Atlantic City and one in some town called Surf City. You can go look them up. There are messages asking for help or guidance from the Blessed Virgin. That's the code name, Blessed Virgin. Who it is, they never told me. Go ahead. Seriously. Look it up. Knock yourself out."

The younger agent got up from his chair without a word and left the room. Before the door closed after him a female agent slipped in with a large blanket and a plastic bag of hotel toiletries. She put the bag on the table and handed the blanket to Mary Kathleen, who immediately wrapped herself in it.

Durkin put down his pen and looked at her. "You've bought yourself a shower, Miss Browne. I am going to check out your story and these newspapers you referenced. If the information you just provided doesn't synch up I'm afraid we're going to have to start all over again. Agent Stinger will take you to get your shower and let you freshen up."

Mary Kathleen stood, pulled the blanket tighter and followed the taller woman out. "It better have a fucking bidet," she said as she left.

Within a minute of her departure the young male agent returned.

"Checks out so far," he said to Durkin. "What do I tell the FBI? Driscoll is running their show and he's getting antsy."

Durkin smiled. "Tell the FBI we have it narrowed down. We think it's AC but it might be Ocean City or Wildwood. Evan's getting a bit too ambitious for my liking lately. Let's put them in the general vicinity but spread them out a little. I don't see any need to share every intelligence detail we've obtained using the Agency's time and resources. "

The agent left without a word. Durkin closed his portfolio, snapped the strap and followed him.

Paramount Air Service
Rio Grande, NJ

Brad thought everyone had left so when he heard footsteps by the banner locker it spooked him.

"Farm boy, what are you doing? You ain't Waxing Wally back there are you?"

It was Yates. His power forward's frame filled the doorway. Brad pushed the wooden box back into the corner and stood up from his crouch.

"Nah, it's not that bad," Brad replied, peering into the darkness.

"You need a lift or something?" Yates asked. ""Cause I'm leaving now and mine is the only car left in the lot."

"I'm OK," Brad said. "My girlfriend should be here pretty soon to pick me up. She needed her car for some stuff today so…"

"Got it," Yates said. "Don't forget we're all going to Tony Mart's tonight. Showplace of the World, man. Three stages. Be at the door around ten and I'll get you in without paying the cover charge. Guy owes me for setting him up with some girls from South Philly who like to hang around the players. Bring your girl. Should be rockin' tonight. If it's not we might drive up north a ways to see some blues band called Sunshine or Sundance, something like that. Anyway, they're playing at a place called The Student Prince in Asbury Park. If you miss us at Tony Mart's just head up there."

"Will do," Brad said. "Thanks."

"Sure hope your girlfriend remembers to come get you. Too

bad you're not a pilot. You could fly home."

"Too bad," Brad said. "I'm sure she'll be here. Traffic out of Long Beach Island was probably heavy."

"Or maybe she got a better offer," Yates said. "Babes are babes, you know. OK, then, Minnie Mouse. Guess we'll see you later, man. But if you're late you'll have to pay the cover to get in." He jingled his car keys and walked off.

Brad waited until he heard the performance engine of Yates' sports car kick into life and the car drive off. He pulled the wooden box from the corner and lifted it up. His arms were tired from the busy day and it felt even heaver then when he'd lifted it out of Candy's trunk telling her it was some hardware he had picked up for the banners. He didn't think she even noticed him do it. Brad hadn't mentioned anything about the previous night. He'd touched the gun. Gone so far as to pull it from the holster. But then he'd slipped it back in and walked around the town until he saw that the police cruiser was gone.

The training plane was about a hundred yards away. Brad glanced around and noticed a small handcart. He walked over and set the box down it. The cart was flimsy and wooden but he thought it would do. Its wheels squeaked as he rolled it out toward the field to the unlocked aircraft. The Carole King song "It's Too Late," popped into his head. There had been no messages, no mysterious female contact telling him to call it off. In the distance the white plane almost glowed in the moonlight.

Brad decided Carole King was right.

It was too late, baby. Definitely too late now.

Surf City

Candy looked at them as if they were all completely crazy.

"That's ridiculous," she said. "Who knows, maybe he found it on the ground at the little airfield where he works. Somebody out there dropped it or it fell out of a plane and he picked it up. Occam's Razor says the simplest answer is usually the correct answer."

"He doesn't care much for the war, does he?" Mickey asked. Her dinnertime chat with Evan Driscoll was on her mind.

"No," Candy replied, "But then neither does *your* boyfriend from what I've heard." She squared her shoulders and crossed her arms, body language Mickey knew was a defensive response.

"And neither do like a zillion other people. I hate to say this about Brad but he's pretty much all talk. He likes to pretend he's Abbie Hoffman or Huey Newton or even Jane Fonda but the truth is he's not. He'd go to a protest rally but he'd never organize one or get up and speak at one. Not to mince words, but he's a chicken-shit when things get real. You know, the kid who suddenly has to go home because he's sure he heard his mother calling." Candy picked up the miniature bomb. "Other than poking you in the ass, this thing could actually hurt somebody?"

Charlie answered her. "That's what Ronnie said. But you have to drop it from real high up."

"How high? Like from the top of the lighthouse? Like that high?" Candy asked.

"More like from an airplane a mile up," Charlie said.

"Well he can't fly a plane," Candy said. "At least he never told me he could. And he said they quit flying those banners at six every night so I even if he rode along they all be back on the ground by now."

"OK," Mickey said. "I get the feeling maybe we're barking up the wrong tree here. Doesn't sound like Brad probably did anything more than, like you said, find this thing laying around, put it in his pocket and forgot about it. Just tell me you don't have a whole carton of them at your apartment."

Candy laughed. "We don't have anything at our apartment. I like Mary T but she counts her pennies like a miser. She gave us one roll of TP and that was it. Said it was the last one they had at the A & P. I mean, who ever heard of a store running out of toilet paper?"

"When does Brad get home?" Dip asked. Mickey noticed that Candy gave him a funny look when he said it.

"He said he was getting a ride back with one of the mechanics so, I don't know, soon or pretty soon I guess. Depends on how much traffic they hit I suppose. Are you going to question him?"

"We don't need to do that, I don't think," Mickey said. "Maybe just ask him if he knows where this thing came from or who gave it to him."

"Sure," Candy said. "No problem." She put the Lazy Dog back on Mickey's blotter, got up from her chair and went to her desk. She slid the wooden chair in front of her as she went.

Mickey shuffled a few papers then turned to Dippolito. "Call Davey and see what he's doing with his assailants." She swiveled in

her chair. "Charlie, see how the young man is doing at Mainland."
Both men grabbed their phones.

Mickey looked at the Lazy Dog. Something about it bothered
her but she couldn't put her finger on it. It was like it gave off some
kind of vibe. She had the Lazy Dog, she thought. Something told
her that now she needed to be looking for the quick brown fox.

▲▲▲

Ronnie loaded the package onto the back of the Royal Enfield.
The motorcycle rear fork didn't budge. He had wrapped the
contents in a bivvy cloth with the exception of the heavy metal
portion. For that he used parachute cord to secure it to the side
of the seat. The two components together weighed, he figured,
around twenty pounds. He had humped packs three times that
heavy though the jungle but he knew it would be the straight
climb up with it that would take its toll on him. Ronnie checked
his watch. He kick-started the bike and pulled into the street. He
was saddled up again and it felt good. It was time to play ball.

-27-

Surf City

"YOU HAVE GOT TO be fucking kidding me," Mickey said. "Tell me you are fucking kidding me."

Charlie shook his head solemnly. "Unfortunately, Chief Cleary, I am not," he said. "And here I was just about to compliment you on your much restrained and highly selective use of profanity over these last two years."

"Well then fuck that and fuck me," Mickey said as if to underscore the comment. "Just fuck me dead."

Dippolito hung up his phone. "I guess that means you heard, right?"

"Yes, I fucking heard," Mickey said. "Andrew signed out of the hospital and claimed he couldn't positively identify any of his attackers other than to say they were white. And now yet another lawyer suddenly materializes with a Judge's Order and springs Davey's perps."

"But they had the kid's ID in their possession," Charlie said.

"They did," Mickey replied. "But now their new story is that they just happened to find it laying on the ground and that they were nowhere near the causeway on the day in question and would never, ever even think of doing such a terrible thing. And I'm sure they added they were all virgins and altar boys to boot."

"Did they say they wouldn't even hurt a fly?" Charlie asked.

"Hey, that's from the final scene of *Psycho*," Candy chirped.

Mickey was just about to reply when her desk phone rang.

She picked it up. "Cleary," she said sharply, skipping the usually scripted greeting the PD's on the Island had grudgingly adopted.

She leaned forward and propped an elbow on her desk. After several minutes of "ums" and "OK's" she said, ".Well I really do appreciate the fact that you'd call me personally. Yes. Yes. I understand. OK, thank you, Judge." She plopped the receiver back in the cradle.

"That was not Chief Justice Warren Burger, I assume," Charlie said.

"Judge Maressa," Mickey replied. "Apologizing that he had to let the assholes walk out of Ship Bottom. He had just gotten off the phone with Davey telling him the same thing."

"Diogenes would be proud," Charlie said.

Mickey looked over at Dip. "Did Andrew say anything before he flew the coop at the hospital?"

"Something like he'd take care of it himself, according to the nurse who wheelchaired him out," he replied.

"That's not good," Charlie intoned.

"Fuck," Mickey said. "Fuck, fuck, fuck." She smacked both palms on her desk. "When did we become a nation of vigilantes?"

"Two hundred years ago," said Candy from her corner. They all looked toward where she sat.

"What does that mean?" Dip asked her.

Candy stood and walked toward the space in the center of the three desks. "That's what we are. It's like, I don't know, our founding principle. If there's one trait that's purely American it's that if we really don't like something we take matters into our own hands to change it."

"No we don't," said Dip.

"Yeah," Candy said. "We do. All the time, in fact. The Boston Tea Party, the American Revolution, the Civil War, Watts, Reverend King's March on Washington, the Stonewall Rebellion . Sometimes it works and sometimes it doesn't. When people think their government is oppressing or misleading them or when they think the law doesn't protect them they rise up – sometimes it's just one person, sometimes a dozen, sometimes millions of them. We're Americans – anarchy is in our, what's that stuff inside your chromosomes called? DNA. Anarchy is in our DNA. If it wasn't we'd still be subjects of the British Monarchy and watching soccer instead of the Iggles. The line between civil disobedience and, what do they call it now - domestic terrorism – it's pretty thin."

Mickey's ears pricked up at the mention of the same phrase Evan Driscoll had used during their dinner meeting at Wally's.

Dip stood up. "That what they teach in college now?" he asked.

"Pretty much," Candy said. "They don't encourage you to be a revolutionary. Well, OK, maybe some professors kind of do but Grinnell is a little different than most colleges. What they do teach you is to try to understand what and why and how things change a society. Why people decide at certain times and not others that enough is enough."

"Popeye," Charlie said.

"Popeye?" Dip asked.

"Yeah, Popeye. A much underappreciated modern philosopher if you ask me. It's like when he says, 'I've stoods all I can stands and I can't stands no more.'"

Mickey laughed out loud. "Charlie, you realize you do not sound anything like Popeye the Sailor Man," she said.

"It's the thought that counts, Chief," Charlie said with a smile.

"I would bet," Candy continued, "That when Andrew found out that the shitheads who beat him up were rich suburban kids he knew he'd never get a fair shake."

"It still doesn't mean you can just take the law into your own hands," Mickey said. "That's what we're here for. That's what the laws and the courts and the government are here for."

"I agree with you," Candy said. "But not everyone sees it that way. Luckily, most people are like Brad or maybe like your boyfriend – they'll get pissed and they might yell and scream but they won't actually do anything crazy."

"Do you think Andrew will do anything crazy?" Charlie asked. "He seemed like an awfully determined young man to me when I talked to him."

"I really only spoke to him for like maybe two minutes, Deputy Higgins," Candy replied. "But I worry that he might think about it. I know if I were him I would be thinking about it."

Mickey eased back in her chair. What worried her right now was that Carlton Dexter and Tommy Santucci were doing something more than just thinking about it.

Rio Grande, NJ

Brad divvied the mess of little missiles more or less evenly into the three plastic buckets he had taken from under Gumby's tool bench. He hoisted each bucket and set it on the passenger seat of the trainer. He did a couple of test lifts to make sure he could raise a full bucket from the seat with one arm. When one of them seemed a little too heavy he took several handfuls of the tiny bombs and spread them on the cracked upholstery of the seat itself.

As each minute passed it was becoming clearer to him that he was a messenger, a wake-up call for a country deeply asleep in its own denial of what it was doing in the world. What it was doing *to* the world. He would provide a taste of what it felt like to be under attack. He would drop the stone into the pond. The ripples would become waves and the waves would spread in all directions, washing clean the hypocrisy and the evil. People would understand the gesture, he now knew, and they would respond.

He closed the plane's right-seat door and took a breath. Though he had been wracked by doubt many times it had evaporated like the morning mist on the airfield when the first rays of the sun touched it. He felt fearless now, invincible.

Brad checked his watch. Candy had taken him to a little jewelry shop on the main street in Riverside to buy it. It was run by on older Italian man who insisted on showing Brad the pink and puckered belly scar from where he said he'd been shot during a hold-up attempt the previous summer. Outside, Candy clarified that the wound had been the result of a local Mafia rift over the payment of protection money. The watch was a Bulova Acutron 259 with a ribbed band and the man said it had a miniature tuning fork that kept it highly accurate. Candy wouldn't tell him what she'd paid but the watch was in a separate felt-lined display and not in the carousel of Timex's, Speidel's and imported Seiko's rotating endlessly in their plastic clamshell cases. Brad jokingly asked if he could trade it on the spot for the Charlie the Tuna watch he spied on a lower shelf in the display case. He recalled that Candy had not been particularly amused. Candy would have a lot of explaining to do by the end of the night, he knew. He realized that before the revelation of the previous evening this would have troubled him. He was not troubled now.

Brad looked around the deserted airfield. All the planes but the trainer were held fast with heavy cords that ran through tie-down rings on the landing gear or under the wings and then to stakes driven into the hard ground. He checked under the plane to make sure he hadn't been distracted by all he needed to do and missed unhitching one in the darkness. Then, like any good pilot, he inspected the length and breadth of the small aircraft, running his hands over its thin stretched-fabric skin. The same way he did over his horse back home before a long ride, he mused. He planned to head south after takeoff and then make the same wide turn Von Don had made out over the Delaware Bay. The Ship John Shoal lighthouse would be his navigational marker since it would be highly visible in the black of the night and the gray of the water. He planned to fly further offshore than the tow route until he saw the glittering cluster of lights out his left window that would be Atlantic City with the brightly illuminated Steel Pier jutting out from the Boardwalk like a giant middle finger into the ocean. As soon as he passed the big resort town he'd adjust his heading by only a degree or two. This would take him over Brigantine. He ran the landmarks again in his mind. North of Brigantine was the stretch of open water in the chain of barrier islands. The next land mass would be the undeveloped and unpaved southern tip of Long Beach Island. When he saw the headlights of traffic appear at the terminus of Long Beach Boulevard in Beach Haven he would adjust course again. He knew he could follow the long, straight road like an elongated string of landing lights the rest of the way. He also knew the crowds would be concentrated on and around the Boulevard, a mass of unsuspecting, undulating humanity stretching all the way north to the rocky jetty that marked the Inlet to Barnegat Bay. He figured there would also be a large crowd gathered for the fireworks at the State Park that ringed the lighthouse.

Brad hiked himself up into the pilot's seat, leaving the door open to let in the cool night air. He waited. He wasn't concerned that he would be late. He knew what he needed to be was early.

-28-

Off U.S. Route 72 & E. Bay Avenue
Mud City
Manahawkin, NJ

THE LONG LINE OF motorcycles came to a stop. Everett Calhoun gave a hand signal and all the engines quit at once. In an instant, the roar of combustion was replaced by the drone of crickets and the chatter of nocturnal predators. Calhoun looked over at Stellwag.

"It's your ballgame," the LT said.

Calhoun glanced at his watch. Stellwag did not think he looked nervous.

"This'll be fun," Calhoun said with a gap-toothed smile. Stellwag gave him a fist-knock on his vest on which, he noticed, Calhoun had pinned his Purple Hearts.

If you were a tourist, Stellwag thought, this was a perfect summer evening. The sky was clear and the stars shone brightly. The moonlight bounced off the chrome of the assembled bikes like a land-locked version of St. Elmo's Fire.

Calhoun checked his watch again. Stellwag knew Garufi and Filisky were already putt-putting their way north offshore of the long, skinny island that lay ahead. The marine forecast was for calm seas and light air. Stellwag knew the little fishing boats that rented out of Mystic Islands were barely seaworthy on a good day. The Ship Bottom diversion was key but Filisky and Garufi were two of his most reliable soldiers. If anybody could pull it off, he knew, it was them.

Calhoun checked his watch a final time. Then he held up his fist and yelled "Move out."

The sounds of the summer evening were split by the growls of engines once again.

Stellwag eased back to let Calhoun lead the pack. Cedar Bonnet Island lay ahead, squatting solidly in Manahawkin Bay. It reminded Stellwag of the night they'd escorted Ronnie Dunn and a battered and bruised Mickey Cleary out of a nightmare in the Pine Barrens and delivered them safely to the old PD station in Surf City. It was one of their finest hours, he thought. Whether this was another would soon be revealed. But either way, the Cavalry was riding once again.

Surf City

Candy knew better than to move her car now. She had been extremely lucky to find the spot she did on a Saturday night and the chances of getting another one was, she figured, astronomically low. The car keys were in the pocket of her jean shorts. The walk from the Surf City PD was only a few blocks. Mary T's store was brightly lit, staying open late to take advantage of the increased foot traffic. She could see through the big plate glass window that there were a fair number of customers inside so the gamble had obviously paid off. Mary T had shared with her one day that the T was for Theresa, in honor Saint Therese of Lisieux, a Carmelite Nun often referred to as "the Little Flower." In keeping with this the shop had small floral appliqués scattered liberally about as well as a little flower stenciled on the front window. Mary T always wore a little flower on her work smock as well.

Candy fished for her keys. She wanted to make sure the Camaro was locked. As she approached it she noticed the trunk was not shut completely. When she got to the back bumper she tried pushing down on it several times to get it to latch but to no avail. She found the trunk key on her ring, slipped it in the lock and opened it. She was about ready to slam it shut when she noticed the rumpled blanket. Brad had been rummaging around when she dropped him off. Something about hardware for the banners he had been told to pick up in Hammonton he'd hastily explained. Her jumper cables were also in a different spot she saw.

She pulled the threadbare plaid blanket, an "Indian blanket" her mother insisted on calling it, out of the trunk and refolded it into a neat square. The car was parked right beneath a streetlamp and it lit up the trunk and its few contents. When Candy went to put the blanket back she noticed a sharp indentation in the carpet that lined the trunk floor. It was perfectly rectangular and had obviously been made by something heavy resting on it. Candy turned the blanket in her hands without thinking. What was it that Mickey had asked her about the little bomb thingies? Something about a box – no, she had asked if she happened to have a crate of them at her apartment. But not a crate – a carton of them.

Candy tried to rewind in her head the images of Brad walking away from the car that morning after he'd closed the trunk. It wasn't a carton he had in his hands, she remembered. It wasn't cardboard. It was a wooden box. And it was heavy, she guessed, because he used both arms to carry it in front of him. A box of those metal missiles would be heavy, she thought. Probably heavy enough to leave a lasting dent in the cheap carpet if it sat there long enough.

Candy threw the blanket back in. She wondered if it would be quicker to walk back to the station to tell Chief Mickey or if she should just run up to the little apartment and use the old rotary dial telephone in the bedroom. The alleyway where the outside steps were had a group of teenage boys milling around in it smoking cigarettes. She decided it would be faster to make the short return trek on foot. She brought the trunk down with a loud bang.

The noise attracted the attention of several passersby on the sidewalk across the street. These included an older couple who stared at her. She was about to turn to leave when she heard a woman's voice call to her.

"Candace?" the woman shouted. "Candace Catanzariti? Is that really you?"

Candy looked at the woman. If she had not just used the bathroom before leaving the station house she knew she would have wet herself in surprise.

300 Yards Offshore
Ship Bottom, NJ

They were standing in six inches of water.

"They really rent these things to people?" Jimmy Filisky asked. "And they actually make it back alive?" Filisky had been a medic during his time and Mike Garufi knew a lot of guys made it back alive because of him.

But Garufi ignored him. He was using a hand pump to overboard the rising water. "We're going to be late," he said. "Here, you pump for a while."

"Sure. Make the old guy do the hard stuff," Filisky said, taking it.

Garufi flipped back the wooden housing on the inboard motor. It was little more than a glorified lawn mower engine connected to a driveshaft and a propeller. He slipped a screwdriver out of the plastic bag of tools the rental company in Mystic Islands had thoughtfully provided. Then he went to work on the carburetor, trying to squeeze just a few more rpm's out of the coughing and wheezing power plant.

"We're carrying too much cargo," Garufi said.

"Anything we can toss over?" Filisky asked.

"Just you, Fat Boy."

"Watch who you're callin' Fat Boy, there, Metal Head," Filisky retorted. They were both dressed comically in gym shorts and tourist t-shirts. Filisky's said "Life's a Beach." Garufi's bore the wildly popular "I'm With Stupid."

The pitch of the engine increased. Garufi tossed the screwdriver overboard. "Like it says in the song," he chuckled, "That's all there is and there ain't no more." The charge he'd rigged up had come from a midnight visit to a construction site near one of the new Parkway Service Plazas. It consisted of a blasting cap with a twenty foot length of primer cord which he figured would give them plenty of time and distance when it blew since the boat would keep making headway after they jumped,. The blasting cap would be set off by a doctored battery-powered alarm clock he'd shoplifted from the Small Appliances department at a Two Guys Department Store.

The water had gone down perhaps an inch. Garufi dead reckoned they were now within two hundred yards of their objective. "Get ready to paddle you old dog," he said to Filisky who dropped the bilge pump and immediately headed for the already listing bow.

Garufi judged the distance again. The primer cord was wrapped around the boat's steering wheel and throttle. "Let's go," he yelled to Filisky who hit the water with a belly-flopping splash. Garufi hit the ALARM ON button on the back of the alarm clock and set it in the open drywell in the tiny cabin. Then he slipped soundlessly over the side.

Dorsal fins broke the surface not far away. Filisky's eyes grew wide. "Sharks?" he said. "Are you fucking kidding me?"

Garufi knew it was only a pod of dolphins surfacing for air but decided it would add significant and much needed motivation to his partner's efforts if he believed otherwise. "Better paddle hard," he said.

Surf City

Ronnie weaved on and off of Long Beach Boulevard trying to maintain a steady speed in the stop-and-go traffic. The Enfield was a little tippy with the weight of the package strapped behind him and also because of the large coil of rope he had slung over his head and under his right arm. Its asymmetry moved both bike and rider's center of gravity just enough that Ronnie had to maintain a slight compensatory lean. It got predictably worse if he had to brake at lower rpm's.

He was approaching 25th Street, the northern boundary of Surf City after which the Boulevard continued on through Long Beach Township. Long Beach Boulevard was technically Ocean County Route 607 but Ronnie had never actually heard anyone refer to it as that. As he crossed the imaginary divide he heard bike engines somewhere behind him. Long Beach Township had a paucity of roads extending toward the beach and eschewed numbered streets. Instead it opted for names like Dolphin Cove and Bar Harbor Drive which made it sound as if the homes there were sitting on something other than a sandbar. He was reminded of Billy Tunell's ill-fated PR campaign to "re-brand" LBI as America's Riviera. He realized that entertaining these thoughts meant he was feeling calmer with each passing block.

He thought he'd passed Mickey's young sidekick back in Surf City. Her name was Candy or maybe it was Cindy, he couldn't recall. She'd been standing on the sidewalk on Long Beach Boulevard next to a white Camaro. A sixty-one or maybe a sixty-two he thought and in pretty good shape from the looks of it. Ronnie checked his watch. He knew it was just a little under seven miles from the dividing street to the northern tip of the island so he throttled down. The inland-facing streets in Long Beach did not connect with one another and so he had no choice but to stay on the Boulevard until the disconnected stretches of Holly Avenue offered him brief westward detours before forcing him back towards the ocean and the main thorofare.

There was a knot of traffic as he crossed into the Harvey Cedars neighborhood with its ruler-straight maze of bayside canals. He could see the lighthouse in the distance. The heavy coil of rope around him shifted throwing him slightly off balance. He yanked it back toward his midline and the bike straightened out. He'd be glad when he could finally unburden himself of it.

Barnegat Light State Park
Barnegat Light, NJ

It was Phil the Thrill Stanley's last summer as a Park Ranger at the lighthouse. And it was this fact that did for once truly thrill him. He was headed back to Pharmacy school in the fall for his final year and the money he'd made over the years as a combination security guard and docent had compounded daily into an amount sizable enough that he would emerge from his studies debt-free.

The light still wasn't the Island's big attraction. The schooner *Lucy Evelyn* drew ten times the number of visitors in a summer. Phil figured it had been there so long people just didn't really see it anymore. It hadn't been a working lighthouse for almost fifty years. When a lightship was anchored eight miles offshore in the 1920's it marked the end of the structure's glory days. The Fresnel lens was ignominiously replaced by first a gas blinker and then, within a period of weeks, by a clear two-hundred-and-fifty watt Westinghouse light bulb. Before the light bulb was eventually turned off, the tower became what one newspaper wag called "New Jersey's tallest streetlamp."

The Eastern States Lighthouse Society had tried to spark some new interest by having the first-order Fresnel lens, the same one that had been removed in 1927, placed back in the lamp room. The lens had been donated to the borough of Barnegat Light but the Society had paid for moving it back into the tower and insuring it for the summer season. Phil had studied the complicated optics of Fresnel lenses over the winter and loved showing and explaining it's amazing power to magnify light to the few visitors who bothered to climb the vibrating metal staircase with him. But the lens hadn't done much to increase business or interest. A lighthouse without a light, in Phil's mind, was just a house. And that made him the housekeeper.

The fireworks had been moved back to ten-fifteen. This was his final Fourth, he thought, and he'd planned on locking the door behind him and watching the show from the observation deck.

A young couple, they looked maybe a little older than teenagers, passed him with a nod. The boy had fair skin and freckles and a mop of curly reddish hair and was cultivating a wispy reddish beard. The girl had dark hair and dark eyes. They carried two beach blankets and a Styrofoam cooler.

"No alcohol or glass containers allowed in the park or on the beach," Phil called to them.

"Just some snacks and some cans of root beer," the boy called back. The girl giggled.

Phil knew he should probably check the cooler but they looked harmless so he decided he really didn't care even if they had a gallon of grain alcohol in there. He waved them on. In the distance he thought he could hear the faint rumble of engines. Sounded like motorcycles, he thought.

Surf City

CANDY KNOCKED ON THE station house's back door.
Dippolito let her in.

"Change of plans?" Mickey asked.

"You won't believe who I just met on the street," Candy bubbled. "Mrs. LaMarro. Mrs. freaking LaMarro. My third grade teacher. Right here. In Surf City. On the freaking Boulevard across from our apartment over top of Mary T's. Mrs. LaMarro, And she recognized me right away after all these years. She knew who I was. She knew my name."

For a moment Mickey couldn't quite process what the excited girl was babbling on about. In the four years she'd known Loretta she had not once heard anyone refer to her as Mrs. LaMarro."

"You mean Loretta LaMarro?" Mickey asked. Her tone was one of mild confusion bordering on disbelief.

"Yes. Mrs. Loretta LaMarro. She taught the third grade at St. Peter's in Riverside when I was little. She was the best. I mean, like the best ever. I loved her. We all did. Even the boys. I just can't freaking believe it. Don't you just love her name? Loretta LaMarro . It's like, like a Hollywood star's name not a grade school teacher's."

Charlie wore an expression of extreme bemusement while Dip looked like a man who just realized he was lost at sea.

Mickey waited for Candy to calm down. "Well I guess it really is a small world, like they say."

"And she says she knows you. That you two are, like, friends. How cool is that? And get this - did you know the mayor, the mayor of Surf City is her freaking boyfriend?"

"We've heard some rumors to that effect," Charlie said, milking even further enjoyment from the girl's giddiness.

"Well I'm glad you two got to reunite," Mickey said calmly. "That must have been a lot of fun for both of you."

"Oh, it was. We're going to meet for lunch tomorrow after church. Mrs. Loretta LaMarro. I'm still in shock I think."

"I can see that," said Mickey. "Did you, um, did you walk all the way back here just to tell us that?"

Charlie and Dip went back to work at their desks.

"No, wait. Fuck. Sorry – I mean no. I mean. Shit. I totally forgot why I was coming back. It's about that little bomb thing, the Lazy Dog or whatever you called it.

Dip and Charlie immediately quit what they were doing. Mickey leaned forward and said, "What about it?"

"Well," Candy said, working hard to get the words out, "I think...I think maybe there might have been a big box of them in my car."

The two deputies stood and moved closer.

Mickey eased back a fraction of an inch. "Might have been – as in they're not there now?"

Candy shook her head.

"Where are they?" Charlie asked.

"I think Brad might have them," Candy replied. "He's had my car since we moved down here. He works all the way out at that banner place in Cape May like I said, so I just let him drive it back and forth and he puts gas in it. But he asked me to drop him off this morning. I was doing something in the trunk and I saw the outline and I remembered-"

"Slow down, child," Charlie said gently. "You looked in your trunk and-"

"And I saw there was this perfectly square, well rectangular actually, perfectly rectangular dent in the carpet. Like something heavy had been laying there. You know, the way furniture legs make dents in the rugs at home?"

"What did you remember?" Dip asked.

Candy took a breath. "I remember that after Brad got out of the car he asked me to pop the trunk. There's a little lever under the dash if you don't feel like getting out. He went back there and took something out. It was a wooden box about this big." She stretched her arms out in front of her and touched her finger tips together. "You could tell it was heavy because he had to use both hands, both arms to carry it."

"Did he say what it was?" Mickey inquired.

"He said it was some stuff from a hardware store in Hammonton he was told to pick up. Fittings or brackets or something he said. For the banners. You don't really think-"

Mickey looked at Charlie and then at Dippolito.

"Is Brad home now?" Charlie asked.

"No," Candy answered. "He was supposed to get a lift back like I said before. I haven't heard from him all day. Seriously, I mean seriously, there's just no way that he...is there?"

"Probably not," Mickey said without an abundance of conviction. "But let's start by making make sure he's OK. Since he's sort of overdue on getting home to you."

Dip started to speak up. "I can go ch-"

"NO," Mickey, Charlie and Candy said nearly in unison.

"Dip, I mean Dennis," Mickey said, "Get on the horn with Hammonton PD. Do we know anybody there?"

"No," Dippolito answered. "But Davey Johnson does. Some buddy of his from the Academy."

"OK," Mickey said. "Call Davey and get a name. Wait, never mind. That's not going to help us. Candy, where did you say this airport was?"

"It's not an airport," Candy said, "I saw it. It's just a field with a bunch of planes and some buildings and a shed or maybe it was a small barn. There might be a runway but I didn't really look too hard. It's in Cape May County, I know that much. It's called Paramount Air. You know, like Paramount Pictures. I remember because Riverside had a Paramount Theatre when I was a kid. Until it burned down. Wait, I might be wrong. It might have been the Fox Theatre that burned down. But it's definitely Paramount Air."

Charlie grabbed the telephone book and started rifling the pages. "Here it is. Rio Grande. Now who in their right mind names a town in New Jersey Rio Grande? Lord Almighty."

"I got it," Dip said. He had unfolded a Texaco road map on is disk. "Shit, it really is in the middle of nowhere. I don't think it's even a real town."

"Probably unincorporated," Charlie threw out. He grabbed another thicker book from the collection on his desk

"What's the closest municipality?" Mickey asked.

"Middle Township, maybe?" Dip asked.

"You'd think so," Charlie said. "But this Directory of New Jersey City Services says it's actually part of Lower Township."

"Do they have a PD?" Mickey inquired.

"Checking right now," Charlie replied.

Candy had wandered to her desk in the corner and was watching with a stunned look on her face.

"Yes," Charlie replied. "On Bayshore Road. I'll try them now."

"Dip, "Mickey commanded. "Call the State Police. Tell them I need to speak to Major George Joo as soon as possible. Even if he's off for the holiday. Tell them to call him at home. Make sure you spell it for them, J-O-O so we don't end up talking to every Trooper they have named Joe."

"On it, Chief," Dip said and started dialing.

Mickey got up and walked over to Candy's little desk. She thought the girl looked ready to cry. "We're probably overreacting," Mickey said although she did not believe it in the least. "But I do think we need to make sure Brad is safe. There's probably a simple explanation like...the guy left without him or they broke down or ran out of gas and they're stuck in a ditch on the side of Highway 9 somewhere. Candy just nodded several times.

"What if he knows, what if he found out that I-"

"Even if he does," Mickey said, "I guarantee you that it has nothing to do with this." She reached into her pocket and pulled out the Lazy Dog. "Like I said, we're probably-"

The Dispatch Radio crackled loudly and the normally calm and collected voice of Arlene Shields filled the room.

"Attention all LBI Police and Fire Units this is LBI Dispatch," Arlene said. There was an element of tension in her voice that Mickey could sense even through the low-tech speaker. "We have multiple incidents at multiple locations. Please respond to the one closest to you regardless of official jurisdiction. Repeat. Multiple incidents at multiple locations. Please respond to the one closest to you regardless of official jurisdiction. Say again. Regardless of jurisdiction. Incidents as follows. Multi-vehicle motorcycle accident with violent altercation in progress. East 26th at Long Beach Boulevard North Beach Haven. Proceed with caution.

Participants may be armed. Next. Small craft offshore explosion and fire. Ship Bottom Beach at 4th Street. Casualties expected. Repeat. Casualties expected. Next. North Long Beach Township."

Mickey listened with one ear as Arlene described a series of coincident mash-ups and minor disasters that she found hard to believe. And they were all occurring at major pinch-points along the Boulevard.

"OK, Thanks, Captain," Mickey heard Dip say. He hung up his phone and turned to her. "Major Joo is at a reception at the Governor's Ocean House on Island Beach but he's ordering two trooper units to check out the airstrip in Rio Grande. He says he can't leave at the moment but the Captain I talked to said Major Joo would call here as soon as he had any information. Here's the Captain's number." Dip tore off the piece of paper with the phone number and gave it to Mickey. She stuffed it in the breast pocket of her uniform blouse.

"Lower Township is rolling out to the airstrip," Charlie chimed in. "They said it would probably be deserted at this time of night but they'll check it out anyway as a favor to, as they put it, the legendary Chief Cleary." Mickey rolled her eyes. "Where do you want us to respond, Chief?"

"You go see if-"

The Dispatch Radio squawked again. "Dispatch here," Arlene said, dispensing with any of the scripted formalities this time. "Citizens report being harassed by, quote, hoodlums, unquote, Surf City 21st Street and the Boulevard. Approach with care."

"How about if you take that one," Mickey told Charlie. He pulled on his gun belt. Mickey knew he was now carrying a Colt .45 ACP Government semi-automatic that had been his late brother Darnell's sidearm in Vietnam. Cole Prejean had somehow acquired the weapon and given it to Charlie as both a gift and a show of good faith that his brother would not be forgotten. Charlie popped out the clip, checked that the magazine was full and slipped it back in. He racked the slide once and put it in his holster.

Mickey turned to Dippolito. "Hustle over to Ship Bottom – their situation sounds like it might get complicated." Dip holstered his Magnum and patted his pants for the keys to his cruiser.

"I'll hold the fort until I hear from either the State Troopers or the Lower Township guys about Brad," Mickey said. "Radio me after you've assessed the scenes and let me know where you think

I can be of most help."

Both deputies voiced their understanding and headed out the door. Mickey looked at Candy. "I might need you to stay here," she said. "Can't put you in any situation where you'd come to harm. Can you work the radio?"

Candy still had not spoken and she replied with a nod.

Then Mickey's radio squawked. "Barnegat Light to SCPD. Copy?"

"Copy, Barnegat Light. This is Cleary. Need a hand?"

"Hold on, please," a voice she didn't recognize said.

"Mickey?" a new voice said. It was Mike Belz, the Light's new Chief. He'd gotten the job after years of service as a patrol officer in Beach Haven.

"Mike," Mickey replied. "What do you have going on up there?"

"Listen," Belz replied. "I know it's nuts right now but any chance you can get up here. We, uh, we got ourselves what you might call a situation, I'm afraid."

"Sounds like everybody's got a situation, Mike, including us," Mickey replied. "What do you need me for?"

"Mick, this situation involves somebody you know. 'It's Ronnie, Mick. Ronnie Dunn. I really think it would help if you could find a way to get up here, pronto. We're standing down for the moment so the situation doesn't blow up on us but I can't say for how long we'll be able to do that. Copy?"

"On my way, Mike," Mickey said automatically even though she knew it wasn't true. Her mind was reeling. She realized she now needed to get to the Light somehow but the roads would be jammed and traffic everywhere up and down the Island would be at a standstill. Ship Bottom still had one of former chief Jim Justus' motorcycles but she didn't ride well and she knew it would take too long to get it anyway. "You don't happen to own a helicopter by chance, do you?" she asked Candy.

She wasn't expecting an answer and so she almost didn't hear it when the girl said, "No. But I know Mary T owns a motor scooter."

Barnegat Light State Park
Barnegat Light, NJ

They weren't the first pair of breasts he'd seen or fondled but,

Jeffrey Silverman had to concede, they were arguably the finest.

He was nestled on a blanket in a natural cove formed by the gigantic boulders of the jetty that guarded the south side of the Inlet and kept the ocean from eroding away and thus eventually toppling the beloved lighthouse.

Now Erica Tennenbaum, under Jeffrey's expert yet tender ministrations and manipulations, had her head thrown back, her eyes closed and was murmuring what Jeffrey was sure were incomprehensible vulgarities and obscenities. The mere thought of what she might be saying only stiffened his resolve to press onward and downward.

It briefly occurred to Jeffrey that he had come a very, very long way from his first pubescent fumblings with Heidi Abramowitz, the Golden Shiksa of his adolescent wet dreams. Those had occurred just a few miles further down the beach and what felt like a million years ago, though it had only been four. At the age of twenty Jeffrey was, he decided, an experienced and thoughtful lover. He was confident that for Erica, a distant cousin from a town called Mountain Lakes in northern New Jersey, the fireworks soon to be exploding overhead would pale in comparison to the ones he had planned for her southern territories.

Jeffrey was pondering the challenge of Erica's skin-tight pair of hot pants when she suddenly made the point moot by agreeably wriggling out of them, accelerating his carefully planned timeline and sequence of sexual events. Jeffrey obliged her efforts by tugging down the nylon-tricot swimsuit he'd ordered by mail from a company called Ah-Men in Hollywood, California. He'd seen the ad in a throwaway newspaper that appeared on the Penn campus with some regularity. Even with the foam rubber "swim cup" it had still only cost him ten dollars, plus a half-a-buck for postage. Jeffrey moved to pull the extra blanket over them but Erica kicked it away and shifted her hips. Paradise was literally close at hand, he knew, and ecstasy awaited him. Now it was Jeffrey who closed his eyes. But just as he thought he was ready to "mount the podium," as his brother liked to say, Erica moaned loudly. Only it wasn't a moan. It was a gasp. And then it was a yell. Jeffrey had such an intense concentration of hormones swimming in his veins that he didn't realize what was happening at first. Erica was squirming beneath him but she was not squirming in a good way. It took several more seconds for his testosterone-addled brain to understand that she was screaming for him to get off of her. To get the fuck off of her, to be exact.

He fell onto his back and immediately understood. They were being bathed in a hot, white light that seemed to be coming from heaven above. Erica scrambled for the blanket to cover herself, leaving Jeffrey both exposed and engorged. He looked up and saw a candle or maybe it was a lantern, burning as bright as the sun and descending very slowly courtesy of a small parachute above it. The beach and the rocks and the people in every direction were lit up like noonday.

The people, Jeffrey thought with unbridled horror.

He scuttled under the bottom blanket, the packed sand quickly finding its way into every unmentionable nook and cranny. At first the crowd of previously unseen people just stood and stared, motionless in shocked and silent disbelief.

Then they began to applaud.

-30-

Rio Grande, NJ

BRAD ZIPPED HURRIEDLY THROUGH a cursory pre-flight check and fired up the Lycoming O-235 engine. The plane vibrated excitedly, like a horse pawing at a corral gate. He turned off the cabin light and watched the instruments glow softly. Switching off the radio he buckled himself in. It was hard to see the windsock but there had been barely any breeze when he climbed in so he didn't think it mattered in which direction he took off. With his right hand he eased the throttle forward and the little plane began to move. He glanced at the fuel mixture. For a moment he was back in the duster in Minnesota, ready for the low level passes and the quick climbs he loved to do. He reached over to make sure he could reach all of the buckets on the passenger seat. He fed the engine more fuel and taxied to the edge of the narrow airstrip. Looking down the long, unmarked straightway was like looking into infinity, he thought. The pitted asphalt strip was six-hundred feet long but Brad knew the plane only needed two-thirds of that to become airborne. The moon was still bright but noticeably smaller now and the stars twinkled dully. Brad put his feet on the rudder pedals, jammed the throttle levers forward again and began his roll.

Two minutes later he was at one hundred feet and climbing. He gave the trim wheel a quick turn.

When the altimeter indicated two-hundred feet Brad leveled off. The land mass below was slowly giving way to the dark and moon-speckled wavelets dancing on the surface of Delaware Bay.

He glanced at the compass and angled a few degrees north. Minutes later the Ship John Shoal Lighthouse came into view below. There would be no mournful fog bell tonight given the almost perfect conditions. Brad began to execute his series of left turns. The light flashed white for five seconds and then winked out in constant and monotonous repetition. There was a red sector light marking the port side of the channel and it came into view as the plane arced through the compass headings that would take him in almost the exact opposite direction from the one from which he'd taken off. He was low enough that he could see two of the light's keepers standing on its lookout deck. During their flight Von Don had mentioned that the light station was still manned twenty-four hours a day seven days a week by a rotating crew of three keepers and was open to the public to tour. Von Don admitted that the light fascinated him and that he had made several visits out to it on his days off.

Brad completed the turn and pointed the Cub's nose north parallel to the beaches. He fed a little more of the lean fuel mixture to the O-235's team of one-hundred-and-thirty-five horses and pulled back on the yoke, climbing slowly until the altimeter read three hundred feet. In the pristine night he could see all the way up the coastline that loomed ahead and to his left. For a moment he tried to imagine the terrain as it once was, dark and uninhabited. The moon lit up the water as it ambled toward the beach. Some lonely breakers foamed and then disappeared out in the deeper water. He wouldn't need to adjust course for a little while. He was now following a straight line, he thought to himself. It was almost poetic - the shortest distance between two points of light. Brad checked the fuel gauge. He had siphoned a healthy portion of avgas out of the tank before takeoff in the event he ditched.

Crashing was one thing.

Burning, he knew, was quite another.

Harvey Cedars
North Long Beach Township, NJ

There was literally, Mickey realized, nowhere to go.

No side streets or roads that would not end blindly. The multiple and simultaneous disturbances had turned Long Beach Boulevard into an elongated parking lot. She didn't think the bike would do well in the sand, especially with two riders. Mickey twisted the throttle. Candy squeezed her tighter with the resultant acceleration.

To Mickey's great relief, Mary T's Honda C70 Passport had turned out to be more motorcycle than motor scooter, but without the challenges of a big bike. It had an electric start and only a few simple gauges. And it was blessedly clutchless with a single-cylinder, four-stroke overhead cam engine that shifted itself between three speeds. Mary T said she'd never gone faster than thirty. Mickey took one look at the engine and figured she could get it to do fifty even with two people. The seat was thick and long and flat and easily roomy enough to accommodate two backsides. Plus, this particular Passport was fire-engine red with a snazzy white contrasting section. She thought she might even buy one when this was all over.

Mickey was weaving the bike on and off the sidewalk, beeping the comical Little Nash Rambler horn almost continuously and shouting apologies to the constant near-misses. Her plan was to get to the lighthouse and then send Candy back to the station with the motorbike and instructions for Charlie and Dip. What she would find at the lighthouse, she realized, was anyone's guess. Mickey knew the street layout of the entire Island as did all the other Chiefs. It was part of the Unified Island Law Enforcement proposal she'd inherited from the long-departed and never-missed Chief Jim Justus. If she could continue her current bob-and-weave strategy all the way to 30th Street then she could turn inland. 30th, she knew, would become Bayview Avenue. Bayview would then gently shuck and jive past Viking Village and almost all the way to the State Park. It was the same road, she recalled, she took to meet Doc Guidice the night Shots Caputo had nearly capped her before Ronnie had intervened with extreme prejudice. When Bayview ended she knew she would be forced to turn seaward and she would hit the Boulevard again but by then, she figured, she'd be almost within spitting distance of the light and whatever drama was unfolding there.

A space appeared ahead, like a lead of open water in an arctic ice floe.

"Hang on," Mickey yelled as she pushed the C70 to its factory limits.

"Ahhhhh, shiiiiitttt," was all she heard Candy say.

Barnegat Lighthouse
Barnegat Light, NJ

No one had shot at him this time, Phil the Thrill thought. At least not yet anyway. He shuffled a step to his right.

"You just stay right there now, Ranger Rick," the man in the biker leathers told him. He was huge, Phil noted. One of the biggest men he'd ever seen up close and personal. He didn't seem angry or even perturbed but Phil knew he meant business. He counted four of them. Plus the one who'd entered the Light carrying a large object and a mess of rope. To Phil's knowledge, no one had ever attempted to climb up the lighthouse tower from the outside or had rappelled down from its top. There was a myth that seemed to circulate every summer that you could parachute from the very top and land in the ocean but no one had tried that either. The closest anyone had come was the death leap the crazy guy had taken two summers before. He'd taken a little Chinese or maybe she was Japanese girl hostage, Phil remembered. And as bad as it all was it had turned out better than he had expected at the time. He also recalled that the crazy guy *had* shot at him, although just as a warning. Phil could see the spot in the parking lot where he hit. They could never get the bloodstains out so they eventually just asphalted over it.

The big man jingled Phil's confiscated ring of keys. They stood in a little island of calm. The parachute flare had been just the beginning. Most people, including Phil, thought it was maybe an early start to the fireworks since it was barely past nine-forty five when it happened. Now they were in a swirl of green and yellow smoke. Each of the motorcycle guys had opened a canister – Phil had initially thought they were grenades - and without a breeze to blow it away it was effectively shrouding them.

Phil could hear some shouting from what he assumed were the local cops. With all the civilians in close proximity he figured they were playing it pretty cool so as not incite a panic and a deadly stampede. He'd had to attend some mandatory seminars on crowd control in an emergency. Phil hadn't seen any weapons, unless you counted the flare gun, which made a "bloop" sound when it went off and the smoke cans, so he gave them credit for not making what was already probably a bad situation much worse. He didn't yet feel in any physical danger. The biker boys had been, if anything, polite but focused. They reminded him of soldiers on a mission. There had been a ripple of applause after the flare went off but it came from behind the structure and Phil still had no idea what had prompted it.

As if on a cue, the huge man popped open another smoke canister. Phil quickly realized his three comrades had done the same. At about that time a man approached them. Phil was waiting for a brandished weapon or barked order to back off but the big man seemed to recognize him. The approaching figure soon revealed himself to be a black man in his late twenties. He wore an open military camouflage jacket with no shirt underneath. Phil could see a set of GI dog tags dangling around his neck down to his hairless chest.

"Paxton," the big man said. "What're you doing here, brother?"

"Come to see my artistry on display," the black man replied. "You look good, Calhoun. Real good. I gotta say."

"Thanks, brother. Think it'll go off the way you rigged it?" the big man who Phil now knew was named Calhoun inquired. He wondered if anyone had ever dared to call him Haystacks.

"Guaranteed," the man named Paxton replied. "As you know, my devices do not fail."

Phil spoke up almost without intending to. "Are you guys going to blow up the lighthouse?" he asked. Then he wondered – was that why the cops were keeping their distance? Phil waited anxiously for the reply.

"Guess you'll have to just stick around for the show," Calhoun said.

That answer, Phil thought, did not thrill him.

Surf City

Charlie and Dip arrived back at the station almost at the same time.

"Well that was certainly weird," Dip said.

"Mine was, too," Charlie replied. "Dennis, I have to say this. I think we have been righteously played."

"What do you mean?"

Charlie walked toward his desk. "All this shit going down at the same time? The odds are just astronomical. And they all went off at exactly the same time. You catch my drift? Like 'synchronize your watches' the same time."

"You mean it was planned?"

"Not just planned, Dennis. Planned, organized and this is the key, executed with military precision," Charlie said.

"You mean like the U.S. military?" Dip asked.

"Yes," Charlie said. "Whoever managed this has a military background and military training. Shit, Darnell would have been proud of how efficiently they pulled this one off. Like clockwork."

"Pulled what off?"

"A multifocal diversionary tactic," Charlie said. "Think about it for a minute. It tied up law enforcement units at key locations up and down the Island. It effectively prevented any kind of a coordinated response. Divide and conquer – the oldest military strategy on earth."

"Yeah, but conquer what?" Dip asked.

Charlie sat down in his chair. He picked up the note Mickey had left him and read it. "The Chief and Candy went to Barnegat Light. I'm guessing that's the objective of whatever this mission is."

"How can you be sure?"

"I just know it. Those motorcycle guys whomping on each other in Beach Haven? They didn't have guns, they didn't have knives, they didn't even have chains and they broke it off and scattered way too easy for my money. It was all complete bullshit now that I understand it better. You see any guys from that boat fire in Ship Bottom?"

"Yeah," Dip answered. "Two of them. They waded in from the ocean. But they said their buddy was still on the boat when they jumped."

"These two guys – they look like fishermen to you?" Charlie asked.

"Not really," Dip said, "but they-"

"Yeah. Not really because trust me they were not fisherman. And don't you get it? There was no buddy still on the boat. That just kept everybody tied up even longer, searching for someone who didn't exist. What'd they look like, these supposed survivors?"

"I don't know," Dip answered. "Kind of rough looking?"

"Regular rough or maybe biker rough?"

Dip shrugged. "Could'a been biker rough I guess. But they were wearing-"

"Tourist shit, right?"

"Yeah," Dip conceded. "They were."

Charlie looked at the note again. "This is the Sons of Satan, man. That's who's behind whatever the hell this clusterfuck really is. All those guys did tours in Nam. Some of them are ex-Navy SEALs and Army Rangers. And Stellwag," Charlie laughed. "Stellwag, man, that dude is George S. Fucking Patton commanding the Third Army of the Pines." He rocked back in his chair. "I don't know what they're up to but this is nothing short of tactically brilliant. Shit, can you believe that these are the guys we had fighting for us over there? You best believe if they couldn't win a war it's only because somebody higher up wouldn't let them."

The phone on Charlie's desk rang and he grabbed it. A look of concern passed over his face. "OK, I understand. I'll let her know right away when she returns. Thank you for telling us." He looked at Dip.

"Trouble?" Dip asked.

"It's Patsy Cleary," Charlie said.

"Did you ask him how things are in Mexico?"

"That wasn't Patsy, Dip," Charlie said. "That phone call was *about* Patsy. He's had a coronary. They're doing everything they can."

U.S.L.S. Ship John Shoal Light Station
Delaware Bay

Alan Stewart puffed on his pipe. This Ship John was the only light he'd ever worked. He tried hard to ignore the constantly swirling rumors of eventual automation. Being a light keeper was a sacred occupation in his book. In fact it was more than an occupation, he thought. It was a calling. He looked out over the Bay's unusually placid water. If there was a better job on earth he'd defy anyone to name it.

"Did you think that was odd?" The question came from Michael Oprea, his partner on this section of Stewart's twenty-two day watch. Oprea had worked the seven a.m. to seven p.m. shift but, as was often the case, could not force himself into his bunk so soon after their shared supper. Oprea was a big man, a full six inches taller than Stewart. He'd been an ironworker in Cleveland before he joined the Lighthouse Service.

"What was unusual?" Stewart asked.

"That plane. Don't see that very often this time of night."

Stewart had to agree. He puffed some more. "For a minute I thought it might be that German-sounding pilot. The one that visits every summer. Thought maybe he was taking a joyride up to watch the skyrockets on LBI. He flew over earlier today, didn't he?"

"I think so," Oprea replied. "Hard to tell once it gets dark though."

"Do I need to report it, you think?" Stewart asked. "Call it in, I mean?"

Oprea thought for a moment. "It's just a little plane," he said finally. "I mean, I guess if it was a Japanese Zero or a Russian MiG then yes, I might think about calling it in."

The two men laughed.

"I'll just make sure I log it," Stewart said. "That should be enough."

"Should be," Oprea replied. "OK, then. I'm going to try and read for a while."

"Anything interesting?" Stewart asked.

"Just started, so too early to tell."

"What's the title?"

Oprea scratched his head. "It's one I picked up in the Cape May County Public Library on my way in. It's called 'I Was a Kamikaze'."

Stewart chuckled. "Is that anything like 'I Was a Teenage Werewolf'?"

"Yeah. Exactly like it, I think," Oprea said.

He turned and slipped back inside.

31

Off Atlantic City, NJ
Heading NNW Altitude 500 ft

BRAD WONDERED IF THE Diving Horse ever dove at night. Having grown up with horses he tried to imagine what it took to get one of the highly self-possessed creatures to leap from that tower. It had to be terrifying, he assumed. He believed horses were far more intuitive than people gave them credit for. His own bay mare, Jolie, always seemed to understand him better than a human friend ever had. Certainly better than Candy had.

The lights of Atlantic City passed beneath and to his left. Just ahead lay the jumbled jigsaw puzzle pieces of Brigantine and the marshy islands that squatted near it. Brad could see the Mullica River, its oxbow bend almost connecting to itself before terminating bulbously in the circular bowl of Great Bay. Long Beach Island loomed ahead. He adjusted the rudder pedals and the rear stabilizers. Pressing the yoke forward slightly he brought the nose of the plane down and watched the altimeter respond. At three hundred feet he leveled off again. He'd make the next course and altitude adjustment when he spotted the causeway bridge. He was still well offshore and planned to remain there until he made that final correction which would point him slightly westward at one-hundred and seventy feet above the beach.

Brad rolled down his side window. The cooler air came whistling through the cabin, ruffling some papers behind his seat noisily. He reached across with his right hand and grabbed a handful of the Lazy Dogs. As he passed the gap that gave Great Bay its wide access to the Atlantic Ocean he transferred them to his left hand. Thrusting his arm straight out the open window he let them drop.

The instant they left his grip he lost sight of them. Up ahead in the distance he saw a shimmering light appear and then drift slowly earthward. Brad hoped they started the fireworks display early.

Barnegat Lighthouse
Barnegat Light, NJ

There was a little more wind at the top of the tower than he had anticipated.

Ronnie had run the heavy braided rope twice around the framework of the lamp room and was hitching it to the package he had humped up the two-hundred-and-seventeen pie-shaped metal steps on his back. It felt like it weighed a ton by the time he got to the last step. He made a mental note of the spot where he'd assembled the M-16 and taken out Danny Rags' button man Shots Caputo. He remembered that Shots was blathering on about something to Mickey while at the same time holding a gun on her. He'd had time to pick him off only because he insisted on making a speech.

Ronnie knew placement of the package was critical if he wanted to achieve full effect. He could barely see Stellwag and the three other Sons as they stood in a four-corners tactical formation. They had popped more smoke and it was wafting upwards toward him. He still had the two handheld tube flares in his waistband. They bit into his belly when he leaned against the ironwork.

He peered over the railing and watched what looked like a bicycle with a motor pull up to the base of the light. He instantly recognized the silhouette of the person who dismounted. He didn't have time to worry about what she was going to do, if anything. He was more than a hundred and fifty feet above her.

And he was running out of time

It was Stellwag who greeted her first.

"Evening, Chief," he said cordially. "What brings you this far north on such a beautiful evening? Come to watch the fireworks?" He flashed a sly smile.

Mickey moved to within six feet of the LT. Then she nodded to Calhoun. "So," she asked the big man, 'You're not still mad at me, are you?"

"No, ma'am," Everett Calhoun replied. "What's past is past. But we got this, Chief. You can head on back now. It'll be alright."

Mickey was able to reasonably assess that neither Stellwag nor Calhoun were armed, which surprised her. "By myself?" Mickey asked. "You know, my ride just took off. I was hoping maybe I could talk to the guy up top about hitching a lift home." She tilted her head skyward.

"I'm afraid he's busy at the moment, ma'am," Calhoun answered.

"How's this gonna end, Everett?" Mickey asked.

"How anything ends is always up to the man at the top," Calhoun replied. "That part never changes."

Mickey shuffled her feet and scraped the gravel with her toe. The Park Ranger next to Calhoun was looking more uncomfortable by the minute. "Everett," Mickey said, "Any chance I could just go talk to him?

"I don't believe you have an appointment, Chief," Calhoun said. "So I'm afraid that's impossible at this point."

Mickey unbuckled her gun belt and wrapped it on itself. She offered it to Calhoun. "I'll come right back down." She took off her badge and jammed it in the holster next to the nine millimeter pistol. "Guess now I'm just somebody's girlfriend. Who wouldn't want to be with the most important person in her life at a time like this? You can understand that, can't you, Everett?"

"Let her in," said Stellwag. "She knows what it means if she goes up."

"Which key is it?" Calhoun asked the ranger.

"The big one with the red paint dab on it," the young man replied nervously.

Calhoun picked the key out. "Open it for her then lock it back up," he said to the ranger. He tilted his head toward Mickey in a "well, go ahead" gesture.

Mickey handed him the gun belt and badge as she passed. Calhoun took them without a word. The young ranger fumbled with the lock but then Mickey heard it click. He opened the door and she stepped inside. It immediately shut behind her and she heard the lock's mechanism slide again. She looked up the segmented dinosaur spine from which the steps were suspended. She had run up them at a full gallop two years earlier trying to save a little girl she barely knew.

She wasn't sure who she was trying to save this time.

The Governor's Ocean House
Island Beach State Park, NJ

The blood alcohol level of the invited guests was rising and therefore so was the din. Major George Joo of the New Jersey State Patrol hated political gatherings but had come to understand they were now a part of his life for better or for worse.

A server in a short white jacket was trying to get his attention. He picked his way carefully across the packed room dodging drinks, dignitaries and assorted damsels until he could hear what the older man was saying.

"Another phone call?" Joo asked. "Where can I take it?"

"In the study this time," the man said. "Come with me. I'll show you."

Joo followed the man down several narrow hallways. The server opened a door and held it. Joo walked in. When the door shut behind him the noise of the raucous revelry disappeared completely. The study was small but sumptuously appointed. Joo walked over to a small secretary desk with impressive scrollwork. The phone had five extension buttons but only one of them was blinking. He punched it and picked up the receiver. After listening intently he replaced the receiver in the cradle.

Joo reached into his jacket pocket and withdrew a small leather-bound notebook. He flipped it open and thumbed through the pages until he found the number for Chief Mickey Cleary in Surf City. This time he took a seat at the small, polished desk with the green-shaded reading lamp. He picked up the phone, depressed the same button and waited for the dial tone. As soon as he heard it he began punching in the numbers, the metallic musical tones pinging with each one.

32

Barnegat Lighthouse

IT WAS EERILY QUIET as Mickey approached the topmost steps inside the tower. About halfway up she'd heard a muffled commotion from outside. It seemed like it was a mixture of cheers and boos and a raised level of what she could only describe as crowd nose. She had stopped, placing a hand on the smooth interior brick to see if there was any vibration that might signal an imminent structural collapse. There was nothing so she kept ascending.

Once at the top she surveyed the situation. She didn't see any suspicious packages, devices or hardware. Certainly there was nothing that screamed out "domestic terrorism." She moved quietly but quickly to the little door that gave egress to the observation deck. She couldn't see Ronnie but she could hear him moving above her. He was outside the lamp room on the even less enclosed deck above the observation one. She went back inside and clambered up the wooden steps that would take her inside the lamp room. Once there she saw a glass door that had been propped open and led to the narrower deck outside. She stepped out. The railing was much smaller with wide spaces between the supporting stanchions. There was some kind of tattered netting as well. Probably to keep birds from hitting the glass she figured. She saw ropes that appeared to run around the glass-enclosed lamp room and stepped carefully around them. They disappeared over the side of the tower. Mickey decided she didn't want to spook Ronnie. She got ready to call out his name.

"You call that a motorcycle?" He was right behind her. Mickey tried not to flinch. She turned around.

"It's a motorbike," she said. "Pretty cool one, too. It's a Honda, but still. Automatic tranny, electric start, three-speed single barrel overhead cam. I got it up to fifty but I bet with a little work I could squeeze ten maybe fifteen more out of it easy. I'm pretty good with motors." She looked at his face. "What are you doing way up here, soldier boy?" she asked. "What's this all about?"

"It's already done," he said with a crooked smile. "You're just a little late, I'm afraid."

"Well that's too bad," Mickey replied. "'Cause I was dead serious about the motorbike. Figured the three of us could take it for rides on Sundays."

"The three of us, huh," Ronnie repeated. "I'm not so sure Patsy-"

"Listen closely," Mickey said locking him with her gaze. "I said...the three of *us*."

She saw the realization of what she had just said dawning on Ronnie's face. He stepped toward her but then stopped.

"Look at that," he said pointing over her shoulder and toward the southern expanse of the Island which twinkled in the distance behind her.

She heard the unmistakable drone of an airplane engine.

It sounded like it was getting closer.

▲▲▲

Candy had given up on mastering the Honda in less than two hundred yards. She was walking it back toward the lighthouse when she heard the crowd buzz and then applaud. Or mostly applaud she realized. There were some loud boos and shouts of "Take it down!" Even a few tired references to communist sympathizers. It reminded her of Brad's outburst in the Diving Bell and the reaction it got.

Then she looked up.

Hanging from the lighthouse railing was a long banner. It dangled at the end of rope which allowed it to lay against the white paint of the lighthouse's lower half. It looked like the kind she'd seen trailing behind the little airplanes that buzzed over the beaches all day. Only it wasn't an advertising banner. It hung a little crooked and not quite right. The banner was vertical and not horizontal like the ones in the air. Its giant letters spelled out only three words:

STOP THE WAR

The shouting had subsided. Now people were taking pictures with old Kodak Brownies, Instamatics and small cardboard disposable cameras. She even saw a Polaroid Swinger pressed into service. The booing and the catcalls seemed to quickly die out but at the same time the crowd murmuring was slowly increasing. A black man in an Army fatigue jacket stepped forward and began clapping rhythmically. Candy could see the dog tags on his bare chest bouncing each time his hands slapped together. He said only one thing.

"Stop the War. Stop the War. Stop the War."

His voice, she thought, was actually gaining strength with each repetition. For a moment Candy feared the crowd might set upon him in anger. But several people started to clap along with him. Then two younger men, both in some variant of military fatigues went and stood next to him. They raised their fists in the air and echoed the chant.

"Stop the War. Stop the War. Stop the War."

The Sons of Satan, Candy noticed, had all pulled old military shirts or jackets over their sleeveless leather vests. Some wore jungle hats and some had on red or green berets. They raised their fists and joined the cadence. She could hear the roar of more motorcycles in the distance.

"Stop the War. Stop the War. Stop the War."

Candy dropped the bike. She pulled her pen from her shirt pocket and her notebook from her jean shorts and started scribbling. She had not brought her camera but judging from the number of flashbulbs popping and flashcubes clicking she figured she would be able to find a suitable photograph before press time.

Each time she looked up from writing more people had gathered together and the chant was swelling.

"Stop the war. Stop the War. Stop the War."

It was plain, Candy thought. It was simple. And it was real. It had none of the "What do we want, when do we want it, kumbaya," bullshit heard so often at the issue-indistinguishable rallies she'd attended. It was not a question, she realized. It was not an answer either. No, she thought, it wasn't even a statement. It was a demand spoken from not just one heart but many. It was the simplest solution to so many problems. It was the best solution. It was, she thought and then wrote it down, an "In the course of human events" moment and she was lucky enough to be present for it.

The crowd had rushed together in some spots. And more and more fists were raised, Candy saw. More voices joined the simple refrain. Within just a few minutes it had even drowned out the sound of the small ocean waves lapping at the sand. It was young people and it was older people. There were middle aged women with tears on their cheeks. Had they lost sons? She wondered. Did they have sons who were fighting there right now? She knew that before she left she would ask them.

A Barnegat Light Police officer came up and stood near her. He just looked around, smiled and shook his head. "Power to the people, I guess," he said to Candy and then moved on.

A man appeared at the lighthouse's topmost railing. He lit something that looked from so far below like it might be a stick of dynamite. Candy took a sharp breath in and held it until she realized it was a flare. An incredibly bright flare. The man, it had to be Mickey's boyfriend Ronnie she assumed, waved it back and forth and then held it straight over his head. She recognized the image it made and she immediately knew she had her lede.

She scribbled in her notebook in stenographer's shorthand:

"For just a moment the old lighthouse, dark for decades, was ablaze again signaling not to ships this time but to citizens. Signaling that it was time to end a perilous journey and bring travelers back from a distant shore. And in that moment it became more than a lighthouse. It became a beacon of hope and a plea for peace. In that moment it was a not just a tower but a statue, raising high the burning torch of Liberty."

Candy looked at the words which had flowed out of her almost unbidden. She thought it might be the best single thing she had ever written. The chant was beginning to subside, replaced by a rising tide of thunderous applause as the flare dimmed and died.

Only when the clapping finally faded did Candy hear the sound of the approaching airplane engine.

-33-

BRAD WAS NOW FLYING directly above Long Beach Boulevard, the long straight spine that stitched the Island's summer colonies together. He descended slightly until the tip of the altimeter needle bounced halfway between one hundred and sixty and one hundred and seventy. Brad pulled one of the buckets closer. The main road was clogged with cars and on either side it was thronged with people. He'd been born with hyper acute visual acuity. An astounded optometrist once measured it at 20/10 which, the balding little man with coffee breath had told him, meant that he could see at twenty feet what the average person couldn't see until they were only ten feet away. At the low altitude Brad could see expressions on the upturned faces lit by the regularly spaced series of streetlights. He was on final approach for what he realized was a bombing run. Brad loved watching *12 O'clock High* – "a Quinn-Martin Production!" he remembered with a smile. In high school he'd done a research paper on the Norden Bombsight which his teacher, although it ran contrary to the teacher's own pacifist leanings, had given him an "A" on. Now he had to be pilot, navigator and bombardier simultaneously. He peered below and saw a woman pushing a baby stroller with one hand. A little girl in a red, white and blue jumper held her other hand and walked along with her holding a large pinwheel.

He grabbed another handful of the Lazy Dogs and rolled down the window.

Barnegat Lighthouse

Ronnie kicked the spent tube flare toward the lamp room so it wouldn't tumble over the side.

"He's flying right on top of the Island," Mickey said, peering intently into the dark southern sky. "I didn't think you could do that."

Ronnie stood next to her now. "Could we discuss this 'three of us thing' for a minute?" he asked.

"Now?"

"We may not have a lot of private time for a while depending on how willing various government agencies are to forgive and forget."

Mickey was still looking at the plane which continued to drone louder. "I think it's coming straight at us. I mean really straight at us."

Ronnie walked to the edge of the platform and grabbed the rail. "Probably just going to buzz us," he said. "Pilots in Nam did it all the time. Buzzed the towers. You'd be amazed at how close they can come. Like reach out and touch close."

Mickey noticed it was becoming harder to hear him. A breeze had kicked up and was wrapping itself around the light and converging where they stood. It blew their voices out to sea.

The sight of the little plane was mesmerizing. The prop was a blur and the ever-enlarging sound had now changed from drone to whine.

"We need to get inside right now," Mickey yelled. "He's not just going to buzz us. He's going to fly right into us."

Ronnie pushed her forward. She stumbled toward the little door but found that her foot was entangled in a tangled loop of excess rope. At the rate the plane was approaching she wasn't sure either of them could make it inside in time. She started to unlace her boot. Ronnie pushed her to the deck. "Stay down," he shouted. "Just stay down as low as you can." He disappeared into the lamp room. She realized with disbelief that he had left her out there by herself.

The whine was deafening now as the plane bore down. Mickey said a quick and fervent prayer to the Blessed Virgin Mary and put her cheek against the rough concrete of the iron-reinforced walkway. She reached inside her blouse and fished around until she found her St. Christopher's medal. She squeezed the silver disc tightly and repeated the prayer. The one Innocentia had taught them all those years ago. Hail Holy Queen enthroned above, she murmured. *Salve Regina.*

A brilliant light shone around her.

If this was really it, she decided, then she was ready. She thought of the child that she, that they would never know. A tear trickled from one eye.

Barnegat Lighthouse

BRAD NOW REALIZED HE had waited too long. He'd already heaved one group of the Lazy Dogs out the window but he wouldn't have time for any more. The lighthouse lay dead ahead. To his surprise there were at least two people on its outside deck. Then he saw the sign and thought perhaps he was hallucinating from the stress and the adrenaline. It rippled gently to-and-fro against the stark white of the tower. He knew he had only seconds to decide if he wanted to put the plane in a hard turn. But then what? Put the Cub down on the calm ocean and just swim away? Go down with the ship? Head inland until he ran out of gas and then hope to disappear into the vast Pine Barrens?

Time was slowing down for him even if the air speed indicator said otherwise. He was amazed at how calmly he was able to mentally tick off his options and evaluate them. He saw the top of the lighthouse clearly now even through the spinning propeller.

Luftwaffe, he thought. The plane is the weapon.

He lifted the nose and then he killed the engine. Once the prop quit rotating he could see perfectly out the windshield.

Then, in the next instant, he couldn't see anything at all.

▲▲▲

Ronnie pulled the remaining flare from his waistband. It was slightly different from the other one which had ignited and burned despite its age and its long period in storage. Ronnie knew he needed lightning twice. The printed markings on the tube in his hand had long worn off but he didn't think it was a *fusee*, a railroad flare, which would burn red and not accomplish what he wanted.

He searched for the hinges on the huge Fresnel lens that would allow him access to its interior. Once he located them he swung open the exquisitely crafted and highly polished glass door. Ronne peeled the tape from the larger end of the old flare and pulled off the waxed cardboard cap, exposing the black igniter button. The cap had a rough surface on its top that was designed to abrade the igniter button creating a spark which lit the flare. He hoped the cap would be rough enough to do the job after being exposed for so long.

Ronnie glanced outside and saw that the plane was still bearing down on them.

This is not an exercise, he thought as he worked.

It suddenly became quieter. It took Ronnie a second to comprehend that the plane's engine had either quit or been shut down. Another glance revealed that it was still coming at them.

Ronnie scuffed the igniter button with the cap.

Nothing.

He did it again.

Nothing.

On the third try the stick burst into life and burning particles singed his hands. He thrust the flare inside the Fresnel lens and propped it upright. Then he went to get Mickey.

▲▲▲

Candy heard the whistling and then the crashes and the pops. She turned her head and saw a car windshield explode fifty yards away. There was a bang of metal on metal somewhere. Chips of concrete and chunks of asphalt flew up. She waited for screams but none came.

Then it got very quiet. It seemed like everyone had their necks craned upward. The plane which had been almost overhead was still there but its propeller wasn't turning anymore and its whining, dental-drill engine had gone silent. It was now gracefully gliding toward the top of the lighthouse.

Candy had done a little story for *The SandPaper* on the installation of a Fresnel lens, something she knew nothing about before her research. It occurred to her that if the plane struck the lighthouse the incredibly expensive lens would be lost forever. Then she saw movement at the top. This shocked her back into the present and the sickening realization that the movement she saw was Chief Cleary and Ronnie. They were still up there.

And she knew that it was Brad was at the controls of the airplane.

Despite the large crowd of people around her there was a strange, stunned silence. It was as if everyone were holding their breath at the same time. Then she saw the light. She had learned from writing her story that there was still no lamp at the top of the tower. Her brain struggled to reconcile what she knew with what she was seeing.

The light seemed to burst forth in every direction. It illuminated the ground, the cars, the rocks on the jetty, the upturned faces and the water for what looked like a thousand yards out to sea.

It occurred to her she would have to rewrite the lede.

For the moment anyway, Old Barney was a real lighthouse again.

▲▲▲

The magnification of a first order Fresnel lens was extraordinary, able to take a two-hundred-watt incandescent light bulb and turn it to something you couldn't stare at without damaging your retinas. The tube flare had a candlepower rating of around fifteen thousand. With the power of the lens it was like looking into the eyes of the sun. Ronnie cupped a hand over his own eyes like a makeshift visor. The sudden radiance had ruined his night vision. He only hoped it had done the same to whoever was piloting the plane.

Ronnie stumbled out through the glass door. He ran into Mickey before he could see her. He dropped down on top of her.

"Are we dead?" she asked. She had her eyes squeezed shut.

"Nah," he said. "The three of us are OK." He looked at her predicament. The combined twenty-pound weight of the banner and its attached tow bar had pulled a looped section of the rope taut around her ankle. He would have to pull the banner back up at least a foot or two to create enough slack for her to slip free.

"I have to pull the banner up," he said. "As soon as you feel the rope go slack pull your leg out. OK?"

"OK," she said. "Just don't go anywhere without me this time."

"Promise," he replied and moved off toward the railing. The sound of the plane's engine had been replaced by a high-pitched whistling noise. It was now gliding, Ronnie knew.

The multiply refracted and magnified light from the torch still made it almost impossible for him to see, He felt along the tick rope until he came to the railing. The whistling was getting louder. He hooked a leg around one of the iron stanchions and pulled. He felt the tow bar and banner elevating and pulled in the two feet of rope he figured he needed. Then he unhooked his leg from the stanchion and backed up. The section of rope behind him loosened.

"I'm out," he heard Mickey yell.

The whistling hurt his ears and he felt like it was almost on top him. And now, along with the whistle there was a flapping sound. His hand was curled under and over the rope, held there by the weight at the end. As he worked to slide it out a gust of air knocked him backward just as the rope pulled him forward.

For the next few seconds Ronnie had the distinct feeling not that he was falling, but that he was flying.

▲▲▲

Candy watched along with everyone else as the plane drew closer to the lighthouse as if it were being pulled in by an invisible wire. Some reflexively turned their heads or covered their eyes the way she used to do during the Saturday matinee monster movies in the balcony at the long-charred Fox Theatre. But she could not force herself to look away.

As the plane approached the tower a collective "Ooooohhhhhh," went up from the crowd in anticipation of what was surely about to occur. There were a few screams and scattered shouts of "NO!" and the requisite number of "Oh my God!" exclamations. To Candy it all seemed to be happening in slow-motion.

But then, as if waved away by a miraculous, unseen hand, the plane's left wing suddenly tipped up. It appeared to pass directly over the top of the circular railing that surrounded the lamp room without touching it. She couldn't tell whether it missed by an inch or by ten feet. But she now knew one thing.

It had missed.

She watched as the aircraft veered seaward. For a moment Candy thought it was going to dive straight into the ocean. But then it seemed to regain its balance and, still soundless, it banked slightly to the left and disappeared into the night sky heading north.

▲▲▲

The brilliant light was beginning to fade but Mickey was still having trouble seeing.

"Did you hear what I said?" she called. "I'm out."

She didn't get a reply so she pulled her boot back on and laced it then pushed herself up until she could stand. She blinked several times and tried to find some way to get her night vision working again.

"I said I'm out," she called again. "Hey, Dunn, where are you?"

Still there was no reply. Mickey moved cautiously around the deck. As her vision improved she realized something unthinkable.

Ronnie was no longer on it.

-35-

Barnegat Lighthouse

MICKEY LEANED OVER THE rusted little railing and stared down in disbelief.

"Little help?" Ronnie asked looking up at her. He was about ten feet below her toes.

"How the fuck-. Are you OK?"

"I think so," Ronnie called. "Nothing's broken or dislocated I don't think."

"Can you pull yourself up?" Mickey asked.

"I'm not sure," Ronnie replied. "The yank overboard tore up my palm pretty badly. I don't think I can grip well enough to go hand over hand. Anyone ever asks you, you tell them this is way worse than gym class."

The absurdity of the comment in the situation made Mickey laugh out loud.

"Copy that," was all she could answer. The breeze had dropped and in the still air high above the ground she thought she could feel the tower vibrating.

"You feel that?" Ronnie asked.

"Yeah," Mickey said.

"Even if he nicked it with a wing it shouldn't fall down, right?"

"Not a chance," Mickey said although she had no idea if this was the truth. She recalled Loretta's Rock of Gibraltar comment. "You alright for a minute until I figure out how to get you back up here?"

"Sure," Ronnie said. "It's a nice night and, like John Glenn said, oh, that view is tremendous." He gave her a smile but she could hear strain and fatigue in his voice. The vibrations increased. "You positive? I mean about the whole not-falling-down thing?" he asked.

"It's like the Rock of Gibraltar," Mickey said. "It's actually two towers. One inside the other. They're not both gonna come down."

"If you say so," he replied. "I just hope they didn't cancel the fireworks on my account."

"Nah. I doubt anybody even noticed you were up here."

"OK," Ronnie said. She watched him draw his knees up and lock his angles around the rope. "Sure. Yeah. Let's go with that for now. You feel that, right?"

Mickey did. The vibration was getting stronger.

Then she heard metal creaking and groaning.

Then footsteps. Then voices and echoes of voices.

They all got louder and the vibrations got stronger. She understood what was happening. They were humping it up the steps double-time.

"Hey, Private Dunn," Mickey called down.

"Yes, Chief Cleary," he replied.

"Hang on, soldier," she said. "Cavalry's almost here."

Ronnie exhaled a laugh. "Great news. Got an ETA?"

"I can guarantee you they will not be de-layed," she said.

"Good to hear," he said. "Hey, while we still have a minute. There isn't any chance we could rig this to make it look like I rescued you, is there?" He was breathing slightly faster now she noticed.

"Sure. I'll lie about it as long as you'll swear to it," she replied.

"Deal," he said. "Any other last minute words of wisdom?"

Mickey could hear what the voices were saying now. And who they were. She recognized Stellwag and Calhoun, amazed at the big man's heart in what had to be for him an almost superhuman physical effort. They sounded like they couldn't be more than a few steps from the top.

"Nope. No words of wisdom," she said. "But I do have a direct order"

"Yeah?" Ronnie asked. "What's that?"

Mickey smiled at him.

"Don't let go of the rope."

Barnegat Light State Park

Candy looked at the pair of unsmiling State Troopers and wondered how they'd gotten here so fast. The lights on their cars were flashing a patriotic red, white and electric blue strobe pattern and it bounced off everything and everyone in kaleidoscopic combinations. It reminded her of a Pink Floyd concert she'd attended in Omaha. The Barnegat Light officers were flanking the two Troopers. All of them had their eyes on the little door that led into the lighthouse vestibule. Candy took out her notebook and pen and approached the Trooper who looked most likely to be in charge.

"Excuse me," she said, tapping him on the razor-sharp crease in his uniform shirt.

"Can I help you ma'am?" he asked.

"I'm Candy, Candy Catan," she said, immediately realizing this would be her new pen name from now on. "I'm a reporter. Do you know the identity of the man who just saved Barnegat Light?"

"Excuse me, ma'am? The man who did - what did you say?"

"The identity – the name or anything about the man who just saved the lighthouse."

The Trooper gave his partner a questioning look.

"Ma'am," he said to Candy, "All I can say is we're here because of a report of trespassing and possible destruction of government prop-"

"Ronnie Dunn," a voice called out authoritatively. "That

was Ronnie Dunn that just saved Old Barney." It had come from man with salt-and-pepper hair wearing a Barnegat Light Police uniform. He thrust his hand at the Trooper.

"Belz," he said. "Chief Michael Belz. Barnegat Light PD. Happy to assist in any way we can. How'd you all get here so fast?"

"We were establishing a perimeter around the Governor's Ocean House on Island Beach," the Trooper said. "He's hosting a number of important guests this weekend."

"Fat cats with open checkbooks I imagine," Belz replied. "Well that certainly explains the truly magnificent response time."

"Now maybe it's just me but I don't see that any government property has been destroyed or even damaged for that matter," Candy interjected trying to do her best Lois Lane impersonation. They apparently hadn't yet noticed the divots in the concrete and the cars damaged by the Lazy Dogs. "I don't see any graffiti either. Do you?" She scribbled madly and theatrically in her notebook. "Could I have your name?"

"My name?"

"Your name. And rank if you don't mind. For the article in the newspaper."

"Article?"

"The one I'm going to file shortly with my paper in the city on the man or maybe it's men who just saved Barnegat Light from being either completely destroyed or irreparably damaged by an out of control airplane."

"Ma'am, I think perhaps you're mistaken," the Trooper said. "We're here to take into custody whoever is responsible for the message that's displayed up there." He pointed at the banner.

"So let me get this right," Candy said. She scribbled some more and flipped a page for effect. "You're going to apprehend – is that the correct term, apprehend?'

"Uh, yes, ma'am. I believe it is."

"You're going to apprehend someone who just saved a national treasure not to mention a local landmark over a *sign*?"

The Trooper adjusted the brim of his campaign hat. "Ma'am, I would hardly call that just a sign. Now I-"

Belz took a step closer. "Trooper – ah, what's your name there, son?" He squinted at the polished ID badge on his chest. "DeBakke. Good. Now, Trooper DeBakke, let me tell you for the record that the man who just saved the lighthouse is named Ronald Dunn.

He served this country in Viet Nam. He was putting his life on the line when you were deciding who to ask to your Junior Prom. Now I'm just thinking out loud here, mind you, but do you really want the attention, no not attention, do you people really want the notoriety of publicly humiliating a war veteran who just put himself in harm's way again and preserved a damn historical landmark. Who's your superior?"

"That would be Major Joo," DeBakke replied, "but-"

"Well I'm sure Major Joo might want a little heads up before you two drag him – and the Governor, I might add – into what is sure to be a public relations debacle."

"How do you spell your last name?" Candy asked. She felt like they were gaining traction. Then Candy remembered Mickey mentioning a Major Joo from the State Patrol. "Never mind," she said. "I'm sure I can call Major Joo. I'll get it from him. I have his number in my desk back at the newsroom."

"You know the Major, ma'am?"

"I'm a reporter," Candy shot back avoiding the question. "And you can tell the Major that this situation also involves Chief Mickey Cleary of Surf City." DeBakke's facial expression told Candy he recognized that name.

"Will you excuse me for a moment ma'am? Chief?"

Candy and Belz nodded. Both troopers retreated to their cars.

Belz motioned Candy over. "No offense, young lady, but just who in the hell are you?"

Candy noticed the troopers had shut their light bars off.

"Candy Catanzariti," she said and shook his hand.

"And you're a real reporter?" Belz asked.

"Yes," she said shaking her notebook. "Yes I am."

"Might I ask for which newspaper?" Belz inquired further. He took off his wire-rimmed glasses and began cleaning them with his tie.

"*The SandPaper*. You can check when they open again on Monday."

A huge grin spread across Belz's face. "The SandPaper," he said. "And so your paper in the city is in…Surf City?" He put on his glasses. "Well darlin'," he said. "I am very pleased to meet you. And may I be the first to say that I firmly believe that you are someone who is going to go far in this world."

Just as he said this a roar erupted from the crowd. The Sons of Satan emerged followed by Ronnie and then Mickey. A young park ranger handed Mickey her gun belt and badge.

"Don't you want to go get an interview?" Belz asked Candy.

"What? An interview? Oh, yeah. An interview. Thanks, Chief." Candy stuffed the notebook in her jeans and walked off.

"What are we going to do with that, Chief?" one of Belz's officers asked, pointing to the banner luffing gently in the night breeze. "You know the Park Service is going to want it taken down right away."

"Just tell them it's evidence," Belz replied. "And as such it needs to remain untouched and in place for twenty-four hours. It's about damn time somebody took a stand on something important around here."

Belz put on his hat and began moving away.

SUNDAY
JULY 4th, 1971

-37-

Winding Way
Merion Station, PA

BRENTON STERLING "BIFF" BRETT had just dropped off Billy Pennisi two blocks from his home and told him to say nothing and speak to no one until Biff could get things sorted out. He'd told the same thing to Lance Pruitt before leaving him a country mile from his parents' acreage. The neighborhood was deserted, a fact Biff believed worked heavily in their favor.

His wife, the former Suzanne "Sukie" Bradford was at home making sure nothing was amiss and doing reconnaissance for any snoopers, cops or nosy neighbors. She was also looking for ways to make sure people continued to believe they were not at home. Sterling Bradford "Bix" Brett, aged fifteen, sat sullenly in the passenger seat next to him.

"And the same goes for you, obviously," Biff said to the boy. "No phone calls, no sign language, no semaphore, no smoke signals, no nothing. You sit in your room and you stay there. I don't want to hear your voice or see your face for a month."

"We didn't *do* anything to her," Bix whined. "Like nothing at all. The little slut."

Almost reflexively Biff's left hand shot out and cuffed the boy square on the cheekbone. Bix began to cry.

"Shut up, you big fucking baby," Biff said almost spitting the words out. "You and your slimy friends completely disgust me. I don't think disgust is even a strong enough word."

"I told you," the boy sniffled. "We didn't do anything."

"You bought alcohol on fake driver's licenses. You gave alcohol to Betsy Dexter who probably had never taken a sip before in her life. Then you let her drink enough of that alcohol that she passed out. And then you molested her. Did you hear what I said? You…fucking…molested her and she's a child. Great job Bix – put that on your application to Princeton. Oh by the way, I am a child molester. But I have good grades and SAT's so it's all OK, right?"

Bix sniffled and snuffled and shifted in his seat.

"Do you know this could cost me my job if we can't bury this whole mess ten feet deep?" Biff said. "Do you see anyone else in our house earning a living? Do you?"

"No," Bix replied.

"Right," Biff said. "So, if you don't want to be going to public school in the fall and then hoping you get in to some shit college that happens to need a child molester to fill its affirmative action quota, you will do exactly as I tell you. Understood?"

"Understood," Bix said almost in a whisper. "Hey, what's that guy doing up there?"

In the center of road ahead was a thickly built man in a shirt and tie and cheap looking slacks. He was waving a red metal gas can. There weren't any sidewalks so Biff had no choice but to slow down and then stop when the man did not move. He hit the button on his armrest and the driver's side window on the Mercedes SL450 slipped silently into the door.

"Morning," the man said. "Thanks for stopping."

"You didn't give me much choice there, old sport," Biff replied coolly.

"Well, I've been walking for almost two hours. Knocked on every door. For a ritzy neighborhood it sure looks like a ghost town today. Where is everybody, anyway?"

"Down the shore I suppose," Biff. "Fourth of July and all that."

"That makes sense," the man said. His tie was loosened and large sweat stains ringed his underarms Biff could now see. And like the character in the Dick Tracy comics, Biff mused, he had B.O. Plenty.

"So can you help me out?" the man asked. "I don't know if I'll even see another car the way things are going. I think there's a Gulf Station up on Montgomery Avenue that's open all the time. I'd sure appreciate it. That your boy?" He motioned to Bix.

"My son, Bix. Say hello, Bix."

"Hello, sir," the boy said.

"Bix," the man said with a chuckle. "That is one bitchin' name. Bet the girls like it. And no need to call me sir."

Biff saw that the man already had the rear driver's side door open and was sliding his formidable bulk onto the leather back seat. He placed the gas can on his lap.

"You can put that in the trunk if you want," Biff said, looking in the rearview mirror.

"I'll just hold it," the man said. "Don't want to dirty up a nice car like this any more than I have to."

The response struck Biff as an odd one but he decided to ignore it.

"So what's your name?" Bix asked without turning around.

"It's a funny one," the man said. "Oreste. It's Italian. Real old-school Italian. But nobody uses it. Everybody I know just calls me Rusty."

THURSDAY
AUGUST 12th, 1971

-38-

Tavistock Country Club
Haddonfield, NJ

"CAN'T WE TEE OFF earlier than one o'clock?"

The question came from a sandy-haired boy wearing a pink Lacoste shirt with banded sleeves and madras plaid golf shorts.

Greg Raecker was the Club Professional.

"You know it's Ladies' Day," Raecker replied pleasantly. "One o'clock. Go to the range, practice putting. You three go to college. I'm sure you can amuse yourselves for thirty-five minutes."

"And you know my family is one of the founding members of this club," the boy answered.

"I do. Because you remind of that fact every time you play." He tapped a little green pencil with gold lettering on the glass counter top. "It's still one o'clock on Ladies' Day. No exceptions, I'm afraid. A mandate from the Board of Directors which, if memory serves, includes your lovely mother, who should be making the turn right...about... now."

The boy's two companions were comparing a shipment of TaylorMade putters that had arrived since their last round.

"And there's no way we can score a couple of carts? It's the freaking Mojave desert out there today, Greg," the boy said.

"It is warm, I'll give you that," Raecker said. His affable manner seemed as unshakeable as granite. "But it's a dry heat, as they say. Half the fun of playing golf is the walk. If you're any good, that is. The marshals will be out so do mind your pace of play."

The boy leaned in. "I know you think you're hot shit because you played on the PGA Tour but you never won a major or anything. I looked it up," he said.

"I do so enjoy our little chats, Mr. DeVary. But the reason I think that I'm, as you so articulately stated, hot shit, is that I've teed off as a professional at St. Andrews, Harbor Towne and Pebble Beach. I was in a final pairing with Lee Trevino. I can respectably call Palmer 'Arnie' and Nicklaus 'Jack' and at nearly twice your age I can still hit a golf ball twice as far as you can. Now, do enjoy your round and remind your friends that they are guests and as such are expected to respect the Club's rules and conduct themselves like gentlemen at all times."

Chip DeVary III decided to let it go. "So no carts," he said. "But we do at least get a caddy, correct?"

"If you wish," Raecker said. "But unlike a public defender, one will be provided to you at no charge even if you can afford one. It is a hot day, as you pointed out. And you will be asking your caddy to lug three bags for eighteen holes. We do encourage you to tip him generously at the end of your round."

"Does he get a salary?" DeVary asked.

"The Club provides him a minimum guaranteed wage, yes," Raecker said. "But it's customary to-"

"So just pay him a better salary," DeVary interrupted. Then he walked away.

At twelve-fifty-four DeVary and his friends walked up to the #1 tee box. There to greet them was an athletically built African-American man. He had muscled forearms and wore a Timex wristwatch with a silver Twist-O-Flex band.

DeVary skipped any pleasantries. "You want to check your Rolex there and see if it's one o'clock yet, Uncle Remus," he said. "Sure feels like one o'clock to me."

"Five 'til," the young black man said ignoring the slur. Never take the bait he'd learned over many years. He already knew that they weren't going to tip him. He also knew that this time it didn't matter. "Maybe you all should take a few practice swings. Loosen up a bit. It'll smooth out your swing some."

"Listen, Sambo," DeVary said. "How about if we golf and you caddy. Pretty sure that's what the Club has in mind here. If I need any advice from you I'll be sure to ask for it."

"Fair enough," the young man replied with a smile. He went to collect the bags and set them on the cart path beside the elevated tee. He rubbed at the scar beneath his left cheekbone.

"Fuck it, it's close enough," DeVary said to his friends. "Let's just go."

The young man watched the trio of wildly errant tee shots and listened to the ensuing torrents of profanity without comment.

The three golfers clambered down the spike-marked railroad ties that served as steps. DeVary was the last one down. "Don't you say a word," he growled.

Two and a half hours later they approached the fifteenth tee. It was the furthest point on the heavily wooded course from the huge timber and stone clubhouse. They had stopped keeping score after four increasingly disastrous holes and had not paused at the clubhouse when making the turn onto the back nine.

There were no groups either directly in front or directly behind them.

"We better drink these beers before they get warm," DeVary said. The Club's roving snack and beverage service was a modified Club Car driven by a comely young girl Chip DeVary referred to as "the cart wench." She had engaged them at several points along the course and now the heat and the alcohol were beginning to exact a toll. They each popped open a can of Coors Banquet Beer, a relative delicacy east of the Mississippi River which the Club dispatched a truck all the way to Golden, Colorado once a month to procure.

"You want one?" One of his guests asked motioning to the young man with the bags.

"Caddies don't drink during a round," DeVary snapped. "They caddy. By mandate of the Board of Directors I'm pretty sure."

"That's OK. I'm all good," the young man said.

"Besides, they like the heat," DeVary said. "Reminds them of their cotton choppin' days on the ol' plantation."

The other of DeVary's guests let out an exasperated sigh. "Jesus, Chip," he said. "That's enough. Seriously, man?" Then he said to their caddy, "You haven't told us your name."

"It's Drew," the young man said. He pulled a driver from one of the bags and looked hard at DeVary. "And it's a Timex not a Rolex."

"No shit, Sherlock Homeboy," DeVary shot back. "Did you really think I was serious about it being a Rolex?" He reached for the club. Drew did not offer it to him.

Then Drew asked him, "You do know what they say about a Timex? Right, white boy?"

"Who the fuck you think you're talkin' to? Gimme the club, Rastus." DeVary snapped his fingers.

"A Timex," Drew said. He let DeVary grab the grip but not did not let go of it, "A Timex," he said again, this time snapping the club forward until it hit DeVary square in the chest, sending him tumbling backwards. "They say a Timex, well now it might take itself a licking but one thing you ought to know, motherfucker - it just keeps on ticking."

Victoria, Minnesota

"Name again? The pleasant woman asked with a kind smile. Her name badge identified her only as Mary Pat.

"Kristen," the younger woman answered. "Kristen Ollenburg."

"Pretty name," Mary Pat said filling in the squares on the form in front of her. "Is it Scandinavian?"

"Swedish mother, German father," Kristen replied.

"I'm sorry, did you say Kirsten or Kristen?" Mary Pat inquired, lifting the pen from the paper. "I always get them mixed up."

"Kristen," Kristen answered. "Just Kris, to most people. Like Kris Kringle."

"OK," Mary Pat continued. "Any aliases?"

Kristen hesitated at the question.

"Isn't it funny how they phrase that?" Mary Pat said. "Aliases? Makes everyone sound like they're on the run from the FBI or something. It's silly I know, but that's what it says on the form. Aliases. So, anything like a married name, a professional name or a pen name or anything else official that might say something different than Kristen Ollenburg?"

"Nope," Kristen replied. "Like the kids all say, that's my name, don't wear it out."

Mary Pat laughed. "If I had a dollar for every time one of my four said that. OK, then. Well, I think I have all we need. Let me be the first to welcome you to Queen of Peace Parish. We're not that big. I'm sure you'll make new friends here right away."

"Yes, I'm really looking forward to that," Kristen said.

"You know," Mary Pat said. "I really thought that with a name like yours you'd probably be –"

"Lutheran?" Kristen asked.

"Well, yes," Mary Pat said.

"Oh, I hate lutefisk," Kristen said. "Although I've always admired Martin Luther's willingness to challenge not only entrenched beliefs but also to take on an institution with overwhelming power."

Mary Pat looked at her oddly.

"Sorry. I took a course that was all about him when I was a student at the University of Mary. It's in North Dakota." Mary Pat nodded. "You don't sound like you're from Minnesota," Kristen said to her.

"Oh no, dear. I'm not. I'm from Omaha, Nebraska. Husker Country. Bob Devaney. Go Big Red. This is going to be our year. You watch." Mary Pat tucked the form in a bright red folder and handed her a small pamphlet. "Summer Mass schedule is on the back and so are the Rectory hours. You'll like Father Mike. Gail is the Parish Secretary and she's the real brains of the operation. But that Father Mike, now he is definitely from Minnesota. You know. Yah sure, you bet'cha all the way. Don't worry dear, you're going to fit right in here. I can tell."

"I'm sure I will," Kristen replied. "I've always been extremely adaptable to new roles."

Iowa Baptist Medical Center
Des Moines, Iowa

The back side of the Emergency Room was littered with cigarette butts. The sun was hot and Charlie was sweating. He checked his shirt hoping he wasn't pitting out. A moment later a tall brunette woman in a white lab coat over a purple scrub suit walked out. She glanced around and then headed toward Charlie.

"Mr. Higgins?"

"Doctor Rivers," Charlie said. "Thanks for agreeing to meet me."

"My break is only fifteen minutes so would you rather talk or listen?"

Charlie pulled out his notebook and pen.

Twelve minutes later he had filled eight pages.

"Are you taking a risk?" Charlie asked the young doctor.

"No more than you are," she said. "No more than Darnell did." She scanned the empty E.R. parking lot again. "He didn't deserve what happened to him. Nobody does."

"Are you being watched?" Charlie asked.

"I am until proven otherwise, as we doctors are fond of saying," Jessica Rivers replied. "And I believe the people who murdered Darnell are still running their game and that they will go to any lengths necessary to make sure it keeps running."

"I have a contact at a major newspaper on the east coast. Would you be willing to speak with him?"

Rivers hesitated. "As long as my name or where I work never sees the light of day. But tell him I want a cool alias – you know, like Diana Prince."

"That's Wonder Woman, you do realize," Charlie said putting away his notebook.

"I know," Rivers said. "That's what it's going to take, I'm pretty sure. You leave first. I'll kill a couple more minutes out here and then get back to work. Just in case." She looked around again.

"Payback is hell," Charlie said.

"Yeah," Rivers replied. "That's exactly what I'm afraid of."

SUNDAY
MAY 14th, 1972

-39-

Surf City

THERE WASN'T ROOM FOR everyone inside the house so the little wooden deck with the new picnic table and chairs handled the overflow. Billy Tunell sat with Ronnie's parents and Father Joe Feeney. The sun was bright and the air was warm and humid but the salt breeze was brisk enough to ripple the fringe on the large green umbrella so no one was complaining.

"Now tell me again why you are leaving us for a cultural backwater like Dublin?" Tunell asked. His own Irish roots ran generations deep. "Some obscure pamphleteer you said?"

Feeney sipped at his spiked lemonade. "Poet," he corrected. "Gerard Manley Hopkins. He was English by birth but taught Classics at University College in Dublin. That's where he did most of his writing as well. He wrote the 'Terrible Sonnets' there. And he was a Jesuit priest just like I am. The Society has graciously granted me two years of scholarly activity. I hope to write a book about him when I'm finished." He sipped again. "You have to realize, Billy, most Jesuits are not parish priests."

"Now why would you or anyone for that matter spend two years studying someone who wrote terrible sonnets?"

"*The* terrible sonnets," Feeney corrected. "Not terrible as in bad. Terrible as in depressing and desolate in their subject manner."

"He sounds like a real hoot," Tunell quipped. "Two years? Hmm. Be sure you bring plenty of Bushmill's. No, not Bushmill's. That would be like coals to Newcastle. Have you ever heard of Templeton Rye? Bring that. And as for as the huge void you're so inconsiderately creating here, the Diocese will probably give us some damn Franciscan," Tunell continued with a twinkle. "And you know how *they* are. We'll all be doing Penance long after we've died."

"I hoped Father Angelo might be coming but he's apparently needed for another tour of duty in Hammonton. I don't know really much about Father O'Mahoney."

Despite his sources deep within the diocesan hierarchy Tunell knew only that Finbar O'Mahoney would be arriving in June and that this would be his eighth parish in twelve years. Beyond that the door was closed as to the reasons for his hopscotch pastoral assignment record.

"Well," Tunell blustered, "I suppose he can't be any worse than you, old friend." Everyone at the table laughed including the impish padre.

A sliding glass door opened and Loretta LaMarro leaned out. She had on a white summer dress with tiny blue polka dots. "She's awake," she said. "Everyone come inside."

The little group shuffled into the house. Ronnie had rearranged the furniture to accommodate the gathering. Mickey walked out from the back bedroom holding her baby. Smiles, "ohhhs" and "aaahhhs" filled the room.

"Everyone," Mickey said, "I'd like you all to meet Eileen Johanna Cleary Dunn." The infant yawned and then demurely passed a raspberry of gas. When the laughter died down Doc Guidice said, "That's the Patsy in her for sure," and everyone laughed again.

"If my father were here," Mickey said. She paused and the room grew quiet. She gently rocked the baby who was thinking about fussing. "If my father were here," she repeated a little louder. The front screen door opened.

"I'm here, I'm here," Patsy Cleary said. He scooped up his dog Pixie and carried her with him. "We had some outside business to take care of," he said. He set the little Chihuahua down and she scurried into the kitchen. "What did I miss?"

Mickey looked at her father. The heart attack the summer before had scared him. He'd lost twenty more pounds, quit surreptitiously smoking Benson & Hedges and laid off the Ballantine. He was older but he seemed healthier to her than he had in a long time. She wasn't as sure about what he called a "totally unromantic" friendship with Sherry the real estate agent. But she was cutting more slack everywhere these days it seemed.

"Just introducing your granddaughter," she said. The little crowd clapped. "I know my mother isn't here to greet her personally," Mickey went on and began to tear up. "But I'm sure she's watching over us right now from her little corner of heaven. I always thought there could only ever be one Eileen Cleary but I'm glad I was wrong." The baby grasped her extended index finger. "In case you don't know, Johanna was my grandmother's name. My mother always told me she was a woman of great strength and, as she put it, uncommon forbearance."

"And opinions," Patsy chimed in. "Especially about me." Laughter rippled again.

"I just want to thank all of you for sharing this Christening Day and this Mother's Day with Ronnie and me. Now, please eat and drink as much as you want and stay as long as you'd like. Doc Guidice brought two huge Italian Rum Cakes, there's a gallon of homemade anisette in the kitchen courtesy of Tony Mart and the Showplace of the World and there's cold beer in the coolers."

The little group applauded again. Ronnie came and stood next to her. "I think she needs a change," Mickey said. "The big kind of change. It's your turn. Man's work." Ronnie took the baby from her.

"Latrine duty," he said to his father as he passed him.

Christopher Dunn snapped off a smart salute. "Carry on, soldier," he said. Ronnie disappeared down the hall.

Arlene Shields touched Mickey's arm. "I have to scoot," she said. "Gorgeous baby. So much dark hair."

"Thanks. Little Black Irish. Oh, and thanks for the Slinky," Mickey laughed.

"She can have her own Magic 8-Ball when she turns five," Arlene said and slipped out.

There was a knock at the front door. "I'll get that," Loretta said. "You should get off your feet for a while."

Mickey went to the refrigerator and retrieved a Tab. Loretta tapped her on the shoulder. "Someone at the door for you."

"Tell them just to come on in," Mickey said popping the top on the soda bottle.

"He said it would only take a second," Loretta replied.

Mickey took the cold bottle of Tab and walked to the door. She stepped outside where Tommy Santucci was holding a brightly wrapped present.

"Congratulations," he said and handed her the gift. "Don't worry. Diane picked it out. It's cool. You'll like it. She'll like it, I mean. Your daughter. It's a St. Christopher's medal."

Mickey took the gift and tucked it under her arm. "Sure you can't come in for a second?"

"Nah," Tommy said. "The girls are waiting for Diane to open their Mother's Day presents to her. All homemade. Fashion accessories you might call them. We waited until after church."

"Not your first rodeo, obviously," Mickey said and sipped the Tab.

"With four girls I've had lots of practice. Say, did they ever find the kid who was flying the plane that night?" Tommy asked. "I was always curious about that."

"Nope," Mickey answered. "Still gone with the wind. In the wind."

"Word is he set that plane down out in the middle of the Pines without a scratch on it. Not his first rodeo either it would seem. They say it would take a hell of a pilot to land it where and the way he did."

"*Who* says?" Mickey asked.

Tommy smiled. "Some guys I know."

Mickey cocked her head and looked at him. "Well, that's funny," she said. "Because some guys I know said Brenton Brett reported a mysterious car fire that totaled his brand new Mercedes last summer. Burned on the Fourth of July, actually."

"See? That's why you should always buy American," Tommy replied nodding to the red Corvette convertible idling and double parked in the street.

"And," Mickey continued, "some guys I know said right around that same time the Brett kid and two of his friends got their private parts dyed blue. And that the stuff they used takes years to fade away completely."

"Huh. I guess I didn't hear that one," Tommy said. "Kids and their pranks, right? Maybe it was, oh, what do they call it now, hazing?"

"Yeah. Maybe that was it. Who bought their house, anyway?" Mickey asked.

"You mean here or the one in Merion?"

"Let's start with the one here."

"Nice couple from Palmyra. Pennsy, not Jersey. Couple of kids. Neff or Nepp or Ness, something like that. Works with these new computers. I guess it's a real thing although I can't see how it can last."

"You better hope it's not Ness," Mickey said with a smile.

"Yeah," Tommy replied chuckling. "I'm pretty sure it's not Ness now that I think about it."

"Tommy?"

"Yes, Chief Cleary?"

"This is still my town. Let's keep that in mind, OK?"

"OK," Tommy said. "But remember what I said about that beautiful friendship. Times are changing, Mickey. You gotta keep up. Does the name Jim Frichionne ring a bell?"

Mickey thought for a moment. "Can't say that it does. Who is he? Not your new boss, that's - what's his name again? Little Nero? I heard he's still looking for a date to take to his Junior Prom."

Santucci smiled. "Domenico represents a new kind of youthful energy. That's all I'm going to say."

"So now who is this Jim Frichionne character?"

"You might know him as Jimmy the Fixer. He's a North Jersey guy."

"Still nothing," Mickey said. "What does he fix?"

"Problems," Tommy said and arched his eyebrows. "Just file the name in your Rolodex for future reference."

"I'll certainly do that, Tommy," Mickey replied. "Thanks. Now are you sure-"

The door opened and Loretta popped her head out. "Mickey. Mickey. Come around back. Quick. You have got to see this."

When Mickey turned back Tommy was already climbing into the Corvette. She followed Loretta into the house.

"Come on. Quick or you'll miss it." She led Mickey through the now-empty rooms and out the back door where everyone was gathered. Mickey heard the drone of an airplane engine. The hair on the back of her neck stood up. Her guests all had their heads tilted up and were gazing into the endless azure expanse of the eastern sky. When Mickey looked she saw a small plane towing what she assumed would be an advertisement for The Dunes or maybe Zaberer's.

"Ah, the first banner of summer," Billy Tunell exclaimed. "As I always say, it's like seeing the first robin of spring."

"The first banners you mean," Guidice corrected. "Look."

It was a line of planes and banners Mickey now realized. And each one tipped its wings as it passed. She counted five in all. Loretta read aloud the messages as they paraded by like an aerial tickertape.

WELCOME EILEEN CLEARY DUNN
HAPPY MOTHER'S DAY
FROM PARAMOUNT AIR
SUMMER AT THE SHORE
HERE WE GO AGAIN !

Ronnie came and stood next to Mickey, holding little Eileen.

"Did you arrange for this?" she asked him.

"Wasn't me," he said. "But you know what they say. It never hurts to have friends in high places."

The Evening Bulletin *Building*
3100 Market Street
Philadelphia, PA

Candy checked the clock.

The newsroom was empty except for the rewrite crew which was hustling to clean up sloppy prose, jumbled paragraphs and highly questionable syntax. She had already missed any chance of making the christening party down the shore. Now she was in danger of missing her mother's baked ziti on Mother's Day. The Sports desks were quiet, the Phillies having fallen to the Dodgers the day before with Steve Carlton taking the loss. Mike Gannon had gotten her the summer job and she did not want to let him down. But it felt like all her best ideas were being quashed. She had wanted to do a Mother's Day story on unwed mothers in Camden but was told it was not "family friendly." Likewise for her idea for a three-part feature on the local Soul Music scene which focused on Archie Bell and the Drells, a Houston group who'd made the pop charts in 1967 with "Tighten Up" and had been recording in town since 1968 after signing with Philadelphia International Records. She loved the title she'd worked up, "TSOP – STOP in the Name of Soul." The editors had smiled and then politely suggested that she focus instead on Frankie Avalon, Fabian Forte and perhaps even Bobby Rydell. And Candy thought if she were assigned one more society shindig at The Peale Club she would drive to Surf City, take Dennis' .357 and shoot herself. Perhaps twice. Plus, Gannon had her working on his "X File" project about a military drug smuggling ring, something the editors knew nothing about and which would likely get them both fired if they did.

Candy looked at the framed page of *The SandPaper*. Her story, "Barnegat Light's Shining Moment," had won a New Jersey Press Association prize for Best Original Reporting, Local or Regional. But she knew Gannon still coveted his neighbor's Pulitzer and he was not above using her and her connection to Surf City and Charlie Higgins to get it.

She decided she could not disappoint her mother. And she loved baked ziti. She would just have to drive back later and finish. As Candy shuffled the papers on the desk a postcard fell out of her stack of mail. She hadn't noticed it before. She peeled it from the dirty floor. On the glossy front side was a full-color picture of airplanes with pontoons instead of wheels. "Greetings from Red Lake, Ontario!" it shouted. Candy turned it over. The little fine-print descriptor in one corner told her the photo showed "A flotilla of Norseman Float Planes on Ontario Province's Red Lake ready to fly adventurous anglers North for the trip of a lifetime."

There was no message, just a handwritten signature.

Lars Svensson.

The guys at the rewrite desk heard the commotion and came running over.

The new girl reporter, they saw, had fainted dead away.

ACKNOWLEDGEMENTS

Fiction is the product of an author's imagination. A novel is the tangible proof that it did not remain only a figment of that author's imagination. And it requires more than just the storyteller to put it into a reader's hands. I hope I don't miss anyone but this author would like to sincerely thank the following people who helped bring this story to the page : my critical readers Dr. Kate Galluzzi, Bruce Forshay, USN (Ret.) and Jim Sauer, CRNA; prolific author Sheldon Siegel; Terry Persun for his formidable formatting skills; Jim Zach of *ZGrafix* for another inspired cover concept and layout; Kellie Jo Heimer at Control Print Creative for eye-catching ads; Rick Theilen for his classic car expertise and access to the Chevy Brookwood; Dale Gibson, CCP, USMC for his encyclopedic tactical and firearms knowledge; Kristen Ollenburg, Esq. for her legal and corporate counsel and Ryan Martz and Doug McCarthy at Fire & Pine for the use of another of their exquisite maps.

I would also like to thank those friends, colleagues and mentors who graciously allowed me to attach of their names or the names of loved ones to characters in this book: William P. Tunell, MD, Thomas F. Santucci, Jr., DO, James C. Guidice, DO, Mary Beth Harman, DO, Michael Ganon, DO, Mark Nepp, DO, Karen Durkin, Esq., Linda Johnson, Michael Belz, CCP, Valerie Gann, PA-C, Arlene Shields, RN, George Joo, N.J. State Police (Ret.), Barbara Tomalino and Paramount Air Service, NBA veteran and pilot Barry Yates, Phil Stanley, DO, Mike Garufi, SNC, Jim Filisky, SNC, Alan Stewart, SNC, Larry Forbes, SNC, Mike Slivka, SNC Louis A. Petroni, Esq., Bob Rocca, Ms. Margaret Collier, JoLynne Maressa, Daniel J. Ragone, MD, Greg Raecker, DO, Bob "Bobby Nads" Dugoni, J.D., Kristen Ollenburg, Esq., Mary Pat Green, Joseph J. Feeney, S.J. and Cape Coral's own Jim Frichionne. I'd also like to mention the names of those who are lamentably no longer with us but are fondly remembered: Mrs. Loretta Lamarro, Sister Innocentia, John Durkin, David A. Johnson, DO, NJ State. Sen. Joseph Maressa, Karl Mizener, SNC and Mike Oprea, RNFA.

I am forever indebted to best-selling author, friend and mentor Robert Dugoni who helped me find my author's voice and "fix my swing" and to Prof. Laura Hope-Gill, MFA, my Master's Program Director at Lenoir-Rhyne University's Thomas Wolfe Center for Narrative who guided me in developing that voice in ways I would have never imagined.

A special and sincere thank-you to Barb Tomalino of Paramount Air Service who helped beyond measure with the myriad technical details of aerial advertising and the story of the company founded by her father, Andre Tomalino, a former fighter pilot, when he returned from WWII. It remains as much a part of being down'a shore today as it was when the first banner flew over the beaches; and a shout-out to Barry Yates who played for my beloved Philadelphia 76'ers and really did fly for Paramount Air. Also thanks to Doreen Cramer at *The SandPaper*; Alice Smith and Brittany Rae at the Riverside Historical Society for their assistance in getting the small details of my hometown right and Reilly P. Sharp at the Barnegat Light Historical Society for the "inside" scoop on Old Barney.

BOOKS BY DANIEL J. WATERS

A Heart Surgeon's Little Instruction Book

A Surgeon's Little Instruction Book

Surf City Confidential

Threshold

Ship Bottom Blues

Barnegat Dark

"SHIP BOTTOM BLUES"

WRITER'S DIGEST AWARD WINNER!

"*This Vietnam era thriller works well on many levels. The book is well-written, with tension driven suspense. The structure is taut, the plot is solid. There's tension in every line making it a page turner. The musical references and the cars add to the real-life details that make the reader feel part of the scene. It's a great read and hard to put down, and comparable to John Sanford, Robert Dugoni and Jeffrey Archer.*"
—WD Judges' Review

AVAILABLE ON AMAZON IN PAPERBACK
AND E-BOOK FORMATS AND
AT SELECT BOOKSELLERS
OR VISIT www.bandagemanpress.com TO ORDER

ABOUT THE AUTHOR

Daniel James Waters, D.O., M.A. is native of southern New Jersey. He graduated from of Bishop Eustace Preparatory School, St. Joseph's College (Phila.) and the University of Medicine & Dentistry of NJ. He holds a Graduate Certificate in Narrative Healthcare and a Master of Arts in Writing from Lenoir-Rhyne University (Asheville, NC). He published his first story in 1981 and has been writing steadily since then. His work has appeared in major medical journals and university literary magazines and he is a frequent contributor to online health professionals' platforms. In addition to numerous articles, stories and essays he has authored two books of surgical advice, three prior novels, two published poems and one award-winning play. He retired following a thirty year career performing open heart surgery and lives with his wife in Clear Lake, Iowa.

VISIT OUR WEBSITE: www.bandagemanpress.com

CONTACT THE AUTHOR: drdan@bandagemanpress.com

Made in the USA
Monee, IL
31 October 2021